PRAISE FOR *ALL THEY NEED TO KNOW*

"This straightforward tale of a woman taking back her power is a good fit for readers who appreciate a heartfelt story of romantic love and female friendship with a dollop of suspense in the vein of Nora Roberts's Three Sisters Island trilogy."

—*Booklist*

"An emotionally riveting read from start to finish."

—*Midwest Book Review*

ALSO BY EILEEN GOUDGE

Fiction

All They Need to Know

Swimsuit Body

Bones and Roses

The Replacement Wife

Woman in Red

Woman in Blue

Woman in Black

The Diary

Otherwise Engaged

Immediate Family

Trail of Secrets

The Second Silence

Stranger in Paradise

Taste of Honey

Wish Come True

Blessing in Disguise

One Last Dance

Such Devoted Sisters

Garden of Lies

Thorns of Truth

Nonfiction

Something Warm from the Oven

the house on mountain laurel lane

A Novel

EILEEN GOUDGE

This is a work of fiction. Names, characters, organizations, places, events, and incidents are either products of the author's imagination or are used fictitiously.

Published by Lake Union Publishing, Seattle
www.apub.com

Amazon, the Amazon logo, and Lake Union Publishing are trademarks of Amazon.com, Inc., or its affiliates.

EU product safety contact:
Amazon Media EU S. à r.l.
38, avenue John F. Kennedy, L-1855 Luxembourg
amazonpublishing-gpsr@amazon.com

ISBN-13: 9781662518140 (paperback)
ISBN-13: 9781662518133 (digital)

Cover design by Eileen Carey
Cover image: © Westend61, ©Sinisa Kukic, © Jon Lovette / Getty;
© Simone Anne / Stocksy

Printed in the United States of America

To the "Dallas Gals" of the Widows' Journey—Kay Murcer, Babs McMahan, Beth Pribulsky, and Claudia Knake Spears—who inspired me in sharing their journeys

Every day is a journey, and the journey itself is home.
—Matsuo Basho

Not the glittering weapon fights the fight, but rather the hero's heart.
—Proverb

1

The sun was setting when Jo pulled up in front of the house. *You shouldn't have come. You're only making it harder for yourself,* said the voice in her head. She ignored it and climbed from her car. She wouldn't stay long. Just a quick stop before continuing to Melanie's bridal shower. She stood gazing at the sixties-era split-level, painted sunflower yellow with white trim, on a quarter acre, bordered by grass and flower beds, backlit by the vermilion sky. Nothing special, some might say, apart from its views. The last house on the tree-lined cul-de-sac, it looked out on the forested foothills and snowcapped peaks of the Sierra Nevada. But it was special to her. Because it was their dream house. Hers and Sean's.

Their first sighting had been random. Back when they'd been saving to buy a house, they used to cruise their target neighborhoods on weekends in search of inspiration. That day, their meanderings had brought them to Mountain Laurel Lane, in one of the older residential neighborhoods of Gold Creek, a fifteen-minute drive from town, and there it was. They'd stopped to take pictures of the house for their virtual vision board. It was neither large nor fancy, but it had curb appeal and they couldn't beat the location. The kind of house they'd hoped to own someday, where Jo could envision their daughters growing up. Except Sean hadn't lived to see "someday."

Two weeks later, they'd sat in the oncologist's office looking at a very different view: the MRI showing the mass on Sean's brain. The diagnosis was even scarier: glioblastoma. After that had come the chemo treatments with their side effects, prompting Sean, who'd lost his hair but not his sense of humor, to dub himself The Incredible Shrinking Bald Man. By fall of that year, he was gone. She felt a stab of loss and absently massaged her chest.

Sean, I miss you so much.

She thought of Betty from her grief group, who'd swum San Francisco Bay, a rough crossing of almost three miles, at the age of sixty-four to get unstuck when she'd still felt stuck two years after her husband's death. Her "epic encore," she'd called it. While Jo was merely treading water to keep from going under. When Jo left the group, Betty had been making plans to hike the Appalachian Trail next. How did other people do it? Why couldn't she seem to move on?

Today was their twelfth wedding anniversary and the second she'd celebrated without her husband. If you could call the pity party she'd be throwing for herself after tonight's bridal shower a celebration. *Some epic encore.* This was why she'd dropped out of her grief group after four months. She was good at her job—everything from finding and framing the perfect shot, the one that told a story or revealed something about its subject, to wrangling family members who hated each other into group shots at weddings without them killing each other—and making a decent living as a photographer since she'd quit her job in advertising to go freelance five years ago. She was a good mother, or she tried to be, despite not having quite got the hang of single parenting yet. But she sucked at self-motivation. It had been a year and a half since Sean died, and she was no closer to moving on than she'd been on day one. Her vows to do better, try harder, embrace her "inner warrior," as one podcaster put it, crumbled like sandcastles with the next wave of grief that rolled in.

Now here she stood, outside their dream house, fantasizing about what might have been. She saw herself relaxing in the Adirondack chairs on the covered porch with Sean on a warm summer evening. She saw Sean shooting baskets with their daughters in the basketball hoop above the garage door. She saw a garden planted with tomatoes and chili peppers like the ones he used to grow in pots on the postage stamp–size patio of their rented duplex. He'd loved spicy foods, the spicier the better, and every year he'd made a giant batch of his extra-spicy salsa preserves, which they'd given away as gifts at Christmastime. She still had half a dozen jars labeled "Sean's Secret Salsa" in a kitchen cupboard at home. She hoarded it like gold, even though it was too spicy for her taste. Because once it was gone, it would be one fewer thing to remember him by.

She was roused from her reverie by the front door swinging open. A man wearing jeans and a sweatshirt emerged from inside, locked the door behind him, and descended the three porch steps. He headed toward the older-model green pickup parked in the driveway. He was somewhere in his late sixties or early seventies, tall and lean, with snow-white hair that he wore pulled back in a ponytail. The fact that he'd locked up suggested he lived there. Possibly a military veteran, from the sign posted on the lawn below the porch that read A Hero Lives Here. He paused to peer in her direction, calling, "Can I help you?"

"Uh, no . . . wrong address," she stammered before ducking back into her car. The kind of help she needed neither he nor anyone else could provide.

The bridal shower she was working tonight was hosted by the matron of honor, Priya, at her home in the same neighborhood. Jo counted twenty guests, including the bride-to-be, Melanie. The party had food and drinks and party games, the highlight of which was the making of the traditional toilet paper wedding dress. By the time the other women were done with her, Melanie resembled an animated mummy swathed in her "Princess Charmin" dress. She was also more than a little drunk. When she went to refresh her drink at one point, Jo could have predicted what would happen next. Before she could call out a warning, a dangling piece of toilet paper brushed against the lit candle on the bar as Melanie reached for the pitcher of sangria beside it, with the inevitable result. Jo flew across the room toward her, propelled by adrenaline, one hand anchoring her camera on its canvas strap around her neck. She reached Melanie in under three seconds. Grabbing the soda siphon on the bar, she loosed a jet of water, dousing the flame and drenching the bride-to-be in the process. For a beat or two, no one moved. Then the smoke alarm began to blare and a voice shrieked, "Oh my GOD," and suddenly everyone was in motion, swarming around Melanie. Priya fetched her a towel, while several others peeled the sodden remnants of her dress from her body. Luckily, she was unharmed.

Someone started to giggle, and within seconds the room erupted in howls of laughter. Jo understood the need to break the tension. In her grief she'd developed an unfortunate tendency toward inappropriate laughter. She'd become an emotional jack-in-the-box, never knowing when the grinning clown head would pop out, like it had at a memorial service she'd attended recently, when she'd been seized by a fit of giggles. On that occasion she'd slipped away before she could embarrass herself further. Now, she captured the moment on camera as Melanie danced in her underwear to "Girls Just Want to Have Fun" to the cheers of her audience, while the host's cairn terrier worriedly eyed the puddle on the floor as if he'd caused it. Photos that might not make it into Melanie's wedding album but would make a great story for her to tell her children someday.

"Jo, you're a lifesaver," said Melanie as she changed back into the dress she'd worn to the shower. "Thanks to you, I won't be spending my wedding day in the burn ward at the hospital."

Jo shuddered. She knew from personal experience how suddenly your fate could turn. One minute you might be living the dream, and the next you'd been plunged into a living nightmare. "No thanks necessary," she said as she helped Melanie with her zipper. With her curvy body and cascade of red curls, Melanie was a Pre-Raphaelite portrait come to life. "I'm just glad you're okay."

"I refuse to let anything postpone this wedding. It took me long enough to find Jayesh."

Jo wished every client were like Melanie, who was so thrilled to have found her soulmate at the "ripe old age of forty-two" that the details of the wedding itself were of lesser importance. Jo had been lucky to find her soulmate when they were both eighteen. She'd never looked at another man after meeting Sean. Even now that he was gone, she still wore her wedding ring. She pressed her lips together before she could blurt out *Enjoy it while it lasts* or something equally inappropriate. "I'm happy for you," she said instead. "Love is a beautiful thing."

"Listen, why don't you take the rest of the night off? You earned it."

"Thanks. I think I will." Normally, Jo was the last to leave when she was working an event, but it was late and she was tired. She'd been awakened by Jess, who'd had a nightmare, at three that morning and been unable to get back to sleep after soothing her daughter and checking to see that there were no monsters under the bed or in the closet. "I'll email you tonight's photos after I've uploaded them onto my computer," she said as she packed up her camera gear.

"Jay will love the ones of me dancing in my underwear."

"See you next Friday!" Jo called over her shoulder as she headed out the door.

Melanie had opted for the full bridal package, which included any prewedding events in addition to the wedding. Jo had photographed the engagement party Melanie's parents had hosted two months ago. Next week, she'd work the bachelorette party on Friday and the wedding on Saturday.

As she drove the hilly, winding road to her rented duplex on the other side of town, her thoughts returned to her anniversary. She and Sean had a tradition, starting when they were newlyweds and struggling to make ends meet, of exchanging gifts on their anniversary that weren't store-bought. For their one-year anniversary, Sean had surprised her with a moonlight cruise on Brambleberry Lake in a borrowed boat, complete with a picnic supper. For the last anniversary they'd celebrated together, she'd made him a photo album with pictures going back to when they'd first met. Their daughters had decorated the cover with stickers and the words "Mommy and Daddy's Big Adventure" spelled out in felt letters. Sean had loved it. One day a few months later, she'd found him sitting up in bed leafing through the album—he'd become bedridden by then—and when he looked up in that unguarded moment, she'd seen on his gaunt face all the pain and sorrow he normally kept hidden. He must have known he wouldn't live to celebrate another anniversary with her.

The memory ripped through her like an icy mountain wind. When she blinked to clear her tear-filled eyes, she saw that she'd strayed across the center line. Her heart lurched in her chest as she corrected her course. *Jesus. Get a grip. Your children can't afford to lose another parent.*

It was 10:40 p.m. by the time she arrived home. The building was dark and silent. She'd arranged for the girls to spend the night with Rosaria, the neighbor with whom she shared the duplex, also a single mom of two. They often took turns watching each other's children, who were close in ages and playmates. Although if Jo were being honest, it was usually Rosaria, who worked as a paralegal and was home most evenings, doing the childminding. Tonight was the second time this week that Jess and Emma had stayed over, Jo thought with a twinge of guilt.

As she entered her house, she was greeted by the faint odor of mildew. The "Taj-Mahole," as Sean had dubbed their rented digs, was poorly insulated, and as a result became damp during the rainy season. The cramped living room, with its dingy beige carpeting and equally dingy moss-green walls, scuffed where the paint had rubbed off in some spots, added insult to injury. It was also a reminder of her failure to move on. During the years she and Sean had been saving to buy a house, it seemed like for every dollar saved, there had been two dollars' worth of some unexpected expense, like when Jess broke her glasses falling down on her school playground and needed a new pair, or when they were socked with expensive car repairs. But the fact of the matter was she could afford better digs now. Sean's life insurance policy, although not a huge sum—$50,000—was enough for a down payment on a modest home. Yet she hadn't spent a dime of it, or so much as glanced at a real estate flyer. How could she without being reminded that Sean had had to die in order to realize their dream? Besides, wherever they lived, they'd be living there without him.

Snickers had made herself comfortable on the sofa in Jo's absence, as usual. Their chocolate Lab wasn't allowed on the furniture, but she'd become lazy in her old age and Jo was too indulgent to enforce the rule. "Hey, girl. You miss me?" Snickers lifted her graying muzzle from her paws and thumped her tail against the sofa cushions, eyes slitted with contentment, as Jo scratched the sweet spot behind her ears.

Snickers climbed down, and Jo took her outside for one last potty break before bed. The outdoor space at the Taj consisted of the fenced patio out back, which was roughly the dimensions of the average prison cell, so Jo took Snickers for a short walk to give her some exercise. The house was so quiet she could hear the ticking of the Felix the Cat clock in the kitchen when she returned. Too quiet. She poured herself a glass of white wine and carried it to her bedroom, Snickers trailing after her. The old Lab curled up in her Orvis dog bed. Jo, after changing into her pajamas, stretched out on the queen bed, which had become a desert island on which she was marooned nightly in Sean's absence, with a sigh. Her head propped against the pillows at her back, she reached for her iPad on the nightstand to check her email. But she didn't open it. Instead, she sipped her wine and closed her eyes, drifting out to sea on the tidal pull of her past.

2

They'd met at a campus mixer hosted by UC Davis's LGBTQIA Resource Center in the fall of their freshman year. Jo had gone with her roommate, Carmela. They'd been making their way through the crowd, headed toward the refreshment table beneath the pop-up canopy at the other end of the quad, next to the one with gay pride merch for sale, when Carmela paused to greet someone, a short, stocky boy with a blond Afro.

"Hey, Reggie. What's up?"

"Carmela, my love." He kissed her on both cheeks. "How is it you're more beautiful every time I see you?"

She laughed and rolled her eyes, though she was in fact gorgeous. In her fitted red dress, which was the same shade as her lipstick, she looked like an actress playing the lead in *Carmen*. Jo had noticed several girls at the party checking her out. Jo felt washed-out in comparison, with her milky skin and pale eyelashes, her even—and some might say forgettable—features. She wore her strawberry-blond hair below her shoulders, parted down the middle. Her nicest feature was her eyes, which were the blue of bachelor buttons. She was also more dressed up than usual tonight, if only because Carmela had insisted on it. Instead of her usual uniform of a T-shirt and jeans, she wore the silk spaghetti-strap dress, leaf green with bluebells on it, that her mom had managed to sneak into her luggage when she'd been packing for college.

"Who's your date? He's cute." Carmela turned her attention to the boy Reggie was with, who was a head taller than he was, with a lanky frame, messy brown hair, and soulful brown eyes like those of a nineteenth-century poet. He wore a Green Day T-shirt and faded jeans, torn at the knees.

The tall boy grinned and stuck his hand out. "Sean Myers. Nice to meetcha."

"Carmela Rodriguez, and this is my roommate, Jo Hunter," Carmela said as they exchanged handshakes.

Jo felt a sizzle of attraction shoot up her arm as Sean's strong fingers closed over hers. She could've sworn it was mutual when their eyes locked. But how could he be attracted to her? He was Reggie's date. She'd known of only three openly gay students in her class at Lyndon B. Johnson High, so her knowledge of the LGBTQ+ community was derived mostly from TV and films. Nor was she sexually experienced, although the fact that she was still a virgin at eighteen was due to lack of opportunity rather than choice. She'd only ever had one boyfriend. Rob had been a reporter at their school paper, where she'd been the photographer. They'd become friends covering school events and games together, and started hanging out outside school. All they'd ever done was kiss, though, and there'd been no sparks. Eventually they'd gone back to being just friends. It didn't hurt her feelings when he asked another girl to their senior prom.

Sean Myers, gay or not, was the real deal. As she gazed into his eyes, her heart raced and her mind went blank. She couldn't think of a thing to say other than "Hey."

Carmela, on the other hand, was vocal in her assessment. *"Carne caliente,"* she declared with an exaggerated roll of her *r*'s as her gaze traveled over him in a leisurely fashion. Which Jo knew from the Spanish classes she'd taken in high school meant "hot meat" in English.

Carmela wasn't shy and her comments were often unfiltered. She blamed it on her being the youngest in her family of six. She'd learned from an early age that she had to speak up in order to be heard. She was "loud and proud," as she liked to say. Still, Jo wished she hadn't drawn attention to Sean's hotness. He acted like she'd been joking, while Jo's tingly awareness of him said otherwise.

"Playing for the visiting team now, are we?" Reggie teased.

"With all the talent on the home team? No way." Carmela tucked her arm through Jo's as she spoke. She was being playful; the truth was, they were strictly friends. "How goes it with rehearsals?"

"I think I finally have my character nailed," Reggie reported.

"Dude, you play the part of a plant. How hard could it be?" said Sean. "That would be the bloodthirsty plant in *Little Shop of Horrors*," he explained for Jo's benefit. She'd seen the posters around campus advertising the drama department's upcoming production of the musical.

"I may not have as many lines as some, but mine is the seminal role of the show," Reggie countered with a flip of his hand. He threw his head back to bellow, "Feed me, Seymour!" loud enough to have heads turning their way. He followed with a more sinister version of the same line, delivered in a lower register. "Which should I go with, version one or version two? I can't decide."

"I don't know how a bloodthirsty plant is supposed to sound," said Jo.

"Don't do the growly voice," said Carmela. "You sound like my uncle Leon after he had his throat surgery."

"I'm staying out of it," said Sean. "I've only heard, like, eight hundred versions."

Reggie smirked at him. "Ladies, you'll have to excuse my philistine friend. He has no appreciation for the arts. This is what comes of too much screen time. Let that be a lesson to you kids."

"You'll change your tune when I'm a tech billionaire and you're looking for investors for your first Broadway show," Sean tossed back at him.

"Honey, I'd love you if you were in retail. *Especially* if you were in retail." Reggie leaned in to plant a kiss on Sean's cheek. Sean rolled his eyes and gave him a playful poke in the ribs.

Damn. Why were the good ones always taken?

Jo didn't see Sean again until several weeks later. She'd gone to the opening-night performance of *Little Shop of Horrors* with Carmela and her girlfriend, Roxy, and spotted him in the lobby during intermission, while Carmela and Roxy were getting some fresh air. Her heart leaped. He stood at the refreshment table helping himself to a cup of complimentary punch provided by the alumni association. In faded jeans and a beat-up leather jacket over a dark-gray polo shirt, he was as gorgeous as she remembered. He broke into a wide smile as she approached.

"Jo, hi! Great to see you again." He'd remembered her name. "Enjoying the show?"

"Very much. Reggie's amazing. I didn't know a plant could be so . . ."

"Emotive?"

"Right."

"Nobody puts Reggie in the corner."

She laughed at the *Dirty Dancing* reference. "He's a star in the making for sure. His parents must be so proud."

Sean's smile fell away. "You would think."

"Is there a problem?"

"Reggie's parents don't approve of his 'lifestyle,'" he said, making air quotes. "Which is why they're not here tonight, despite having been invited and Reggie leaving tickets for them at the box office."

"God. How awful."

"After he came out to them when he was fifteen, they tried to get him to enlist in 'Bible boot camp,' as he calls it. They seem to think if Jesus could turn water into wine, he could turn a gay boy straight. Naturally, Reggie refused. He moved in with his older sister after they kicked him out."

"I can't imagine." Jo was the square peg in the round hole of her parents' ordered existence, but she knew she was loved and they'd never reject her. "It's their loss, and they're missing out tonight, but still . . ." She shook her head, feeling awful for Reggie. "How's he taking it?"

"He acts like it's no biggie, but I can tell he's hurt."

"How could he not be? I'm glad he has his sister. And you," she remembered to add. "How did you two meet?"

Sean's smile returned. "So, funny story. My first day on campus, I'm in my dorm room unpacking when in walks this dude belting a show tune. I figured he was either going to be the most annoying person I'd meet on campus or the most interesting. By the time he left, I knew."

"He seems like a great guy."

"He is, with a heart as big as his talent."

"What about you? Are you really out to become a tech billionaire?"

"I know my way around software and coding, which might lead to something," he replied with a shrug. "It may not make me rich, but I believe in doing what turns you on. What turns you on, Jo?"

You. She became lost in his eyes, scarcely aware of the theatergoers milling around them, before pulling herself back into the moment. "Me? That's easy. Photography."

It had started with the Kodak point-and-shoot her grandparents had given her for her thirteenth birthday. Initially, it had been a buffer at the parties her parents had frequently hosted and expected her to put in an appearance at, during a time in her life when she'd been at her most awkward socially. It had saved her from having to interact with the guests—she could hide behind her camera and take pictures of them instead. Over time, however, photography had become her calling. She was captivated by the marriage between the camera and the images she captured with it.

"I'd love to see some of your photos," Sean said with what seemed like genuine interest.

She pulled out her phone and scrolled through her camera roll. "These are from my summer vacation." She showed him a few of the photos she'd taken while vacationing in Colorado with her friend Natalie the past summer.

"Wow. You're good," he said, studying the photo of a buffalo herd in Estes Park.

"The ones I took with my camera are better."

"I'd like to see them sometime." She couldn't tell if he was just being polite or if he was really interested. He seemed sincere. "Do you plan to major in photography?"

"Yes. Although my parents have other plans for me." The mention of which acted on her like a spoonful of vinegar in a glass of milk. Her stomach curdled.

"Like what?"

"My dad wants me to major in business, so I can work at his accounting firm after I graduate. My mom hoped I'd become a star in the beauty pageant circuit like she was when she was my age. A dream that was dashed, I might add, when I was five and competed in my one and only baby beauty contest, which I totally blew. Now she'd just like to see me in a profession that I could easily step away from if and when I become a wife and mother someday."

"Well, from what you showed me, you have talent. So, if you want my advice, I say follow your dream. Your parents will make peace with it, if they love you."

She nodded. Right now, she was fantasizing about him kissing her. Talk about foolish! She tore her gaze from his. "Even if it turns out to be a dead end?"

"You won't know unless you try."

They chatted some more until the intermission was over. She learned that Sean was an only child like her, and that he'd been raised by his aunt and uncle after his parents were killed in a car accident when he was nine. He was from a mountain town up north called Gold Creek. She told him about growing up in Fairview, Texas, a planned community in outer Houston with its own golf course and country club, where if you didn't play golf or tennis or enjoy socializing, you were an outlier.

"Aren't you going to drink that?" she asked at one point, noticing he wasn't drinking his punch.

"I'm scared to. Looks vile, doesn't it?" He peered into the cup in his hand, filled with a mixture that was a noxious shade of red. "I don't know what's in it, but I'm calling it Cherry Chernobyl."

"The question is, will it make you glow in the dark?"

"Only one way to find out. But I'm not doing this alone. You in?" She grinned and snagged a cup of punch. "Here's to being adventurous." He tapped his cup against hers.

"Am I glowing yet?" Jo asked after they'd each taken a hefty gulp.

"Oh yeah." Their gazes locked, and there were those sparks again, causing her to tingle all over. Why was he looking at her like that? Like . . . *he wanted to kiss her*. She must have been imagining it. Either that or the sugar rush from the overly sweet punch had gone to her head.

She didn't see him again until several months later. One blustery day in January, she was strolling hand in hand in the campus arboretum with Colton, the boy she'd been seeing at the time, when she spotted a familiar figure whizzing toward them in the bike lane. Sean. Her heart jumped, and she paused to watch as he drew near. He spotted her and became distracted, which caused him to lose control of his bike. He swerved to avoid hitting another biker and crashed. With a cry of alarm, she dashed over to where he lay sprawled, his long legs tangled in his bike frame.

"Oh my God. Are you all right?"

"Um. I think so." He disentangled himself from his bike and stood, with some assistance from her. Removing his bike helmet, he ran a hand over his head as if to make sure his skull wasn't cracked, which caused his unruly dark hair to stand up in a halo of corkscrew curls. "Nothing appears to be broken."

"You're bleeding." She pointed to the blood trickling down his left leg below the blue Lycra shorts he wore.

"Oh." He glanced down as if surprised to see that both his knees were skinned. "It's nothing. I'm fine. Totally my fault. I didn't look where I was going. When I saw you with that guy . . ." His gaze moved past her for a second. "Your boyfriend?" His tone was casual but she sensed it was a loaded question.

"Huh? No." She'd forgotten all about Colton until that moment. She glanced behind her to see him still standing on the path where she'd left him, his blond head now bent over his phone. As if he'd determined the situation wasn't urgent and didn't require his assistance. She felt annoyed before she realized his lack of empathy worked in her favor, in a weird way. It was one more reason to break up with him, which she'd been planning to do. "Why do you ask?"

"It's just . . . I thought you were into girls."

"What? No. Why would you think that?"

A look of confusion came over his face. "You and Carmela aren't, you know, together?"

"I love Carmela. As a friend," she added pointedly.

"Oh." His face lit up, and he broke into a grin. "So much for me making assumptions."

"You could've asked."

"I was afraid if you knew I was interested, it'd get awkward."

"Wait. You're interested? In me? I thought you were with Reggie." Suddenly it became clear: They'd each jumped to the wrong conclusion about the other. Understandably, given the circumstances of their first meeting. Jo started to giggle at the comedy of errors, and Sean joined in.

"Oops," he said, looking past her again. "Looks like your boyfriend got tired of waiting."

Jo followed his gaze and saw that Colton had indeed left without her. Either he was pissed off because she'd been paying attention to Sean and not him, or he'd seen the handwriting on the wall. "Whatever." He was already history. "And FYI, he's not my boyfriend. We went out a few times, is all."

Sean's eyes in the sunlight were the golden brown of maple syrup poured over buttered pancakes. "In that case," he asked, his voice low and husky, "would it be all right if I kissed you?"

She nodded as if in a trance and he dipped his head, his lips brushing over hers, tantalizing and leaving her wanting more. Their kiss deepened, and . . . *kaboom*. Sparks flew as their bodies melded in an explosion of heat and desire that left her trembling. She'd never experienced anything like it before. She'd thought it was just in romance novels. Another thing she'd been wrong about.

"Wow," he said after they drew apart. He looked as dazed as she felt.

"Yeah."

When they finally broke eye contact, he bent to pull his bike upright and straddled it. "Hop on," he said, and handed her his helmet.

"Where are we going?" she asked after she'd done as instructed. She'd planned to go back to her dorm after her date with Colton and finish the essay that was due in her humanities class the next day, but right now all she wanted to do was play. With Sean. Homework could wait.

He turned his head to smile at her. "You tell me."

"Surprise me," she said, and off they went. Jo never looked back.

3

They'd gotten married in the small stone church in Gold Creek where Sean had been baptized, on a gorgeous day in May, followed by a reception at his aunt and uncle's ranch, where they'd danced their first dance to K-Ci & JoJo's "All My Life," with cattle lowing in the background. Gliding over the dance floor in Sean's arms, she'd never felt more certain about anything than she did about marrying him. A certainty that never wavered in the years to come, even when they squabbled or were consumed by the needs of their babies as new parents. While she'd launched her freelance career and he'd been working on the app he'd created with his partner, Rohit, when he wasn't working his day job in IT, their time together had been catch-as-catch-can, but somehow they'd made it work. People said they were too young to get married, barely out of college, but they'd proved them wrong. Sean had been, and would always be, the One.

Jo returned from her trip down memory lane to find her wineglass empty and her face wet with tears. She didn't remember either drinking her wine or crying, but it appeared she'd done both. It was almost midnight by the time she got around to checking her email. She saw that she had three new messages. Two were work related, and the third, which came with an attachment, was from Reggie, sent at 7:04 p.m., according to its time stamp. The subject line read "For Your Eyes Only." Curious, she clicked on the message to open it.

Baby girl,

Happy anniversary! I hope you're doing okay. I know it's a bittersweet occasion for you. Which is why I'm writing. The attached is a video Sean made for you before he died. I was instructed to deliver it on your anniversary this year. That's all I know. I haven't watched it. He threatened to come back and haunt me if I so much as took a sneak peek. I hope it brings you some peace.

Call me after you've watched it, if you need to talk. Even if it's late. I'm here for you. I love you.

xxxxoooo

Reggie

Her head spun. Sean had made a video before he died? And Reggie had been holding on to it all this time? She clicked on the attachment and hit play, and then gasped as the image of her dead husband appeared on-screen. He was gaunt and hollow-eyed, but he seemed alert, which suggested he'd forgone the morphine drip he'd used to manage his pain in order to be clearheaded while filming the video. His smile, undimmed by pain or the shadow of death, lit up the screen. She smiled back, despite the golf ball–size lump in her throat.

"Happy anniversary, babe. I'd have sent flowers, but it wouldn't have had the wow factor, and you know I'm all about the wow factor. Also, if you're watching this, it means I'm dead. I'm sorry about that. And I'm sorry I wasn't there for last year's anniversary and that I'm not there for this year's. You know the worst thing about dying? It's not feeling like crap all the time. It's having to say goodbye to the people you love. You and the girls most of all. I hate that I won't be around to watch our daughters grow up, or for you and me to grow old together. Best day of my life was the day I proposed and you said yes. I still can't believe you took a chance on a broke-ass entrepreneur when you could've had anyone, but I sure am glad you did.

You've made me so happy, Jo. And I wish I could be there to celebrate our anniversary with you in person. We had some good ones, though, didn't we? Who can ever forget the year of the doughnut cake?" She'd made him a chocolate cake for their second anniversary and had cut out the middle, where it was underbaked and had sunk. She burbled a wet laugh at the memory. "Though I gotta say, babe, the tattoo you surprised me with on our tenth takes the prize. If your intention was to make me hard without taking your clothes off, you succeeded. It's hot as hell."

Jo brushed her fingers over the heart tattooed on her ankle. Wreathed in roses, it bore their initials and the word "Forever."

"Good times. And, yeah, it sucks that we're running out of time, but I'll be waiting on the other side with open arms when you get there someday. Which brings me to the second reason for this video. Jo, you have many more years ahead of you, God willing, so don't mourn me forever, please. I want you to be happy again after I'm gone. I want you to do the things we talked about doing. Starting with buying a house, if you haven't already. The money from my life insurance policy ought to cover the down payment, and Uncle Brad and Aunt Dorothy offered to cosign the loan." Sean's aunt and uncle had moved to Costa Rica after they retired and sold their ranch, but they'd kept in close touch. "Last but not least, I want you to date again. Find someone who'll love you like I do and who'll be a father to our girls. I know it's a big ask, which is why I had Reggie hold off delivering this until you'd had a chance to grieve and might be more open to it. But do it anyway. Go live your life." With those words and his signature crooked smile, he crushed her. "Now, I know what you're thinking. Worst. Gift. Ever. You just gotta trust me on this, babe. I love you. See you on the other side." He blew a kiss, leaned in, and the screen went dark.

"No!" she cried as if she could bring him back to life somehow. She felt gutted. It was a minute before she could catch her breath, she was crying so hard. When she finally reached for her phone, she could barely see through her tears to punch in Reggie's number. He picked up on the second ring.

"Damn you," she said.

"Don't shoot the messenger." Reggie's voice, normally deep and resonant enough to be heard in the back row when he performed onstage, a cross between James Earl Jones and Steve Harvey, sounded meek.

"I thought you were my friend!"

"I am. But I was his friend, too, and I was given strict instructions."

"You could've told me. I didn't even know the video existed! You . . . you could've told me."

"If I had, you would've wormed it out of me somehow, and Sean was specific about the delivery date. He didn't think you'd be ready to hear whatever he had to say before now."

"Guess what? I'm still not ready."

"I know, baby girl. I know." Reggie allowed her some space as she sniffled without speaking before he continued. "So, tell me what he said because, honey, the suspense is killing me."

"He wanted me to buy a house."

"That's it?"

"What did you expect?"

"Something along the lines of *Dark Victory* or *Terms of Endearment*." Reggie was a film buff, in keeping with his career as an actor. It wouldn't have surprised Jo to learn he'd seen every movie ever made. She hadn't watched either of the movies he'd referenced, nor did she intend to if they were tearjerkers. She'd done enough crying, though you wouldn't know it looking at her now.

"He also wanted me to date again."

"Wow."

"I know. Crazy, huh?"

"Actually, I was thinking it's about damn time."

She frowned. "What are you saying?"

"Do I need to spell it out? Girl, if ever there was someone who needed to get laid, it's you."

"Thanks for that insight," she said.

He ignored her sarcasm. "Honey, you don't have to be in love with someone to sleep with them."

"Is that why you slept with half of the men in Hollywood?" Or so he'd claimed.

"That was before I met Marco." Marco was his fiancé, whom he was due to marry in six weeks. "And we're talking about you, not me. You're too young to pack it in. Sean was right about that."

"No one could ever replace him. What we had was special."

"True." Reggie knew this better than anyone. He'd been there from the beginning. And he'd been the best man at their wedding. "But the fact is he's gone, and a woman has needs. Or so I've heard."

She reached for the box of tissues on the nightstand. "My sex drive is in sleep mode."

"Dear Lord. Don't tell me you haven't even—"

"No."

"Well, now I know what to get you for Christmas. I'll give you a hint: It comes with batteries."

"Can we please talk about something else?" She blew her nose into a tissue with an unladylike honk that prompted Snickers to investigate. Jo gave her a pat on the head, and thus reassured, the old Lab returned to the comfort of her plush bed. "How are the wedding plans coming?"

"Peachy. When Marco isn't channeling his inner *Mommie Dearest*," he reported. "First, it was the venue he couldn't decide on. Now it's the guest list, which is growing like unwanted hairs. His relatives on this continent alone would fill a banquet hall, and now he's insisting we also invite his Italian relatives, which would bring the head count to just shy of a cast of thousands. When I gently suggested we pare the guest list just a *tad*, he accused me of ruining this entire experience for him." She heard the sound of a breath being forcibly expelled at the other end. "I mean, I've heard of bridezillas, but who knew there was such a thing as groomzillas?"

"They're rare but they exist."

"So, girlfriend, what's it to be?" Reggie circled back to her situation. "Do you plan to remain celibate for the rest of your life out of misguided loyalty to your dead husband, or will you honor his memory and your own needs—however sublimated at the moment—by fulfilling his dying wish?"

"Well, when you put it that way . . ."

"Ha. I knew you'd come to your senses."

"I was being sarcastic!"

"It's what Sean wanted. You heard the man."

"What about what *I* want?"

"So, to be clear, you're refusing to honor your husband's dying wish?"

"No. He was right about one thing. I need to find a place to live that isn't a dump and that has a yard big enough for Jess and Emma to run around in. They—we—deserve better than the Taj Mahole."

Reggie enthusiastically endorsed this. "Just say the word and I'll fly up to aid in your house hunting."

"Thanks, but I can manage on my own. I'll send pictures, though."

"And the other thing?"

"How can I date when I still feel married?" She absently twisted her ring on her finger. A baguette diamond flanked by two smaller, square-cut diamonds on each side set in a rose-gold band, it had belonged to Sean's late mother.

When he'd asked her to marry him, Sean had said, "If it's not your style, we can shop for one that is. Don't feel you have to wear it because it was my mom's."

To which she'd replied, not entirely in jest, "You'd have to take it from my cold, dead hand." Instead, she was still alive, and it was Sean who was dead. She shivered.

"Baby steps. Starting with sex. The partnerless kind," Reggie clarified before she could protest.

She laughed. "You're incorrigible."

"I'm also right. And FYI, I'm not waiting until Christmas, so expect a package in the mail."

Jo was awakened the next morning by the sound of running feet. She cracked one eye open to see a pair of human cannonballs hurtling toward her. "Mommy! Mommy!" they chorused. "We're home!"

"Sorry," said Rosaria, coming up behind them with her two children, Pablo and Alicia, both as round-faced as her, with the same thick dark hair and big brown eyes. "I told the girls we should let you sleep in. I figured that's what you were doing when you didn't answer my text. But they insisted. I let myself in with the spare key you gave me. I hope that was okay."

The girls pounced. Jo couldn't help grinning as she gathered them in her arms, even though she could've used another hour or two, or week, of sleep. "Did you have a fun sleepover?" she asked. They both bobbed their heads. "It's me who should be apologizing," she told her neighbor. "I should've collected them before now. I didn't plan to sleep this late." It was only a few minutes past eight thirty, but she was usually up by six at the latest.

"Rough night?" Rosaria eyed the empty wineglass and pile of used tissues on the nightstand.

Jo nodded but offered no explanation. She didn't like talking about Sean in front of the girls. They were grieving, too. They didn't need to be constantly reminded of their loss. For the same reason she'd taken down the family photos that used to hang on the walls. There was just the one framed 5 x 7 of her and Sean, from their wedding day, that sat on her dresser.

"I fed them breakfast," Rosaria said. "Bacon and eggs."

"Thanks. And thanks for keeping them overnight. I'll be over for their stuff as soon as I'm dressed."

"No rush. I had to run a few of their things through the wash. They're still in the dryer."

Rosaria wasn't specific, but Jo could guess which things. *Emma.* While she wasn't outwardly grieving—she'd been three when Sean died, too young to fully grasp the concept of death—she'd reverted to her babyhood habits of sucking her thumb and wetting the bed. It was why Jo had held her back a year rather than enrolling her in kindergarten this year. Emma must've wet the bed again last night. Jo felt bad for her and guilty that it'd caused extra work for Rosaria. She'd make it up to her neighbor by inviting Pablo and Alicia for a sleepover and giving her a night off.

"Vamos, chicos," Rosaria said to her children, and they followed her out the door.

"I'm hungry," announced Jess.

Jo knew better than to ask. Jess, a naturally picky eater, had developed a pathological aversion to new foods, or any that were prepared differently from what she was used to, since Sean died. Even if she'd been hungry when Rosaria had served breakfast, she wouldn't have eaten it unless the fried eggs were cooked through, the bacon just shy of burned, and the toast browned just so. Whereas Emma would eat anything on her plate. Once, even sushi, to Jess's utter horror.

Her two daughters couldn't be more different from each other. Jess, who'd just turned seven, was the image of her father, with his mess of dark curls and soulful brown eyes behind purple-framed glasses. Five-year-old Emma looked like Jo did in the photos of her at that age, with her pixie face framed by flyaway strawberry-blond hair and bachelor button–blue eyes. A girly girl, she liked wearing pink, preferably with ruffles, and favored her stuffed animals and dolls over her other toys. Jess was a bookworm who wouldn't have been caught dead in a ruffled dress. She collected mineral rocks and dreamed of becoming a geologist when she grew up.

"You can have cereal," Jo told her. "But"—she held up her index finger to indicate she wasn't finished yet—"only on the condition that you eat whatever I fix for dinner tonight."

"No fair," Jess grumbled.

"That's the deal. Take it or leave it."

"Fine," Jess mumbled. "But no yucky green stuff."

"If by 'yucky green stuff' you mean vegetables, there's a good chance you'll be eating them."

Jess eyed her narrowly, as if she suspected it was a trick. The truth was, Jo did sometimes have to resort to trickery with her, or negotiating, as she preferred to think of it. Otherwise, Jess wouldn't eat any healthy foods.

"Do we have any Frosted Flakes?" Jess asked.

"No, but we have Corn Flakes."

"I want some, too!" said Emma. She probably wasn't hungry, but she aped everything her big sister did.

The girls went racing off to the kitchen, and Jo got up to tackle the day. As she swept the used tissues from her pity party the previous night into the wastebasket, her thoughts returned to Sean's message from beyond the grave. She shivered, pressure building behind her eyes. Sean's dying wish that she start dating again was a hard pass. As for the other thing he'd urged her to do . . . For the first time since he'd died, she could see herself and her daughters in a home of their own.

She knew of a Realtor, Lynette Woodson, whom she'd met at a wedding she'd worked recently. She'd call her today and make an appointment. It was time. Past time, if she was being honest.

4

"Are you sure this is the right address?" Jo stared out the windshield as they pulled up in front of the house she'd come to see today. She couldn't believe her eyes. Because it wasn't just any house. It was her and Sean's dream house. The house on Mountain Laurel Lane.

"It's one of my listings, so yes," said Lynette. "A pocket listing, which is why you don't see a For Sale sign. It won't officially be on the market until tomorrow. I'm giving you a sneak peek. Is something wrong?" she asked when Jo made no move to climb out.

"No." Jo shivered as though a goose had walked over her grave, to borrow an expression from her meemaw. "It's just . . . I've been here before."

"You know someone who lived here?"

"No. I've never been inside. I've only driven past." For some reason, Jo didn't mention the photos of the house on her vision board. Maybe because it would require an explanation she wasn't prepared to give. Or maybe it was because she didn't want to jinx this opportunity, if that's what it was.

The house, with its yellow clapboard siding and cheery red door, looked as inviting as she remembered. The same white-haired man she'd seen on her previous visit was mowing the lawn. The rosebushes lining the front walk were in bloom. She was dying to see inside, but there was something she needed to know before she got her hopes up.

"How much?" she asked. She groaned when Lynette quoted a sum that was 30K above the top of her price range. "You're killing me."

"It doesn't cost anything to look," Lynette replied breezily as she climbed out. In her early fifties with a sleek silver bob, she was stylishly dressed today in a houndstooth pencil skirt paired with a cropped white jacket. Jo felt like a poor relation tagging along as they headed up the front walk, wearing the shorts and T-shirt she'd pulled from the pile of clean laundry that she hadn't gotten around to folding, with her hair scraped back in a ponytail. "And there might be a way you can afford it. We'll get to that after you've had a look around, if you like what you see."

Jo wondered what she meant. Would the seller consider a lowball offer? If so, why? "What's the catch?" she asked, raising her voice to be heard above the droning of the power mower.

"Catch?"

"Black mold. Termites. Cracked foundation. Leaky roof." Jo listed some of the flaws that might cause a seller to entertain a lowball offer. Then something else occurred to her, something even more off-putting than any of the aforementioned, and she came to a dead stop. It was a beautiful June morning, the sun shining, but she suddenly felt chilled. "Was someone murdered here?"

"You watch too much TV," replied Lynette with an amused shake of her head. *Or maybe my mind goes there because I've experienced the worst losing Sean.* "No cracks, leaks, or infestations that I'm aware of, and the previous owner, Mrs. Applegate, died of natural causes at the age of ninety-two."

"There's something you're not telling me, then. I don't see how it's possible—"

Before she could finish the sentence, a voice called, "Morning, ladies!" The man operating the mower shut off the engine and began walking toward them. Somewhere in his seventies, he wore navy board shorts and a Hard Rock T-shirt, both faded from many washings. His stubby white ponytail poked from under the Giants ball cap covering his head. His blue eyes twinkled, the lines at their corners curving down toward his smiling mouth. His face was the very definition of "craggy."

"I know you weren't expecting us until eleven. I hope it's okay that we're here early," Lynette said after they'd exchanged hellos. It was ten to eleven.

"No problem. I'm just finishing up here." He gestured toward the half-mowed grass. "Front door's unlocked. Key's on the table just inside. If you'd be so kind as to put it in the lockbox when you're leaving, I'd be obliged."

"Of course. Hank, this is my client, Jo Myers. Jo, this is Hank Goodwin."

Jo saw a glint of recognition in Hank's eyes as they were introduced. Did he remember her from her last visit? It didn't seem possible. It had been dark, and he couldn't have gotten more than a glimpse. "Pleased to meet you," he said. "You have any questions while I'm here, just give me a shout."

"I do have one question," Jo said. "How long have you lived here?" He didn't look old enough to be the widower of the deceased homeowner unless theirs had been a May–December romance. A son, perhaps?

"Almost twelve years," he answered.

A wistful expression crossed his face, prompting Jo to ask, "May I ask why you're selling?" Out of the corner of her eye, she saw Lynette shoot her a startled glance. She didn't imagine it was the kind of question prospective buyers normally asked of homeowners. But then, she hadn't encountered any homeowners at the properties she'd toured thus far. And she was curious.

"Oh, I don't own the place," he said. "I rent the downstairs. Or I did when Martha was alive. After she died, her children asked me to stay on and see to the upkeep until the place sold." Jo perked up. This must be what Lynette had meant when she'd said there might be a way she could afford this property. Rental income could be a game changer.

"Martha and her husband were the original owners. I didn't move in until after their kids were grown and Martha's husband had passed. When I answered her ad for a lodger, I was between addresses, looking for someplace permanent. I didn't expect to stay long. But, as you can see, I'm still here. Martha was a good woman."

His expression turned mournful.

"I'm sorry for your loss," she said, her heart going out to him. She motioned toward the sign she'd noticed on her previous visit. A HERO LIVES HERE, it read. "Would that be you?"

He nodded, looking embarrassed. "That there was Martha's doing. She put the dang thing up without my knowledge and refused to take it down even after I told her there were no heroes in 'Nam."

"Why do you say that?"

"Don't get me wrong. I fought alongside some brave men when I was in country, but those of us who came back were jeered instead of cheered. Public sentiment wasn't in our favor."

"Anyone who fought for their country deserves recognition," Jo declared. Both her grandfathers had served in the military. Grandpa Bob had fought in the Korean War. Pappaw had fought in Vietnam.

A smile eased its way back onto Hank's craggy face. "Those were Martha's exact words."

"She sounds like a good friend."

"She was." His eyes glistened below the brim on his ball cap.

"Where will you go after the house is sold?"

He shrugged. "Got my name on the wait list for VA housing, and I've put some feelers out elsewhere in the community. Something's bound to turn up." He sounded resigned, but she didn't miss the slight downturn of his mouth or the look of regret in his eyes. *This is his home.*

"Good luck," she told him.

She and Lynette continued up the path, and Hank resumed his mowing. As they walked through the house, Lynette pointing out its features,

Jo's excitement grew. Its floor plan consisted of a living room, kitchen and dining nook, two small bedrooms and a Jack-and-Jill bathroom upstairs, and an en suite bedroom and sitting room downstairs, which had its own entrance. The rooms were on the small side, but the house didn't seem cramped with light pouring in every window. The original hardwood flooring, built-ins, and wood-burning fireplace made up for the outdated plumbing fixtures and appliances, and overall shabbiness. The property abutted state forestlands to the east, and the view from the deck off the rear entrance was of the large, leafy backyard, with forested hills and layers of mountains stretching into the distance beyond. She pictured her family eating meals on the deck in summer, or gathered in front of a cozy fire inside in winter.

"Where do I sign?" she said at the end of the tour.

Lynette beamed at her. "I knew you'd love it."

"The question is whether I can afford it. How much does the downstairs rent for?"

Lynette entered some numbers into her calculator app and turned her phone so Jo could see the total on its screen. "This would be your monthly payment on a thirty-year mortgage factoring in the rental income." The figure seemed doable. Just. But her hopes were dashed by Lynette's next words. "But there's something you should know before you consider making an offer."

"What?"

"The rent Hank pays includes kitchen and laundry privileges."

Jo stared at the Realtor in shock and dismay. "You've got to be kidding me." Of all the deal-breakers she'd imagined, this was not one of them. But it was a deal-breaker, nonetheless.

"The arrangement seems to have worked with him and the previous owner."

"She was elderly and lived alone. Maybe she enjoyed the company. I, on the other hand, value my privacy. I also have my children to consider." How would they—Jess especially—react to a stranger traipsing through their house? They'd been traumatized enough by their father's death. They needed stability now more than ever.

"It could still work."

"No way." Jo shook her head. "And who's to say he would even want to stay on under new ownership?" Especially if the new owner was a single mom of two energetic young children.

"I've spoken to him about it. He said he'd be open to it."

"That may be, but—"

"He's the dream lodger, according to the sellers. Not only did he pay his rent on time, but he also did chores and helped take care of their mom when her health was failing. They came to rely on him."

Jo softened, hearing about Hank's reliability and good deeds, but it didn't change her mind. "I'm sure he's all those things, and he seems nice. But the fact remains I don't know him." If it were just the outdoor spaces and laundry room, she might consider it, but sharing the kitchen with someone who'd be using it several times a day at minimum if he ate most of his meals at home, was an entirely different matter. It wasn't a large kitchen. They'd be tripping over each other if they were both using it at the same time. "What if the rent didn't include kitchen privileges?"

"Then you'd be getting anywhere from a third to half of what Hank pays."

Jo's heart sank, along with her last hope of owning the home. She couldn't afford it on her income alone, which varied from month to month, depending on the time of year. The wedding season in Gold Creek was June through early October. The rest of the year, bookings were fewer. And as a freelancer, she had to pay out of pocket for health insurance, a benefit she'd enjoyed as a salaried employee. Even if she were to buy the house and keep Hank on, it would be risky. What if he were to move out? She'd have to find another lodger. And who knew what she'd get?

It seemed her and Sean's dream house was destined to remain just that—a dream. "Well, I guess we can cross this one off the list," she said, trying to hide her disappointment.

She exited the building to see the grass was cut. Hank was gone, along with the pickup that'd been parked in the driveway when they arrived. She waited while Lynette locked up and deposited the key in the lockbox.

"May I make a suggestion?" Lynette asked as they walked back to her car.

"Does it involve waving a magic wand?"

"If only." Lynette gave a chuckle. "Why don't you meet Hank for coffee? You could discuss your concerns with him. See if you can work something out. The property won't be listed until the start of business hours tomorrow. There's still time to make an offer if you change your mind."

Jo was opening her mouth to say, "What would be the point?" when she remembered something Sean used to say. *If a window of opportunity appears, don't pull down the shade.* He'd lived by his motto, as an optimist and entrepreneur. He'd conceived of MashUp, the app he'd designed to allow fans of performing artists to track their tour dates, purchase concert tickets and merchandise, and enter contests to win prizes, such as bling and backstage access, across multiple music-streaming channels and social media platforms. He'd written the code, and he and his business partner, Rohit, had worked tirelessly in courting the artists and their managers along with potential investors. Their start-up would've succeeded if fate hadn't intervened, she was certain. Once the investors learned Sean had brain cancer, they'd evaporated. Even Rohit conceded that their enterprise was doomed without Sean.

She knew what Sean would have urged her to do in this situation.

"I suppose," she said, "there's no harm in meeting him." It would probably lead nowhere, but she owed it to herself—and Sean's memory—to at least explore this opportunity.

Cowboy Coffee, the bakery-café in the heart of Gold Creek's historic district, was where Jo often met with clients and where she and her closest friends, the five women who called themselves the Tattooed Ladies, met for dinner regularly. It occupied the ground floor of a nineteenth-century redbrick two-story, co-owned by her friend Frannie and Frannie's sister, Vanessa, who were descendants of the town's first Creole settlers. Several smaller businesses, one of them Frannie's tattoo parlor, Red Ink Tattoos, occupied the upper floor. Today, Cowboy Coffee was where Jo was meeting Hank Goodwin. Lynette had arranged the meeting, which was scheduled for 1:30. Jo arrived at the appointed time and spotted Hank, in tan chinos and a blue chambray shirt, seated at one of the wrought-iron café tables on the brick forecourt. On the table before him were two take-out coffees.

He pushed one toward her as she sat down. "You seem like a cinnamon latte kind of girl, but I can get you something else if you'd prefer."

"No, this is perfect. Thanks." She pried the lid from her cup and inhaled the heavenly aroma of coffee and steamed milk infused with cinnamon and nutmeg before taking a sip. She was on edge, and the warm brew and Hank's thoughtful gesture hit the spot. "And thank you for meeting me."

It was a mild, sunny day. Most of the outdoor tables were occupied by coffee drinkers and people lingering over their lunches. It was tourist season, as evidenced by the steady trickle of passersby on the sidewalk beyond. The clopping of hooves announced a horse-drawn stagecoach moments before it came into view on the street—stagecoach rides were a popular tourist attraction in Gold Creek.

"My pleasure," Hank said. "I understand you're considering making an offer on the house?"

Her stomach flipped. "Depends on whether I can afford it. Without its rental income, it'd be out of my price range."

"And you'd like to know what to expect if I were to stay on?"

"Well, yes." He was blunt, no beating around the bush. "Nothing against you. I don't know you. It's just . . . I've never lived with anyone who wasn't family. Aside from my roommate when I was in college."

"Then you need to know I don't smoke, drink to excess, do drugs, or throw wild parties. Nor do I keep late hours. I'm retired but stay active, in case you're worried I'm one of those old folks with nothing better to do than bend your ear. Is there anything else you'd like to know about me?"

"What sort of activities do you do? I mean, besides gardening."

"Mainly volunteer work, though I've been known to do the occasional odd job for friends and neighbors. I also belong to a motorcycle club—the Graybeard Bikers' Club. Maybe you've heard of us?"

"No, but I noticed the Harley parked in the garage. I'm guessing it's yours and not Mrs. Applegate's."

"You guessed right. Although I used to take Martha for a spin on it now and then."

Jo smiled at the image of the nonagenarian roaring around on the back of a motorcycle. "She sounds like my kind of old lady."

"She wasn't one to spend her golden years in a rocking chair, that's for sure. She walked two miles a day, rain or shine, until her heart started to give out. She had a regular Friday poker game going with her friends, and when she hosted it at the house, it'd get raucous, speaking of wild parties."

"I want to be her when I grow up."

He chuckled. "She called it 'growing old disgracefully.' Martha didn't believe old people should act their age. Which is why we hit it off and why I stayed for as long as I did. That, and neither of us was in the habit of leaving messes for the other to clean up. Which is important when you're sharing spaces with someone."

"To be honest, that's my biggest concern. You know, sharing spaces. How often do you normally use the kitchen?"

"Right now it's just me, so I come and go as I please. It was the same when Martha was alive. But it'd be different if you owned the house. I don't imagine you'd want some stranger popping in and out. I'd be happy to work around your schedule so we wouldn't be in each other's way."

One by one he was knocking down her objections like so many bowling pins. She didn't know whether to be worried or relieved. Her biggest fear was that she'd be lulled into buying the house, only to discover too late that she'd made a mistake. Time to show him what *he'd* be getting out of the bargain.

"I don't know how much Lynette told you about me."

"Just that you were a single mom with two young children."

"And a dog."

"How old are your children?"

"Jess is seven and Emma is five. They're very active, so if you're used to peace and quiet, you'd be in for a rude awakening. Literally, as in being woken early in the morning by the pitter-patter of little feet overhead."

He seemed more amused than put off. "Martha was deaf as a post and refused to wear her hearing aid. When she watched her TV shows, she'd turn the volume up so loud the neighbors could hear it. It wasn't until I got her a hearing device that plugged into her TV that I got any peace."

"Children don't come with an off button."

"I'm aware."

"It wouldn't bother you?"

"Not in the least. When you're old, you miss things that might've bothered you in your youth. I volunteer at the Morningside Home for Veterans here in Gold Creek. Can you guess what happens when grandchildren and great-grandchildren visit?"

"They disturb the peace?"

"Sure, but that's part of their appeal. Some of the residents don't get out much. Children are a breath of fresh air, and a reminder of when they were young. The old boys are always happy to see them come and sorry to see them go. Otherwise, life in an assisted living facility can seem pretty dull."

"I never thought of it that way. Do you have family of your own?"

"As in next of kin? You want to know that it wouldn't become your problem if I should fall and break my hip or suffer a stroke?"

Her cheeks warmed. "The thought crossed my mind."

"I have a brother back in Ohio, where I'm from, but I don't see much of him. And there's my grandson, Ian. He's in the air force, currently stationed overseas. My daughter-in-law, Cherise, is my emergency contact. She lives in the Seattle area and works as a nurse. She'd come and take me off your hands in the event I should become incapacitated."

"I wasn't—"

"Sure you were," he countered mildly. "And I don't blame you one bit. You have every right to know what you'd be signing up for, if you were to take me on as a lodger."

"I've never . . . this is all new for me."

"First-time homebuyer?"

"How did you know?" she said dryly.

"Lucky guess." His blue eyes crinkled with good humor.

They sat drinking their coffees in companionable silence for a minute or two. At the grander Italianate-style brick building across the street that housed both the Washburn County Sheriff's Department and Washburn County Detention Center, uniforms came and went. Two doors down at the Gold Nugget Ice Cream Parlor, a little boy ate an ice cream with his mom. Next door at Mother Lode Mercantile, someone was checking out the sandwich board advertising the chance to pan for gold in its sluice, a replica of the ones miners used back in the day.

"What did you do before you retired?" she asked, returning her gaze to Hank.

"I was a pilot in the military. After I retired, I flew for an air transport company. You?"

"I'm a photographer. Weddings mostly."

"You must be good if you can make a living at it."

"Good enough." Her unique style had gained her a modest reputation. Where traditional wedding photographers might focus on the highlights, she favored the unscripted moments. Her favorite was the photo she'd taken at an outdoor wedding in a local park. Its subject, an elderly woman, was a passerby who'd stopped to watch the ceremony. She was depicted in close-up against the backdrop of the wedding party in soft focus, her expression a mix of wonder and wistfulness.

"Is your children's father in the picture?"

His question caught her off guard, and she felt the familiar clench in her throat. She shook her head. "He passed away recently."

"I'm sorry." She was grateful when he didn't dwell on the subject, although the look of compassion on his face suggested he was no stranger to loss. "Anything else you'd like to know about me?"

"No. I think that about covers it."

"Call me if you think of anything else."

"I will."

They exchanged contact info and he rose to leave, picking up his empty cup to discard. "One more thing, Jo, and I'm not saying this because I have a dog to hunt. I don't think you'd regret buying the house, regardless of whether you were to keep me on or not. It's a good house to raise a family in. Martha's children, Ruth and Mark, both have fond memories of growing up there."

"I'll keep that in mind." She didn't mention that she'd envisioned living there with her family long before they'd met, while Sean was alive. "Thanks again for the coffee."

Sean would've liked him, she thought as she watched him walk away. Heck, she liked him. She also knew if she didn't make a preemptive offer, there would be multiple offers on the house by this time tomorrow. Desirable properties didn't stay on the market for long in this community. Known as the "jewel of the gold country," Gold Creek boasted a population of just under ten thousand, which tripled from May through September with the tourists and summer folk. Prospective buyers who lived here year-round competed against out-of-towners looking to buy second homes. View properties tended to generate bidding wars and sell for sums well in excess of their asking prices. Yet it was a huge decision.

One thing was for sure: Hank Goodwin hadn't made it any easier.

5

Red Ink Tattoos was closed, with a hand-lettered sign on the door that read *Back in 30 minutes*, when she popped upstairs to see Frannie, so she headed for her car, parked down the street. She stopped at Buckboard Books on the way. The family-owned business run by her friend Marisol was the oldest bookshop in Washburn County and second oldest in the state of California. Founded by Marisol's ancestress Milicent Macgowan, who'd peddled dime novels and periodicals door to door from her buckboard wagon in the early 1900s before it became a brick-and-mortar store, it'd been owned by four successive generations of Macgowans, of which Marisol and her father were the last surviving members in Gold Creek. Housed in a two-story built of sandstone in the Edwardian style with a front bow window, arched pediments, and a gabled roof, it wouldn't have looked out of place on a cobbled backstreet of London. A striped tabby was curled up, snoozing, on a stack of books in the window when Jo pushed open its glass door.

Inside, books lined the walls and warren of freestanding shelves in back, with overstuffed chairs creating cozy reading nooks where there were gaps. Featured titles were displayed on the vintage tables dotting the space. Persian-style rugs were scattered on the hardwood floor. Half a dozen customers browsed, and in the children's section a young mother sat reading aloud to her toddler.

Jo spotted Marisol in back assisting a customer, a grumpy-looking middle-aged man, and waved. Marisol held up two fingers, mouthing the words "two minutes." She wore purple velour leggings paired with an oversize Dr. Seuss T-shirt, which went with the Cat in the Hat tattoo on one arm, and rhinestone-studded glasses. Marisol had her own unique style, a quirkiness that sometimes fooled people into not taking her seriously, despite her being a successful business owner.

A marmalade cat sauntered past as Jo stood waiting. Buckboard Books partnered with Wee-Care, a local feline rescue shelter. On any given day, anywhere from three to a dozen felines roamed the premises in search of future owners. Currently there were thirteen, a baker's dozen.

Marisol hurried over to her as soon as she was free. "Perfect timing. You saved me from dropping the f-bomb on Mr. Sourpuss." She watched as the grumpy man she'd been speaking with stalked past on his way out after handing her the book he'd been holding. As Jo learned with Marisol's next words, he wasn't a customer, as she'd presumed. "Stanley is one of our local authors. He's angry because we don't carry his title here." She rolled her eyes and glanced down at the copy of his book that he'd given her. "Like people are lining up to buy his self-published memoir."

"They might if he led an extraordinary life."

"He's a retired postal worker."

Jo suppressed a smile. "Who knows what he's seen while delivering mail? Anyway, this is probably all he's got." She nodded toward the book in Marisol's hands. She felt sorry for him.

"You're right. I need to try harder to be more tolerant. Working in retail would make a grouch out of Santa Claus." Marisol was in fact one of the nicest people Jo knew, beloved by her customers and the authors whose events she hosted. "Can I help you with anything, or did you just stop by to say hello?" Before Jo could respond, she said, "Wait. Don't tell me. You found a house."

Since she'd started house hunting, Jo had kept her fellow Tattooed Ladies entertained and horrified in equal measure with her descriptions of the properties that she'd looked at. The ones in her price range were either fixer-uppers or infested with vermin, mold, dry rot, and in one case, a tenant turned squatter. Or they were in undesirable locations, like the house under a flight path and the one next door to a landfill. Her friends had been sympathetic. They'd also aided in her efforts. Suzy had gone with her to look at a house for sale in her neighborhood. She, Marisol, and Frannie asked everyone who came into their places of business if they knew of any properties for sale by owner. Kyra's boyfriend, Coop, had offered to sell Jo a parcel of his thirty-acre spread in the country, where he and Kyra lived in an old farmhouse, at a rock-bottom price. Jo had been tempted by the setting and the prospect of having Kyra and Coop as neighbors, but it would've meant building a house, which would've been too much for her in addition to the demands of her job and children.

Her stomach did another flip. "How'd you guess?"

"Your face. You look like the people in those Publishers Clearing House ads do holding those giant checks. Like you don't know if it's real or not."

"That about sums it up."

Marisol's dark eyes danced behind her bedazzled cat-eye glasses. Adorable and curvy, she had the features of her Filipina mother. But she'd gotten the spray of freckles across her nose and red highlights in her chin-length black hair from her Scottish father. "I can't believe you found a place in your price range that isn't a dump."

"Me either. It's perfect except for one thing."

"What is it with this one?"

"There's someone living in it."

"Oh no. Not another squatter!"

"No. He's—"

"Hi, guys!" called a voice from behind.

Jo turned around to see their friend Kyra coming toward them, in jeans and a white button-down, with her rescue dog, Ranger. She looked like a model, tall and willowy, with dark hair she wore in a long braid, huge hazel eyes, and cheekbones that could cut glass. Her shepherd mix looked like a cross between a bear and a wolf. Smarter than many humans, Ranger had taught himself tricks like how to open doors and power down a car window. He also knew better than to tangle with the store cat, a black tom with one torn ear, that'd wandered into his path and now stood hissing at him. "I came to pick up that book I ordered," she said to Marisol. Glancing over at Jo, she asked, "What were you two talking about? You looked thick as thieves when I walked in."

"Jo found a house," said Marisol. "Only there appears to be an issue."

Jo sketched out the situation. "So you see my predicament. If I buy the house with its resident lodger, I could be buying a whole new set of problems along with it."

"Or it could be a good thing," said Marisol. "Not to be sexist or anything, but if he's handy and mows the grass, that'd be a plus."

"You know what they say—no risk, no reward," said Kyra. "I hate to think where I'd be today if I'd stayed in my marriage. Dead, probably." She shuddered visibly. When she'd first arrived in Gold Creek over two years earlier, jobless and knowing no one, she'd been on the run from her abusive ex. A former art teacher, she'd since reinvented herself as a forensic artist, and was working for the local sheriff's department. She'd also found love at last.

"And look at you now. You're living the dream, solving crimes with your wonder dog . . ." Marisol glanced down at Ranger, who grinned and wagged his tail. "And shacking up with your hot boyfriend."

"That," said Kyra, her eyes sparkling, "was just the icing on the cake."

The glow she radiated cast a spotlight on Jo's loveless existence. She felt her heart wrench.

"Life is full of surprises," Marisol said.

Not all of them good. Jo remembered, with a pang, the day she'd learned Sean had inoperable brain cancer. The day life had ended as she'd known it. Now she was faced with a decision that could negatively impact the rest of her life, and the lives of her children, if she chose wrong.

"I need to decide before the start of business hours tomorrow," she said. "That's when the house goes on the market." Her stomach executed a cartwheel in slow motion. "I don't know what to do."

"I know one thing," said Marisol. "This calls for an emergency meeting of the Tattooed Ladies Club."

One thing about becoming a widow that Jo had learned: It showed you who your true friends were. People she'd thought were her friends avoided her now like she was a known COVID carrier at a Christmas party. She'd become the dreaded third wheel and an uncomfortable reminder of their own mortality. Liz, one half of a couple with whom Jo and Sean had socialized on occasion, had at least had the decency to be honest about it. "It's not the same without Sean," she'd confessed. Jo's best friends and fellow Tattooed Ladies were the polar opposite. They'd revealed themselves, like evergreens in winter, to be true friends in her time of need. They'd taken turns cooking and cleaning for her, and babysitting her children, while she'd taken Sean to his doctor appointments and chemo treatments, and after he'd died, when she'd been paralyzed by her grief. They had lifted her up when she'd been low. They'd given her a kick in the butt when she'd needed one.

That evening, they were there to give her some much-needed advice. The five women met at the wine bar down the street from Suzy's hair salon, Shear Delight. Press, with its extensive wine menu and trendy decor, accented by retro touches like an antique wine press by the entrance and vintage beer sign above the bar, attracted a more upscale crowd than the touristy bars in town, and tonight it was packed as usual. Jo, Marisol, Kyra, and Suzy were seated at their table, drinking wine and nibbling from the charcuterie board they'd ordered, when Frannie, the last to arrive, blew in.

"Sorry I'm late," she said as she dropped into the vacant chair at the table. "My last appointment of the day was a beast."

"Your customer?" asked Suzy.

"No, the tattoo he requested. It took three hours and five different colors of ink."

Marisol poured a glass of chardonnay and pushed it across the table toward Frannie. "Not to worry. We didn't start without you. But now that you're here, Jo has some news."

Kyra preempted her. "She found a house."

"Wow. So we're celebrating?" Frannie appeared confused. "In your text you said it was an emergency."

"It is. I need you guys to talk me out of doing something I might regret," Jo said as her stomach performed gymnastics. She took a drink of her wine to calm her jitters.

"What, buying the house or passing on it?" asked Kyra. She was here without her trusty sidekick. Ranger had stayed home with her boyfriend—Ranger's second-favorite human, according to Kyra.

"That . . ." Jo raised her voice to be heard amid the loud conversation the party of four at the next table was having. "Is what I need help deciding."

"If two heads are better than one, there's no problem five can't solve." Frannie helped herself to slices of prosciutto and cheese from the charcuterie board, layering them on a piece of bread.

"Speaking of which, yours is looking a little shaggy," said Suzy, assessing her oldest friend with a professional eye. "Call me and we'll schedule an appointment for a haircut. I can fit you in next week. On the house," she added.

Frannie just smiled and shrugged.

Frannie and Suzy were both "sixty-six years young," as Suzy liked to say. They'd been best friends since kindergarten. Aside from that, and the fact that they were both divorced, they had little in common. Suzy was a self-described "fashionista grandma" who'd once declared that she intended to die with her face and heels on. Jo had never seen her when she wasn't stylishly dressed, in full makeup, with her blond hair blown out. Tonight she wore a gauzy black tunic dress with a silver-and-turquoise conch belt fastened loosely above her slim hips, and silver sandal heels. Frannie was the earth-mother type. She wore her curly silver hair short so she wouldn't have to fuss with it, and didn't bother with makeup. Her preferred attire was denim and cotton. Today, she wore her work uniform of khakis and a Red Ink Tattoos T-shirt. Both women were beautiful, each in her own way, although Suzy fought the battle against wrinkles and gray hairs with her arsenal of beauty products and hair dyes, while Frannie was content to grow old gracefully.

Jo produced her phone and tapped on its camera roll. She passed it around so everyone could see the pictures she'd taken of the house when she toured it with Lynette. "It's gorgeous," pronounced Suzy. "The decor could use some updating, but other than that, it's perfect."

"The views are incredible," said Marisol.

"I can picture you relaxing on the deck," said Kyra.

"Looks familiar," said Frannie. "Where have I seen it before?"

"My vision board," Jo reminded her. The day she'd gone to Red Ink Tattoos to get the heart tattoo with which she'd surprised Sean on their tenth anniversary, she'd shown Frannie the photos of the house on the vision board she'd created on Pinterest. "It was Sean's and my dream house."

"Right." Frannie looked up at her. "Talk about kismet. It's as if—"

"It was destined." Kyra finished the sentence for her.

Jo felt a shiver go through her. "Except for one thing."

Jo explained, for Frannie's and Suzy's benefit, about its resident lodger and how he factored in. Suzy wasn't shy in giving her opinion. "I don't know about you all, but someone else's dirty dishes in the sink and their tighty-whities in the wash would be a deal-breaker for me. Someone I wasn't sleeping with, that is, and even then, I'd expect him to clean up after himself."

"Hank claims to be tidy," Jo said. "And I'd prefer not to think about his choice of underwear."

"Are you worried he might accidentally catch sight of you in *your* underwear?" asked Marisol. "Because, you know, this situation has 'rom-com' written all over it." When Jo gave her a withering look, she added, "Just saying."

"No," she said. "And there's nothing the least bit romantic about it. He's old, for one thing. He fought in the Vietnam War."

"Hey, watch who you're calling old," protested Suzy. "Some of us were alive back then."

"What's he like?" asked Frannie, taking a bite of her ham-and-cheese-topped bread slice.

"He seems nice. Maybe you know him. Hank Goodwin?" Frannie, a fourth-generation Gold Creek native and local business owner, seemed to know everyone in town, newcomers and old-timers alike.

"Name doesn't ring a bell. What else can you tell us about him?"

"He drives a Harley and belongs to a bikers' club."

"He's in a biker gang? Oooh. Now we're talking." Suzy grinned and waggled the cooked asparagus spear she held in one hand in a gesture that might've been interpreted as suggestive.

"It's not the Hells Angels. They call themselves the Graybeard Bikers' Club."

"I've heard of them," said Frannie. "One of their members is a customer of mine."

"I don't care what he drives," Jo said. "What matters is, I'd have a stranger living in my house. It'd be weird for the girls. Emma would probably be okay with it. She likes everyone. But Jess isn't one to roll with change, as you know, and she's having a hard enough time coping with her father's death."

"Maybe you could find someone you do know to rent the downstairs," suggested Marisol. Tonight she wore one of her vintage finds, a fifties swing dress, robin's-egg blue with cherries on it, paired with a red cardigan, in which she looked as though she'd just come from a sock hop.

"Or you could do a house flip," said Suzy, delicately biting off the tip of her asparagus spear. "A paint job and floor refinishing wouldn't break the bank, and you could sell for a profit."

Jo shook her head. "I don't know anyone who's looking to rent, and I'm not interested in doing a house flip—too risky."

"We can all agree on one thing," said Kyra as she sipped her wine thoughtfully. "Change is hard."

"Here's to you getting a fresh start." Marisol raised her glass in a toast. "Speaking of which, have you given any more thought to the other thing Sean wanted you to do besides buy a house?"

Jo felt her chest constrict. She'd told her friends about Sean's surprise anniversary message. They hadn't watched the video—it was too private to show anyone—but they'd gotten the gist of it. "No," she said. "There's nothing to think about. Dating is out of the question."

"Especially when you're still wearing your ring," said Suzy dryly, her gaze dropping to Jo's left ring finger.

"It's my Do Not Disturb sign," Jo replied, tipping her chin up in defiance.

"It does send a signal," Frannie agreed.

Suzy suggested, "You might consider taking it off. You know, while you're not thinking about dating."

"Never," Jo declared, and placed her hand on her lap, where it was out of sight.

"You never know," amended Suzy. A veteran of online dating, she got more action in her sixties than most of the single women Jo knew in their thirties and forties. Currently she was seeing a divorced, fiftysomething pharmacist named Cliff, whom she'd met on Match.com.

"I thought I was doomed to become a spinster cat lady before I met Cal," Marisol said. She and her boyfriend had met when he'd been working as a guide for Gold Creek Tours while taking a gap year between his undergrad and postgrad. Buckboard Books had been one of the stops on his tour. Over time, their friendship had blossomed into romance, despite their twenty-year age difference.

"Will he be coming home for the summer?" asked Kyra. Cal was currently attending NYU film school in New York City.

"That's the plan. I'm already counting the days. It's been weeks since his last visit, and phone sex does have its limitations. Unless you're the NSA listening in, then I imagine it's hot stuff."

"TMI." Kyra covered her ears, and then they were all giggling like teenage girls.

After they'd drunk the wine and talked some more, it was time to go. Jo said, as she stood, "I still don't know what to do about the house. And I only have until tomorrow morning before it's listed."

"Why don't you sleep on it?" advised Frannie. "The way forward is usually clearer after a good night's sleep."

"In the immortal words of Scarlett O'Hara, 'Tomorrow is another day,'" quoted Kyra.

Jo wondered what tomorrow would bring.

She arrived home at 9:40 to find the house quiet. Her babysitter, Allison, sat on the sofa with her laptop open and Snickers curled at her feet. She looked up, flashing a mouthful of braces. "Hi, Mrs. M. The girls are asleep. I fed them and made sure they both took their baths." Allison was sixteen, a junior at the local high school, but looked all of twelve. She reminded Jo of herself at that age.

"Everything go okay?" Jo worried, even when her girls were in trusted hands.

"Yeah. Jess claimed she had a tummy ache, but I could tell she was faking."

"How did you know she was faking?"

"When I'm sick to my stomach, even the smell of food makes me want to throw up, but she ate a brownie and asked for seconds. Oh, that's another thing—we made brownies. I hope that was okay."

"Of course." Jo kept boxed brownie mixes on hand at all times for that purpose.

"I said no to the second brownie. Should I have called you?" Allison looked worried suddenly.

"About her alleged tummy ache? No, although I'm sure she was hoping you would. It's not the first time she's faked an illness." The nurse at Jess's school had become concerned enough to suggest that Jo take her to see a child psychologist. She'd given her the name of a therapist, and Jo had made an appointment with Dr. Shaw for next week. She felt guilty she hadn't done it sooner. What kind of mother was she, that she couldn't see past her own grief to help her daughters cope with theirs?

Jo paid Allison and watched from her stoop as the teenager walked to her house four doors down. After letting Snickers out for her evening potty break, Jo headed off to bed, pausing to check on the girls on the way. They were both fast asleep, looking like two little angels, one dark and one fair. Emma had kicked off her covers in her sleep and lay on her back with one arm flung over her head. Jess was curled in the fetal position, clutching her stuffed dog Bowwie, her stuffie since she was two. Jo felt her forehead to make sure she wasn't running a fever. She wasn't.

"Mommy," Emma murmured sleepily as Jo pulled the covers over her.

"I'm here," Jo whispered, dropping a kiss on her forehead. "Go back to sleep."

Emma was burrowing under the covers when suddenly she froze and her eyes flew open. "Mommy," she said again, this time with a whimper.

"What is it, sweetie?" Jo sat down on the bed, smoothing Emma's strawberry-blond hair where it stuck up in one spot.

"The bed wetted me," she whispered.

"It's okay, sweetie. It happens." Jo's heart ached for Emma, seeing her distress, and she wondered if she'd made the right decision in turning down her parents' offer. After Sean died, when they'd flown in for the funeral, they'd proposed she and the girls move into the guest cottage on their property. Had she been too hasty in refusing them? It wasn't too late to change her mind. Would the girls be better off in a more stable environment where they'd be near their grandparents? Where she'd have a support network and free housing, which would mean she wouldn't have to work so hard?

Then she remembered she had a support network already—her friends.

"Let's get you cleaned up and I'll change the sheets." She spoke in a low voice to keep from disturbing Jess.

After she stripped the bed and made it with fresh sheets, she helped Emma into a clean nightie and took her to use the bathroom before tucking her back into bed. Emma fell asleep at once. Jo paused in the doorway on her way out, the soiled sheets bundled in her arms, looking back at her sweetly slumbering children. *My babies.* She might have let them down in her grief, but they had been her reason for living during her darkest days, when she hadn't seen how she could go on without Sean. They were the reason she got up every morning, knowing they depended on her to feed and care for them. She realized something else: It was her job to set a good example for them as well. So they'd grow up to become strong, confident women who wouldn't be afraid to take risks in life.

The next morning, she called her Realtor. "I'd like to make an offer on the house," she said.

6

She offered the asking price of $599,000 and was surprised when it was accepted. The sellers could've gotten more for the property in a bidding war, but it turned out they cared more about doing right by Hank than getting top dollar. They were deeply grateful to him for having helped care for their mother toward the end. When they learned he'd be able to stay on as a lodger under the new ownership if Jo were to buy the house, they'd both agreed it was what their mother would have wanted.

Jo drove to her Realtor's office downtown to complete the paperwork. By two o'clock she was exiting with a signed purchase agreement. She wondered how her children would react when she told them her news. She'd kept her house hunting on the down-low. Otherwise, Emma might've expected a home of their own to magically appear like an inflatable bouncy castle, and Jess might've fretted unnecessarily. Jo had figured it'd be best to present it to them as a done deal once she found a house. Now that she had, she was sure they'd love it. Their lodger was another matter, which would require delicate handling. She'd wait until she'd laid the groundwork before introducing them to Hank. Hopefully, once they were all living under the same roof, it wouldn't be a problem if he used the kitchen and laundry room at prearranged times, as they'd discussed. His presence would be low impact. Or so she told herself. She was still nervous about it.

She walked to her car, which was parked several blocks away, the only spot she'd been able to find. It was peak tourist season, when parking spaces and reservations at popular eateries were as scarce as the gold that had once proliferated in these hills. The day was sunny with scattered clouds, the temperature in the low eighties. She passed the quaint mom-and-pop stores lining Sutter Street. Loopy Llama was advertising a sale on its alpaca yarns. At the Copper Kettle, the shop next door that sold high-end kitchenware, she paused to admire a set of Portmeirion dishes she coveted in the window. She stopped briefly to say hello to Art Henshaw, one of the owners of Petal Pushers, the florist shop on Sutter Street, who was freshening up his sidewalk display. She'd gotten to know Art and his husband, Curtis, through her business. They'd been the florists for most of the weddings she'd worked.

Passing Sutter Park, the two-block stretch of green space where the four main streets of Gold Creek's historic district intersected, she could hear the splashing of the mosaic-tiled fountain in the plaza at its center and see people strolling the paths in the park through its trees.

It wasn't until she reached her car that it fully sank in. *Holy crap. I bought a house.* She didn't know whether to shout with glee or call Lynette and tell her she'd changed her mind and decided not to go through with it. She did neither. Instead she halted in her tracks, her heart pounding.

The voice in her head spoke. *Proud of you, babe.*

It's not the same without you.

I know. But it's still pretty freaking amazing. You did good.

Once she was in her car, she texted her friends with her news. First Reggie, then the Tattooed Ladies in a group text. She received a stream of congratulatory messages punctuated with smiley face emojis in response.

Reggie: OMG. I'm crying. Like for real and not because I'm auditioning for Angels in America.

Marisol: AWESOME!!!
Suzy: Woo-hoo! This calls for a celebration. Lunch tomorrow? My treat.
Frannie: Congrats on becoming a homeowner! Thrilled for you!
Kyra: WOW WOW WOW.

She headed home, stopping to pick up Jess and Emma along the way. The drop-off for their day camp was at the Lutheran church in their neighborhood, and she was there to meet the bus when it arrived. This was Jess's third summer attending Little Explorers Day Camp and Emma's first. Situated on ten wooded acres north of town, the camp offered activities such as guided nature walks, arts and crafts, and the planting and tending of a vegetable garden every summer. The campers ranged in age from five to thirteen. This year Jo's parents were paying the tuition. Jo had been hard-pressed to refuse when they'd offered. Now that she was supporting her family on what she earned, she couldn't afford nonessentials and had been loath to dip into the insurance money. As much as she appreciated her parents' generosity, however, she couldn't help feeling a tad resentful, knowing it was bolstering their argument that she couldn't manage without their help.

They'd be less than thrilled when she told them she'd bought a house. They still hoped she'd change her mind and move back to Texas. And the girls? How would they react? Jo felt a tug of anxiety as she watched them deboard along with the bus's other pint-size passengers and head in her direction. Emma's pigtails flopped like a spaniel's ears as she ran. Jess followed at a slower pace, pausing at one point to pick up something on the ground that had caught her eye—an interesting rock, no doubt. Jo's heart swelled with love for them. *It'll be okay.* Even if they were initially resistant, they'd come around once they saw the house. Nevertheless, she decided to wait until they got home to tell them about it.

"What did you do today at camp, girls?" she asked as they drove home. Jess and Emma, both in the back seat, were rosy-cheeked from the outdoors and smelled of sunblock.

"We can't tell you. It's a surprise," said Emma.

"Let me guess. You built a soddy?" Constructing a scaled-down version of a soddy, a log structure with a sod roof, like the ones built by pioneers, had been one of last summer's camp activities.

"Noooo." Emma smiled secretively in the rearview mirror.

"You milked a goat?" The camp owners kept a few farm animals on the property.

"Uh-uh."

"I give up, then."

"We made flowers!" Emma burst out.

"Duh. You spoiled the surprise," Jess said. "And we didn't make flowers. We made *pressed* flowers. For bookmarks," she informed Jo. "Miss Caitlin showed us how."

"Sounds like fun. I can't wait to see yours."

"They're for *presents*, Mommy. You can't see yours until you open your *present*."

Jo smiled. "Oh. Well, then I'm sure I'll love it."

Upon arriving home, she fixed them snacks—peanut butter toast and apple slices—and sat with them at the table in the Taj's narrow galley kitchen, which was a shrine to the seventies with its bronze appliances, while they ate.

"Speaking of surprises . . ." she began. "I have one for you."

"A kitten?" asked Emma hopefully. She'd been begging for a kitten ever since Rosaria had gotten one for her children.

"It's not a kitten, dummy," scoffed Jess. "Mommy already said no, like, a million times."

Emma scowled at her. "I'm not a dummy. Mommy, Jess called me a dummy!"

"Jess, don't call your sister names. Say you're sorry," Jo ordered.

"Sorry," Jess muttered unconvincingly.

Jo sighed. This was not going well, and she hadn't even told them her news yet. She wished for the millionth time that Sean were here. That they were building toward a better future as a family and not hobbling along in the three-legged race created by Sean's absence. "No, sweetie," she told Emma. "It's not a kitten. We can't afford another pet. You'll have to make do with the one we've got." She reached down to stroke their Lab's silky head. Snickers sat alertly below the table in the hope of a dropped crumb. "It's a house. I bought us a house."

"Yay!" exclaimed Emma.

Jess stared at Jo in shock. "Why?"

It wasn't the reaction Jo had hoped for, although it was typical of Jess, who approached new experiences like someone entering a hazmat zone. She might need some time to get used to the idea.

"Because that was always the plan. Don't you remember when Daddy and I were saving to buy a house?"

Jess's expression darkened at the mention of her father. "No," she said, although the flicker in her eyes behind her purple-framed glasses suggested otherwise.

This was why Jo normally avoided bringing Sean into the conversation. It was too painful for all of them. "Maybe you forgot. Anyway, this house was only supposed to be temporary until we bought a home of our own. One big enough for all of us."

Minus Sean now that he's gone, she thought with a pang.

"I want to stay *here*," Jess said.

"You haven't seen our new house yet. I think you'll love it."

"Does it have a pool?" asked Emma. A swimming pool, like the one at her grandparents' house in Fairview, Texas, was another thing on her wish list.

"No, but it has a big backyard for you and your sister to play in, and a chimney for Santa to come down."

She immediately regretted her words. She wouldn't put it past Jess to seize the opportunity to inform her little sister that there was no Santa Claus, which she'd deduced on her own when she was Emma's age. Sometimes she was too smart for her own good. She was also grieving, and it seemed like she couldn't bear to see others happy when she was unhappy. Jo breathed a sigh of relief when Jess let the Santa reference pass. But her next words acted on Jo like a wrecking ball.

"It won't be the same without Daddy."

Jo felt herself start to crumble. She concentrated on taking slow, even breaths until she'd composed herself and could speak again without her voice breaking. "No," she agreed, "it won't. But Daddy would be happy to know I was making our dream come true and making a better life for us all."

Jess seemed unconvinced. "Will I still see Pablo?" Pablo, her playmate since they were babies, was also in her class at school and, Jo suspected, her only friend. She'd never asked anyone else over to play.

"Maybe not as often as you do now, but we can arrange playdates."

"But I'll still see him in school?" An edge of desperation crept into Jess's voice.

"Well, no. You'll be going to a new school."

"I have to *change schools*?" Jess looked horrified.

Jo felt awful. If she'd thought this through, she might've predicted Jess's reaction. Instead, it'd been a case of wishful thinking. She'd failed her daughter. Now all she could do was damage control. "Sweetie, I know it's a big change, and change can be scary, but—"

"I won't know anyone at my new school! I won't have any friends!"

"You'll make new friends."

"I don't *want* new friends." Jess's voice rose on a quavering note.

Jo stood and pulled Jess into her arms. Jess clung to her, sobbing. Jo's heart ached for her child. She wished she could comfort her as she had when Jess was a colicky baby, and Jo used to sing her to sleep while rocking her in her arms. But Jess was too old to be soothed by lullabies and too smart not to see this for what it was: a change in circumstances that would alter life as she'd known it.

Suddenly, this whole thing seemed like a terrible idea. What had she been thinking? "It'll be okay, sweetie. You'll see." She stroked Jess's curly, dark head in a soothing motion, which seemed to have the opposite effect on her.

"No, it won't. It's never gonna be okay."

She's not wrong about that. "Okay" had left the building on the day Sean died. Jo could only play the hand they'd been dealt as best she could. And clearly she was doing a piss-poor job of it.

She noticed that Emma had grown quiet and glanced over to see her youngest watching them while she sucked her thumb, her eyes pooled with tears. Jo knew she'd be looking at a China Syndrome–size meltdown involving both her daughters if she didn't act fast to defuse the situation.

"Who wants ice cream?" she heard herself ask in a chipper voice. Jesus. She sounded like the cruise director of the Good Ship Lollipop. She grimaced inwardly. Had she sunk so low as to resort to bribery? She used to be judgmental of parents who bribed their children with treats to get them to stop crying or acting out when they were having a meltdown.

It did the trick, though. Jess's sobbing ceased, and she asked, "What kind?"

"You have your choice between vanilla and chocolate." The list of foods Jess wouldn't eat included any flavor of ice cream that wasn't vanilla or chocolate. Luckily, Jo had stocked up on a quart of each last time she'd shopped.

"Can I have both?"

"Yes, but only half a scoop of each."

"Do we have to wait till after supper?"

"No, you can eat it now." It would spoil their appetites, and they'd be bouncing off the walls, but anything to avoid a total meltdown.

Emma unplugged her thumb from her mouth to ask, "With chocolate sauce?"

"You bet. And sprinkles."

Emma broke into a grin. Jess didn't so much as crack a smile, but at least she'd stopped crying.

Jo, as she scooped ice cream into bowls, thought, *I'm the world's worst mother.*

"Jess, would you like to see my fish?" asked Dr. Shaw when they arrived at her office on Monday.

Jess didn't answer. She hung back, pressing her body against Jo's side, refusing to make eye contact.

"She's a little shy," Jo said.

The psychologist seemed unfazed. "They're tropical fish. All kinds. Angelfish and mollies and neon tetra, to name a few. My favorite are the panda cory. They look like miniature pandas with fins instead of fur." Dr. Denise Shaw was a sixtyish woman with spiky, dyed-red hair and a warm smile. She wore a long cotton skirt and flowy batik top. Her office was welcoming like her, with a comfortable sofa and pair of armchairs, a play area, and a rainbow painted on one wall.

The talk of fish got Jess's interest. She finally looked up at Dr. Shaw.

"Some people find it relaxing to watch fish swim," Dr. Shaw went on, "and I confess I'm one of them. Better than TV, no remote control needed. Would you like to see mine?" She waved toward the open door to her inner office, through which Jo could see fish swimming in the aquarium built into one wall. "Mommy can wait here while you and I have a chat in my office, if that's okay with you."

Jo willed Jess to engage. She needed help. They all did, as a family. The kind only a trained professional could provide. She let out the breath trapped in her lungs when Jess took the psychologist's proffered hand. It seemed a good sign. Normally, Jess was mistrustful of strangers.

She watched as they disappeared into the inner office, Dr. Shaw closing the door behind them. She spent the next thirty minutes—the length of the average therapy session for young patients, she'd been told—watching YouTube videos to keep from fretting as she waited for her daughter to reappear. When she did, she seemed . . . okay. None the worse for her experience, anyway, Jo was relieved to see.

The following day Jo met privately with Dr. Shaw to discuss her observations about Jess from their session. "I asked her to draw a picture of her family. I didn't specify the time frame. This is what she drew." The psychologist produced a crayon drawing of a family—a mom and dad, their two children, and a dog—standing next to a house. They were all smiling, even the dog.

Jo studied the drawing through a film of tears. "It's from . . . before."

"It would seem so."

"What do you make of it?"

"Other than she has fond memories from when her father was alive? Not much. Although I got the sense when we were talking that she escapes into her fantasy world to cope with feelings that are too painful to unpack."

"Her fantasy world?"

"Magical thinking, in shrink-speak. If you refuse to face something that's painful, you can pretend it doesn't exist—or so the thinking goes. But of course it doesn't work that way, as we all know."

"Should I be worried?" More worried than she already was.

"Worried? No. But it's something to pay attention to."

"She's grieving."

"Yes, but children grieve differently than adults, and to varying degrees depending on their age."

"Jess was five when her father died. Emma, my youngest, was three."

"How would you say Emma is coping?"

"She seems fine most of the time, but she's started sucking her thumb and wetting the bed again like she did when she was younger. Do you think she needs to be in therapy, too?"

"It wouldn't hurt to bring her in for an assessment, but with children that age, behaviors like the ones you described are usually temporary. Unless you suspect there's a deeper problem?"

"No. I don't know how much she remembers about her dad."

"Probably not as much as Jess does. And preschoolers can't conceptualize death the way older children can. To them it's something temporary and that person will return. A five-year-old, especially one as bright as Jess, realizes that death is real. Sometimes they feel responsible."

Did Jess feel responsible for her father's death? How could she? No one could've prevented Sean's death. But since when did feelings make sense? She felt suddenly sick at the thought of Jess suffering guilt on top of her grief. "Jess is afraid of anything new—new people, new places, new foods. And right now, a new neighborhood and a new school. Did she tell you we were moving?"

"It came up during our session, yes."

"She's always been fearful, but it's gotten worse since her dad died. I'm surprised she trusted you."

"As much as I'd like to claim credit, I don't think I was the main attraction." Dr. Shaw smiled and motioned toward the aquarium. "My superpower, such as it is. Few children can resist."

"Curiosity trumps shyness."

"Also, children are more likely to open up to adults when they're distracted."

"What else did you learn from talking with her?"

"Her biggest fear is that something bad will happen to you like it did to her father."

Jo had suspected as much. Jess was clingier than before. She panicked if Jo was three minutes late picking her up from school. But under the circumstances . . . "That's normal, isn't it?"

"It's not uncommon for children who've lost a parent to worry that their surviving parent won't always be around to take care of them, but it seems to loom larger for Jess than for most."

"I do my best to reassure her, but . . ." Her shoulders sagged in defeat. "I can't promise I'll always be there." She regarded the drawing Jess had done of their family in happier times, her heart heavy. "Anything could happen at any time. Like it did with my husband." Her throat tightened.

"That's another thing."

Jo looked up. "What?"

"She seems to be picking up on your fears."

"My fears?"

The psychologist responded with a question. "Are you afraid?"

"Afraid? I'm terrified! What if I got sick and died, or was killed in an accident? My children would be orphaned. Or what if they grow up to become as messed up as their mom? How can I give them what they need when I'm barely keeping my head above water?"

"You seem to be doing a pretty good job of it."

Jo gave a cheerless laugh. "You caught me on a good day."

"You don't have to be strong to appear strong." The psychologist leaned forward in her purple, plush recliner, her elbows resting on her knees. "That's what we do best as parents, and why it comes as a shock to our kids when they're teenagers and discover we're flawed human beings."

"Fake it till you make it?"

"Something like that, only I don't advise hiding one's emotions. It's better to let children know when you're feeling sad so they know it's okay for them to feel sad, too. And so they can see that it's possible to be sad without falling apart. Otherwise, they tend to keep their emotions under wraps so as not to rock the boat. Jess needs to know the captain of her ship won't allow it to sink."

Jo struggled to process it. Had she somehow infected her elder daughter with her fears? But how, when the mere mention of Sean caused Jo to come undone, could she talk to her daughters about him without appearing unstable? What if the ship capsized despite her best efforts to stay afloat?

That night she read the girls the rest of *The Velveteen Rabbit*, which they'd started a few nights earlier. It had been Jo's favorite book when she was a child, her copy as well worn as the stuffed rabbit of the tale. Tonight, with Dr. Shaw's sobering insights in mind, she hoped to use the story as a talking point to get her girls to open up about their grief. "How do you think the boy feels when the doctor orders his toys be burned?" she asked them when she closed the book after reading the last chapter.

"Sad," said Emma, her mouth turning down.

They sat snuggled together on the sofa in the living room, Snickers curled up at Jo's feet. "Yes, because he has to give up his beloved toy rabbit. Jess, how do you think you'd feel in that situation?"

Jess shrugged.

"Honey, it's okay to feel sad about losing something, or someone, you love. Not talking about it doesn't make it go away. It just makes things worse." *I should know.*

"But the rabbit gets real after he's took," Emma pointed out.

"Yes, and the boy is happy to see him hopping in the garden."

"But he can't *hold* him." Jess frowned. "It's a dumb story."

Jo suppressed a sigh. This wasn't a boo-boo she could kiss away. And how could she help her daughters heal when she was hurting? When she was usually so drained at the end of each day, after juggling her work and her chores and the girls' schedules, that she had neither the time nor the energy to fill her own bucket, much less her daughters'? It seemed an impossible task.

"Time for bed," she announced. It was actually fifteen minutes past their bedtime, despite which they engaged in their usual stall tactics, begging for another story, requesting glasses of water, insisting they needed to go to the bathroom one more time, before she finally got them into bed.

Jo returned to the living room and was cleaning up the kernels from the microwave popcorn they'd eaten while watching TV before story time that were scattered on the floor and sofa cushions when her phone rang. She glanced at the screen and sighed before dutifully picking up. "Hi, Mom."

"Thank God. I was expecting your voicemail. Again," her mom said peevishly.

She had called twice earlier and left a message on Jo's voicemail both times. Jo hadn't returned either of those calls. "I'm sorry. It's been a crazy day. I was going to call you tomorrow."

"You know I worry when I don't hear back from you. I was about to start phoning hospitals."

Jo suddenly felt like she couldn't catch her breath. Like she was in one of those movies where the survivors of a building collapse are trapped underneath rubble with their air supply running out. It was how she'd often felt with her parents when she was growing up and why, when she'd been looking at colleges during her senior year, she hadn't considered applying to any of the ones in her home state. In the end she'd gone to UC Davis, much to the despair of her parents, who'd declared California to be the land of "hippies, pot smokers, and tree huggers."

"Was there something you wanted to talk to me about?" she asked.

"Your father had his six-month checkup today. I thought you'd want to know how it went."

Her annoyance gave way to worry. Six months earlier, her dad had suffered a heart attack, which would've been scary under any circumstances but which had hit Jo especially hard so soon after losing Sean. She couldn't bear the thought of losing her dad, too. He'd made a full recovery, but still . . . "How'd it go?"

"His doctor gave him a clean bill of health."

She let out a breath and felt her tension ease. "Whew."

"I can't tell you what a relief it is, although I'm not a bit surprised. He exercises every day and he's down thirty pounds since his heart attack. I told him he'd thank me someday for making him stick to the diet his doctor prescribed. Maybe now he'll eat his egg-white omelets without bellyaching."

"I'm with him on that," Jo said. Ugh. She'd sooner skip breakfast than eat an egg-white omelet.

"How are you? How are the girls?"

"We're good."

"How have you been sleeping lately?"

"Better some nights than others." She'd developed insomnia while taking care of Sean. At first it was because she'd slept with one eye open, alert to any change in his temperature or other sign of infection requiring immediate medical attention. Now it was because she slept alone. Besides missing him, she worried about how she was going to manage without him.

"The medication your doctor prescribed isn't helping?"

"No."

"Maybe if you had him up the dosage . . ."

"Her, and I stopped taking it."

"Why on earth would you do that?"

"I didn't want to get hooked."

"Nonsense. An Ambien or two as needed never hurt anyone." *Say the legions of patients who've become addicted to the drug.* "How can you possibly manage if you're not getting enough sleep?"

Jo felt a prickling on her skin like hives she couldn't see or scratch. Her mom treated her like she was still sixteen. Never mind she'd been a rebel, in her own quietly stubborn way, from the time she was four and rejecting the outfits her mom had picked out in favor of wearing what she wanted. When she was in school, she'd hung out with the fringe crowd instead of the kids whom her parents had deemed "socially acceptable." She'd married the man she loved, and not one of the privileged sons of their social set whom they would've preferred.

"Who says I'm not managing?" she replied testily.

"No one said you weren't. It's just . . . well, I know these last couple of years have been difficult."

"Difficult? That's one way of putting it."

"Honey, I can only imagine, but it doesn't have to be this hard. Life would be easier if you moved back home. Your dad and I would be on hand to help with the girls and anything else you needed."

Jo wondered again if she should've at least considered her parents' offer. Her children would surely benefit from living closer to their grandparents—in this case, a stone's throw away in their guest cottage—and the prospect of rent-free accommodations and free childcare was admittedly tempting. But it would come at a steep price. Her mom and dad, however well meaning, were the Black Hawks of helicopter parenting. They would attempt to control every aspect of her life, from how she raised her children to how she handled her finances. Also, she'd have to start over from scratch with her business in building a client base in the Houston area. No, she'd made the right decision.

"Mom, I appreciate the offer, but my answer is still no."

"It's not too late to change your mind."

"Actually, it is."

"Why is that?"

"I bought a house today."

Her announcement was met with silence at the other end. Then: "You bought a house? Without discussing it with your father and me first?"

"I wasn't aware I needed your permission."

Her mom ignored her sarcasm. "A heads-up would've been nice."

"You knew I was looking at houses."

"Yes, but we were hoping . . ." Her mom's voice trailed off.

Jo felt a stab of guilt. She wouldn't have been in a position to buy a house if not for her parents. Their wedding gift to her and Sean had been a prepaid life insurance policy. At the time, she'd thought it was a weird gift, although typical of her parents, and Sean had joked, "Seems I'm worth more dead than alive." They'd been young, and death had been a distant rumor rather than a fact of life. Until it wasn't. When the unthinkable occurred, she'd had a financial cushion thanks to her parents. They'd also helped out when she'd had her hands full taking care of Sean, visiting when they could and taking the girls to Disneyland once for a long weekend. Mindful of this, and the fact that they were paying the girls' tuition for day camp, Jo reined in her impatience.

"Mom, I'm thankful for everything you and Dad have done for me, so please don't see this as a rejection. I love you both, and it goes without saying you're always welcome to visit and we'll visit you."

"So tell me about this house." Her mom sounded somewhat mollified.

"It's perfect for us, on a quiet street. I'll text you a photo."

She sent one she'd taken of the exterior. "Who's the man mowing the lawn? Is he the gardener?" her mom asked. Trust her to single out that one detail. This was, after all, the same woman who could spot a microscopic stain and tell the difference between a designer handbag and a knockoff from a hundred feet away. Jo considered kicking this can down the road, but it was only a matter of time before her parents discovered her new home came with a lodger.

"That's Hank," she said. "And he's not the gardener."

"Who is he, then?"

"He lives there."

"The house comes with a rental property?"

"Not exactly. He rents the downstairs. I arranged for him to stay on after I close on the house."

"I see." Her mom sounded dubious. "I assume the downstairs has a separate entrance."

"Yes, but . . ." Jo paused to draw a bolstering breath. "His rent includes kitchen and laundry privileges."

Her mother's next words came with the suddenness and force of a tornado. "Sweet baby Jesus in the manger. Joellen Marie Hunter, have y'all lost your mind?" Jo imagined those in her parents' social set would be surprised to learn the always poised and perfectly put-together Carol Hunter, née McGraw, had grown up poor in the hill country of Texas. Through sheer determination, combined with beauty, smarts, and a talent for twirling a baton, she'd escaped poverty via the beauty pageant circuit. She'd reigned as Miss Crocket County the year she was eighteen, and was voted first runner-up in the state division of the Miss America pageant the following year. Along the way she learned to dress, speak, and comport herself like a lady, and how to make an entrance in an evening gown and heels. After marrying her husband, a partner at the prestigious accounting firm he'd cofounded, she settled in Fairview and became a mother, devoting herself to raising her only child, hosting parties, and doing charity work. Only when she was under extreme duress did her humble origins reveal themselves.

"Do you mean to tell me y'all are letting a strange man have the run of your house?"

Even Snickers, snuffling under the sofa like a truffle-hunting pig, looking for dropped popcorn kernels, must've sensed the shock waves from the blast of parental displeasure because her ears and tail went down and she retreated to the other side of the room, where she made herself small.

"No. Just the kitchen and laundry room, and only during prescheduled times when the girls and I won't be using them." He'd also be sharing their outdoor spaces, but the small patio off his quarters, where presumably he spent most of his time when he was relaxing outdoors, was hidden from view below the deck.

"What do you know about him?"

"He seems like a nice man."

"That's what they said about Ted Bundy."

"Jesus, Mom. He's not a serial killer."

"How do you know? You don't know the first thing about him."

"I didn't know Carmela, either, before we roomed together."

"That was different. She was your college roommate. And a very nice girl," she added. *For a lesbian.* Jo mentally supplied her mother's unspoken qualifier. "Also, you didn't have children to think of then."

"And your point is?"

"He could be a pedophile, for all you know."

Her mom had a point. Which was why Jo had asked her friend Coop to have one of his cop buddies run a background check on Hank. She doubted it'd reveal anything that he hadn't already told her, but it paid to be cautious—in that respect, she was her mother's daughter. She also planned to install a nanny cam in the girls' room. For the nights, at least in the beginning, she had the baby monitor she'd used when the girls were babies. None of which she shared with her mother because it would only have fueled her mad spinning of worst-case scenarios. Instead, she replied, in a mild tone, "I'm sure that's not the case. Besides, I'm not in the habit of leaving my children alone with people I don't know."

"Aha. So you don't trust him."

"I didn't say that. All I'm saying is it takes time for someone to earn my trust."

"Can you name one thing to recommend his character?"

The first thing that popped into Jo's head was something Lynette had reported about Hank. "He took care of his former landlady when she was dying."

Her testament to Hank's good character bit her in the ass with her mother's next words. "His landlady died while she was in his care and you don't find that suspicious?"

"No. She was in her nineties and died of natural causes."

"Did they do an autopsy? How do we know he didn't hasten her demise by holding a pillow over her face?"

"Why would he do that?"

"Maybe he was expecting to inherit."

"For God's sake, Mom. Are you even listening to yourself?"

"Don't you sass me, Joellen Marie!" Growing up, Jo had known she was in trouble whenever her mom called her by her full name. "What else can you tell me about him? Something that isn't fodder for *Dateline*."

"He fought for our country."

"Well, that's something," her mom said. Her parents were diehard patriots. The US flag flew proudly outside their home, and after their neighbor's son was reported missing in action, they'd kept a yellow ribbon tied around the oak tree in their front yard until he came home. Her dad's firm favored veterans in its hiring policy and made an annual donation to a charitable organization that trained service dogs for disabled vets. Every year on Veterans Day, he and her mom volunteered at their local VFW chapter's annual pancake breakfast honoring its veterans. Jo's mom couldn't deny Hank his due.

"Gotta go, Mom. I have an early work thing, and if I don't get some rest, I'll be no good tomorrow." She had an outdoor photo shoot scheduled for 8:00 a.m., when the morning light was optimal, with a newly engaged couple who'd requested a photo for their wedding invitation at the archery range where they'd first met. "Give Dad a hug from me and tell him I'm thrilled that he got a clean bill of health. Not that I was worried," she lied. "He's too stinkin' stubborn to die."

Her mom gave a snort of laughter. "You can say that again."

It was the one thing they could agree on.

After ending the call, Jo stretched out on the sofa and closed her eyes. Her head throbbed, and she felt so drained she didn't think she could get up even if an intruder were to break in. Suddenly, the cumulative effect of the day's events—buying a house and the blowback from Jess and her mother, the worrisome discovery that she might have infected Jess with her fears—came crashing down on her. When she felt a rough tongue lick her cheek, she cracked one eye open to find Snickers regarding her woefully. Her expression seemed to say, *We both know this won't end well.*

She sighed and stroked her dog's head. "Hey, a little support? I'm doing my best here."

7

The closing took place on the last Friday in June. With the keys in her possession, Jo went to work making her house a home, starting with picking out paint colors. She hoped to engage Jess's interest by getting her involved. Emma was excited about their new home, but Jess remained resistant.

"You can have any color you like as long as you both agree," Jo told the girls when they were at the house deciding on a paint color for their room. She produced the color wheel she'd picked up at the hardware store.

"Pink!" declared Emma. If it were up to her, the room would be painted the color of her Barbie Dreamhouse.

"What do you think?" Jo asked Jess. "Pink, or would you prefer a different color? Purple, maybe." Purple was Jess's favorite color, as evidenced by her choice of eyewear and the nickname Sean had given her, "Purple People Eater," after the sixties song. Jess shrugged. "How about we paint Emma's side pink and yours purple? Take a look at these samples and pick out the shade you like best."

Jess refused to even look at the color wheel. "I don't care," she replied flatly.

"You say that now, but . . ."

Jess showed a flash of emotion. She shot her a molten look. "I like my room at our house." Meaning the Taj.

"I know you do, honey," Jo said gently. "But you might feel differently once we're living here."

"I won't. If you make me, I'll run away."

"We'd miss you a lot if you did that, and you might get homesick."

Jess glowered at her. Jo sighed, feeling defeated. Emma regarded her sister nervously.

The move was scheduled for Monday of the following week. In the meantime, Jo haunted flea markets and garage sales whenever she had free time while the girls were at camp. She found a sixties-era dinette set for the dining nook and a cute dresser for the girls' room, which she stripped and refinished. Her plan to convert a section of the garage into a home office someday when she could afford it became possible sooner rather than later when Hank proposed he do the work in exchange for his continued use of the space in the garage where he kept his tools and motorcycle. She had only to pay for the materials. He promised to have the work done by the time she moved in.

One morning she was at the house pulling up the shag carpeting in the main bedroom, which might once have been gold but had become a nasty shade of Dijon yellow with age and ground-in dirt, when she heard the sound of approaching footsteps. An intruder? Had she forgotten to lock the front door? She sprang to her feet, pulse pounding, imagining being hacked to pieces by the friendly neighborhood axe murderer. Oh, God. What would become of her children?

Seconds later, Hank appeared in the doorway and she let out a shaky breath. She felt silly for letting her imagination run away with her. She hadn't always been this way, but now that she was a single parent, she couldn't drive a car or fly in a plane—or be alone in a building, it appeared—without fearing the worst. If she were to die or become incapacitated, who would take care of her children? Her parents? Dear God. Hank took in her flushed face and heaving chest and asked, "Is everything okay?"

"Yes. You just surprised me, is all." She hadn't seen his truck in the driveway when she'd arrived.

"Sorry. I would've knocked but . . ." He gestured behind him, indicating that he'd come by way of the interior stairs rather than entering through either the front or side doors. Was this how it'd be from now on, with him popping up unannounced? So much for thinking she could arrange it so they crossed paths only at set times. "I heard you banging around up here and came to see if you needed a hand." His gaze dropped to the partially torn-out carpeting. "Looks like you could use some help."

"Don't you have anything better to do?" she asked, and flushed at the sharpness of her tone. What she'd intended as a polite refusal had come out sounding like a rebuff. What was wrong with her? Hank had been nothing but helpful. He was building her an office, for cripes' sake.

He didn't seem to take offense. "Not at the moment. And two can get the job done faster than one."

"Thanks, I could use the help," she said in a more appreciative tone. "Besides, the sixties is calling and it wants its carpeting back."

He chuckled. "I'm not so sure about that. I can reliably report that shag carpeting was ugly even when it was in style."

Forty minutes later, after they'd removed the last piece of carpeting, she gazed around her in satisfaction. "I can't believe anyone ever thought it was a good idea to cover this gorgeous wooden floor."

"That'd be Martha and her husband. In their defense, every floor in every house in America that wasn't covered in linoleum was carpeted back then. And I imagine this carpeting looked better when it was new."

"Maybe, but it's still hideous."

"I offered to tear it up and refinish the floor free of charge, but Martha wouldn't hear of it," he said. "She was of the generation that believed if something had life left in it, it was worth keeping."

"She sounds like my eldest. To say Jess is averse to change is putting it mildly."

"How's she doing with the move?" he asked as he bundled up strips of torn-out carpeting to be carried out to the trash.

"Not well." Jo's stomach clenched. "She's having trouble adjusting."

"When's moving day?"

"Monday of next week." She felt suddenly overwhelmed at the prospect. As much as she loved her new house, she was not looking forward to the move, which would involve a ton of work and a million details to attend to, all while trying to be there for Jess. "I need to get the floors refinished and the walls painted before then."

"I could help with that."

"Thanks, but I've got it covered." Kyra's boyfriend, Coop, had offered to do the floor refinishing for the cost of renting the equipment, and her friends had volunteered to help with the painting. For which she was beyond grateful. Her bank balance was dangerously low and her credit cards all but maxed out due to this month's house expenditures and the deposit she'd paid the movers. "Besides, you've done enough already. I appreciate your help today."

"My pleasure. I like staying busy."

She envisioned Hank in the role of the lovable but annoying building super in *One Day at a Time*, the seventies sitcom she'd watched in reruns. A character known for appearing at inconvenient times and offering unsolicited advice, and often unwanted help. "That may be," she said, "but if this arrangement of ours is going to work, I can't be taking advantage of you." They'd agreed to a thirty-day trial period before committing to a lease, during which time either of them was free to back out of their arrangement without penalty. Although the background check Coop had run on Hank, which showed only that he'd been honorably discharged from the military and gainfully employed from that time until his retirement, confirmed the positive impression he'd made, Jo still had reservations about their unorthodox living situation. Only time would tell whether it was a good fit.

"Martha and I didn't stand on formalities," he said.

"I'm not Martha."

He regarded her thoughtfully before replying, "Fair enough. May I offer you some iced tea, then?"

"I'd love some." She was parched from her labors and the dust they had stirred up.

Minutes later, as she watched Hank move around the kitchen, grabbing a couple of glasses from one of the cupboards and a pitcher of iced tea from the fridge, she had the oddest feeling of being a stranger in her own home. It was more than a little disconcerting.

"Sugar?" he asked after he'd poured the tea.

She made a face. "No thank you. I can't abide sweet tea."

He raised an eyebrow at her. "A Southerner who doesn't drink sweet tea? Now, that's a first."

"How'd you know I was from the South? Was it my accent?"

"Yes, though it's hardly noticeable. What part of the South are you from?"

"Texas, and I'd know you were a Yankee even if you hadn't told me. No self-respecting Southerner would add sugar to iced tea before serving it. In some parts of the South, that could get you run out of town."

He chuckled. "Duly noted." He added a lemon slice to each glass along with a handful of ice, and handed her one. "How is it normally made?"

"You're asking the wrong person," she said, taking a drink. "All I know is that it takes days and a bucket of sugar to make proper sweet tea. I'm an outlier by my parents' standards," she explained.

"Why is that?"

"In Texas they worship God, country, and football, not necessarily in that order. I love my country, but I'm a fan of neither football nor religion."

"Not a churchgoer, huh?"

"I used to be. I stopped going to church after . . ." She trailed off, taking another drink of her iced tea to force down the lump rising in her throat. "Let's just say God has some explaining to do."

"About?"

"Why good people die young and bad people get to live."

Hank sipped his tea, leaning back against the counter. "I had the same question after I lost my son, and when I was in 'Nam before that. Don't know the answer. I guess some things aren't ours to know."

His revelation sent a shiver down her spine. "You lost a son? Hank, I'm so sorry."

"It was a long time ago." Not long enough, from the pained look that crossed his face.

"How did he die?"

"He was killed in action during the Gulf War. Awarded a Medal of Honor posthumously."

"Does it help knowing he died fighting for his country?"

"Sure, but I'd rather he have lived an unexceptional life than died a hero."

"Do you have any other children?"

He shook his head. "Ben was my only child."

"You mentioned a grandson."

"Ian. Ben's son." At the mention of his grandson, Hank's sad face lit up.

"Didn't you say he was in the military?"

Hank nodded. "He's a pilot, like his father and grandfather before him. Except his dad and I were army and Ian's air force. Two tours in Iraq, currently serving as a flight instructor at the Ramstein Air Base in Germany."

"Presumably where he's out of harm's way."

"Until the next time he's deployed to a war zone, anyway."

"Must be hard having him so far away."

"Sure, but we stay in touch via WhatsApp and FaceTime. Unlike when I was serving overseas and any news from home was old news by the time I got it, we don't have to rely on snail mail."

"When will you see him again?"

"He's due home on leave sometime next month. He plans to spend some time with his mom in Seattle before making the trip down to see me."

"Well, I look forward to meeting him."

She wondered if her lodger would still be around then. Hank might decide to decamp once he got a good look at life in the Myers household, with all its problems and chaos. She hoped not. She needed the rent money. And, she was beginning to realize, maybe she needed Hank, too.

"The marines have landed," announced Marisol as she and the others trooped inside early the following Saturday, dressed in old clothes suitable for painting. "And we bring fortification."

Marisol carried a cardboard tray of coffees and Suzy carried a box of pastries, both from Cowboy Coffee. Frannie carried a picnic hamper. Kyra had brought her dog, sporting a paisley bandanna around his furry neck. Jo wouldn't have been surprised to learn Ranger, who was smarter than the average three-year-old child, possessed the ability to use a paintbrush. He grinned and wriggled his butt as she bent to greet him before setting off to explore his surroundings.

"Bless you," she said as she helped herself to a coffee and a blueberry Danish. "I made coffee, but Maxwell House isn't a patch on Cowboy Coffee's house blend." She moaned as she took a bite from her Danish. "Oh my God. Better than sex," she mumbled around a mouthful of pastry.

She regretted her offhanded remark when she saw her friends exchanging glances. Her sex life—or rather, lack thereof—was apparently a matter of concern among them. When she'd shown them the vibrator Reggie had sent her, along with a gift card that read "You'll thank me later," they'd hooted with laughter, but it had been knowing laughter.

"Breakfast of champions." Marisol bit into a bear claw.

Kyra was busy checking out the view from the slider. "Wow. Amazing."

"I may be broke, but at least I have million-dollar views," Jo said. The state parklands that abutted her neighborhood covered over twelve thousand acres. The fire tower rising above the treetops in the distance was the sole visible man-made structure. It was a reminder of the downside to living in a densely wooded area: the danger of forest fires.

"The pictures don't do it justice," agreed Frannie. "Nice digs, too." Emptied of its furnishings, the living room appeared twice as big as it had when it was furnished.

"Coop did a great job on the refinishing," remarked Marisol. The living room's wood floor gleamed in the morning light.

"He's a man of many talents," Jo said.

"I won't disagree with that," said Kyra, smiling.

"Is that a wood-burning fireplace?" Suzy crossed the room to the brick fireplace. Even in old clothes, she managed to look chic, with her dungarees rolled at the ankles and the collar of her shirt turned up.

"Yes, but I'll need to get the chimney swept before I can use it." One of the many items on her ever-growing punch list. "Hopefully, I'll have it operational before the cold weather sets in."

"I'll ask Coop to bring over a load of firewood," said Kyra. Deadfall was plentiful year-round on their spread in the country, and Coop owned a chainsaw. "Could you also use more eggs?" One of Coop's brothers kept chickens, which produced more eggs than he and his family could eat.

"I'll take whatever's going," Jo replied. "I have no shame."

"You may regret those words when I'm bombarding you with tomatoes and zucchini from my garden come August. None of you is safe," Kyra threatened, her gaze traveling around the room.

This elicited groans and pleas for mercy.

"Seriously, guys, I appreciate all your help. It's above and beyond." Jo took another bite of her Danish.

"You'd do the same for any of us," said Frannie.

"All for one, and one for all," echoed Suzy.

When Kyra had first arrived in Gold Creek, jobless and homeless, the Tattooed Ladies had befriended her and provided a soft place for her to land. Suzy had given her a job and Frannie a steer on a rental property, which in turn had led to Coop, who'd been Kyra's landlord then. Whenever Suzy's troubled relationship with her son got her down, the others gave her solace and support. The same had been true for Marisol when her mother died, and when she'd agonized over whether to make the first move with Cal. After Sean died, Jo couldn't have survived without her friends—they'd been her rocks.

They talked zucchini recipes while they finished their coffees and ate their pastries. Afterward, Jo gave her friends the grand tour, such as it was, before directing them to the cans of paint and painting supplies that she'd placed on a tarp in one corner of the living room. "Feel free to start wherever you like," she told them. "I labeled each can so you'd know which color goes where."

"First, I need to put these sandwiches in the fridge." Frannie picked up the picnic hamper from where she'd placed it on the floor, then headed for the kitchen with Jo leading the way.

When Frannie had offered to stop in town and pick up some takeout for lunch on her way here, Jo had expected to reimburse her for it. Now, watching Frannie unpack the contents of the hamper—two different kinds of sandwiches, roast beef with bacon jam and turkey and Swiss on sourdough; house-made potato chips; a variety of fruits and soft cheeses; Cowboy Coffee's signature triple-chocolate espresso brownies; and a selection of bottled beverages—she worried about how she was going to afford it. All this bounty must've cost a fortune.

"How much do I owe you?" she asked with trepidation.

"Not a cent," Frannie said as she stowed the perishables in the fridge. "It's Vanessa's housewarming gift." Frannie's sister, Vanessa, was the owner of Cowboy Coffee and as kind a soul as Frannie.

Jo was touched and relieved. "I don't know what to say. That was so generous." She'd call and thank Vanessa later.

"Where are the kiddos?" Frannie asked.

"At home with their babysitter. Where there's paint, young children can't be trusted."

"How's Jess doing? She still upset about the move?" Frannie placed the last of the bottled beverages in the fridge and turned to look at Jo, her expression one of understanding. She, too, had faced challenges as a single parent, so she knew what Jo was going through. Her daughter, Hannah, had been in and out of mental health facilities since she was a teenager. For the past two years, Hannah had been staying with Frannie while she got her life back on track after going through a bad patch.

"More than ever. She met our lodger."

Jo felt her stomach twist, remembering the day she'd come to the house with the girls to measure for curtains and encountered Hank. He'd been coming up the stairs as they were leaving.

"Well, hello there." He paused at the top of the stairs, his smiling gaze shifting from Jo to her daughters.

Jess froze, staring at him as if he were an intruder. "Mommy, who is that man?" she whispered loudly.

"Girls, this is Hank. Remember, I told you he's renting the downstairs?" Admittedly, she'd glossed over the details, such as the fact that he'd be sharing some of their spaces, which, she could see from Jess's shocked face, had been a mistake. "Hank, these are my daughters, Jess and Emma."

"Pleased to meet you," he said. "Your mom's told me a lot about you."

Emma seemed more curious than taken aback by the strange man who'd appeared as if out of nowhere. "Do you like it here?" she asked him.

"I do."

"Me and Mommy and Jess are gonna live here, too."

"Yes, I know. Won't that be nice? How do you like your new house?"

"It's amazeballs." Her new favorite word, and a reminder of the dangers of too much screen time for children. "Mommy says we can have a swimming pool, and maybe a treehouse someday."

"An inflatable pool," Jo corrected her.

Hank turned toward Jess. "What about you, Jess? Do you like your new house?"

Jess stared at him wordlessly.

"I like the paint colors you and your sister picked out for your room," he went on. "Pink and purple go together, although if I had to choose one, it'd be purple. Reminds me of when I used to read my grandson *Harold and the Purple Crayon* when he was little. Do you know that book?"

Jess remained mute.

Hank turned to Jo. "I was going to fix myself a sandwich, but it can wait if this isn't a good time."

"No, it's fine. We were just leaving," she told him. She didn't know which was worse, the cold reception from Jess or the look of horror on her face at learning their lodger would be using their kitchen. *I really should have said something.*

Now, as if on cue, the sound of a car engine announced Hank's return. He'd gone to the hardware store to exchange one of the paint colors, which she'd decided was the wrong shade of blue. How exactly he'd become a member of today's painting crew, she wasn't entirely certain. As she remembered it, she'd declined his offer to help, saying she didn't want to take advantage of him. Yet here he was. Although he was never intrusive, Hank had a knack for appearing when he was needed.

A minute later, he entered through the side door carrying a gallon-size can of paint. "Sorry it took so long. They didn't have the color you wanted in stock, so I had them mix up a batch, and—" He broke off, noticing Frannie. "Hey, there," he greeted her. "You must be with the band."

"Frannie." She stuck out her hand. "And you must be Hank."

"Pleasure," he said as they shook hands.

"There's coffee, and I saved you a pastry." Jo gestured toward the coffee maker, with its mostly full pot, and the bear claw on a plate beside it.

"Thanks, don't mind if I do," he said.

"So, Hank, what's a biker dude like you do for fun around here?" asked Frannie, watching as he poured himself a cup of coffee.

"Jo told you I drive a Harley, did she?" He looked up at her, his eyes twinkling.

"You ride with the Graybeards, I'm told. I know another member of your gang. Rolph Heineman."

"I wouldn't go so far as to call us a gang. We're better known as 'The Mild Bunch.'" The membership of the Graybeard Bikers' Club was exclusively male, roughly two dozen in number. The youngest member was sixty-five and the oldest in his eighties. The one thing they all had in common, besides the fact that they owned motorcycles, was their belief that there was more to life after retirement than golfing, fishing, and touring the country in an RV. Unlike the Hells Angels, they weren't known for run-ins with the law or terrorizing the local citizenry. "How do you know Rolph?" He picked up the bear claw and took a bite, chasing it with a swig of his coffee.

"He's a customer of mine."

"What do you do for a living?"

"I'm a tattoo artist. I own Red Ink Tattoos."

"Ah, yes. I know of it. Was it you who did Rolph's bald eagle tattoo?"

"Why, yes."

"That's some fine work there. The detail is amazing."

She seemed pleased by the compliment. "Thank you. It's one of my original designs. Where'd you get yours?" She eyed the Chinese dragon tattoo on Hank's right arm, which snaked from his forearm to his bicep before disappearing underneath the sleeve of the Rolling Stones T-shirt he wore.

"Back-alley tattoo parlor in Saigon in 1972. Looked a lot better before it got all wrinkly," he added, glancing down at his arm.

"Didn't we all?"

"Ain't that the truth. But I don't see any wrinkles on you, so either you're a lot younger than me or you discovered the fountain of youth."

Frannie pressed her lips together as if to keep from smiling. "I'll have you know I protested against the war in Vietnam, which tells you how old I am. I'm guessing you fought in 'Nam?"

He nodded. "I hope you won't hold it against me."

"Regardless of my political views, I thank you for your service. I'm glad you made it back in one piece."

"You and me both. And you might be surprised to learn my views on the war aren't so different from yours."

"Good to know."

They locked gazes for a beat or two. The space between them crackled as if with static electricity. Jo remembered something her grandpa Bob had once said. *There may be snow on the roof, but there's fire in the furnace.* From what she was witnessing, the fires in Hank's and Frannie's furnaces were still burning. They were obviously attracted to each other, despite Frannie having claimed she was done with men after her last failed relationship, years ago.

Jo lingered, listening to the two boomers reminisce, slipping into the slang of their era and referencing rock bands she'd never heard of, while Hank drank his coffee and ate his pastry. The free-love vibe of their generation seemed alive and well when Hank asked Frannie, in a flirty tone, "Care to join me in the bedroom?" as they were exiting the room to go to work. Frannie came to a halt, her eyebrows shooting up. "Thought I'd get started there . . . on the painting."

Frannie burst out laughing. "If that was a proposition, I give you points for originality."

"Is that a yes?"

"Sure, why not?"

Watching them head off together, laughing and talking like old friends, Jo ached for Sean. She remembered how easy it'd been with him from the very start, how perfectly they'd fit together—*like peas and carrots,* Sean used to say. As if they'd been together in another lifetime.

That could be yours again, babe.

Not with you, it can't.

No, but if we hadn't met, you'd have met and fallen in love with someone else.

But we did meet. What's your point, anyway?

Don't let your past get in the way of your future.

They broke for lunch at noon. It was a beautiful day, with the temperature in the high seventies. Sitting in the shade of the umbrella at the redwood table on the deck, they ate their lunch, while Ranger patrolled the perimeter, watching for any dropped crumbs. Jo was pleased to see her friends get along with Hank, Frannie in particular. She was more animated than usual.

After they'd eaten, Hank excused himself to go back to work and Ranger went chasing after a squirrel in the backyard, while the women lingered on the deck. They discussed decorating ideas. Suzy showed Jo a set of dishes on the Pottery Barn website that she wanted to get her as a housewarming gift with her approval. Jo accepted on the condition that her friends be her first dinner guests once she'd moved in. Frannie and Kyra, the two artists of their group, had each promised her an original painting to hang on her walls. Marisol had offered to provide as many books as she might need to fill her built-in bookshelves, from her overstock of advance reader copies.

Before heading back inside, they posed for a group selfie. As they all squeezed into the frame, cheek to cheek, arms looped around one another's waists, Jo did the honors. "Say cheese!" she directed as she lined up her shot, holding her phone above her head to get everyone in the frame.

"Cheese!" they chorused.

Click.

In that moment, standing on the deck of her new home with the sun shining and her best friends gathered around her, Jo felt content. She'd almost forgotten the feeling, it had been so long. *Enjoy it while it lasts,* whispered the voice in her head. Because, as she knew better than most, life didn't stand still. It was as changeable as the weather. The next bad thing could come crashing down at any moment.

8

"Mommy! I can't find Kermit! He's goooone," wailed Emma on the day before moving day.

Jo had left the girls' room for last in packing for their move, in the hope of making it less traumatic for Jess. She hadn't expected Emma to be the one in tears. "He's got to be here somewhere." She abandoned the box she'd been packing and headed off to help search for Emma's missing stuffie. Emma followed, sobbing as though it were a crisis on the scale of an Amber Alert. She seldom went anywhere without her stuffed Kermit the Frog and slept with him every night.

Kermit failed to turn up, however, after she'd conducted a thorough search of the premises. He wasn't in the house or car. Nor had he been accidentally left next door, reported Rosaria. Jo was beginning to panic when it occurred to her that Jess was behaving oddly. Although she'd aided in the search, she seemed neither bothered nor mystified by Kermit's disappearance. Jo became suspicious.

"Jess, honey, do you have any idea where Kermit might be?" she asked.

"No," Jess said.

"Are you sure you didn't take him and put him somewhere? Because if you did, you need to tell me. I promise I won't get angry. But your sister will be really, really sad if we don't find Kermit."

The guilty flush spreading across her eldest's cheeks confirmed Jo's suspicion. Jess dropped her gaze, staring down at her feet as she mumbled, "I might know where he is."

Emma stopped sniffling and glared at her sister.

"Show me," Jo ordered.

Jess led the way through the slider onto the patio, where she crossed to the hibachi that stood at one end next to the covered bucket that was used to dispose of its ashes. She lifted the lid of the bucket to reveal Kermit lying on a bed of ashes, his green plush body smudged with soot. Emma snatched him up with a cry, scattering ashes down the front of her Hello Kitty top as she hugged him.

Jess looked so miserable, Jo didn't have the heart to scold her. "Thank you for telling the truth," Jo said. "What I don't understand is why you would do such a thing. I know you're not a mean person."

"I thought if you couldn't find Kermit, you'd keep looking and we wouldn't have to leave."

Jo crouched down, placing her hands on Jess's slumped shoulders. Jess lifted her head to meet her gaze. "Honey, I know this is hard. Moving to a new place where you don't know anyone can be scary. But I promise it'll be okay. Even if you can't see it now, can you try to have faith that it'll work out?"

"It won't be the same without Daddy."

Jess's words and the heartbroken look on her face hit Jo like a blow to her chest. She ached for her daughters, who'd been robbed of their father. "I know, sweetie. But we're still a family—you, me, and Emma. And home isn't just where you live, it's about the people who are in it."

A memory of Sean dancing around their living room with three-year-old Jess on his toes to the tune of John Lennon's "Imagine" surfaced. She saw him holding their daughter's small hands clasped in his as he guided her—as he would have in every aspect of her life had he lived to watch her grow up—while Jess gazed up at him with complete trust. Jo's eyes grew misty. She wondered if Jess remembered, or if she'd been too young. She was opening her mouth to ask her when she stopped, thinking better of it. Why bring up a memory that would only cause more pain?

Instead, she said, "Now say sorry, and then I want you to think about how you can make it up to your sister."

"How?"

"That's for you to decide, but it should be something that shows you're sincere. Like, for instance, if you broke something that belonged to someone else and gave them something of yours."

Jess scrunched her forehead in thought. "I guess I could let her borrow Bowwie. But only for a day." Jo knew what a sacrifice it would be for her to part with her stuffed dog even for one day. Bowwie was to her what Kermit was to Emma. But it was a good sign that she was making an effort.

"How about you let Emma borrow Bowwie just while I run Kermit through the wash?" she suggested. Jess nodded, looking relieved. "Emma, would that be okay with you?" Emma was on board with that idea, too.

"I'm sorry I took Kermit and hid him," Jess said to her sister.

"Okay, but don't do it again," replied Emma agreeably. She wasn't one to hold a grudge. She also adored her big sister and could never stay mad at her for long.

"I won't."

The crisis resolved, Jo extracted the sooty Kermit from Emma's embrace. "Into the washing machine for you, mister." His googly eyes seemed to stare up at her with reproach, as if to say *Really? After the crappy day I had?* "I know," she told him. "It's not easy being green."

The movers arrived at 9:00 the next morning. Two hours later, after everything they owned had been loaded into the movers' van, it was time for them to go. As they said their goodbyes to their neighbors, Jess wept and hugged Pablo as if she'd never see him again, even though Jo had already arranged for Rosaria to bring him and his sister over for a playdate the week after next. She hoped Jess would find a friend in their new neighborhood. She'd seen kids' bikes in front of some of the houses on Mountain Laurel Lane. Maybe one of them belonged to a kid Jess's age. Meanwhile, there would be plenty to unpack, besides the boxes that held their belongings, during Jess's next session with Dr. Shaw.

Arriving at their new house, Jo hit the ground running and never stopped moving. The temperature soared into the high eighties, and it wasn't much cooler indoors with one of the AC units on the fritz. By midafternoon she was dragging, with dog hairs stuck to her sweaty skin from when Snickers had crawled onto her lap the one time she'd sat down to catch her breath. Jess wasn't the only family member who was anxious about their move.

As the movers were leaving, a white panel truck with the name Petal Pushers painted in gold letters on one side arrived to deliver two dozen pink roses in a vase tied with a pink ribbon. The gift card attached read, "In the immortal words of Dorothy, 'There's no place like home.' May you and the Munchkins enjoy many happy years in your forever home. Love, Reggie & Marco."

Jo was deeply touched by the gesture, which was just what the doctor ordered after her stressful day. She fired off a text to Reggie: Thank you!!! The flowers are gorgeous. And thanks for being my wingman.

Bubbles appeared on-screen.

Reggie: Always. How's it going?

Jo: I'll let you know once the dust settles.

Reggie: Now that you're a homeowner, your next mission should you choose to accept it . . .

Jo: Ugh. No. But I appreciate the early Xmas gift. She had yet to use the vibrator, but it was good to know it was there should her deactivated libido ever emerge from its sleep mode.

Reggie: You're welcome. And just so you know, I'm not giving up.

Jo: You're as bad as Sean.

Reggie: I was his wingman before I was yours.

She was in the girls' room, helping them unpack their toys and clothes, when she heard Hank's voice call, "Say, Jo, where would you like me to put your TV?" moments before he appeared in the doorway, wearing board shorts and a Margaritaville T-shirt. He'd been making himself useful since they'd arrived, doing small repairs, hanging curtains, and assembling bed frames. He'd installed her desktop and printers—one for paper and one for photos—in the home office he'd built for her. Presently, he was installing her home entertainment system in the living room.

"Corner to the right of the fireplace," she instructed. "Oh, and Hank? Thank you. You've been a big help today."

"You're welcome. Happy to pitch in." His gaze shifted to Emma, who was busy arranging her stuffed animals on her bed. "That's quite the menagerie you've got there, young lady."

"What's a ma-jory?" Emma looked up at him.

"A fancy word for 'zoo.' Do your animals have names?"

"Uh-huh." Emma proceeded to rattle off each of their names. There was Ollie the gorilla, Flora the parrot, Pinky the rabbit, Bubbles the dolphin, and last but not least, Kermit the Frog. She picked him up and manipulated one of his spindly arms to make it look like he was waving to Hank. "Kermit says hi."

"Hey there, bud," Hank greeted him. "You look like you could use a bath, if you don't mind me saying so." Kermit's plush body was more brown than green, despite having been laundered.

"He had a bath already," Emma said.

"In that case, he might've missed a few spots."

Emma giggled. She'd taken to Hank immediately.

Jess, on the other hand, was intent on ignoring him. Right now, she was busy organizing her rock collection in the bookcase on her side of the room, which was painted purple, in contrast to Emma's side, which was painted pink. Her hobby had begun with a tour of one of the abandoned mines in the area when she was five. At the end of the tour, she'd declared that she wanted to be a geologist when she grew up. She'd since acquired a good-size collection of rocks and minerals, which included phosphates and silicates, sulfides and crystals, and uncut semiprecious gemstones. The geodes took up most of one shelf. The largest was the size of an ostrich egg.

"Hank, if you're not doing anything later, why don't you join us for supper?" Jo said as he was turning to leave.

He paused in the doorway. "Appreciate the offer, but I wouldn't want to put you to any trouble."

"It's no trouble. I was planning to order a pizza. I'll get an extra-large if you're coming."

He grinned. "I never say no to pizza."

"Mommy, why is that man still here?" demanded Jess after he'd left. She had yet to refer to him by name.

"Hank lives here. You know that."

"You said he lives *downstairs*."

"Yes, but today he's helping us with our move."

"What about after today?"

"We'll see him sometimes. You know, when he fixes his meals or does his laundry." She'd explained all that to the girls after their first encounter with Hank, when she'd been caught off-guard.

"Will he eat with us every night?"

"No. It's just this once, to thank him for all his help today. It was the polite thing to do." Jess frowned, her lower lip quivering. "Sweetie, what's wrong?" Jo went over to her, pulling her into her arms.

"Daddy wouldn't like it."

Jo understood it had been an emotional day for her. She herself had been surprised to feel a tad nostalgic watching the Taj recede in the rearview mirror. However humble, it'd been home for the past decade. It was where her babies had been born and where she'd lived with Sean.

"I know it's not what we planned, but do you think you could give Hank a chance? This is new for him, too. Also, he and the lady who used to own this house were good friends. I imagine he misses her."

"Okay, but if I still don't want him here after I give him a chance, can we ask him to leave?"

"No."

"Why not?"

Jo was sweaty and exhausted. She didn't have the energy or patience to explain again why she needed the rent money, so she said the one true thing that was inarguable: "He was here first."

Jess had nothing to say to that, though she didn't look happy about it.

Later, Jo was on her way to the kitchen when she heard voices. Through the archway to the kitchen, she could see Emma perched on a stepladder at the counter where Hank was unpacking a box labeled COOKWARE. She paused to watch as he passed an item covered in Bubble Wrap from the box to Emma, then guided her small fingers as she unwrapped it. She smiled, witnessing the interaction, and then remembered something her dad had said about Hank when she'd been FaceTiming with her parents the other day. *Doesn't he have any family of his own? Or is he that annoying relative that no one wants to be stuck with? Mark my words, he'll be glomming on to you and the girls if you don't watch out, and then* you'll *be stuck with him.* What if her dad was right? Was Hank trying to inject himself into her family out of loneliness? She was instantly ashamed for questioning his motives. Was she becoming like her parents, who were quick to judge and slow to trust?

Any lingering concerns she'd had about Hank were put to rest after the incident that occurred the following day. Jo was arranging the books she'd unpacked in the built-in bookshelves in the living room when she heard Hank's voice call, "Jo, have you seen my Willie Mays baseball?"

She turned around to find him standing at the top of the stairs looking worried. She remembered that he collected sports memorabilia. His collection, displayed on the floating shelves in his sitting room downstairs, included valuable baseball cards, several Super Bowl rings, a baseball bat signed by the legendary Yankees ballplayer Bobby Murcer, and a baseball autographed by the late, great Willie Mays.

"Not since you showed it to me," she told him. "Why? Is it missing?"

He nodded. "It was in its usual spot before I went out earlier, and when I got back, it was gone."

"Maybe you accidentally knocked it off the shelf and didn't notice? Did you check under the sofa?"

"It was in its Plexiglas cube. The cube's still there. It's just the ball that's missing."

Jo, recalling the recent disappearance of Emma's Kermit the Frog, suddenly had a bad feeling. Her gaze darted to her children, whom she could see playing in the backyard with Snickers through the screen door of the open slider. Jess was tossing something the size and shape of a baseball for their dog to fetch. *Oh no. No no no no.* Jo flew out onto the deck and down the stairs to the yard, dread pooling in her stomach.

When Jess and Emma saw her coming, they both froze, wearing guilty expressions, while Snickers trotted toward them with the object she'd fetched in her mouth, tail wagging. A baseball. Jo bent to pry it from her jaws. Through the dirt and dog slobber covering it, she could make out the signature *Willie Mays*. She didn't think her heart could sink any further, but it found a new low.

"Is that my ball?"

She turned around to see Hank jogging toward them, worry lines etched into his face. "Oh, Hank. I'm so sorry!"

He took the baseball from her, staring at it in disbelief. "Shit."

Normally, she'd have objected to him cursing in front of her children, but she could hardly blame him under the circumstances. He looked stricken as he stared down at his formerly valuable and now worthless collectible. Jo felt sick about it, knowing her daughters were responsible.

She turned to confront them. "Girls, what did I tell you about staying out of Hank's room?" she said sternly.

Emma looked up at her with wide eyes, her thumb plugged into her mouth.

"The door was unlocked," Jess said in their defense.

"That's no excuse. You disobeyed and took something that didn't belong to you. Now it's ruined."

"We didn't take it. We only borrowed it."

"Without asking, which was very naughty of you. You both know better." Even as she scolded them, she felt partly to blame. After picking them up at their bus stop and feeding them their snacks, she'd become distracted by the mountain of boxes still to unpack. She should've kept closer watch over them.

Emma mumbled something around her thumb that sounded like "Sorry, Mommy."

"Tell it to Hank. You both owe him an apology."

"Sorry, Hank," the girls chorused, although Jess sounded less contrite than Emma did.

When Hank didn't respond, Jo grew fearful. Suppose this proved to be the last straw on top of Jess pretending he didn't exist and the chaos of their household. If he moved out—and who wouldn't, from a home inhabited by children who couldn't be trusted?—she'd be unable to make her mortgage payments. She'd have to find another lodger, and who could she find who'd be as agreeable as Hank?

"Girls, go to your room," she ordered. "We're not done discussing this. I'm very disappointed in you both." Jess and Emma trudged off toward the house, heads down, while Snickers stayed behind, tail wagging and her eyes on the ball in Hank's hand like she thought the game was still on. "Hank, I don't know what to say. I feel terrible. Do you think you can replace it? I'll reimburse you, of course." She had no idea what it would cost to replace a baseball signed by Willie Mays, but she was pretty sure it was more than she could afford. Maybe he'd be willing to accept payment in installments.

He raised his head to focus on her like someone coming out of a trance. "I'm not taking your money, Jo."

"But . . ."

"The girls meant no harm."

"Maybe not, but they know better than to take what doesn't belong to them."

"It was partly my fault. I neglected to lock up before I went out earlier." He referred to the privacy door to his quarters at the foot of the interior staircase. "I won't make that mistake again."

"So you're not leaving?"

He seemed surprised by her question. "No, why would you think that?"

"I just thought . . . well, it's a sorry state of affairs when you have to lock the door to keep out resident bandits."

"Kids will be kids," he replied with a shrug.

"Still. You must think I didn't teach mine to respect other people's property." She worried it was indicative of a deeper problem with Jess, who was no doubt the instigator of today's mischief. She planned to discuss it with Dr. Shaw before Jess's next appointment, which was set for Thursday of that week.

Hank's keen gaze met hers. "You're a good mom, Jo."

"Am I?"

"Why do you doubt it?"

"I feel like I'm failing my children. I'm usually either too busy or too tired to give them my full attention. I also get impatient with them. The other day I snapped at Emma after she accidentally spilled her milk while we were eating breakfast." She'd been mopping up more than spilled milk after Emma broke into sobs, and she'd felt awful about being the cause of it. "Today I took my eye off the ball. No pun intended." Her lips twisted in a dry smile.

"My dad once told me 'All parents are amateurs.' I didn't understand what he meant until I became a parent myself. Sometimes we get it right. Sometimes we don't. We're only human. When all is said and done, the only thing that really matters is that our children know they're loved. From what I've observed, you haven't failed yours in that regard. Take it from someone who did."

"Your son?"

He nodded, his expression sorrowful. "I was nineteen when Ben was born and a soldier in the army. A week later, I was deployed to 'Nam. Ben was two by the time I got back. I was a stranger to him. It didn't help that my civilian job involved a fair bit of travel. After his mom and I divorced, he saw even less of me. I never forgot a birthday, and there were always presents from me under the Christmas tree, but often weeks would go by between visits. I missed more games and school plays than I attended. I wasn't there to see him make the winning touchdown when his team won the state finals, and I never did get around to taking him on the camping trip I promised him when he was twelve. I told myself I'd make it up to him someday, but I blinked and he was grown, a soldier with a wife and child of his own. Then he was gone."

Jo was moved by his tale. "Oh, Hank. I'm so sorry."

He gave a short nod, his eyes glistening with unshed tears. "After Ben died, I relocated to Seattle so I could be near my grandson, and took a job there that didn't require travel. Ian was a baby when his dad died and doesn't remember him, but I made damn sure he knew his granddad."

"So he was your do-over?"

"You could say that. I like to think I did a better job as a grandpa than I did as a father."

"What's the story with Ian's mom?"

"Cherise?" His expression brightened. "She's an amazing mom, but a boy needs a man to show him how to pee standing up, and how to talk to girls when he's older."

"She never remarried?"

"No, and she wasn't close with her parents, so it was just her and me and Ian. She's like a daughter to me."

Jo felt ashamed for having entertained the notion, however briefly, that her lodger was attempting to worm his way into her family because he had no family of his own and nowhere else to go. Clearly, that wasn't the case. Her next thought was unsettling: *I need him more than he needs me.*

"I guess I should be thankful I have daughters. They didn't have to be taught how to pee standing up. Though apparently I didn't do a good job of teaching them to respect other people's property."

Hank's gaze returned to his ruined baseball. He absently toyed with it, lost in thought, and then in a sudden move that caused Jo to start, he launched it toward the back fence with a long throw, which sent Snickers racing after it. "It's just things, Jo. Things are replaceable. People aren't."

She thought of Sean, and the knife in her heart gave a painful twist. "No, they're not."

9

She had a talk with her girls. They were both contrite, even Jess, who'd made it clear she wished Hank gone. They hadn't acted out of malice, nor had they known the baseball was valuable. They promised to be good from now on. Jo knew with children good intentions usually lasted only until the next temptation, but she let them off with a warning and had them each apologize to Hank in writing. Emma's apology came in the form of a crayon drawing of a stick figure with tears spouting from it like water from a fountain below the word *sorry* in crooked block letters.

Jo slept poorly that night and awakened the next morning while it was still dark out. Her first thought as her feet hit the floor was *Where am I?* She could make out the familiar shapes of her bedroom furniture, but nothing was in its proper place. Then she remembered. "We're not in Kansas anymore, Toto," she said to Snickers when her dog rose and padded over to her.

Jo braced for the usual gut punch that came with the news, delivered fresh daily to her brain upon awakening, that her husband was gone, but this morning it didn't come. Huh. Weird. She chalked it up to the fact that she was in a different setting, a house where there were no ghosts.

The house was quiet, the girls asleep in their beds when she paused to poke her head into their room on her way down the hall. She let Snickers out, leaving the sliding door cracked open so she could get back inside after she'd done her business, and headed for the kitchen to start the coffee. She was measuring grounds into the filter when she heard voices drifting from outside.

"You're up early, Pop-Pop. It's, what, six o'clock where you are?"

"Couldn't sleep," said a voice she recognized as Hank's. "This a bad time?"

"Nah. I'm on duty but between training exercises at the moment. What's up? Why couldn't you sleep?"

"Dunno. Must be getting old."

"You? Never."

From the gist of their conversation, Hank was talking with his grandson in Germany. Which would explain the reference to him being on duty. It was midday on the other side of the Atlantic.

"Happens to the best of us. What's new with you, son?"

"Our new base commander, that's what. He arrived last week and is shaking things up around here. I believe you know him. Captain Kellogg. Claims you and he fought together in 'Nam."

"Corny Kellogg? Well, I'll be damned. Haven't heard that name in years. Yeah, we fought together once. This was during a mission that involved both the army and air force."

"So he said."

"One of these days I'll have to tell you the story. It had us flying over the jungle, rescuing a platoon trapped behind enemy lines, while taking fire. Two other helicopters were shot down. Miracle the rest of us survived." He added wryly, "Both the mission and the night of drinking that came after."

"I'd love to hear it sometime."

"I'll save it for your next visit. Tell the old bastard I said hello."

"Will do, but I won't quote you. He may be an 'old bastard' to you, but he's my commanding officer. How's it going with the new landlady? She kicked your sorry ass to the curb yet?"

Jo realized with a guilty start that she was eavesdropping. When she went to close the slider to give her lodger some privacy, she saw him seated at the table on the deck, his face illuminated by the glowing screen of his laptop in the darkness. He glanced up and called softly, "Morning, Jo! Hope I didn't disturb you. Wi-Fi downstairs was wonky, so when I saw the lights on upstairs . . ."

"You're not disturbing me. I was up anyway," she told him.

"I'm talking with my grandson. Come say hello." He beckoned to her.

Jo's inner child balked. Growing up, she'd hated it when her mother had dragged her over to meet so-and-so or put her on the phone to say hello to someone, as she'd been in the habit of doing. If her mom was a social butterfly, Jo was a social caterpillar. But to refuse Hank would be rude, especially after yesterday's incident. So she set aside her discomfort, put on a smile, and stepped out onto the deck.

The sun was peeking over the horizon and the air cool. Mornings in the mountains tended to be chilly even in summer, and she was glad to be wearing her robe. As she neared, Hank scooted over to make room for her on the bench where he sat, giving her an unobstructed view of the man on-screen. He looked to be in his mid-thirties with a square jaw and vivid blue eyes like Hank's, which stood out in contrast to his light-brown skin. He was in uniform and appeared fit. His curly dark hair was cut in a military fade.

"Well, that was awkward," he said, smiling.

Disarmed, she smiled back. "Not half as awkward as if I had kicked your grandpa to the curb, which I assure you I have no intention of doing. Although he'd be entirely justified if he decided to leave."

"Why is that?"

"There was an incident."

"Uh-oh. Dare I ask?"

"Our dog ate his Willie Mays baseball. This was after my daughters borrowed it without asking."

Wait. What had possessed her to bring *that* up? To someone she'd just met, no less. She blamed her oversharing on the early hour and the fact that she hadn't had her coffee yet.

"Damn." Ian shook his head.

"I offered to reimburse him, but he wouldn't hear of it." She darted a guilty glance at Hank.

"I've moved on," Hank said.

"At least now I know what to get him for Christmas," said Ian. "He's the worst person in the world to buy gifts for. He always claims there's nothing he wants or needs."

"Because it's true," said Hank. "Besides, Christmas is for kids."

"Speaking of which, how old are yours?" Ian asked Jo.

"Seven and five, respectively. And, despite the impression you may have formed, they're usually well behaved. Yesterday's incident was not the norm and hopefully never to be repeated."

"That was nothing compared to some of the stunts I pulled when I was a teenager. I was incorrigible."

"Really. No one would guess to look at you."

"Ask Pop-Pop if you don't believe me."

"Believe it," said Hank. "He's responsible for every white hair on my head."

Jo laughed. Ian was easy to talk to, and she found herself curious to learn more about him. It was with reluctance that she said, "Well, I'll let you two get back to it. It was nice meeting you, Ian."

"Likewise," he said. "Hopefully, we'll meet in person next time I visit."

"When might that be?"

"If my request for leave is granted, I'll be home later this month. I plan to spend some time with my mom in Seattle, and then fly down to visit Pop-Pop."

"Will you stay with him while you're in town?"

"If it's all right with you. It'd be just for a few days."

"You don't need my permission, assuming you'll be bunking with your grandpa." The sofa in the sitting room downstairs was convertible and her lodger was permitted to have the occasional overnight guest, per the terms of their informal agreement. "Anyway, you're more than welcome."

"You might run into me getting coffee in the mornings."

"Not a problem. I'm an early riser. Besides, I'm guessing you've stayed here in the past."

"Yes, but that was under the old administration."

"Well, I think you'll find the new administration to be equally hospitable."

"Much appreciated." He flashed her a grin. "You know, you remind me of Martha. Not that you look anything like her. I mean, she was old and you're . . ." He trailed off, looking awkward suddenly.

"What Ian's trying to say is that you're young and beautiful," Hank finished for him.

Jo felt her face warm, and she absently ran a hand through her sleep-tangled hair. Beautiful? She couldn't remember when she'd last felt beautiful or had even cared about her appearance.

She was in the kitchen mixing pancake batter when Hank entered a short while later. "Sorry about that," he said, wearing a sheepish expression. "It wasn't until after I called you over to say hello that it occurred to me you might not feel like talking with a stranger first thing in the morning."

"No worries. I enjoyed meeting Ian," she said.

"He's a good kid." She heard the pride in Hank's voice.

"Despite his alleged crimes as a teenager?" she said dryly.

"He straightened out, by the grace of God and the military school he attended after getting into trouble with the law."

Ian had been a juvenile delinquent? She was dying to know more but reined in her curiosity.

"Coffee?" She gestured toward the freshly made pot.

"Thanks." Hank grabbed a mug from the cupboard over the coffee maker, one of the two he owned, red with the slogan STARTER FLUID. "May I make a suggestion?" he said as he filled his mug. "How about we take turns making the coffee in the mornings. Then I wouldn't disturb you on the days it was my turn. I could program the coffee maker the night before. One reason Martha and I got on so well was because we both liked our coffee strong and neither expected the other to make it."

She stirred a handful of blueberries into the batter. "Good idea." She appreciated that he was being considerate. "Coffee strong enough for you?" she asked after he'd taken a sip of his.

"Just the way I like it. Say, Jo, I was wondering . . ." Color crept into his cheeks and his expression grew shy. "You wouldn't happen to know if your friend Frannie is seeing anyone, would you?"

His question surprised her, though it probably shouldn't have after witnessing the chemistry between him and Frannie when they'd met. "Not that I know of. Why? Are you planning to ask her out?"

"That's for me to know and you to find out," he replied with a wink. "Thanks for the coffee. My turn tomorrow." He raised his mug and headed off, pausing to pet Snickers as she was coming back inside.

Watching him go, Jo pondered the irony of romance blooming between a pair of boomers while she, a woman in her prime, withered on the vine. Hank and Frannie seemed like the perfect match, and she was all for her friends finding love, but at the same time, she couldn't help feeling left behind.

10

The next two weeks flew by. Jo was busier than ever. When she wasn't working an event or a scheduled shoot, she was at her desk editing photos or doing paperwork. One shoot was with a local author who'd needed an author photo for her soon-to-be published mystery novel. Another was with the CEO of a small company who'd requested a "sexy" photo of him with his marketing team for their website—like there was anything remotely sexy about a manufacturer of outdoor furniture. Most of the events she covered were wedding related, although one was for a couple celebrating their golden anniversary. The rest of the time, when she wasn't doing household chores or on mom duty, she spent unpacking the remaining boxes. Gradually, she was settling into her new digs.

She was also getting to know her neighbors. Kelsey and Mike, the newly engaged young couple who lived next door, had hired her as their wedding photographer after checking out her website. Then there were Burt Clemmons, the retired policeman who was head of their neighborhood watch, and his wife, Janine. And Mrs. Atkins, the old lady who lived across the street, had brought over homemade brownies to welcome them to the neighborhood. When Jo had gone to return the Tupperware the following day, Mrs. Atkins had invited her to stay for tea.

Emma had made friends with a little girl from down the street named Greer, who'd had her at "dollhouse." Jess, however, had refused to approach any of the neighborhood kids her age. At home, she was moody and withdrawn. The only thing that seemed to give her any pleasure, besides her rock collecting, was going to her day camp. When Jo had shared her concerns with Dr. Shaw, the therapist had advised her to be patient. "Rome wasn't built in a day," she'd quoted.

One day Jo was in the kitchen, organizing the drawers, where she'd tossed items at random when she'd been unpacking and now couldn't find anything, while the girls colored in their coloring books at the table in the dining nook, when Hank appeared carrying a gift-wrapped package. He handed it to her. "For you and the girls."

She was touched but couldn't help feeling awkward. She wasn't just being polite when she said, "Hank, you shouldn't have. You've already done so much. And I owe you after . . . you know."

"No idea what you're talking about." He pretended to have forgotten about the incident with his baseball. "Anyway, it's no big deal. Just a little something I made for you as a housewarming gift."

She sat down to open Hank's gift while he and the girls looked on. She tore off the wrapping paper, uncovering a rustic 8 x 10 picture frame, handcrafted from wood and decorated with pieces of tree bark. It was beautiful, but that wasn't what made her gasp. It was the photo in the frame: one of her and Sean and the girls taken during a family excursion, three years earlier. They'd gone skiing that day at a local resort and were dressed in ski gear and posing on a snow-covered slope, ruddy-cheeked and beaming. Emma, who'd been two at the time, stood no taller than Sean's kneecap.

"I noticed there were no family photos around the house," Hank said. "I got this one from Frannie."

Jo remembered it was Frannie who'd taken the photo. A veteran of the slopes, she'd gone with them that day. She swallowed. "Th-thank you, but you shouldn't have."

This time her words came out sounding harsh. Hank looked worried suddenly. "Did I overstep? I assumed there were no photos because you hadn't gotten around to unpacking all your stuff yet. I didn't think . . ."

"No. It was kind of you," she said, recovering her manners. "Just . . . unexpected."

She looked up to see that the girls had crept up alongside her and were gazing raptly, hungrily almost, at the family photo from happier times. "Can we put it in our room?" asked Jess, glancing over at her sister.

Hearing the eagerness in her voice, Jo had a sobering realization. She'd thought she was protecting her girls from memories that might be painful, but it seemed she'd been depriving them instead. She felt a stab of guilt. She rearranged her features in a semblance of a smile. "I think that's a fine idea. Then you'll always have it to remind you of the good times we had with Daddy."

Jess's face lit up, and when she cast a glance at Hank, Jo counted it as a minor victory. It was the first time she'd so much as acknowledged him since they'd moved in. She put her arms around her girls and pulled them close while they studied the photo in the beautiful frame that Hank had made.

"Is there snow in heaven?" asked Emma.

"I don't know, honey, but if there is, Daddy's probably skiing the slopes with the angels."

"I miss skiing," said Jess wistfully. Sean, who'd been an avid skier, had had the girls skiing the bunny slopes as soon as they'd learned to walk. They hadn't gone skiing since he'd died.

"I'll take you skiing this winter," Jo promised. She was by no means an experienced skier, but she could handle the easy slopes. And perhaps she could get Marisol's boyfriend, Cal, who'd worked as a ski instructor at the Timberlake Lodge here during the off-season when he wasn't working as a tour guide, to give the girls skiing lessons when he got back from New York.

After she hung the photo in the girls' room, they reminisced about other fun family adventures they'd had. For Emma, the highlight was their trip to Disneyland, the last one they'd taken as a family. For Jess, it was the time she'd gone spelunking with her dad in one of the caves in the area.

Afterward, the girls went back to their coloring books and she went to find Hank to let him know she appreciated his gift and apologize for being less than gracious in thanking him earlier. Snickers followed as she descended the stairs to his quarters. "May I come in?" she asked after he answered her knock.

"Of course." He stepped aside to let her and Snickers in.

As she entered, her gaze swept over the tidy space. They were in the sitting room. On one side stood a sofa, with a standing lamp at one end, opposite a pair of armchairs, with a Shaker-style coffee table on the Kilim rug in the center. The shelves lining one wall held his sports memorabilia and family photos. Through the door to the en suite bedroom beyond, she could see his bed, neatly made. The walls were painted a calming shade of blue and hung with more photos and a couple of prints.

"Thank you again for your gift," she told him. "It's lovely, and I could see you put a lot of work into it."

"You're welcome. It was simple enough to make, and the wood and pine bark I used were foraged." He gestured toward the view of the forest through the slider to his private patio.

"It was thoughtful of you. And I was a jerk."

"You're sure I didn't overstep?"

"No. You couldn't have known why I haven't put up any family photos."

"Why is that, if I may ask?"

"I was afraid it'd be painful for the girls. You know, to be reminded."

"Memories can be painful," he agreed. "But for every tear I shed at my son's grave, there was a happy memory."

His gaze fell on a framed 8 x 10 photo on one of the shelves of a tall, strikingly handsome man in a military uniform, with Hank's eyes and mouth, who could only have been his son. Her chest spasmed with sorrow. Sorrow for Hank's loss and for her own. "Does it ever get any easier?"

"You never stop grieving, but it becomes bearable over time. That was my experience, anyway."

"You mean there's hope for me?"

He placed a hand on her shoulder, his kind eyes meeting hers. "It's different for everyone and some days are tougher than others. The secret is to give yourself some grace on the tough days."

She swallowed and nodded. "Just FYI, I'll be out of town next weekend," she told him as she was leaving to go back upstairs.

"Business or pleasure?"

"Both. My friend Reggie and his partner are getting married. I'm their wedding photographer—it's my gift to them. I arranged for the girls to stay with my friend Suzy while I'm away." Suzy had invited them for the weekend. Her daughter and granddaughters, who lived in DC, would also be visiting, and the four girls would keep one another entertained, according to Suzy.

"Thanks for letting me know. I'll look after the place while you're away. I could take care of the old girl, too, if you like." His gaze dropped to Snickers, who'd parked herself next to him like she intended to stay. She seemed to have decided that Hank was her new master in Sean's absence.

"Well, if you're offering . . ." She'd planned to board Snickers at the kennel where she usually stayed when Jo was away but knew their dog would be happier at home. "Are you sure you don't mind?"

"Not in the least. We'll keep each other company, won't we, girl?" Snickers wagged her tail in response and looked up at him adoringly as he bent to scratch behind her ears.

Her dog wasn't the only one keeping Hank company these days. Marisol had reported seeing Hank and Frannie having lunch together one day last week, and today the photo in the picture frame Hank had given Jo, which could only have come from Frannie, had confirmed her suspicion that they'd become romantically involved. Not that either of them had said a word about it. One thing the two boomers had in common, besides the fact that they seemed to know every seventies rock band that ever existed, was that they were both private people. Whatever they were up to, or however serious their relationship, they were undoubtedly having more fun than she was. It was a depressing thought.

It doesn't have to be this way, babe.

Says you.

You know I'm right.

I'm not listening to you. You're dead.

True. But you're missing the point.

Which is . . .

You're not.

The following Friday Jo arrived at LAX to find Reggie waiting in baggage claim. He was easy to spot even in a crowd in his lime-green linen blazer over a Hawaiian shirt and blue suede loafers, with his tangerine Ray-Bans pushed up into his blond 'fro. She waved to get his attention. A moment later, she was engulfed in a rib-crushing hug and a cloud of Polo by Ralph Lauren.

"Thank God you're here. And not a moment too soon," he said as they went to find the baggage carousel for her flight.

"Where's the fire?" she said. "The wedding's not until tomorrow."

"Not if I call it off. Either that, or murder my fiancé. Whichever comes first."

"Uh-oh. What'd he do this time?" The two had been fighting about one thing or another ever since they'd set a date.

"I'll give you a hint: memories."

"As in making them?"

"As in the song. Marco wants us to dance our first dance at the reception to the signature song from *Cats*. Can you imagine?" He gave a theatrical shudder.

"Why that song?"

"He claims it's *our* song because it was playing when we first met."

"Wait. Didn't you two meet—"

"In an elevator. Exactly."

"Okay, you have a point, but I still don't see the problem." They found the baggage carousel and staked out a spot among the other passengers from her flight. "It's a great song."

"I don't disagree. But after listening to it approximately nine billion times, most recently at my niece's sixth grade talent show, I think it's fair to say that it's been overdone."

"There are worse things than dancing to elevator music at your wedding."

"Name one."

"Marrying the wrong person. Which is not the case here. You and Marco are soulmates."

Like Sean and me. Her vision blurred. This wedding was bittersweet for Jo because it was bringing up memories of her wedding, when Reggie had stood beside Sean at the altar as his best man. She remembered the toast Reggie had given at the reception, in which he'd alluded to the series of misunderstandings that had nearly scuppered her and Sean's relationship before it got off the ground. *Their gaydar may be faulty, but their hearts are true,* he'd said. Except now hers had a Sean-size hole in it.

"That was before Marco morphed into a groomzilla," said Reggie. "It's not just his questionable song choice we disagree on. Instead of the small wedding I proposed, he's getting the huge wedding he wanted, to which every relative of his, both here and abroad, is invited. Oh, and did I mention his Sicilian relatives are rumored to have mob ties?"

Jo took the "rumor" with a grain of salt. Not only was Reggie known to overdramatize, but he was also a fan of the *Godfather* movies. "And you're so easy to live with, are you?"

"I never said I was."

"Admit it, you'd be lost without him."

"Be that as it may, I'm at my wit's end."

"It might help if you remembered his good qualities."

"I can't think of any at the moment."

"What made you fall in love with him, then?"

"That's obvious. He's hot."

"Besides that."

Reggie's expression softened. "He's thoughtful. And funny—he makes me laugh when he's not dancing on my last nerve. He's also a great cook and we like the same movies. Not to mention, the man can dance the horizontal salsa like nobody's business."

"*And* he puts up with you."

"That, too," he conceded.

A buzzer sounded and the carousel started to revolve, spitting bags from its chute. Jo spied her bags amid the logjam making its way toward her and snagged her suitcase while Reggie grabbed the hard case containing her camera gear. Her camera, an older-model Nikon DSLR, was in her carry-on. She never let it out of her sight when she traveled. Besides being the chief tool of her trade, it had sentimental value. Sean had given it to her for Christmas the year she'd been pregnant with Emma. At the time, she'd still been at Redmond Advertising, debating whether to go freelance. With another baby on the way, she'd worried they couldn't afford to give up her steady paycheck. But Sean had believed in her. When she learned he'd sold his dad's Gibson guitar to buy the camera, she'd cried. His dad had been a musician, good enough to perform in clubs, and his Gibson was the one thing of value Sean had had left of his dad after his parents were killed. Sean hadn't seen selling it as a sacrifice, though. *My dad didn't live to become the next Eric Clapton,* he'd told her, *but* you *could become the next Annie Leibovitz.* Which was why, even if she could afford to buy a state-of-the-art camera, she'd never part with her Nikon.

"What's new with you?" asked Reggie as they crawled through traffic, en route to the condo in Santa Monica he shared with Marco. The classic T-Bird he drove, baby blue with a cream interior in factory-mint condition, he'd purchased after receiving his first six-figure paycheck, for his role as a dog groomer to the stars in the hit sitcom *Who Let the Dogs Out?* that ran for three seasons. "You all settled in at your new place?"

"Not quite, but I'm getting there." She refrained from mentioning the problems she was having with Jess. Reggie had enough problems with his wedding drama without her adding to the mix.

"How's it working out with your lodger?"

"Better than I expected. Not only does Hank keep a low profile and clean up after himself, but he also helps out around the house. He even does the gardening. He wasn't going to charge me, but when I insisted, he quoted me a ridiculously low hourly rate that even I can afford."

"If he were thirty years younger, he'd be perfect for you."

She frowned. "I don't need a man in my life."

She'd had the perfect man. Anyone other than Sean would be a poor substitute. If she was feeling left behind now that Hank and Frannie were dating, it was because she knew she'd never find love again.

Reggie changed lanes, advancing several car lengths before traffic slowed again. The sunlight backfiring from the surrounding vehicles was blinding. "You're not getting any younger. More to the point, you're not getting any."

"I have your 'early Christmas present.'"

"Did you even take it out of its packaging?"

"Yes."

"Did you insert . . ."

"No!" she screamed.

"The batteries that were included?"

"No," she repeated, weakly this time.

"I rest my case."

"I'm not ruling out the possibility of having sex again someday," she said grudgingly. "If it's with the right person."

Reggie lowered his sunglasses to give her his comic-react look. "What is this I'm hearing? When we last discussed the subject, you were on the fast track to becoming a nun. What's changed?"

"Apart from my change of address? Nothing much. But who knows? I might find myself in a different place in my life someday. Or not," she added.

"Is that your backassward way of saying you wouldn't be opposed to getting laid at some point?"

She shrugged. "Anything's possible."

"Well, praise the Lord and pass the biscuits," Reggie sang out in his churchy voice. "Honey, I'd dance the Watusi at my wedding if that's what it'd take to get you laid."

"Don't get too excited. I haven't met anyone I'd want to sleep with."

"There'll be plenty of eligible men at the wedding, not all of them gay."

"I'll be working," she reminded him.

"Only because you wouldn't let us hire a photographer. Not that Marco and I don't appreciate the generous gift of your services, but we'd rather you attended our wedding strictly as our guest."

"Can't I be both?"

"Yes, but I expect you to dine with our other guests. And dance," he added pointedly.

She frowned. "You didn't say anything about dancing."

"If I have to dance to elevator music at my wedding, you can take a turn or two on the dance floor. You look gorgeous, by the way. Did you do something with your hair? Or is it your makeup?"

"I've had the same hairstyle since you knew me in college and I don't wear makeup. But thank you."

"That's it," he said with a snap of his fingers. "You look like yourself."

"How else am I supposed to look?"

His grin gave way to a somber look. "Honey, you haven't looked like yourself since Sean died."

Jo winced at the truth of his words. In the weeks after Sean's death, she hadn't bothered to so much as comb her hair or take a shower unless she'd had to make herself presentable for work. She couldn't eat or sleep. She'd lost fifteen pounds and looked like an extra from *Night of the Living Dead.* It wasn't until Frannie had said, "You're scaring me. And if I'm scared, imagine how your children must feel. If you don't start taking better care of yourself, how will you be able to take care of them?" that she'd taken a good look at herself in the mirror. It'd been the wake-up call she'd needed. She'd since regained the weight she'd lost along with the color in her cheeks. She was even making conscious wardrobe choices. Today she wore a jean jacket over a granny dress and knee-high leather boots. "I guess I had to rejoin the land of the living sometime."

"I'm glad to hear you say that because there's someone I'd like you to meet."

"Oh no you don't." She narrowed her eyes at him.

"What? I'm not suggesting a blind date. He'll be at the wedding. I'll introduce you."

"Fine. I'll meet him, but I'm not sleeping with him."

"Whatever you say." Reggie smirked at her, and she had a sinking feeling she was being set up.

The rehearsal dinner that evening was held at a neighborhood Italian restaurant. It was a lively affair with Marco's parents, both sets of grandparents, and six siblings and their families filling most of the seats at the long table. But although Reggie's relatives in attendance were fewer in number than Marco's, they included his parents, with whom he'd recently reconciled after a lengthy estrangement, in addition to his sister and her family and one cousin, which was cause for rejoicing. Everyone seemed to get along, and the toasts became more effusive as the evening wore on.

Jo didn't pick up on any friction between Reggie and Marco, despite Reggie having threatened to call off the wedding. They were as affectionate as ever. They were also living proof of the theory that opposites attract. Marco, who worked as a personal trainer to the stars, was six foot four and could bench-press his own weight. Reggie was a head shorter with a physique that betrayed his fondness for sweets. Marco was normally even-keeled, while Reggie was known to be a drama queen.

"Jo, did this one bitch to you about my plebeian taste in music?" Marco asked when dessert was being served. He cast a wryly affectionate look at Reggie, seated to his right. Reggie heaved a long-suffering sigh, but the effect was spoiled when he took Marco's hand.

"I heard something about a disagreement over a song choice," she said.

"What's your opinion?"

"My opinion doesn't count. It's *your* wedding, and if you decide to dance to elevator music, it'll be just the two of you in the 'elevator.'"

She remembered her first dance with Sean at their wedding reception. As they'd glided over the dance floor, created of pine planks and enclosed by hay bales, in the glow of the lanterns suspended from the rafters of the barn at his aunt and uncle's ranch, they'd danced like no one was watching.

"You okay?" Reggie's whispered voice brought her back to the present.

She brushed away the tears in her eyes and mustered a smile. "Just feeling a little nostalgic."

He nodded in understanding. "Your wedding was the most romantic ever. Apart from Julie Andrews and Christopher Plummer's in *The Sound of Music*, that is." He made as if he were swooning. "Watching you and Sean together, I could believe it would happen for me someday. And so it has." His gaze softened as he glanced over at Marco. "Thanks, by the way. Nice save."

"You're welcome."

"I miss him, too, you know." His brown eyes glistened.

She squeezed his hand. "I know."

The day of the wedding dawned cool and gray. The coastal fog characteristic of the summer months lingered until late in the afternoon. By the time the wedding party gathered on the terrace at Sandrine's, the beachside hotel in Santa Monica where the ceremony was set to take place at sunset, Reggie was in full drama-queen mode. The terrace was so fogged in, he complained, the guests wouldn't be able to see past their noses. "Our wedding photos will look like stills from *The Mist*," he wailed. While Darnell, the aspiring actor and friend of Reggie's who'd been hired to assist her, helped Jo set up the LED light stands inside for the posed shots to follow the ceremony, Marco did his best to calm Reggie's nerves, without success. Reggie grew increasingly stressed as the guests, ghostly figures amid the fog, began to arrive and fill the seats on the terrace. Then, minutes before the ceremony was due to commence, the fog lifted as if by direction of a celestial stage manager, revealing the terrace in all its wedding finery and stretch of shoreline beyond, bathed in the glow of the setting sun.

Jo was in position to the right of the flower-bedecked wedding bower, when the string quartet began to play an instrumental rendition of "Memories," which made her smile, and the procession began. First came the five groomsmen, then the two flower girls, Marco's young nieces, scattering rose petals as they went, and last the grooms, who wore matching white linen jackets and purple bow ties. Each was escorted by his parents, which was all the more meaningful in Reggie's case. Both looked as though nothing could spoil their happiness today and the drama of the weeks leading up to it had been but a blip on their radar. Jo captured it all on camera while darting this way and that, bobbing and weaving, to get shots from every angle while remaining unobtrusive.

At one point, she grew emotional listening to Reggie deliver his speech. "Marco, when I first saw you, I thought you were the most gorgeous man I'd ever seen. And because we were in an elevator, my first thought was, 'Whichever floor he's getting off at is where I'm going.' My second thought was, 'Lord, I have *got* to take that man shopping.' Because, honey, you looked like you were dressed for a Disney cruise." This was met by laughter from the audience. "Once I got to know you,

I saw the beautiful heart inside the beautiful man I'd fallen for. Over the past five years, my love for you has only grown, along with your wardrobe, I might add. Baby, you've given me the ride of my life, and the best is yet to come."

Jo was seized by a sudden, fierce yearning for what she'd once had and lost. She wasn't looking for love, because how could she be with another man without feeling like she was betraying Sean or settling for second-best? But she missed seeing the love shining in the eyes of someone who adored her.

After Marco's speech came readings by the mothers of the grooms—Reggie's mom read a passage from the Bible and Marco's a Tennyson poem—before the grooms recited their vows and they each slipped a ring on the other's finger. Jo got a shot of them kissing against the backdrop of the sunset sky, which she knew, even without seeing any of the others she'd taken, was the money shot. All the while, she ached inside—an ache as fathomless as the ocean glittering beyond.

Afterward, with Darnell's help, she corralled the wedding party into the staging area inside, where she took group photos and ones of just Reggie and Marco. Darkness had fallen and the reception was in full swing by the time she reemerged. The terrace was lit by the glow from inside and the fairy lights strung overhead. Guests mingled and servers circulated with trays of canapés. Drinks were being served at the open bar beneath the cabana at one end. The dining area consisted of rows of pine trestle tables, each beautifully set with floral centerpieces spaced at intervals down its center. She was snapping photos when she spied her name on the place card at one of the table settings and remembered her promise to Reggie. She wasn't sure about the dancing but she had to eat, she supposed.

Later, she was photographing the spread at the grill station, where the steaks—a choice between beef and salmon—were being fired and the buffet supper was being served when she heard a voice ask, "Can I get you something to eat?"

She turned around to see a man standing behind her. "Excuse me?"

He stuck out his hand. "Hi, I'm Scott. Reggie's friend. He said I should introduce myself." He was somewhere in his mid-thirties, attractive in an LA hipster kind of way, with sandy hair tousled just so and gray-green eyes. He wore an unstructured linen jacket over a black silk T-shirt.

Clearly he was the "someone" Reggie had wanted her to meet. She grew flustered but quickly recovered her manners and shook his hand. "I'm Jo."

"Pleased to meet you, Jo. Listen, why don't I get you a plate while I'm getting mine? You can join me when you're ready." He motioned toward the table where she'd seen the place card with her name on it, indicating that their assigned seats were next to each other. Reggie had left nothing to chance. She made a mental note to strangle him after he returned from his honeymoon.

"Thanks, but I can get my own food." It seemed too intimate somehow, having him get it for her, like something a boyfriend or husband would do.

"You could," he agreed. "But what's the point in us both waiting in line?" His gaze traveled over the long line of people snaking past them. "Please, allow me." He flashed her an engaging smile.

"All right," she relented. "I'll have the salmon. Oh, and thanks," she remembered to add.

A short while later she found herself seated next to Scott at their table, with a plate of food in front of her—grilled salmon steak with sides of roasted fingerling potatoes and charred-corn salad. Her mouth watered at the delicious aromas. She hadn't realized how hungry she was until now.

"How do you know Reggie?" she asked as they started digging into their food.

"We met on a movie set," said Scott as he cut off a piece of his New York strip, cooked a perfect medium rare.

"You're in show business? Should I have heard of you?"

He smiled. "Not unless you were in the industry. I work behind the scenes. I'm a location scout." He popped the piece of steak into his mouth and chewed.

"Really?" She'd never met a location scout before. "What does your work involve besides, you know, scouting locations?"

"I also do the footwork in advance of the film crew once the location is locked. Everything from negotiating thc use of public and private property to securing lodging and sourcing any local services or equipment that might be needed."

"Sounds complicated."

"It's part of what makes my job interesting. How about you? I know you're a photographer because you're here taking pictures and also because Reggie told me. Do you do it for a living?"

"Yes, although I'm not charging for this job—it's my gift to the grooms. Reggie's an old friend."

"So he said. What else can you tell me about yourself?"

My husband died and I'm still wearing my ring, in case you hadn't noticed, so if you're looking to get laid, you're barking up the wrong tree. She blushed at the direction her thoughts had taken and said, "Well, I'm a mom. I have two daughters, ages seven and five." Who she was missing something fierce right now. "We live in a small town up north called Gold Creek."

His expression turned serious. "Reggie told me about your husband. I'm sorry for your loss."

Suddenly, her appetite vanished and her eyes grew hot. She gave a nod and changed the subject so she wouldn't make a public spectacle of herself by breaking down. "Have you ever been married?"

"Once." His jaw tightened. "And once was enough." She wondered what his story was, but decided it was none of her business. It wasn't as if she planned to see him again.

By the time they were done eating, the band had struck up and the dance floor was thronged. Scott asked her to dance, and she remembered again her promise to Reggie. *One dance won't kill you.* "All right," she said. "But then I have to get back to work."

Fortunately it wasn't a slow dance and Scott turned out to be a good dancer. After an awkward start, she got into the rhythm of it. She'd forgotten how much fun it was to cut loose on a dance floor, it'd been so long. As she moved to the music, she felt herself relax. She remembered the compliment Reggie had paid her and became aware of herself as a woman. She felt glamorous almost in her emerald-silk dress and pink ballet flats. She was sorry when the song ended.

"To be continued," Scott said as she left to go back to work.

"I don't know if we'll see each other again after tonight, but it's been fun," she told him.

"As it so happens, I'll be in your area on my next assignment. Maybe we could get together then."

She was surprised, and wondered if this, too, had been orchestrated by Reggie before concluding it was too much of a stretch. "Really? What a coincidence," she said, stalling rather than give him an answer.

"I'm scouting for a big-budget Western that's slated for filming there in the fall. Bradley Cooper was just signed to play the lead role."

"How exciting." The words fell from numb lips.

"Any chance I could get you to show me some of the sights while I'm in Gold Creek?"

She hesitated. She'd enjoyed chatting, and dancing, with Scott. But seeing him again was another matter entirely. Would it count as a date? Oh, God. She was not prepared for this! "When are you planning to be in town?" If his dates coincided with her work commitments, she'd be off the hook.

"Sometime next week. I'll be looking at other towns in the area, and I can't say how long I'll be in each one, but I could arrange my schedule depending on your availability. Any day next week would work."

"Let me check my calendar." She pulled out her phone and scrolled through the next week's appointments, buying more time. She had some slots available, but he didn't need to know. She could tell him she was fully booked.

Go for it, babe. What have you got to lose?

The real question is, what do I have to gain?

You won't know unless you put yourself out there.

Jo debated whether to take the plunge or remain on the fast track to becoming a nun, as Reggie had so eloquently put it. Becoming aware that Scott was watching her, waiting for an answer, she came to a decision. "How about Friday morning after breakfast? I'll have some free time then."

He grinned, striking fear in her heart with his next words. "It's a date."

She stopped at Suzy's to pick up Jess and Emma on the way home from the airport the next day. Suzy lived in a cute, cedar-shingled rambler on a tree-lined street in one of the older residential neighborhoods of Gold Creek. Jo climbed from her car and hurried up the front walk, eager to see her children. It seemed like weeks, rather than days, since she'd last seen them.

Suzy greeted her at the door. "They're playing in the backyard with Rose and Lily. I'll let them know you're here." She led the way through her HGTV-worthy house, which was as stylish as the woman who owned it. It was also surprisingly neat for one with weekend visitors, four of whom were below the age of ten. She stopped when they reached the den, which looked out on the backyard.

"Since when do you own a trampoline?" Jo asked, watching the four girls jumping on the trampoline outside.

"Since I became a grandma who can't say no to her grandkids," Suzy answered with a wry chuckle.

"Did the girls behave themselves?"

"They were good as gold, and kept one another entertained, as predicted. How was your trip?"

"Great! The wedding was perfect, despite Reggie's dire predictions and the fog that didn't roll out until showtime. There's nothing more romantic than a sunset wedding at the seashore."

"Speaking of romance . . . Guess who I ran into last night at Sung Hun Lo while I was picking up my takeout order?"

"You ordered Chinese takeout for supper? And Jess ate it?"

"Just some of the fried rice and kung pao chicken." Jo was surprised Jess had eaten any of it, she was such a picky eater. "Anyway, who should I spy but Frannie and Hank. They were having dinner together." Suzy's eyes sparkled with glee at her revelation.

"So they're official?"

"Oh yeah. In fact, if I read their body language correctly, they're sleeping together."

"Wow." This was a major development. "How did she act when she saw you?"

"Busted."

"Why is she being so secretive? I didn't think you guys kept secrets from each other." Frannie and Suzy had been friends forever.

"She's always been weird about that kind of thing. After her Seven Minutes of Heaven with Donnie Ignatz at Bev Lowry's party in eighth grade, she denied they'd kissed."

"How do you know they did?"

"After they went into the powder room together, some of her lipstick was on Donnie when they came out." Jo didn't know which was more shocking: that Frannie had lied about her alleged Seven Minutes in Heaven or that she'd been wearing lipstick. Jo had never known her to wear makeup.

Before she could comment, her children came running inside chorusing, "Mommy! Mommy! You're back!"

Jo hugged them and kissed their rosy cheeks, inhaling their sweet scents. They smelled of cut grass and peanut butter. "I missed you guys so much! Did you have a good time at Aunt Suzy's?"

"We jumped on the trampoline," reported Jess.

"I saw. Looked like you were having fun."

"I found a caterpillar!" reported Emma. "But it got squished."

"I *told* you not to put it in your pocket," said Jess in her bossy big-sister voice.

Emma's mouth turned down.

"Well, you'll know for next time," Jo said to her.

Suzy's daughter, Christina, a younger version of Suzy in yoga pants, came inside with her two towheaded daughters. While the adults exchanged hellos, Jess skipped over to join hands with eight-year-old Rose. "Mommy, can Rose come over to our house to play?"

Jo was heartened to see that Jess had made a new friend. Would wonders never cease? "Of course, if it's okay with her mom. Lily's welcome, too. When do you go back to DC?" she asked Christina.

"Not until Tuesday, and we don't have any plans for tomorrow," said Christina. "I could bring Rose and Lily over after lunch if that works for you."

"I have a Zoom meeting at one. How about two o'clock?"

"Perfect."

Christina took the children into the kitchen to rustle up some snacks. Jo followed Suzy to the guest room the girls had shared to collect their things. "Did you have fun at the wedding?" Suzy asked as they gathered up stray items that hadn't made it into Jess's and Emma's overnight bags.

"Fun? I don't know about that, although it was meaningful watching the ceremony. But then, I was working, so it wasn't the same as if I'd gone strictly as a guest." Jo spied a Pet Shop figurine that'd become separated from its brethren and picked it up off the floor, tucking it into Emma's bag.

"You worked the entire time?"

"No. I ate with the other guests, and I danced one dance." Remembering her "date" with Scott, she felt her stomach flip.

"With whom?"

"Just this guy I met. We sat next to each other at dinner."

Suzy's eyebrows shot up. "Ah."

"What's that supposed to mean?"

"Nothing," she said innocently as she retrieved a pair of child-size underpants from under one of the twin beds. "I was just thinking it's about time."

"It was one dance." Suzy straightened, regarding her with an unwavering gaze. Jo broke out in a sweat, as if she were being interrogated. "Okay, so I may have agreed to see him again. He's coming to town next week and I said I'd show him some of the sights. It's not a date," she added.

"If you say so." Suzy smirked.

"I'm not dating," Jo reiterated. "Whatever Sean might've thought was best for me."

"Are you saying he was wrong?"

"What I'm saying is, he was irreplaceable." An edge of desperation crept into her voice.

"That may be, but just because someone isn't your Mr. Right, it doesn't mean he can't be your Mr. Right For Now."

"Is that what Cliff is to you? Mr. Right For Now?"

"I like him a lot, but . . . yes. We're having fun together. Who knows what the future holds?"

"Do you think you'll ever get married again?"

"Unlikely. My marriage was a shit show. How can I be sure a second time around wouldn't be a case of rinse and repeat?"

"You're older and wiser than when you married Wayne." Her ex-husband had been her high school sweetheart, whom she'd married when they were barely eighteen after she became pregnant.

"True, which means I'm smart enough to stay single unless the perfect man comes along."

"No one's perfect." Sean had had his idiosyncrasies and flaws. He could write computer code but couldn't tie a ribbon on a package. He'd dressed like the average middle-school boy and had had the table manners of a five-year-old. He'd forgotten to put the toilet seat down after he flushed more often than he'd remembered to do it, and his dirty dishes hadn't always made it into the dishwasher. But she'd loved him for his imperfections. "It's just about finding someone who's perfect for you."

She replayed her conversation with Suzy as she drove home with the girls. Had she been looking at this the wrong way? Seeing only what was impossible—that she could ever give her heart to another man—rather than what was possible? She'd had fun hanging out with Scott at the wedding, and dancing with him had been . . . exhilarating. Could he become her Mr. Right For Now?

11

The following week, the last in July, was a blur. Jo had a bridal shower on Tuesday, which was cut short when the pregnant bride went into labor. Wednesday she had a marriage proposal, that of a minor league baseball pitcher who'd popped the question to his girlfriend at the ball field where he played while Jo photographed it from the bleachers. Thursday she met with a new client, Rachel Tennenbaum, who'd hired her to photograph her daughter's wedding in September. When Rachel questioned the need for an assistant as they were going over the budget, Jo explained why it was necessary. The first outdoor wedding she'd worked before she'd had an assistant, the temperature had climbed to over a hundred. By the time she got her equipment set up for the posed outdoor shots, the bride and bridesmaids looked like they'd been caught in the rain, with makeup running down their sweaty faces. Rachel needed no further convincing; she wrote a check for the deposit on the spot.

Meanwhile, her date with Scott loomed. He called on Thursday evening to confirm that they were still on for the next day. It wasn't until after she ended the call that Jo noticed Jess had come into the kitchen, where she was making supper. "Who were you talking to?" she asked. From her tone, she'd guessed it wasn't a business call.

"Someone I'm meeting tomorrow."

"Who?"

Jo made it a practice never to lie to her children. Instead, she filtered information according to what was age appropriate. She was extra cautious with Jess, who had been making progress since she started seeing Dr. Shaw and was starting to come out of her shell but was still emotionally fragile. Jo feared she'd suffer a setback if she learned that her mom had a date. "A friend of Uncle Reggie's. I met him at the wedding. I'm taking him sightseeing tomorrow."

"Why?" Jess's brown eyes regarded her suspiciously behind her purple-framed glasses.

"He's from out of town and doesn't know anyone."

"So you're doing it as a favor for Uncle Reggie?"

"Something like that."

The next morning after dropping the girls off at their bus stop, she returned home to shower and dress for her date. At 8:59 she pulled into the parking lot of the hotel where Scott was staying. She was nervous. Her palms were sweating and the butterflies in her stomach were throwing a party.

Relax, babe. It's gonna be okay.

Tell me again why I'm doing this.

You know why.

Yeah, but suddenly it doesn't seem like such a good idea.

Trust the process.

The Pioneer Hotel was one of the more notable historic buildings of Gold Creek, and an anchor of the main drag, depicted on the postcards sold in its gift shops and on the Gold Creek chamber of commerce website. Dating back to the Victorian era, it boasted twin turrets, gables, and stained glass windows among its architectural features, and had survived more than one earthquake in the century and a half since it was built. She spotted Scott, in off-white chinos and a striped polo shirt, browsing the rack of brochures advertising local attractions in the terrazzo-tiled lobby, as she entered.

"Hey, Scott."

He looked up, breaking into a grin. "Jo, hi!"

"I hope I didn't keep you waiting," she said, even though she was on time.

"No. I got in about an hour ago, and had some time to kill, so I thought I'd check out some of these brochures."

"There's a lot to see and do. We won't be able to cover it all today, but I can show you some of the main attractions. This hotel is one of them. It dates back to the mid–eighteen hundreds."

His gaze swept the grand lobby, with its marble-topped registration desk and historic photos of the town hung above its oak wainscoting. "It's one of the nicer places I've stayed at. Thanks for the steer."

"You wanted historic. It doesn't get more historic than this. Teddy Roosevelt stayed here, among other notable figures. You should talk to the manager, Lewis, who's also the president of the Gold Creek Historical Society. No one knows more about the history of the region than Lewis. Have you eaten? We could stop somewhere for coffee and a pastry if you're hungry." She realized she was babbling and stopped, blushing. Could he tell she was nervous?

"I'm good." He grabbed his backpack from the floor at his feet and slung it over one shoulder. "Shall we? I'm eager to see what else this town has to offer." The look he gave her suggested he hoped to get more out of this visit than sightseeing. The heat in her face intensified.

"I thought we'd start with a short tour of the historic district," she said as they exited the building. "Afterward, we'll go on a hike, if you're up for it. The views from some of the trails at Brambleberry Lake are incredible. We could pick up some sandwiches in town and make a picnic lunch of it. It's not far from Dead Man's Mine, where we're booked for their one o'clock tour."

"Sounds good," he said. "I'm in your hands."

Over the next hour or so, they toured the historic district. They strolled the main drag and climbed to the top of Signal Hill to check out its bell tower, the tallest structure in Gold Creek. On the way down they stopped at the neoclassical building that had housed the town's original courthouse and operated now as a museum. As they passed the Whiskey Barrel, a popular watering hole that had been a saloon when Gold Creek was a boomtown, she paused to tell the story of the notorious outlaw

Black Bart, who was rumored to have shot and killed another man in a dispute over a card game there. She pointed out Buckboard Books but didn't take him inside. She wasn't ready to introduce Scott to any of her friends. Maybe next time. If there was a next time.

Because he was here scouting locations for a movie, Scott took lots of photos with the Leica he carried in his backpack and dictated voice memos into his phone. Before leaving town, they picked up some takeout at Cowboy Coffee, for which he paid, then she drove them to the lake. They hiked up to a ridge with a scenic overlook, where they enjoyed a bird's-eye view of the lake reflecting the snowcapped mountains above while they ate their picnic lunch. He told her about his marriage.

"We both realized it was a mistake before the ink dried on our marriage license. We were friends before we became lovers and should've stayed friends. Now we're barely on speaking terms."

"You still see each other?" Jo couldn't think why they would, being as they didn't have children, unless it was because their work brought them into contact.

"We share custody of our Rottweiler. Modo—that's short for Quasimodo—stays with Courtney when I'm out of town."

Quasimodo? Who named their dog after *The Hunchback of Notre Dame*? "So he's with her more than he is with you?" She tossed a crust from her sandwich to a chipmunk foraging nearby.

"Yeah." He sounded bitter, though she didn't see how his ex-wife could be blamed for the fact that he traveled a lot in his line of work. "What about you? Was your marriage a happy one?"

"Very." Her throat grew thick, and the view of the lake blurred.

"What's the secret to a happy marriage in your experience?"

"Never go to bed angry." Sean's uncle Brad had given her and Sean that piece of advice when they married, and they'd heeded it. They'd had their share of squabbles through the years, but each time they'd made up by day's end. Which, she remembered, had often involved some pretty spectacular makeup sex. "You'd be surprised how few things are worth staying mad about when it's the only thing standing between you and a good night's sleep."

"I'll have to remember that if I ever get married again." From his tone, it didn't seem likely he'd ever remarry.

They were pulling into the parking lot of Dead Man's Mine by quarter to one. One of the abandoned mines for which the region was known, it operated now as a tourist attraction. Jo occasionally brought visitors here, most recently her parents when they'd visited on Thanksgiving weekend last year.

"I hope you brought a jacket." She eyed Scott's backpack as they climbed from the car.

"No. I didn't think I'd need one."

"I'm sorry, I should've warned you it gets chilly in the mine. But I have something you can throw on." She popped the trunk on her car and pulled out the hoodie that was inside.

When she'd finally gotten around to sorting through Sean's things while cleaning out her closets in preparation for her move, she'd donated everything she hadn't disposed of. She'd rescued the hoodie from the box she'd been off-loading at the Goodwill donation center in a fit of sentiment. Now she tossed it to Scott. Which she had cause to regret when the sight of him in the Maroon 5 hoodie sparked a memory of strolling arm in arm with Sean while he wore it. She found herself wriggling her finger through the hole in one sleeve. If she closed her eyes, she could pretend . . .

When Scott took her hand, she was jerked back to reality. It was all she could do to keep from snatching her hand from his. It wasn't his fault he was wearing a dead man's hoodie, she told herself.

The converted mine offices were housed in a rustic wooden building beyond which the entrance to the mine was visible farther up the hill. They joined the group of other ticketholders waiting for the next tour. Soon their guide, an older man, with a full beard as white as the hair on his head, costumed in period attire—button-fly trousers and suspenders, a plaid shirt, and a flat-top hat—appeared.

"Howdy, folks. I'm Jack Wheeler," he introduced himself. "I'll be your guide today as I take you into the bowels of what's known as Dead Man's Mine. Now, a question I'm frequently asked is how did it come by that name? I'll get to that later. First, let me give you a brief history of the mine . . ."

They learned that the gold strike that gave rise to the mine was discovered in 1850 by a prospector by the name of Fergus O'Malley. The mine had operated for a period of eight years in the 1850s before it was tapped out, during which time over a million dollars' worth of gold ore was extracted from it, a fortune in today's money. After giving his talk, Jack took them on the tour. As they made their way through the mineshaft, he explained about hard-rock mining and "drifts," the quartz deposits through which veins of ore ran. He introduced them to mining terms such as "pinched out," "powder monkey," and "fire in the hole." The deeper they descended into the mine, the lower the temperature dropped. Jo grew chilled despite the windbreaker she wore over her long-sleeved tee. When Scott put his arm around her, she was grateful for his body heat. And maybe the fact that his borrowed hoodie still carried a trace of Sean's scent had something to do with it, too.

"This here's what's known as the belly of the beast, folks," said Jack when they reached the innermost chamber of the tunnel they were in. "What you see before you is what the miners called the 'spine' and 'rib cage.'" He gestured around him, taking in the walls and ceiling of the chamber. "Those miners, now, they were a superstitious lot, and mining was mighty dangerous work. They could just as easily be maimed or killed by a cave-in as strike gold. Must've seemed that they were at the mercy of an unpredictable beast."

"Tell us how the mine got its name!" called a boy who was taking the tour with his parents. He looked to be around ten, with inquisitive brown eyes behind his glasses.

"Well, son, I'm glad you asked because I was just getting to that," replied their guide. He hooked his thumbs through his suspenders and, when he had everyone's attention, continued. "This here's the site of a deadly cave-in in the year 1854. The miners, you may recall, used dynamite to blast through the rock face to get to the ore. Who can tell me what 'fire in the hole' means?"

"It's what the powder monkey calls before he lights the fuse on the dynamite," the boy answered. The "powder monkey" being the miner in charge of detonating the explosives.

"You are correct, young man. Except something went very wrong that day. When the dynamite they were using was detonated, it caused the shaft where we stand now to collapse. Five men died. Legend has it the ghosts of those miners haunt the mine to this day."

"Cool." The boy's eyes grew big.

"If you keep an eye out, Billy, you might see a ghost," said his dad, ruffling the boy's hair.

"Right. Everybody knows there's no such thing as ghosts," muttered Scott, loud enough for the others to hear.

Jo grew annoyed at him. It was a harmless ghost story, for crying out loud. Why spoil it for everyone? Especially the boy, who looked embarrassed, like he thought he shouldn't believe in ghosts.

Jack appeared unfazed. "Sir, I have seen and heard things in Dead Man's Mine that defy rational explanation. And . . ." He paused for dramatic effect. "I lived to tell the tale."

Scott snorted. The boy cut him a glance and snickered, one of the cool dudes now. "That's another thing. Shouldn't it be called 'Dead *Men's* Mine' since more than one man died here?"

Now that was just plain rude, Jo thought.

The rest of the tour was uneventful, with no ghost sightings or further disruptions, but Scott had spoiled it for her. She was mad at him for being a jerk. She was mad at her husband, too. She wouldn't be in this position if Sean hadn't died and then urged her to date again in his message from beyond the grave.

On the drive back to town, Scott didn't seem to notice she'd grown quiet. "I had a good time today," he said when they pulled up in front of his hotel. "Thanks for showing me around."

"My pleasure. I hope you got what you needed," she said.

"I did. I plan to do some more sightseeing tomorrow, but I think I may have found what I was looking for."

"For your movie location?"

He nodded. "Subject to approval by the producers I work for. The other towns I visited all have unspoiled views and historic buildings, but this is the only one with whole stretches of the main drag where there's nothing to break the illusion of being back in the days of the Wild West."

"Goodness. I don't know if us locals could stand the excitement of Bradley Cooper being here in Gold Creek," she remarked dryly. "The last celebrity sighting here was Kenny Rogers, when he was renting a summer house out at the lake. This was back in 2001. People are still talking about it."

"You probably wouldn't see much of Bradley. Movie stars tend to keep a low profile, or they wouldn't have a moment of privacy, between the selfie seekers and the paparazzi. But I could arrange to take you on a tour of the set if you'd like. You might even get to shake his hand."

"Imagine that." But she wasn't thinking about shaking the hand of Bradley Cooper. She was wishing Scott would get out of the car so she could be on her way.

Finally, he retrieved his backpack from the back seat and opened the door to his side. "Thanks again for today. It was fun. In fact, I hate to see it end. How about dinner tonight here at the hotel?"

"Thanks, but I'm afraid I have other plans," she told him. Friday night was movie night with the girls.

"Tomorrow night, then?"

"Sorry. I have a work thing." She had a wedding on Saturday night, that of an older couple, Vern and Dot, who'd met on a safari and who were planning a safari-themed reception.

Scott appeared disappointed but undeterred. A guy as attractive and confident as he was probably wasn't used to being rejected by women.

"I'll catch you next time I'm in town, then. You haven't seen the last of me, Jo Myers." He flashed her a flirty smile.

It wasn't until he climbed out and was walking toward the hotel entrance that she noticed he was still wearing Sean's hoodie. She flung open the door to the driver's side and jumped out. "Wait!" she called as she hurried toward him. He stopped and turned around, wearing a quizzical look. "I need—"

Before she could finish the sentence, he moved in to kiss her, like he thought he knew what she needed. Caught off guard, she froze. It wasn't until she felt his tongue push past her lips that she was jolted from her temporary paralysis. She broke away. "What did you do that for?" she demanded.

He appeared confused. "Sorry, I thought—"

"What? That I was asking for it?"

"Look, if I misunderstood, I apologize."

She narrowed her eyes at him. "Was it Reggie? Did he say something? Did he tell you I haven't had sex in a really long time? Did you think I was so desperate, I'd jump into bed with you?"

"No, of course not." His face reddened.

Suddenly, she was furious. Furious at Scott for taking liberties. Furious at Sean for leaving her. Furious at herself for imagining she could ever be with another man, even if it was just for sex and companionship. Judging by how she'd reacted when she was kissed, she'd probably have a full-blown meltdown if she ever got naked with a man. "Good. Because this"—she pointed at him and back at herself—"is not happening. Now will you kindly return the hoodie you borrowed so I can be on my way?"

Scott peeled off the hoodie like it was on fire. He thrust it into her hands and took a step back. "Fine. Whatever. And for the record, Reggie didn't say anything about you being desperate. What he *said* was that you were his girl, and if I didn't treat you right, he'd have to kill me. So do me a favor and don't mention this to him, okay? I don't want to make an enemy of him."

"Oh." Just like that, her anger fizzled. She was mortified to realize she'd misjudged Reggie and completely overreacted with Scott. Heat crawled up her neck, flooding her face.

"It was just a kiss," he said. "I wasn't trying to get in your pants."

"Right. Well, I, um . . ." She glanced past him and spotted the bellman stationed at the hotel entrance, a college-age kid in full livery, who was watching the scene playing out before him like it was a TikTok video. From his expression, he was in full dude sympathy with Scott. Great. Not only did they have an audience but Scott had his own cheering section. "I should get going." With that, she turned and hurried back toward her car. She couldn't get away fast enough.

She picked the girls up from their bus stop on the way home. They were both in high spirits, chattering about having gone horseback riding today at camp. Seeing their happy faces in the rearview mirror was just what the doctor ordered after the mortifying scene with Scott. She cringed, replaying it in her mind. What had gotten into her? Going off on him, and then blurting out that she hadn't had sex in ages. Basically accusing Reggie of pimping her out. Oh, God.

"Let's play horses," Jess said to Emma when they got home, and they took off for the backyard with Snickers. Jo headed for the kitchen, where she encountered Hank in his work uniform, khakis and a blue polo shirt with the Morningside Veteran's Care Home patch on it, reheating something in the microwave.

"Hey, Jo. Be out of your way in a jiffy," he said.

"You're not in my way. I'm just making the girls their snacks," she said as she pulled a half-eaten package of bread from the bread box on the counter. She'd grown accustomed to having him around and couldn't remember why she'd ever worried it would be a problem. Besides being a dream lodger, he'd become a friend. He also provided a sense of normalcy, of family, in Sean's absence.

The microwave pinged, and he removed a mug of reheated coffee from it. "Three cups a day is usually my limit, but after the day I had, who's counting?" He seemed uncharacteristically down.

"Did something happen?" she asked, popping two bread slices into the toaster.

"We lost one of the old boys at the home today."

"Oh, Hank. I'm sorry. Was he someone you were close to?"

He nodded dejectedly. "Ernie, yeah, he was one of my favorites. Great old guy. One of the last of the World War II veterans. Fought in the Pacific theater. Lost part of a leg in Okinawa." He took a sip of his coffee. "How about you? How's your day going so far?"

"You don't want to know." She grimaced. "But at least no one died."

His phone, which was sitting on the counter, rang. She saw his grandson's face on its screen before he picked up. Hank, being naturally friendly, put the call in speaker mode as he answered. "Hi, son."

"Hey, Pop-Pop. I just got off duty, so I thought I'd give you a call. How are you?"

"I've been better. I'm here with Jo. We're both having bad days, but it's good to hear your voice."

"Something wrong?" Ian sounded concerned.

Hank reported the death at the veterans' home, and Ian offered his condolences. "As for why Jo's wearing a long face, you'd have to ask her. Unless you'd rather not talk about it," he said to her.

She told them without going into detail. "I took a friend from out of town sightseeing today, and he said something that rubbed me the wrong way. Things kind of went downhill from there."

"What did he say?" Ian pressed. "What an ass," he declared after she'd recounted the incident in the mine.

"I may have overreacted."

"Trust me, you didn't," said Ian.

"Really, it wasn't that big a deal. All he said was, 'There are no ghosts.'"

"It's not what he said, it's what it says about him. Half the fun of going on campouts when I was a kid was telling ghost stories around the campfire. Anyone who'd spoil a kid's fun for no reason is not a nice person. Next, your friend would've been telling your kids there's no Santa Claus."

"He's not really a friend. He's a friend of a friend."

"Please tell me you're not going out with him again, or I'll lose all respect for you," Ian teased. She imagined this was what it'd be like to have a brother. The thought surprised her because she barely knew Ian. This was only the second time they'd spoken. There was just something about him . . .

"It wasn't a date," she clarified. Her toast popped up. She grabbed the jar of peanut butter from the pantry.

"Really."

"Some might call it a date. For me it was . . . an exploratory mission."

"To see if there's life on another planet?"

"Or to see if the water's warm?" Hank put in.

"I suppose I was hoping to find there's life on Mars despite evidence to the contrary." Specifically, in her case, life after the death of her spouse. "I haven't dated since college," she confided.

"I'm sorry about your husband," Ian said. Hank must've told him.

She blinked back tears as she spread peanut butter over the toasted bread slices. From outside came the whinnying of her girls pretending to be horses, accompanied by the barking of her dog. "Thank you."

"Good for you for putting yourself out there. It can't have been easy."

"No. And from my reaction to his"—she stopped herself before she said "kiss"—"untoward remark, I'm not ready to date." She wouldn't trust herself to go on a date with anyone else, even if she were so inclined, which she wasn't. She might haul off and punch the next guy who kissed her.

"You can't give up after one bad date. There's other guys out there. Nice guys. Some of us even believe in ghosts," he added in a voice laced with humor. "Don't quote me on that, though, or I'll lose credibility here at the base."

"Just because there's no life on Mars, it doesn't mean you won't discover it on another planet," said Hank as he sipped his coffee.

She sighed. "The trouble is, when you've had the best, the rest is just . . . the rest."

"Your husband must've been a special guy," said Ian.

"He was." Her voice cracked.

Hank was sensitive enough to change the subject. He asked Ian if he'd be coming home on leave as planned. "That's what I wanted to talk to you about," Ian said. "I got word today that all requests for leave are on hold until further notice by order of your old pal 'Corny.' It's all hands on deck while reorganization efforts are underway. Sorry, Pop-Pop, I know this is a disappointment. It is for me, too."

Hank's face fell. "God and Uncle Sam," he muttered. "If it's not one, it's the other mucking up our plans."

"Maybe this is God's punishment for putting you and Mom through hell when I was a teenager."

"What'd you do that was so bad?" Jo asked out of curiosity.

"He fell in with the wrong crowd," Hank said in his grandson's defense.

"I made some stupid choices." Ian didn't cut himself any slack. "Got picked up by the police a couple times, the first time on a misdemeanor charge of vandalism, the second time for possession. A dime bag of weed, but it was my second offense. I'd have been looking at juvie if Pop-Pop hadn't intervened on my behalf. He persuaded the judge at my arraignment to give me a choice between juvie and military school. It was the devil or the deep blue sea. I went with the lesser of evils."

"Military school."

"Right. Next thing I knew, I was on a plane to Richmond, Virginia, with Pop-Pop, where we were met by a friend of his who runs the Eastlake Military Academy outside Richmond. I hated it at first, and then grew to love it. Which is the short version of how I ended up in the military."

"And this is what I get for my good deed. You stuck on a military base halfway around the world." Hank shook his white head, frowning. "Damn. I was really looking forward to you visiting."

"You and me both, Pop-Pop." Ian echoed the sentiment.

Jo realized she was disappointed, too. She'd been looking forward to meeting Ian in person.

12

The following Saturday, Jo and her daughters attended the annual regatta at Brambleberry Lake, which took place every year during the first week in August. The sun was shining; it was the perfect day to be outdoors, with just enough of a breeze to propel the sailboats. They watched with Frannie and Hank from the deck at Frannie's cabin as the boat owners on the lake cruised past in their watercraft, from classic wooden Chris-Craft motorboats and sailboats of all sizes to the less sporty pontoons. She hadn't attended the Brambleberry Lake Regatta since Sean's death. She remembered how much fun she and the girls used to have watching the parade of boats with Sean commenting in his sports announcer voice on each one as it passed by and making up stories about its owner.

She was surprised to realize it didn't hurt to remember, which she thought must mean she was moving on. The house on Mountain Laurel Lane had something to do with it. But it also had to do with Hank. He'd provided a sense of family and stability. She felt his presence in their household even when they weren't crossing paths. She'd grown accustomed to waking in the mornings to the burbling of the preprogrammed coffee maker on the days he made the coffee, and hearing him whistle while he worked in the yard or in the garage. So when his thirty-day trial period was up the following week, it was cause for concern. She waited for him to say something, but he didn't mention it. Could it have slipped his mind? Or was he on the fence about signing a lease? He might want a place of his own now that he was seeing Frannie. She panicked at the thought of him leaving.

By the end of the week, when he still hadn't broached the subject, she got up the courage to ask him about it. She was in the kitchen preparing supper and he'd come upstairs to do his laundry. "Hank, I don't know if you're aware, but your thirty-day trial period is up," she reminded him. She stood in the doorway that connected the kitchen and laundry room, watching him load the washing machine. "I'd love for you to stay, so it's up to you. How do you feel about signing a lease?"

He poured detergent over the dirty clothes in the washer. "Well, now, that would be—"

He was interrupted by Jess's voice calling indignantly, "Mommy, Emma's hogging the controller! She won't let me take my turn!" Jo turned around to see her seven-year-old marching toward her, wearing a scowl. Jess came to a sudden halt when she looked past Jo and spied Hank.

He stepped from the laundry room, where the washer now churned. "You want to watch out for that one. I got roped into playing *Mario Kart* with your sister once, and she smoked me good. But I expect you're a way better player than I am. Maybe you could teach me some tricks so I can up my game." From his amiable tone, no one would've guessed that Jess had been a pill toward him.

Jo was shocked when Jess actually spoke to him. She hadn't addressed him directly until now, to Jo's knowledge. "I know you don't like me. You're just being nice because you have to be."

"Actually, that's not true," he said. "Though I can see you're doing your best to make me not like you."

Jess studied him for a moment, as if wondering what to make of his statement, before she turned and fled. By the time Jo caught up with her, she was in her and Emma's room, sitting cross-legged on her bed sorting through her box of found rocks. Her dream was to one day discover gold in an ordinary rock. A dream as elusive, it seemed, as the prospect of her ever being happy again.

Jo sat down next to her on the bed. "Honey, what's wrong? What's bothering you?"

"He doesn't like me, not really," she said. "Nobody does."

She sounded so woebegone, Jo didn't have the heart to suggest that Hank might like her better if she were nice to him. Instead, she said, "That's not true. There's me and your sister and Grandma and Grandpa, and all of your aunties." The Tattooed Ladies weren't blood relatives but they were family, nonetheless. "We all love you, and so did your dad." Her gaze was drawn to the family photo on the wall in the beautiful handmade frame Hank had given them. She felt a sharp tug of yearning.

A tear dripped from under the cloud of dark curls covering Jess's face as she sat with her head down, staring into her box of rocks. "No one wants to be my friend."

"You have Pablo. He's your friend."

"Yeah, except I hardly ever see him anymore."

"What about Shoshanna?" Shoshanna, the daughter of their neighbors from down the street, Jim and Lila Bennett, who was in second grade, had invited Jess over to play. Jess had gone once but hadn't been back since. "I bet she'd like to be your friend, or she wouldn't have invited you over."

"She doesn't like me. She said rocks were *dumb*. She only wants to play dress-up."

"If you showed her your rocks, she'd see what makes them special. And, you know, it wouldn't hurt to play dress-up once in a while. Just to be fair," she added after Jess gave her the side-eye.

"I guess." Jess shrugged.

"Why don't you invite her over tomorrow? Or I could call her mom and arrange it, if you'd prefer."

Jess sniffled and lifted her head, wearing a cautiously hopeful expression. "Would you? If I ask, she might say no."

Eager to make it happen, Jo went to phone Lila Bennett, who was more than happy to set up a playdate with their daughters once it was determined that Shoshanna was on board. They arranged for her to come over after camp tomorrow. By the time Jo ended the call, Hank had left the building. She'd have to wait to get the answer to her burning question. She ground her teeth in frustration.

Her mom phoned later, after she'd put Jess and Emma to bed and taken Snickers out for her evening potty break, when she was in the living room folding laundry while streaming *Stranger Things*, her dog sacked out at her feet. Jo wasn't a fan of sci-fi as a rule, but when one's life was stranger than fiction, monsters were a welcome distraction. She muted the volume on the TV, inserted her AirPods, and switched to Bluetooth mode on her phone before she answered. "Hi, Mom. What's up?"

"Is this a bad time?" her mom asked.

Jo was surprised by the question. When had her mother ever asked her if it was a bad time to call? "No. I'm folding laundry, but I have you on Bluetooth. How are you? How's Dad?"

"We're both well. Did I mention your dad is competing in our club's annual golf tournament next weekend? There's a good chance he'll bring home the trophy this year, with Mitch Dearing out of the running, recovering from knee-replacement surgery. Mitch won the past three years in a row."

"Wish him luck for me. I'll be rooting for him."

"I'll let him know, but that's not why I called. Honey, your dad and I have been talking . . ." Jo felt the muscles in the back of her neck tense. Usually, when her parents "talked," it led to "helpful" suggestions on how she could improve her life. "It's been ages since we last visited. Whenever I suggest dates, it seems like there's never a good time, so we went ahead and made plans. We're coming next weekend. I just need to know if you'll be in town then before I book our flights."

Jo was suddenly swamped with dread. Her mind went blank. "As far as I know," she said after she recovered, "but I'll be working next weekend. How about sometime in the fall instead?"

"Why wait when we can come sooner?"

"You wouldn't see much of me."

"We understand if you have commitments. We don't expect you to drop everything for us. But you won't be working the entire weekend. And when you're busy, we can visit with the girls."

Jo and her daughters had spent the past Christmas with her parents in Fairview, but the last time they'd visited was the previous Thanksgiving. In all honesty she had been putting them off, not because she was too busy with work or because they were a bother—they stayed at a hotel when they visited, being as she lacked guest accommodations—but because they were easier to deal with from a distance. In person, they could be a bit much, and there was no avoiding them like there was when they phoned and she had the option of letting the call go to voicemail. And this time, there was the added complication of her lodger. She shuddered, imagining them giving Hank the third degree Southern style, as in sugarcoated in polite language. Her mother questioning him about the circumstances of his former landlady's death and her father probing into his background. If Hank were on the fence about signing a lease, it could prove the tipping point.

Desperate for an out, she reminded her mom, "Summer's my busiest season."

"If you can spare the time to have a meal or two with us, that's all we ask. And I don't think it's too much to ask," Jo's mom said pointedly.

"No, but I'd rather you came when I could spend more time with you."

"Would you prefer we didn't come at all?" Her mom ladled on the guilt.

"Of course not."

"Wonderful! We'll see you next weekend, then. I'll email you our itinerary once I book our flights."

Jo knew it was useless to fight it. She could no sooner get her parents to change their plans once their minds were made up than she could stop an incoming tide. So, while she folded Emma's Princess Elsa pajamas and the intrepid teenage heroes of *Stranger Things* battled alien creatures on-screen not three feet from where she stood, she gritted her teeth and said, "Great. I look forward to it."

13

The neighbor girl, Shoshanna, came over to play the next day. Jo took her and Jess and Emma for a hike on one of the easier trails that crisscrossed the state park abutting their neighborhood, with Jess pausing here and there to point out the various geological formations they passed. Afterward the two big girls disappeared into Jess and Emma's room. Jo kept Emma occupied with a puzzle so she wouldn't disturb them. When she heard them giggling through the closed door, she took it as a good sign that she'd have something positive to report when she next consulted with Dr. Shaw.

On Monday, after seeing the girls off to camp, Jo met a reporter from the *Sacramento Bee* for coffee downtown, a young woman who interviewed her for an article on destination weddings in the West. Afterward, she walked the two blocks to Suzy's salon, bringing lattes for Suzy and her two junior stylists. The 1940s stucco building that housed the Shear Delight salon resembled a candy box, painted in shades of pink and green, with a green-and-pink-striped awning over the entrance. It was as cute inside as outside, with the same color scheme and redolent of hair products.

Jasmine and Hailey were busy with customers and Suzy was nowhere in sight. "She's in her office," Jasmine informed her after thanking her for the latte. A statuesque young woman with braided hair and a warm smile, Jasmine had developed a following due to her expertise with Black hair.

"You're a goddess!" called Hailey from her station. Petite with blond hair dyed pink at the ends, she'd gotten the job at Shear Delight through Kyra two years ago. They'd met when Kyra interviewed her in connection with a criminal investigation. She was a talented colorist, according to Suzy.

Jo crossed to the door to the private area in back, which consisted of the break room, bathroom, and office, ignoring the sign that read EMPLOYEES ONLY as she entered. She found Suzy seated at the desk in her office going over some paperwork. "Jo. What a nice surprise!" she exclaimed. "What brings you here today?"

"I brought you a latte. A small token of my appreciation." She owed Suzy far more for taking care of her children while she was in LA, but she knew she wouldn't accept more than this. She handed her the to-go cup she carried. "Oat milk. No sugar."

"You didn't have to, but thank you." Suzy pried the lid from the cup, and even when she licked the foam from its underside, she remained the picture of elegance. How did she do it? It was a mystery. "Have a seat." She waved toward the visitor's chair opposite the desk, and Jo sat down.

"I'm not interrupting anything, am I?"

"Nothing that can't wait. I haven't seen you since you got back from the wedding. What's new with you?"

While Suzy drank her latte, Jo told her about her date with Scott, everything from her doubts leading up to it to the unfortunate incident during the mine tour and, finally, her going off on him after he kissed her. "I don't know what came over me. I just . . . lost it. It was like some weird out-of-body experience. What's wrong with me?"

"Why do you assume it's your fault?" Suzy asked.

"It was an innocent kiss."

"Where tongue is involved, it's never innocent."

"He claimed he misread the signals, and he seemed sincere, so I'll give him a pass. Not that I plan to see him again, or that he'd even want to see me. He probably thinks he dodged a bullet."

"Good riddance."

"Yeah, but what does it say about me? Am I doomed to freak out if any guy comes near me?"

"No. It was probably an isolated incident. You might have better luck with the next guy. In fact," she said, thoughtfully tapping her chin, "I might know of someone. Single dad, works as a contractor. He did my friend Sheila's house remodel. We met at her open house. Nice guy. Easy on the eyes, too."

"Not interested. And, anyway, how do you know he doesn't have a girlfriend?"

"I'll ask Sheila." Before Jo could stop her, Suzy was picking up the phone to call her friend. After ending the call, she informed Jo, "His name's Dawson. He's a widower, and he hasn't dated since his wife's death, as far Sheila knows. So you and he have that in common."

Jo rolled her eyes. "Great. We're both members of the club no one wants to be in."

"Honey," Suzy said gently. "You're still young, with years yet ahead of you, God willing. Don't let life pass you by. Take a chance. See what else—or who else—might be out there."

A sudden prickling in her sinuses signaled the onset of tears. Jo looked down at her hands as she struggled to regain her composure. She heard the sound of a drawer opening and closing, and when she looked up, Suzy was holding a box of See's Candies—possibly a gift from one of her admirers since she rarely ate sweets. She offered it to Jo like a therapist offering a box of tissues to a distraught patient. Jo helped herself to a bonbon. Coffee cream, she discovered when she bit into it, her favorite. She'd read somewhere that chocolate was a remedy for a broken heart. She didn't know if it was true, but the little taste of heaven in her mouth lifted her spirits.

Suzy indulged in a single chocolate-covered molasses chip and said, as she nibbled on it, "Sheila offered to text Dawson your contact info, or she can send you his, whichever you'd prefer."

"No pressure," Jo remarked dryly.

"What do you have to lose? If nothing else, you and he could trade tips on single parenting."

Suzy could be very persuasive. Often when a customer came to her with a particular hairstyle in mind, or married to the same one they'd had forever, they left sporting a different, more flattering hairstyle than the one they'd had or envisioned when they arrived. Maybe she was right about this, too.

Jo remembered a summer day after her freshman year of college, when she and Sean had been cruising the backroads of Gold Creek in the old beater he'd owned at the time. Her bare feet propped on the dash and her hair blowing in the breeze from the open windows, laughing at something Sean had said. They'd been so young and carefree. So in love. It made her sad to think that part of her was lost. She might never find love again or be as carefree as she'd been on that long-ago summer day, but it'd be nice to someday ride in a car with a man who made her laugh again.

What do you have to lose, babe?

That's what you said about the last guy.

This one might be a better bet.

Or a worse one.

Only one way to find out.

"All right. Have Sheila send him my contact info." Even as she said it, Jo had a feeling she might come to regret it. "I'll answer if he calls, but I'm not making any promises beyond that."

Suzy smiled and was opening her mouth to respond when she became distracted by the ping of an incoming text. She glanced down at her phone and muttered, "Uh-oh. This can't be good."

"What?"

"A text from my sister. It's about our dad."

"What about him?"

"Michelle suspects the woman he's seeing is a con artist."

"Your dad is seeing someone?" Jo was surprised. Last she'd heard, Suzy's eighty-eight-year-old father, who lived in a retirement community in nearby Pine City, was deeply depressed and still mourning his wife, who'd died some years ago.

Suzy nodded, wearing a troubled expression. "Her name's Sharon. She recently moved in next door to him. Since then, Dad's gone from being practically a shut-in to being the poster boy for active seniors. When he's not playing bingo, bunco, or pickleball with Sharon, they're out for the evening. She even has him taking tango lessons, if you can believe it."

"I don't see the harm."

"Nor did I until Michelle became suspicious. She got me to chip in to hire a PI to run a background check. The report's in, apparently. She said to check my email." Which Suzy proceeded to do.

"What does it say?" Jo asked eagerly, leaning forward.

Suzy frowned as she perused the report. "Oh no. This is bad. I'd hoped Michelle's hunch was wrong, but . . ." When she looked up, her face was drained of color. "Sharon's been arrested twice, once for larceny and once for theft by taking. Both crimes involved elderly victims. No convictions. Either there wasn't enough evidence to make the charges stick, or she had a good lawyer. And that's not all. She was also sued by family members of two of her alleged victims. One of the lawsuits went to trial and the jury ruled in favor of the petitioners. The other is ongoing."

Jo stared at Suzy in disbelief. "Oh my God! That's awful." She'd heard of vulnerable seniors being scammed by con artists, but it hadn't happened to anyone she knew. Until now. Her heart went out to Suzy and her sister, and their dad. And deep down she wondered if it wasn't a lesson in the perils of dating. "What's to be done?"

"Hopefully, it's not too late for an intervention."

"You think this Sharon already has her hooks into his finances?"

"Not yet, as far as I know, but I have a feeling it's only a matter of time."

"What if you showed him the report from the PI?"

"I'm sure Sharon would have an explanation for everything in it. And Dad's so smitten, he'd believe any lies she told him."

"Have you met her?"

"Yes. She was charming and seems utterly devoted to Dad. You'd never guess that she's a snake in the grass."

"What's your next move?"

"I plan to pay him another visit, for starters. If all else fails, Michelle and I will have a chat with Sharon. Once she knows we're onto her, she might back off." Suzy didn't sound too hopeful.

"Do you need me to come with?"

Just then, a voice called from the front of the salon, "Suzy! Your eleven o'clock is here!"

Suzy stood, stepping from behind her desk. "No. Michelle and I can handle it. But thanks anyway."

Jo followed her out of the office. "Is there anything I can do?"

Suzy paused, turning to look at her. "Yes. Go out with Dawson if he calls. Nothing would make me happier than to see you happy."

14

"I got you something." Marisol dug into her shoulder bag, which was big enough to double as a carryall, and pulled out a paper bag with the Swenson's Drugs logo on it. She handed it to Jo.

Jo peered into the bag. "Condoms?"

"You never know."

"I don't plan on having sex."

"On your first date, or ever again?" asked Kyra.

The three women were in the family bathroom at Jo's, where she was being primped for her date tonight. Marisol was plucking Jo's eyebrows, while Kyra watched from her perch on the toilet.

"Both," she said, her teeth gritted against the pain. "Jeez, I haven't even met the guy." She'd spoken with Dawson only once, over the phone. "I'm not sleeping with him. Or anyone," she added.

"I'd sworn off men before I met Coop," said Kyra.

"And we all know how *that* turned out," said Marisol. She looked especially colorful tonight, wearing an oversize purple T-shirt with the logo Book Nerds Have All the Fun, paired with polka-dot leggings.

Jo could hear Coop explaining the proper technique in building a blanket fort from somewhere down the hall. He and Kyra had volunteered to babysit tonight, and right now he was keeping Jess and Emma distracted to give the women some space. Otherwise, they'd have been crowding into the bathroom to witness the spectacle of their mother getting a makeover. They'd be wondering why, too—she didn't normally get this dressed up when she worked an event. Jo had told them only that she was going out tonight, and when Emma had asked if it was a "bride thing," she hadn't set her straight. Jo felt a pang of guilt for being dishonest with them, even if it was a lie by omission.

"Your situation was entirely different," she said to Kyra. "You had nowhere to go but up after your ex." Who was currently serving time in prison. "Whereas I'm sure to be disappointed by any man I go out with after Sean."

"You might be pleasantly surprised tonight." Marisol leaned in, brandishing her tweezers. "Speaking of romance, what's the latest with Frannie and Hank?"

"Ouch." Jo winced as another eyebrow hair bit the dust. "I couldn't say for certain, they're both so private. All I know is, Hank went out last night and didn't come home until this morning."

"You think he spent the night at Frannie's?"

"It wouldn't surprise me."

"Wow. I never thought I'd see the day," Kyra said. "Hank must be really special."

"He is," Jo said. That reminded her, she needed to pin him down about the lease. She'd been afraid to bring it up in case he'd decided against it. One more thing to worry about on top of her parents' impending visit. They were due to arrive on Friday and planned to stay until Tuesday of the following week.

Marisol, satisfied that no unwanted hairs had escaped her tweezers, went to work with her makeup kit. She squeezed liquid foundation into the palm of her hand and dabbed it over Jo's face before blending it with a makeup sponge and dusting it with powder.

"Will I still look like myself after you're done?" Jo asked when Marisol was applying eye makeup.

"Yes, only more so."

"May I remind you it's a pizza date."

"Was that his idea or yours?"

"Mine." After getting her contact info, Dawson had called Jo that night. They'd chatted for a while and he'd sounded nice, but when he asked her out for drinks, she suggested they make it pizza instead. "Meeting someplace family friendly seemed less intimidating than meeting at a bar."

"Coop and I met in a bar," Kyra reminded her. "I suspected he'd been hired by my ex to follow me. He suspected I was on the run from the law. Yet here we are." Kyra hadn't expected to cross paths with him again after their inauspicious first meeting. But weeks later, after Coop's mom unwittingly rented Kyra the Airstream on his property, they'd both been surprised to discover that he was her landlord.

"Did I hear my name?"

Jo looked over to see Coop's huge frame filling the doorway. Brawny and bearded, he stood well over six feet. He looked every inch the cop he'd been before he became a therapist, but she knew him to be a softie, as evidenced by the two small girls clinging to his legs. Crowding in behind them were the dogs, who squeezed past the humans blocking the doorway, grinning with their tongues lolling and their tails wagging.

"We were talking about you." Kyra smiled up at Coop as she gave Ranger a scratch under his chin.

"Telling tales of my manly prowess, were you?"

"I wouldn't dare. If your head gets any bigger, it won't fit through that door."

At the affectionate look they exchanged, Jo felt an ache in her chest.

"In that case, I'll leave you to your girl talk. Come on, ladies, we have a fort to build," Coop said to Jess and Emma before herding them and the dogs down the hall.

Jo remembered when it'd been their dad building forts with them, and the ache in her chest became a sharp wrench. She'd come home one evening after working an event to find the girls asleep next to Sean inside a blanket fort so elaborate it had "rooms" connected by crawl spaces. Suddenly, she was tempted to cancel her date tonight. Even pizza with another man seemed like a betrayal.

"My work is done," announced Marisol finally, stepping back to admire her handiwork.

"Is that really me?" Jo stared in disbelief at her reflection in the mirror. With her smoky eyes and glossy lips, her hair falling in soft curls below her shoulders, she scarcely recognized herself.

"You look gorgeous," declared Kyra, standing up to get a closer look. "There's just one more thing . . ." Her gaze dropped to the ring on Jo's left hand. "You might want to take that off. You know, so it doesn't send the wrong message."

"No." Jo shoved her hand into her pocket, thinking she'd sooner donate a kidney.

"Just for tonight?" urged Marisol. "Otherwise, it kind of defeats the purpose."

Every cell in her body rebelled against it, but Jo reluctantly slipped her ring from her finger and placed it on her right hand, where it wouldn't send the wrong message but would remind her.

Pizza My Heart, owned by a married couple, Gina and Carlo Martinelli, was the kind of place you might pass by without noticing. Its location, in a strip mall between a Foot Locker and a nail salon, was unpromising and its decor uninspired, but it served some of the best pizza west of the Rockies. It was already packed by the time Jo arrived at six. Gina stood behind the counter taking an order, and Jo could see Carlo through the pass flipping pizza dough, both as round as the pies for which they were known. Jo grabbed a couple of menus from the stack on the counter and found a table.

No sooner had she sat down than a man entered, in cuffed Levi's and a blue-and-gray-checked button-down, whom she recognized from his photo on the McCafferty Construction website as Dawson. He paused inside the door, his gaze sweeping the crowded space, and she waved to get his attention.

"Can you tell I'm new at this?" he asked after he'd joined her at their table. He had a nice face, framed by ginger hair, cropped short on top and shaved at the sides, with a wide mouth and green eyes that looked sad. His physique was as hard as his calloused hands, both those of a working man.

"A little," she said, an understatement. He looked more nervous than she felt, if that was possible. She couldn't pretend this wasn't a date, like when she'd taken Scott sightseeing. "But we're in the same boat."

"I haven't been out on a date since my wife died."

"This is only my second date."

When he asked, "How long has it been?" she knew he wasn't asking about her previous date.

"A year and eight months. You?"

"Three years and two months."

They spoke the universal language of the bereaved.

"How did your husband die?"

"Cancer. Your wife?"

"Brain aneurysm." His features twisted with grief.

Any more of this talk, she thought, and they'd be too depressed to eat by the time their food arrived. "Shall we split a pizza?" she suggested, picking up her menu.

"Sure," he said. "You like pepperoni?"

"Yes, but my favorite is the mushroom and prosciutto."

"How about we do half and half?"

"Sounds good."

What do you want to drink?" he asked as he got up to place their order.

"Nothing for me." She had poured waters from the self-serve dispenser on the counter for her and Dawson before she'd sat down.

Dawson left and returned shortly with a pitcher of beer and two plastic cups. He placed one of the cups in front of her. "In case you change your mind. Can I pour you a beer?"

"A small one," she said so he wouldn't have to drink alone. "I don't normally drink when I'm driving, but I don't suppose a few sips will hurt." It wouldn't put her over the legal limit, or even close.

By the time their pizza arrived at the table, Dawson was on his second glass of beer while she was still nursing her first. He was a big man, however, so she figured he could handle his alcohol.

"Do you eat here often?" he asked, taking a bite from his slice.

"Not as often as my girls would like, and we usually do takeout. I save it for those days when even canned soup and grilled cheese sandwiches is more than I can manage."

"I hear you," he said, wiping grease from his chin with his napkin after he'd chewed and swallowed. "Usually, I'm so bushed by the time I get home from work, I don't make it past my recliner."

"How do your kids get fed?" She knew from their phone conversation that he had two children, a twelve-year-old boy and a nine-year-old girl.

"My mom does most of the cooking. I couldn't manage without her."

"She lives with you?"

He nodded, taking another swig of his beer. "My folks are divorced. Mom was living alone when my wife died, so she came to help out. And never left. Ryan was nine at the time, and Katy was six. I was a wreck. Judy . . . she was everything to me." A sorrowful look came over his face.

"I'm sorry for your loss," Jo murmured and steered away from the topic, asking him about his work. He told her he'd worked at his father's construction firm part-time when he was in school before he went on to become a licensed contractor. Now his dad was retired and Dawson owned the business.

"Everything I know about construction, I learned from my dad," he said.

She pulled a string of melted cheese from her slice and rolled it into a ball before popping it into her mouth. "Sounds like you enjoy your work."

"I do, though I enjoy it more when I'm working with my hands than when I'm filling out forms or dealing with building inspectors. What about you? You like being a wedding photographer?"

"It has its challenges, but my job is never boring, because no two weddings are alike." She didn't tell him the work in which she used to take joy had become a source of pain since Sean died. Each time she witnessed the happiest day of most people's lives, it was a reminder of her loss.

"My wife? She was a sucker for weddings. Couldn't sit through one without getting teary-eyed. I used to tease her about it. 'Who died?' I'd whisper in her ear whenever I caught her puddling up at a wedding. I never imagined—" He broke off, his eyes growing misty. "God, I miss her."

He poured himself a refill, and when he went to fill her glass, she covered it with her hand. "Thanks, I'm good." Which was more than she could say for him. She noticed his speech had become slurred. She suspected he'd had a shot of liquid courage before meeting her tonight.

"They say it gets easier with time, but if that's true, I'd have to live to be a hundred. Every day when I wake up, I wonder how I'm gonna get through the rest of this day without her."

Jo suddenly wished she were anywhere but here. She pitied Dawson, but listening to him go on about his dead wife wasn't exactly her idea of a fun date. It was like a vision conjured by the Ghost of Christmas Future showing her what her fate might be if she allowed herself to wallow in her grief.

"I get it," she said, nodding in sympathy.

He pulled out his phone to show her the photo on its lock screen, one of his younger self, with longer hair, posing on a beach somewhere with a pretty, dark-haired woman. "That's her. That's my Judy."

"You both look happy," she said as she studied the photo.

"She was the love of my life." Dawson looked up at her with bleary, bloodshot eyes. "I'll tell you something I've never told anyone." He leaned in to whisper, "I keep a bottle of her perfume by my bed and dab some on my pillow every night before I go to sleep. 'S my little secret."

She smiled. "Hate to break it to you, but your mom knows if she does your laundry."

"She's never said anything to me."

"Trust me, moms always know."

It was getting dark by the time they left. Dawson had finished the rest of the beer along with most of the pepperoni half of their pizza. He was unsteady on his feet as they made their way to the exit, she with a firm grip on his arm, trying and failing to steer a straight course with him weaving from side to side. "Why don't I call you a taxi?" she suggested when they were outside.

"'S okay. Got my own ride." He gestured sloppily toward a white pickup bearing the signage McCafferty Construction, which was parked a few spaces down from where they stood.

"You're in no condition to drive." He ignored her, fumbling in his pocket and pulling out a key fob. She snatched it from his hand. "It's not a matter of opinion."

"I'm jus' down the road." He pointed in the general direction of the housing development abutting the commercial district they were in.

Seeing she wasn't going to win this argument, Jo took matters in her own hands. "Perfect. I'm going that way, so I can drop you off." This time, he didn't object, and she guided him toward her car.

He mumbled his address after they were buckled in and Jo entered it into Google Maps. Minutes later, the GPS lady announced that Jo had arrived at her destination. She pulled into the driveway of a rambler on a quiet street. She looked over at Dawson, and her heart sank when she saw he'd passed out. *No good deed goes unpunished.*

"Dawson, wake up. We're here." He roused briefly when she shook him, muttering something under his breath, before passing out again.

She climbed out with a growl of frustration. It was dark out, but she could see well enough. She went around to the passenger side, getting a blast of pepperoni-and-beer breath when she opened the door and reached across him to unfasten his seat belt. She shook him again, and this time was able to get him out of the car and on his feet. She was steering him up the path to the house when Dawson suddenly came to a halt, swaying on his feet. "Just a little farther. We're almost there," she coaxed, desperate to get him inside, where he wouldn't be her problem anymore.

Instead he sank to his knees before doing a face-plant on the grass bordering the path. Seconds later, he was snoring. *Great. Now what?* She was tempted to leave him there but couldn't in good conscience. What if his kids saw him like this? Instead, she climbed the steps to the porch and knocked on the front door. A minute later, it opened a crack and an older woman in a robe and slippers, with her hair in curlers, peered out. "Yes?"

"Mrs. McCafferty? Sorry to disturb you. I'm with Dawson, and we have a bit of a situation."

"Where is he? Is he all right?" The confusion on the other woman's face gave way to alarm.

"He's fine. He just . . . he had too much to drink, so I drove him home. This is as far as we got." She pointed to the human lawn ornament that was Dawson, visible in the glow of the porch light.

His mom flew out the door and down the steps, rushing over to where he lay. She dropped down beside him. "Dawson, honey. It's Mom. Wake up." She shook him. When he remained unresponsive, she cast a stricken look up at Jo. "I don't understand. He doesn't drink. This isn't like him."

Jo pitied the woman. She could imagine how distressing this must be for her. "Is there someone you can call?" she asked after several failed attempts to get him up onto his feet. He was too heavy to lift, even with the two of them working together.

"I . . . I wouldn't know who to call. We only recently moved into the neighborhood." Jo imagined she was too embarrassed to have any of her new neighbors see her son in this condition.

Luckily, Jo knew who to call. Normally, Hank would've been her first choice, but tonight she had backup in the form of Coop. She breathed a sigh of relief when his black Ford F-150 pulled in behind her car in the driveway ten minutes later. He and another man climbed out. “I brought reinforcement,” he called. As the other man came into view, she saw it was Hank. God bless them.

“Good timing,” Hank said. “I’d just gotten home when you called.”

“Thank you both for coming,” Jo said. “You’re lifesavers.”

“I don’t know about that, but we’re saving this poor fellow from any further embarrassment,” said Hank with a nod toward the prone figure on the grass.

Together, the two men managed to hoist Dawson onto his feet. He came to, after a fashion, and staggered in a forward direction with Coop and Hank supporting him on either side. His mom led the way with Jo bringing up the rear. They got him as far as his bedroom, where he toppled onto the bed and began snoring again. His mother removed his shoes and, with a tenderness that was heartbreaking to witness, covered him with the crocheted afghan that had been folded across the foot of the bed.

“I can’t thank you enough,” she said as she was seeing them out. Standing in the doorway, with her face partially in shadow, she looked ten years older than when she’d answered Jo’s knock. “If his children had seen him like that . . .” She shivered, and Jo suspected it wasn’t from the chill in the air.

“Glad we could be of assistance,” said Hank.

“I don’t know what to say. This is all so distressing,” she said, wringing her hands.

“No judgment,” said Coop. He pulled out his wallet, extracting a business card from it. He handed it to Dawson’s mom. “If he feels like talking to someone after he sobers up, have him call me.” Coop, in addition to being a licensed therapist, was also a recovering alcoholic, five years sober. “See you back at the ranch,” he called to Jo as he and Hank headed down the walk together.

Jo was about to leave when the other woman said, “Where are my manners? I just realized I didn’t get your name.”

“Jo.”

"I'm Veronica." They shook hands. "Forgive me if this sounds selfish, but I'm glad it was you and not someone else he was with. Someone who wasn't as caring as you would've cut and run. And if he'd driven drunk, he could've been injured, or worse. His children already lost their mom. They can't lose their dad, too."

Jo empathized. She often had the same worry about her children. "He's home safe, that's all that matters."

"Yes, of course, although it's a pity you had to see him like this. Honestly, it's so unlike him. I've never seen him drink more than two beers. If he had too much to drink tonight, it's probably because he was nervous. You're the first woman he's been out with since his wife died."

"I get it. Grief does funny things to people." One day, a few months after Sean died, Jo had run into someone from her church at the grocery store, a woman named Peggy whom she hadn't seen since she stopped going to church. After Peggy offered her condolences—a day late and a dollar short, as her mother would've said—Jo walked off without saying a word. She was halfway home before she realized she'd left her groceries in her cart at the store. "I hope he finds some peace."

"Me too. Well, thank you again."

"No need to thank me. I only did what anyone would."

"Ha. His wife would've put him in a cab if he'd gotten drunk on their first date, and that would've been the last he saw of her. Judy wasn't one to put up with any nonsense." She spoke with affection. A thoughtful look crossed the older woman's face. "I don't suppose you'd consider—"

"No." Jo spoke kindly but firmly. Clearly, neither she nor Dawson was ready for prime time. "Good night! And good luck with everything," she called over her shoulder as she hurried off.

"I'm cursed," she said to Hank later.

They were drinking tea in the dining nook after Coop and Kyra had left. Her children were asleep and Snickers was snoozing at her feet. Hank had come up to check on her and stayed to chat.

"Oh yeah? And why is that?" he asked.

"One bad date is lousy luck. Two in a row is a sign from the universe that I'm not meant to date."

He blew on his tea before taking a sip. "Or it could be that you're discovering what it's like for the rest of us." She lifted a quizzical eyebrow, and he explained, "Most people don't get it right the first time around like you did, or ever."

Jo reached for the cookie tin on the table, a gift from a client, and helped herself to a Mexican wedding cake. Powdered sugar rained down the front of her shirt as she bit into it. "What went wrong with your marriage?"

"We married young. Don't know that we'd have put a ring on it, as you kids say, if Lorraine hadn't gotten pregnant. Or at least we would've waited. Suddenly, there we were, both nineteen and married with a baby on the way. Neither of us knew what hit us, much less what we were doing. Marry young, you either grow together, like you and your husband did, or you grow apart. It didn't help matters in my case that I shipped out to 'Nam a short time after Ben was born."

"It wasn't your fault. You were in the army, fighting for your country."

"True, but it doesn't change the fact that I was gone for months at a time and she was left to raise our son on her own. She looked elsewhere for the emotional support she wasn't getting from me."

"She cheated on you?" Poor Hank.

He shrugged. "Let's just say the demise of our marriage was hastened by my deployment."

"Was there anyone after her?"

"A few I was serious about, but none that went the distance."

"Until now?"

He smiled mysteriously. "That remains to be seen."

"Frannie's a special person."

"Without question. Frankly, I don't know what she sees in me," he said dryly.

"That's easy. You're a silver fox, Hank," Jo said, taking another bite of her cookie.

He chuckled. "Martha used to say that she'd marry me if she were twenty years younger."

"I'd marry you if I was twenty years older."

Talk of marriage, even in jest, had a sobering effect on Jo. She grew quiet, looking around her. The dining nook was a work in progress. When she'd been stripping off its wallpaper, with an eye toward painting the walls, she'd uncovered multiple layers—from the nineties-era Laura Ashley bird-on-branch pattern to the flocked silver wallpaper that screamed the eighties and the wallpaper showing Chinese coolies carrying buckets from a pre-Woke era—representing different time periods. Now, she wondered about the life passages that had occurred within these walls over the decades since the house was built. Years in which the people who'd lived here had celebrated wins, suffered losses, given birth, and buried loved ones. She thought of Sean, longing for what was and would never be again.

"None of us knows what the future will bring." Hank's voice brought her back to the present.

"I know one thing. I'll never find love again like I had with Sean."

"Not tonight, anyway," said Hank.

The next day, a Thursday, while the girls were at camp, Jo worked in her office. She was editing the photos from the previous weekend's wedding when Chad, who worked as her assistant on an as-needed basis, called to say he couldn't work next weekend's engagement party as planned. "Family emergency," he explained. As soon as she got off the phone, she called Miranda, her backup assistant, and left a message on her voicemail when she didn't answer. Minutes later, her phone rang. She picked up without glancing at her caller ID, assuming it was Miranda. "Please tell me you can do it."

There was a pause, then a male voice said, "That would depend on what you want done."

"Ian!" Warmth flooded her cheeks. "I thought you were someone else."

"I figured."

"It's nice to hear from you, but why are you calling? Is something wrong?"

"I heard about your date disaster. I called to see if you needed to be talked off the ledge."

She was touched by his concern. "That's sweet of you, but I'm fine. I had a rough night but I've recovered."

"Want to tell me about it?"

"My date had too much to drink, so I drove him home. He passed out on his lawn before I could get him inside."

"Jesus."

"I know. And I couldn't just leave him there. I didn't want his kids to see him like that. So I went and got his mom, who lives with them. We couldn't lift him, and she was too embarrassed to ask any of her neighbors for help. Fortunately, your grandpa and my friend Coop came to the rescue."

"Did he call and apologize after he sobered up?"

"No, and I don't expect to hear from him."

"He's probably too mortified to call. I imagine he's suffering morning-after regret on top of a monster hangover."

"No doubt. But Dawson's not a bad guy. I felt sorry for him, actually. His mom claims he's not an alcoholic. He's just grieving. He lost his wife a few years ago. He thought he was ready to move on. Turned out he wasn't."

"You're very forgiving for someone who had her date get drunk and pass out on her."

"Because I get it. Grief makes you behave in ways you wouldn't ordinarily."

"What was he like?" Ian asked.

"Who, Dawson?"

"No. Your husband."

"Oh." She was surprised to be asked. Most people avoided the subject, either because it was awkward for them or they thought it might be painful for her. They didn't get that it was comforting to talk about a loved one when you were grieving. What was hurtful was people acting like they never existed. A smile crept onto her face, spreading down to warm her chest, as she described Sean. "He was smart and funny, goofy at times, with a big heart and two left thumbs, as he used to joke. He never wore a tie that someone else hadn't knotted for him, but he was athletic—a bicyclist and a world-class skier. Also a genius at writing computer code and usually the smartest person in the room. He had big dreams but always put his family first. He was, in short, amazing."

"How did you two meet?"

"Long story. You sure you want to hear it?"

"I've got time." He laughed when she told the story of how she and Sean met. "Good thing he saw you with that guy, or he might never have known you were straight."

"Sean suggested we invite him to our wedding, if you can believe it. And I'm not entirely sure he was joking. You know, in appreciation for the part he unwittingly played in bringing us together."

"What did you say to that?"

"That I would if I could remember his name."

"Good answer." Ian chuckled. "He sounds like someone I would've liked. Your husband, that is."

"He'd have liked you, too."

They talked for a while longer. Ian told her about his life as a flight instructor in the military and how he'd wanted to be a pilot from the time he'd first flown in an airplane with his grandfather when he was eight. She was surprised when she saw it was almost noon. They'd been talking for almost half an hour.

"Thanks for calling, and for listening," she said as they were saying their goodbyes. "Even if I didn't need to be talked off the ledge."

"My pleasure. And if there's ever a time when you do need to be talked off the ledge, you know who to call. I have one advantage over your friends who might normally be your first call."

"What's that?"

"At night when everyone in your time zone is asleep, I'm usually awake."

"I'll keep that in mind."

Jo was smiling when she ended the call.

15

On Friday, the day her parents were due to arrive, Jo was in the kitchen with the girls preparing dinner—grilled chicken, corn on the cob, baked potato, and peach cobbler for dessert—when she heard a car engine outside. "That must be Grandma and Grandpa," she said. Her dad had texted after their flight had landed. That had been a couple of hours ago, enough time for them to have driven from the airport in Sacramento and checked in at their hotel before coming here. She felt a tremor of anxiety. She prayed their visit wouldn't include any guilt trips, "helpful" suggestions, or interrogation of her lodger. It seemed too much to hope for.

Jess and Emma stood on step stools at the counter, each wearing a flour-dusted apron. They were rolling out biscuit dough for the cobbler under her direction. They both looked up when she spoke, their faces alight with anticipation. "Did they bring us presents?" asked Emma.

Her parents never visited without bringing gifts, usually expensive ones, but Jo was trying to teach her children not to expect presents, so she answered, "I don't know, but what I *do* know is that you'll be happy to see them even if they didn't bring you anything."

"I hope it's not dolls like the last time," muttered Jess.

"If you don't want yours, can I have it?" asked Emma.

"No." Jess wasn't a fan of dolls, but what was hers was hers.

Jo sighed. So much for managing their expectations. "When someone gives you a gift, it shows they were thinking of you, and that's what matters most. Now, both of you wash up while I get the door."

Outside, the sun had dipped below the rooftops, and the long shadows of late afternoon stretched across the landscape. Jo waved to Mrs. Atkins across the street, who was pruning the roses in her yard, before her attention was drawn to the black Lincoln Town Car idling at the curb. She watched, with an uneasy mix of love and dread, as her parents climbed from the back seat, her mom in heels and her dad carrying a canvas tote from which a gift-wrapped package peeked.

"How was your trip?" Jo asked after they'd exchanged hugs.

"Uneventful," her dad reported.

"Honestly, Pete. How can you say that?" Jo's mom cast him a disbelieving look. "It was a nightmare!" she told Jo. "I don't know when I've had a bumpier flight. At one point, I was saying my prayers." Jo, who was accustomed to her mother's histrionics, took her account of the flight with a grain of salt. "Thank heavens we made it here in one piece without the plane crashing!"

They were both dressed as if for a daytime function at their country club, in color-coordinated outfits, accessorized by chunky gold jewelry in her mom's case. Jo's mother looked ageless, as always, due to a combination of the face work she'd had done, her daily beauty regimen, and regular Botox injections. Her hair was dyed champagne-blond and worn in the style known in the South as "dyed, fried, and shoved to the side." Thin to the point of skeletal, she resembled a human breadstick, although a glamorous one. The surprise was her dad, who'd dropped a good thirty pounds since she'd last seen him prior to his heart attack. Fit and trim, with his golfer's tan and full head of silver hair, he might've stepped from a *Modern Maturity* magazine cover.

"So this is your new place? Nice," her father remarked.

"Cozy," said her mom once they were inside.

The expression "damned by faint praise" came to mind, but at least they'd found nothing to criticize.

"We brought some things for you and the girls." Jo's dad handed her the tote.

"How thoughtful, but I hope you didn't go overboard," she said. For Christmas last year, they'd given her a gorgeous shearling jacket, which had probably cost more than she earned in a month, and the girls each got an iPad mini as their main gift. Their overgenerosity, at a time when Jo had been lacking both in funds and Christmas spirit, had made Santa seem like Scrooge in comparison.

"What are children and grandchildren for if not to spoil?" replied her dad.

"Speaking of, where are my little princesses?" asked her mom, peering past her into the living room as they stood in the foyer.

Jess and Emma appeared, running toward them, trailed by Snickers at a slower pace, with her tail and ears down. Their Lab seemed to sense, as animals do, that her parents weren't dog people. When Jo had begged for a pet as a child, her mom had refused, claiming that a dog or a cat, or even a parakeet, would only create messes for her to clean up. "Grandma! Grandpa!" the girls chorused.

They'd done as they were told and both had clean hands. Emma had on the pink tutu and leotard that she'd worn trick or treating on Halloween for the past two years in a row. Jo remembered when Sean had gotten her the ballerina costume, the last year he'd taken the girls trick or treating, and felt a rush of grief along with a painful awareness of how long it had been since he'd died. The costume had been a size too big for the then three-year-old Emma and was a size too small for her now. Jess wore shorts and her T-shirt from the rock museum in Auburn they'd visited once on a family outing, which read I Rock. They hurled themselves into their grandparents' open arms.

"My goodness, you've both grown a foot!" Jo's dad declared. "It appears our plot to smuggle you out of here in our suitcases has been foiled. You wouldn't fit in them."

The girls giggled.

"They'll be wearing makeup and heels before you know it," said Jo's mom. She winked. "Along with a tiara, if either of them decides to follow in their grandma's footsteps."

Over my dead body, Jo thought.

The girls were thrilled with their gifts—an American Girl Doll for Emma and a coffee table book on mineral rocks for Jess. And although Jo had little use for the set of fancy wine goblets she'd received, being as she rarely entertained, she appreciated the gesture. Afterward, they all went outside. While her parents relaxed on the deck, enjoying the chilled white wine and crudités with yogurt-dill dip Jo had served, and the girls played in the backyard, Jo fired up the grill. As she got started grilling the chicken, she told her parents about the plans she'd made for the weekend.

"I arranged for us to go boating at the lake on Saturday, and hiking on Sunday if you're up for it. I have evening events both Saturday and Sunday, but I'm all yours for the rest of the weekend."

"Sounds good, honey," said her dad.

"We're in your hands," said her mom. "And I'm sure we can find plenty to do with the girls while you're working."

Jo was surprised they weren't giving her grief about the fact that she had to work for part of the weekend.

The chicken was almost done when she heard a car engine in the driveway and, minutes later, voices from below. Hank was home, and he wasn't alone. She peered over the deck railing and saw him and Frannie coming around the side of the building, headed toward the downstairs entrance.

"Is that your lodger?" Jo's dad asked.

"Yes," Jo said, making no move to catch Hank's attention. Fearing it might lead to a grilling of something—or rather, someone—other than the chicken, she felt suddenly paralyzed. Hank was no fool. He would know if he was being interrogated, even if it was sugarcoated in Southern hospitality.

"Aren't you going to introduce us?" her mom prompted.

Jolted back into action, Jo called to him and Frannie, "Guys! Come say hello to my folks!" When Hank gave an affirming wave, she was gripped with dread.

He and Frannie headed for the stairs to the deck, pausing to greet Emma and Jess along the way. The girls were playing with the Hula-Hoop they'd unearthed from the treasure trove of old playthings Jo had discovered in the garage after they'd moved in, which included a pogo stick and board games such as Chutes and Ladders and Candy Land. Emma ran toward the newcomers, dragging the Hula-Hoop with her, calling, "Hank! Frannie! Look what I can do!" while Jess hung back. Jess had thawed slightly toward Hank since their talk, if you could call it that, when she'd accused him of not liking her and he'd denied it, although she had yet to warm up to him.

The adults watched, from above and below, as Emma put on an unintentionally hilarious show that involved a series of jerky movements as she attempted to spin the Hula-Hoop around her waist. When she finally managed to complete a revolution, they all applauded and Emma beamed.

"Hank, meet my parents, Pete and Carol. Mom, Dad, this is Hank." Jo made the introductions after Hank and Frannie had joined them on the deck. "And you remember Frannie."

"Yes, of course. Good to see you again, Frannie," said Jo's mom, kissing her on the cheek. If she was surprised to see Frannie with Hank, she didn't bat an eye.

"And under happier circumstances," her dad put in.

The last time they'd seen one another had been at Sean's funeral. Jo felt her mood grow even darker, remembering that awful day. Frannie must've been remembering it, too, because her smile dimmed slightly. "Indeed," she said. "You're both looking well. Pete, it appears the rumors of your health scare were greatly exaggerated. And Carol, how is it that you never seem to age?"

"You're too kind." Her mom of course lapped up the compliment before turning toward Hank. "At last we meet our daughter's famous lodger." She was all smiles, but Jo didn't trust her one bit.

Don't mess this up for me.

"We've heard so much about you, Hank," said Jo's dad as they shook hands. "And yet we know so little."

Jo broke out in a nervous sweat. Before either of her parents could start quizzing Hank, she offered, "Can I get you two something to drink? I have beer, wine, lemonade, and iced tea."

Hank and Frannie both requested iced teas. Jo transferred the chicken from the grill to a platter and carried it inside to keep warm in the oven until dinner was served. She returned carrying the two tall glasses of iced tea she'd poured, each topped with a lemon wedge and sprig of mint. She found her company seated around the low table that held the crudités and dip, conversing pleasantly. Where some might have seen an innocent gathering, she saw a trap, one into which the unsuspecting Hank had been lured. Her anxiety mounted as she handed him and Frannie their iced teas.

"I was just telling your folks about our plans for the evening," said Frannie. "Hank's taking me to dinner at the Mill." The Mill, a converted nineteenth-century flour mill housed in a quaint stone building on the banks of Bear River, was one of the top-rated fine-dining restaurants in the area. Frannie was dressed for the occasion, in a batik shift and sandal heels, a silver choker around her neck.

Jo's mom said, "Pete and I ate there once, with Jo. Lovely setting, and the food was divine. Honey, don't you remember?"

Jo nodded. Her parents had insisted on taking her out to dinner when they'd visited a few months after Sean died. What she remembered was putting on a brave face and barely tasting her food.

"Believe it or not, I've never eaten there, even though it's been in business for ages. Too fancy for the likes of me," said Frannie with a smile that suggested she wouldn't have it any other way.

"What's the occasion?" asked Jo's dad.

"Nothing special," said Frannie. "Neither of us is celebrating a birthday, and Hank and I haven't been dating long enough to be counting anniversaries."

"How long have you two known each other?" asked Jo's mom as she sipped her wine. Her gaze was innocent and her smile unwavering, but Jo detected a glint of something hard in her eye.

"A couple months," Hank said. "We met when Jo was sprucing this place up before she moved in. We both helped with the painting, along with her other friends."

Jo's parents exchanged a glance, and Jo felt her gut clench. *Here it comes.* She expected them to start questioning him about his past, in particular where it involved his former landlady. Instead, much to her surprise and relief, her mother said, "Hank, Jo tells us you do volunteer work."

Hank nodded and scooped up some of the dip with a celery stick. "Here and there," he replied modestly. Hank served on the boards of several nonprofits that Jo knew of, in addition to his other charitable activities. "Mostly, I volunteer at the Morningside Veterans' Care Home here in Gold Creek."

"What does your work involve?"

"It varies from day to day, although there's always at least one person who needs a shave or needs help getting dressed. Sometimes I act as escort when someone wants to leave the building. I also read to anyone who requests it. Quite a few of the residents are visually impaired."

"They don't listen to audiobooks?"

"Sure, but some are lonely and want the company."

"Hank's also the silver surfer instructor at the home," boasted Frannie.

"Silver surfer?" Jo's mom asked in confusion.

"I teach a course in basic computer skills," Hank explained. "Most of my students don't know how to operate a computer before they sign up for my course. By the time they graduate, they're emailing and surfing the internet. It allows them to stay in closer touch with family and friends."

"It must be gratifying for you," said her mom.

"Yes, although I don't know who gets more out of it, them or me. I enjoy spending time with the old boys and listening to their stories. Many of them fought in wars, and boy, do they have stories to tell."

"I understand you served in Vietnam," said Jo's dad.

Hank nodded, his expression shuttered. "I was lucky. I made it back in one piece. Others weren't as fortunate. Some of the men I've met at the veterans' home lost limbs or suffered permanent brain damage. I consider it a privilege to do whatever I can to improve their quality of life."

Score one for Hank. Even her parents seemed impressed. But Jo remained on edge. Because she knew their objection to Hank wasn't really about him—how could it be when they didn't even know him? It was about her having gone against their wishes in buying this house. Did they have an ulterior motive in coming here? Did they hope to drive Hank away and, in doing so, leave her with no choice but to sell this house and move back home?

She didn't know what to make of it when her mom gushed, "Why, I think it's just wonderful what you're doing for those men and for your community." Eyes shining, she placed her hand over her heart like she did when reciting the Pledge of Allegiance or when the national anthem was sung at football games, and declared, "God bless you, Hank. And thank you for your service."

As her mom and dad both beamed at Hank, Jo thought, *Who are you, and what have you done with my parents?*

On Saturday, the girls spent the morning with their grandparents while Jo caught up on some work at home in preparation for her evening event, starting with breakfast at their hotel and ending with a train ride. The Roaring Camp steam train, a relic from the lumber industry's heyday, still operated on the five-mile-long spur that had once been used to transport logs from the lumber camps to the old sawmill, as a tourist attraction these days.

In the afternoon they all went boating on the lake with Frannie in her pontoon. Hank had to work, so he was unable to join them. It was a sunny day, the water still as glass, reflecting the trees, a mix of pine and hardwoods, fringing the lake. At one point, Frannie dropped anchor where there was a sandbar so they could go swimming. She was the first one in the water, and she assisted the girls as they climbed down the ladder at the stern, wearing life jackets over their swimsuits.

Jo was all set to join them when her mother placed a stilling hand on her arm. "Jo, a word?" She was in full makeup, as usual, and wore a cover-up over her swimsuit the likes of which you might see poolside in Palm Beach. A wide-brimmed straw hat and designer sunglasses completed the picture. "Your father and I have something to say."

"About what?" Jo asked warily. She anticipated either a criticism or an announcement that would disrupt her plans, and possibly her life, like when they'd informed her they were coming to visit.

Her mom's next words confirmed her suspicion that they were pod people posing as her parents. "We owe you an apology."

Jo was stunned speechless. She couldn't recall her parents ever apologizing to her or anyone. Why would they, when they were never wrong? "For what?" she asked when she found her tongue.

"We were wrong to pressure you to move back home. We're sorry."

"We were worried about you," said her dad. "After Sean died, you were struggling. We thought if we were on hand to help out, it would make your life easier. Our guesthouse seemed the ideal solution."

"Needless to say, the offer is still open if you change your mind," said her mom.

"I won't. But thank you," Jo remembered to add.

"We still wish you lived near us. Partly for selfish reasons, I admit, and not just because we think it'd be best for you and the girls. We've missed out on so much already. We weren't there when the girls were born, or when they took their first steps. Or when Sean—" She broke off with a small, choked sound.

"He was the son we never had." Jo's dad's voice was hoarse with emotion.

Jo swallowed against the lump in her throat as she watched the girls splashing in the shallow water off the sandbar with Frannie. Sean might not have been her parents' first choice for a son-in-law; they would've preferred she marry someone from their social set. But they'd grown to love him, and he'd had a genuine affection for them. He'd also negotiated peace between her and her parents when they'd clashed by helping them find a middle ground where they could meet. Whenever she'd become fed up, he'd reminded her that they loved her, however misguided their actions at times.

"He loved you, too," she said when she could speak in her normal voice again. "As do I. I hope you know I wasn't rejecting you when I said no to your offer. Which was most generous," she added. "It's just that moving back home would be a step backward, and I need to get on with my life."

"We understand," said her dad. He put his arm around her, and she dropped her head onto his shoulder, remembering when she was little and he used to carry her in his arms. She felt a wave of affection wash through her. "Whatever we did, it was done out of love. We only want what's best for you."

"We do have a favor to ask, however." Jo's mom pushed up her sunglasses to dab at her moist eyes with the handkerchief she'd fished from her straw bag.

"Just one?" Jo teased.

Her dad chuckled. "Yes, and it's a small one. Your mom and I would love for you to be our guest at this year's dinner-dance at the club." Every year on the Saturday of Labor Day weekend, the Fairview Country Club hosted its annual dinner-dance for its members to mark the end of the season. "I realize it's last minute and you might have other plans, but we wanted to ask you in person after we apologized for our past transgressions. If there's any chance you're free that weekend, it would mean so much to us if you could come. We hardly ever have an opportunity to show off our beautiful, talented daughter. Bring the girls and make a weekend of it. All expenses paid, naturally."

"It might be our last chance to visit with the girls before school starts in the fall," her mom said.

Jo didn't know what to say. It *was* last-minute, only two weeks away, but coincidentally, the wedding she'd booked for Labor Day weekend had been called off, just days ago, after the bride-to-be caught her fiancé in bed with another woman. As a result, Jo not only had an opening in her schedule, but she also got to keep the deposit, so she wouldn't have to scramble to fill it. Still, she hesitated. Her memories of the club functions she'd attended in the past were anything but fond. Yet how could she refuse her parents after their heartfelt appeal?

"As it so happens, I'm free that weekend," she said. "I'd love to come, and I'm sure I can find something to wear to the dance."

"Never mind about that. I'll take you shopping for a dress," said her mom. "Oh, this'll be so much fun!" She clapped her hands with glee, her tears of a moment ago replaced by happy anticipation.

"I'll book the flights," said her dad.

Jo bit back her lingering reservations, seeing how happy she'd made them. They were trying. The least she could do was meet them halfway. Why, then, did she have the feeling she'd been played?

"Something tells me I'm going to regret this," Jo said to Frannie later that day.

They were relaxing on the deck at her cabin after their boat ride, while Jess and Emma fished off the dock below with her dad, and her mom looked on. At the moment, Jo's dad was showing Jess how to bait her hook, which she was having none of—she was not a fan of worms.

Nor was Jo's mom, from the look of disgust on her face as her husband threaded the wriggling worm onto the hook.

"I can think of more fun things to do on a Saturday night than go to a country club dinner-dance," agreed Frannie. The two women reclined on matching chaises in the shade of the deck overhang, Jo sporting a mild sunburn, the curse of the redhead, despite the sunblock she'd slathered on prior to their boat ride. "But it probably won't be as bad as you envision. Nothing ever is."

"I suppose, although the last dinner-dance I attended at the club, when I was fifteen, was possibly the worst night of my teenage life."

"Why is that?"

"I got stuck dancing with the son of one of the club members, who tried to feel me up when he wasn't stepping on my toes."

Frannie made a face. "I see what you mean. But you're not a kid anymore, and it's just one night."

"If you don't count going shopping with my mom for a dress to wear to the dinner-dance. Knowing her, she'll insist on picking one out and won't allow me to pay for it."

"Poor you," replied Frannie in a dry tone. Jo realized to her chagrin how ungrateful she'd sounded. Compared to some—like Frannie, whose parents had been unfit to raise her and her sister, and Kyra, who'd been dragged from town to town by her mom to evade bill collectors—Jo had been blessed in that regard. "Think of it as the mother-daughter experience she was denied with your high school proms."

"I went to my proms. I just didn't go in formal wear with a date." Jo had attended both her junior and senior proms strictly in her capacity as photographer for her school paper, dressed accordingly.

"I rest my case."

"I'm being a brat, aren't I?" she said sheepishly. Frannie didn't disagree. "You're right. It could be worse. And Mom does have a great sense of style." *Even if it doesn't happen to be my style.*

"She does."

"It's just that she tends to forget I'm not twelve anymore."

"It's a fine line between mothering and smothering, which I'm sure I've crossed any number of times with my daughter."

"It's different with you and Hannah."

Frannie's daughter had been in and out of mental health facilities and group homes since she was diagnosed with schizoaffective disorder when she was fourteen. The cruel irony of her mental illness was that she was stable when she took her meds, but that was also when she was at greatest risk. She'd become convinced she didn't need to be on meds and stop taking them, which would cause her to go into a downward spiral. She'd been staying with Frannie for the past two years while getting her life back on track after her most recent spinout. She was currently working as a cashier at the Walmart in Pine City and had a steady boyfriend.

"Yes, but I still have to watch that I don't hover."

"How's she doing?"

"Never better." Frannie's face lit up. "She just got promoted to head cashier. And she and Darren are planning to move in together." She seemed less enthusiastic about the latter than the former.

"That's great. Moving in with her boyfriend, though, is a huge step. How do you feel about it?"

"I'm of two minds. I want her to be happy and Darren makes her happy. But so did her previous boyfriends before they dumped her after seeing what she's like when she's off her meds. Each time, she wasn't just heartbroken, she was broken. And I was the one left to pick up the pieces."

"She's lucky to have you."

"I wouldn't have it any other way. It's just hard sometimes."

"Being a single parent is hard even in the best of circumstances," Jo agreed, "and you've had more than your fair share of challenges with Hannah." Hannah's father was useless, and the responsibility for raising Hannah had fallen squarely on Frannie's shoulders.

Jo's gaze was drawn to the sweet domestic scene below, her children sitting on the end of the dock with their feet dangling in the water, fishing poles in hand, watched over by their doting grandparents. It did her heart good to see her girls having fun, especially Jess, and she had to admit her parents had played a part in it.

"Now you know what your folks went through when they were raising you," Frannie teased.

"Except I wasn't a problem child."

"It's all a matter of perspective."

"I take your point," Jo conceded. She'd been an obedient child, but stubborn when it came to resisting her parents' efforts to mold her in their images. Even at a young age, she hadn't shared their goals and values, and now they saw her way of life as a rejection of theirs. "Which is why I'm flying two thousand miles to be trussed like a turkey and trotted out at their club's dinner-dance. I guess I owe them."

Jo was distracted by a squeal from below. She looked down to see that Emma had caught a fish. Scarcely bigger than her thumb, it might have been a trophy catch from how excited she was. They all watched as Jo's dad extracted the hook from its mouth and tossed it back into the lake.

Jo changed the subject. "How was your date last night?"

"Wonderful."

"What? The food, the ambience, or the company?"

Frannie smiled. "All of the above."

"I'm glad you and Hank found each other."

"Me too. Funny how life works out. I had to wait until I was in my sixties, after I'd gone through a string of losers, before I found someone who treats me like a queen and who makes me happy."

"Do you think you'll ever marry him?" Jo wanted them to have their happily ever after. They were perfect for each other. At the same time, she knew it would mean Hank moving out and worried about how it'd affect her. Leaving aside her financial concerns, Hank had become a part of her household, and she'd grown used to seeing him every day. She'd also come to rely on him.

"We haven't discussed marriage. Frankly, I don't know that I'd even consider it."

"Why not?"

"Seems like I've spent my whole life accommodating other people. My parents, my husband, my daughter. Now it's my turn to do as I please."

"Hank's not one to make demands."

"No, but when you live with someone, you have to be considerate of their needs, and I've grown selfish in my old age. I'm looking forward to having this place to myself again once Hannah moves out. If I have to work late, I won't have to cancel any plans I've made with someone else. I can eat when I want and stay up as late as I like. I can watch TV without having to share the remote."

"But if you love someone, you don't mind sharing." That was her experience anyway.

Frannie gazed thoughtfully out at the lake, where a breeze ruffled the water and a family of loons, a mated pair and their half-grown babies, paddled in a V formation. "Love isn't always enough."

"For me it was everything."

Jo remembered a woman she'd met when she used to accompany Sean to his chemo treatments, the wife of another patient whom she'd gotten to know a bit. She seemed to find being a caregiver a burden, whereas Jo had considered it a privilege. Because every moment spent with Sean had been precious, even when it had involved cleaning up after he'd vomited or emptying a bedpan. She understood what Frannie was saying, but their realities were worlds apart. Frannie's past relationships had made her gun-shy, while Jo would've given anything to have Sean back.

16

That evening's event was relatively painless. It was a church wedding, followed by a reception at the home of the bride's parents, with approximately fifty guests. The candlelight ceremony created some technical issues—Jo had to keep adjusting the settings on her camera to get the exposure just right—but the venue, the old Quaker church on Cherry Street, was lovely, and the people she met were nice. She was home and her parents, who'd babysat, were on their way back to their hotel before midnight.

The following afternoon they went on a family hike in the neighboring park. She took one of the easier trail loops, although she needn't have worried about the others being able to keep up. Her children had energy to burn and raced each other up the trail. Her parents were in better shape than she was—her mom took a Pilates class that met every weekday, and her dad had become a fitness fanatic since his heart attack. If not for her elderly dog setting the pace, she would've been lagging behind.

On Monday morning she drove her parents to the Little Explorers Day Camp so they could see what they were getting for their money. Kristin, the camp director, gave them the tour, and they marveled over the fact that their grandchildren were building a birch-bark canoe, making candles, and growing vegetables, to name just a few of the activities. Jo observed a big difference in Jess since she'd last visited, earlier in the summer. Before, she'd hung back and hadn't interacted much with the other campers. Now she seemed more engaged. Even Kristin remarked on it. It warmed Jo's heart to witness. She didn't know if either of her children would ever be in a situation requiring them to build a canoe, but Jess was becoming a person someone else might want in their lifeboat. She was clearly benefiting from her therapy, and maybe the house on Mountain Laurel Lane had something to do with it, too.

On her parents' last evening in Gold Creek, they took Jo and the girls out to dinner at the Grubstake Café downtown, where they feasted on buffalo burgers and fries and milkshakes for dessert. Jo didn't see them again before they left for the airport early the next day. It had been a successful visit, and nothing like she'd been dreading, though she still didn't know what to make of her new-and-improved parents. She couldn't shake the niggling suspicion that all was not as it appeared.

On Thursday morning of that week, Jo was dropping Jess and Emma off at their bus stop when Jess asked for the umpteenth time, "You won't forget about the cupcakes, will you, Mommy?"

Tomorrow marked the occasion of the camp's annual Harvest Festival, which was held every year in August at the close of the summer session. The campers put on an eco-friendly play, after which there were food and games. The vegetarian meal that was served buffet-style at picnic tables outdoors was prepared by the campers, with adult supervision, and parent volunteers, from vegetables grown in the camp garden. Jo, acting out of guilt, the foe of every working parent, had volunteered to bake cupcakes. Three dozen organic, sugarless, whole-grain, nut-free carrot cupcakes to be precise. She was already stressing out about it. But she'd find the time. Somehow.

"I won't forget," she told Jess.

From Jess's worried face, she had her doubts. Jo had given assurances to her daughters in the past that had proved false, like when she'd assured them their dad wouldn't die while Sean had been battling cancer. Emma, who was forgiving by nature, didn't seem to hold it against her, but Jess had trust issues as a result. Jo, as she watched her girls board the bus, vowed to do her best to rebuild her eldest's trust, starting with cupcakes.

Unfortunately, her workday didn't go as planned. The photo shoot scheduled for that afternoon was delayed by almost an hour due to her clients' late arrival. Things went downhill from there. Or, technically, uphill, since the shoot took place at the scenic outlook atop a mountain where her clients, Brian and Beth, had become engaged. The climb billed by the pair of avid hikers as "a piece of cake" turned out to be a mile long, made more arduous by the fact that Jo was lugging her camera gear.

Beth and Brian, who were both in their early twenties but had wealthy parents who were footing the bill for the wedding, had opted for Jo's full bridal package, which in their case included photographing of the marriage proposal. Jo had done only a few proposals in the past and they'd been in real time, but being as Beth and Brian's had taken place in the wild, they were doing it as a reenactment, which was today's assignment. And which would've been easy if Beth, who wanted it picture-perfect for her socials, hadn't ordered Jo to take a million shots for every one she approved. Jo did her best to comply while cursing herself for not having specified a block of time for the shoot and gotten the details on the location in advance. At the very least, she should've rescheduled after Beth texted to say they'd be late. It was just that she'd never experienced anything like this before.

"Now get some from my good side," Beth directed at one point as she stood at the scenic overlook, with Brian on bended knee before her. She had on the outfit she'd worn on the day of her engagement, a Taylor Swift concert tee, boyfriend shorts, and hiking boots, although Jo doubted whether she'd been in full makeup with her hair done at the time.

"Sure thing," she said, gritting her teeth as she silently repeated her mantra: *A happy client is a future referral.* She sidestepped around the couple, carefully, so as not to fall over the edge of the overlook and into the canyon below and make orphans of her children. She shuddered at the thought.

"For the love of God, make it quick," said Brian from where he knelt on the ground, his jaw clenched in pain. "Man, I'm dying here." Like Beth, he was dressed for a hike. Unlike her, he wore a frown.

After she'd taken a dozen shots from Beth's "good side," Jo edged her way back to where she wasn't one step away from plunging to her death. Brian, looking enormously relieved, started to rise and was stopped when Beth placed a hand on his shoulder, pushing him back down. "We're not done yet," she told him. "I don't think I looked excited enough in those last shots. It has to look real."

Brian muttered something under his breath that might've been a curse word. Twenty minutes later, when he slipped the ring on the finger of his bride-to-be for the last time before she called it a wrap, his thoroughly disgusted expression suggested she might become his bride-not-to-be.

It was a quarter to five by the time they were done. Jo had arranged for Lindsay Crawford, one of the other camp moms, to pick Jess and Emma up from their bus stop along with her kids. Jo was supposed to come get them by five, but there was no way she could be there on time. She kicked herself for not doing a better job of managing both her time and Beth's demands. She tried calling Lindsay but couldn't get a signal on her phone. She saw that she had three missed calls from her. Damn. It was another fifteen minutes before she'd descended the mountain to where she was within cell range. She phoned Lindsay from her car.

"Jo, thank God. I've been trying to reach you." Lindsay sounded frantic. Jo could hear a baby crying in the background.

Jo grew worried. Had one of the girls become sick or injured? "I'm so sorry. I was delayed, out of cell range, or I would've called sooner. Is everything okay?"

"Taylor has an ear infection. I have to take her to the ER. My mother-in-law said she'd watch Braden and Tatum . . ." Taylor, she remembered, was Lindsay's one-year-old. Braden and Tatum were her five-year-old twins. "But she can barely handle my twin terrors. I can't dump your children on her along with mine. I need you to come and get them. Oh, and by the way, I fed them supper."

Jo was relieved to learn no one was hurt or seriously ill, but the fact that Lindsay had managed to feed the older children while dealing with a sick baby, while she couldn't even manage to be on time, made her feel even guiltier. "I'm still thirty minutes out, but I'll send someone to pick the girls up. Again, I'm so sorry. I hope your little one feels better soon."

After ending the call, Jo tried her other friends and got their voicemails. In desperation, she phoned Hank. She hated to impose, but what choice did she have? Luckily, she caught him at home. "No problem," he said after she'd thrown herself on his mercy. "I'll head over there now and meet you back at the house." She texted him Lindsay's address, which GPS showed to be six minutes from their house.

She felt a surge of relief, even as she worried about how Jess might react when Hank showed up in her place. Though Jess no longer acted like he didn't exist, she still viewed him as an interloper. Jo feared this could cause a setback.

It was 6:02 when Jo arrived home. She was headed inside when she remembered about the cupcakes, which had slipped her mind in the midst of today's madness. She groaned. If she failed to deliver, Jess might never trust her again. She couldn't do that to her daughter. Which meant she'd be up until late tonight baking cupcakes after doing a grocery store run.

And she'd thought her day couldn't get any worse.

She paused inside the door, arrested by the sounds emanating from somewhere in the house. Happy sounds. The girls chattering, interspersed with Hank's voice. *I must be dreaming,* she thought at the scene she encountered as she entered the kitchen, where baking supplies were spread over one counter and the girls, both wearing aprons, were measuring ingredients while Hank supervised.

"Mommy! We're making cupcakes!" announced Emma.

"I took the liberty after I was informed you'd promised them cupcakes for their camp do tomorrow," Hank explained. "I figured it'd save you time if we got the production line rolling. We stopped at the store on the way home to buy ingredients. Miss Bossy Pants here"—he tilted his head toward Jess, standing on a step stool beside him spooning flour into a measuring cup—"said they had to be *healthy* cupcakes, so we went all out on the crunchy front. Organic eggs and flour. Monk-fruit sweetener. Coconut oil. Our one cheat is the rainbow sprinkles we got for toppings."

"We're elves!" said Emma.

"I told them the story about the shoemaker's elves," he said.

"The one where the shoemaker's children go barefoot because he's too busy to make them shoes?" said Jo with a dry lift of her brow and a twinge of guilt.

"Yours will have cupcakes at least, and the girls know you would have made them even if we hadn't gotten started without you. Hope I didn't overstep." His smile gave way to a worried look.

Jo realized she'd forgotten to thank him in her surprise at arriving home to a scene from a Hallmark movie instead of the one she'd envisioned. "God, no. You saved me. I'd have been up all night. I meant to stop at the store on my way home, but . . ." Heat rose in her cheeks as she shot a guilty glance at Jess.

"It's okay if you forgot, Mommy," said Jess. "Hank said you wouldn't, but I thought you might when you were late. This is better, anyhow, 'cause we get to help."

That was when Jo saw something she hadn't seen in a long time and feared she might never see again: a huge grin on Jess's face. It was like Christmas in August. A minute ago she'd been tired and downbeat, and now she felt energized and in good spirits. She swooped in to hug her daughters. "You two are the best elves ever. And I know these will be the best cupcakes I ever ate."

"We can't eat them. They're for the *festival*," Jess said, wriggling free from her embrace.

"We'll make extra," said Hank.

While Jess and Emma got busy peeling the carrots from the camp garden that they'd brought home for the cupcakes, Jo said to Hank, "You have no idea how much I needed this after the day I had."

"Some days we work harder for the money than others," he commented after she told him about her day. "But we've got you covered at this end."

"Yes, I can see that." She blinked back tears of gratitude. "Thank you."

He waved away her thanks. "It was a joint effort. You've got a couple of budding Martha Stewarts there." He gestured toward the girls, who were bickering over who was doing a better job peeling the carrots.

"And looks like you've got yourself a new friend." Jo cut a meaningful glance at Jess, lowering her voice as she added, "And I was worried I'd come home to find you packing to move out."

He chuckled as if she'd been joking. She hadn't been. "Oh. That reminds me, I have something for you." He left the room, and she heard footsteps on the stairs. He returned shortly, carrying a document. He handed it to her. "It's a standard lease form I found online. Why don't you look it over when you have a moment, see if there's any changes you'd like to make before we sign it? That is, if you haven't decided to kick me to the curb," he added with a twinkle in his eye.

Jo smiled and shook her head, her heart overflowing. "Never. This is your home."

It was half past eight by the time the cupcakes were done. Jo ran a bath for the girls, who were both sticky with frosting in their hair, and sprinkles in Emma's case. Once they were bathed and in their pajamas, she read them a story and tucked them in. Later that evening, she was getting ready to turn in when her phone pinged. She saw she had a text message from Ian via WhatsApp.

I heard it's official. So Pop-Pop passed the test?

She texted him back. More like we passed the test. How he puts up with us, I'll never know.

He doesn't see it that way.

I know. He and the girls made cupcakes today. I helped. We saved one for when you visit.

I don't know when that might be.

It'll keep in the freezer. How are you?

Good. How was your day?
I almost fell over a cliff taking pics of a bridezilla, but except for that, it's all good.
??????
Long story. I'll save it for when I see you.
Glad you survived.
Me too. What are you up to?
Coffee. It's 6 a.m. here. You?
Brushing my teeth before bed.
Did you remember to floss?
LOL

It was nice, she thought as she was climbing into bed after signing off with Ian, to have a friend who was just starting his day when hers was ending. Almost like having someone to keep watch while she slept.

17

The cupcakes were a hit at the Harvest Festival. Better yet, Hank had gone from zero to hero in Jess's eyes. Since then, she'd become his shadow. She'd taken to hanging out with him in the kitchen or the garage when he did his woodworking projects and small engine repairs. He taught her how to do the simple stuff that didn't involve sharp tools, and together they built a birdhouse, of which Jess was prouder than if it were an actual house where people lived. Sometimes he and Frannie took the girls on outings, and once he'd taken them to visit the veterans' care home where he volunteered. They'd returned home agog from the tales told to them by the old-timers they'd met.

Life at the house on Mountain Laurel Lane settled into a normal routine, or what passed for normal these days. Workwise, Jo was busy with all the bookings packed into the last days of summer before the weather turned too cool for outdoor weddings. Before she knew it, Labor Day weekend was upon her. On Friday of that week, she flew from Sacramento to Houston with the girls, arriving at lunchtime.

"There you are, the three loveliest ladies in all of Houston!" declared her dad when he met them at the airport. Jo was glad to see him, and the girls were ecstatic. After collecting their baggage, they trudged through the hot soup that was summer in Texas in passing from the air-conditioned terminal to her dad's air-conditioned Mercedes.

"Thanks for coming to get us," she told her dad as they cruised the southbound lane of 288 en route to Fairview. "You didn't have to."

"It's no bother. Besides, I never would've heard the end of it from your mom if I'd left you stranded at the airport."

"We could've taken an Uber. I know it's the middle of your workday."

"Nothing's more important than spending time with my girls. Your mom and I are thrilled you came, honey bear." Jo felt guilty, hearing him call her by her pet name, for suspecting her parents of having an ulterior motive in persuading her to come. "Girls, we have some fun things planned for this weekend," he called to Jess and Emma in the back seat.

"Can we go to the Lego store?" asked Emma.

"You bet. I'll take you there tomorrow while your mom and grandma are shopping. I thought we'd do the aquarium afterward. Remember the last time, when we went through the shark tunnel?"

"Yes, but maybe we could skip the shark tunnel this time," said Jess nervously.

"Not a fan of sharks, are you? Neither am I, between you and me," he said.

Soon they arrived at the gated entrance to Fairview. Her dad punched in the gate code and then they were crawling through the familiar streets of the planned community, where the speed limit of fifteen miles per hour was enforced by speed bumps installed every fifty feet or so. The effect was that of sailing a gently rolling sea. The homes they passed were built on a grand scale in one of three styles—Cape Cod, Colonial, or Tudor—each painted in HOA-approved colors and surrounded by beautifully landscaped grounds. Jo's childhood home was one of the Colonials, painted white with black trim. Its porticoed entrance was flanked by a square column on either side. Rows of multipaned windows with exterior shutters stretched up three stories. Mature oaks dotted the manicured grounds, through which wound gravel paths bordered by lush flower beds. Stepping inside, Jo was assailed by the aroma of fresh-cut flowers and delicious cooking smells.

"You're just in time." Jo's mom appeared to greet them. "Juana is serving lunch on the patio. Girls, go wash up." Jess and Emma scampered toward the powder room off the front hallway, while Jo's dad carried their luggage upstairs to the guestrooms.

They ate lunch on the covered patio overlooking the swimming pool and guesthouse beyond, gazpacho and spinach quiche for the adults, tuna salad sandwiches and potato chips for the girls, served with the obligatory pitcher of sweet tea. Jo complimented Juana, her parents' housekeeper, on the meal when she came to clear the table. A sturdy-looking woman in her late fifties with graying dark hair, she'd worked for Jo's parents for the past decade and prepared most of their meals.

"Tomorrow after breakfast we'll all head over to the Galleria," Jo's mom announced while they were eating dessert, homemade lemon sorbet served on half of a lemon rind with its pulp removed. "Dad can take the girls shopping while you and I shop for a dress for the dinner-dance," she said to Jo.

Jo couldn't think of anything she'd enjoy less than browsing the shops at Houston's super mall with her mom, trying on formal wear, but she remembered her resolve to be a better daughter and said, "Sounds like a plan."

The next day she was feeling considerably less agreeable after she'd tried on half a dozen dresses at the Ooh La La boutique, their first stop in the Galleria, during which her mom had provided running commentary from her seat in the changing room.

"Not that one—pink washes you out."

"Red is not your color, dear."

"Ugh, no, take it off at once. You look positively funereal in black."

"Green is a good color for you, but the cut of that dress does nothing for your figure."

"How about this one?" Jo asked as she modeled the one dress she'd picked out. Knee-length with cap sleeves and a flared hem, it was made of silk fabric in teal blue that flowed over her body like poured water.

Her mom narrowed her eyes in an assessing gaze. "It suits you, but I'm afraid it won't do."

"Why not?"

"Everyone knows you don't wear semiformal to a formal affair."

"I like it."

Her mom sighed. "I suppose you could make it work with the right jewelry, if you do something with your hair."

"I didn't bring any jewelry."

"You can wear something of mine."

Jo's mom insisted on buying her the dress, and once Jo saw the price tag, she didn't object. She couldn't have afforded it. Afterward, they took the escalator to the next level down to look for a pair of heels to go with the dress. They were passing through the cosmetics department at Nordstrom on their way to the shoe department when her mom came to a halt. "You know what you need," she said, eyeing a saleswoman who was brushing powder over a customer's face. "A makeover."

Jo was opening her mouth to say enough was enough but was stopped by the look of eager anticipation on her mom's face. She'd been denied the mother-daughter experience most moms get to have when their daughters go to their proms. Why spoil today's experience for her when it was obviously giving her pleasure? Instead, she said, "I'll pass, but I wouldn't say no to a mani-pedi."

Her mom smiled and tucked her arm through Jo's as they continued. "I know just the place, and we don't need an appointment. Wait until you see what they can do with acrylics."

That evening when she kissed the girls goodbye, they were so busy with the Lego sets their grandpa had bought them, they scarcely noticed she was leaving. Besides, they knew and loved Juana, who'd be taking care of them while Jo was out. Ten minutes later she was arriving at the Fairview Country Club with her parents, in her new dress and the shoes her mom had bought her to go with it, a pair of silver-and-gold sandal heels that showed her blue-painted toenails, which matched her fingernails. Her hair was pulled back in a sleek bun. Her jewelry consisted of sapphire drop earrings and a matching necklace on loan from her mom.

Jo's mom was resplendent tonight in an off-the-shoulder, full-length ivory chiffon gown that floated around her ankles as she moved, her champagne-blond hair styled in an upsweep. Her dad looked like the lead actor in a forties movie, whom you'd expect to see zipping around in a roadster or mixing martinis in a silver cocktail shaker. "How lucky am I to be escorting the two most beautiful women here?" he said as he entered with his wife on one arm and his daughter on the other.

Jo's mom tilted her head coquettishly at him. Jo blew him a kiss. "Love you, too, Dad."

The Fairview Golf and Country Club was housed in a stately two-story built in the style of the Texas White House, as the LBJ homestead was known, with white clapboard siding and wooden shutters, painted the blue of the US flag that flew outside. It boasted a covered balcony, where club members could relax and take the air as they enjoyed a sweet tea or a mint julep while gazing out at the golf green it overlooked. As she made her way through the building, it was slow going, with her parents pausing frequently to greet fellow club members and make introductions in passing. It seemed an eternity before they exited onto the terrace at the rear, where the cocktail hour was in full swing.

Outside, the temperature was in the mid-seventies but felt cool after the day's triple-digit high. The fairy lights strung around the perimeter and Japanese lanterns suspended overhead cast a warm glow in the darkness. Servers circulated with trays of drinks and canapés while women in floor-length gowns and men in formal jackets chatted in small groups. The air was scented with honeysuckle, which grew along the back wall of the terrace. Through the row of French doors to the dining room, Jo could see red-jacketed waiters putting the finishing touches on the table settings in preparation for the dinner-dance portion of the evening.

Jo snagged a flute of champagne from a passing tray before she was dragged over to meet a group of people, an older couple chatting with a younger man across the terrace. "Jo, honey, you remember our dear friends Duke and Sissy Wheatleigh," prompted Jo's mom when they reached the group. "And this is their son, Trevor, who I believe you've also met." She gestured toward the younger man, who looked vaguely familiar, as did his parents. He gave her a cold look.

Dude, what's your problem?

Then it came to her: He was the boy with the two left feet and roaming hands who she'd danced with at the dinner-dance she'd attended here when they were both fifteen, grown up. With his wavy brown hair that curled over the tops of his ears and piercing gray eyes beneath thick black brows, he resembled the dark-and-brooding hero of a gothic novel. Mr. Rochester in *Jane Eyre*. Frankly, she'd never seen the appeal. Jane was welcome to him.

"You," she blurted out.

Recognition flared in his eyes. "We've met," he said tersely to no one in particular.

"Jo, the last time we saw you, you were just a slip of a girl," drawled Sissy. "And look at you now, all grown up and prettier than ever. Why, you're the spitting image of your mama."

Jo acknowledged the compliment with a smile. She didn't consider herself beautiful, not like her mother, who'd been a true beauty in her youth, but to demur would only have called attention to herself.

"Jo's visiting for the weekend with her daughters," Jo's dad said. "She calls California home these days, but she'll always be a Southern girl at heart." He put his arm around her shoulders, beaming.

"Trevor's a doctor," her mom informed her. She turned to him. "Orthopedics, isn't it?" He nodded, expressionless.

"Best bone doc in all of Harris County," boasted Duke, who resembled his son, only heavier and with gray hair and jowls. "He's in a group practice in Houston. Me and the missus are awful proud of our boy, and awful glad to have him back home where he belongs. We missed him while he was away during his internship and residency." He gave Trevor a hearty clap on the back. Trevor winced.

Sissy was a head shorter than her husband, even with her teased silver coif adding several inches to her height. Thick around the middle with thin arms and legs, she resembled a ladybug in her red gown sewn with jet beads. "Too bad our older son and daughter couldn't join us tonight," she said. "They had family commitments. Trevor's the only one of our brood who isn't married."

Trevor suddenly looked like he'd bit into something sour.

"How's retirement treating you, Duke?" Jo's dad asked.

"I'm busier than ever, although none of it's making me any money," Duke reported. "But that's why I busted my butt working all those years, so I could retire while I was still young enough to enjoy life." He looked at Jo, his expression sobering. "Me and Sissy were real sorry to hear about your husband. Damn shame, young fella like him."

"Such a tragedy." Sissy reached over and squeezed Jo's hand.

At the expressions of sympathy, Jo's grief, which ran like an underground spring below her surface, bubbled up. She blinked back tears. "I'm sorry for your loss," she heard a soft voice say beside her. She was surprised to see that it was Trevor who'd spoken. He'd sounded almost human.

"Thank you," she murmured.

After she was pulled away to meet other friends of her parents, Jo thought she'd seen the last of Trevor Wheatleigh. Until dinner, when she arrived with her parents at their assigned table and found herself seated next to him. Her heart sank. It was no coincidence, she was certain. Suddenly, it all made perfect sense: her parents' odd behavior when they'd visited and their eagerness to have her attend this dinner-dance. They hadn't given up on luring her back to Texas, it seemed; they'd merely resorted to devious tactics where persuasion had failed. By setting her up with a doctor who practiced in Houston and who'd give her a reason to relocate if they were to fall in love and marry. She glared at her parents across the table, which they either didn't notice or chose to ignore.

Trevor appeared no happier about it than she. But, unlike him, she at least made an effort to engage him in conversation during dinner, if only because it was easier than shouting to be heard by the elderly man seated to her left, who was hard of hearing. Trevor seemed distracted and not the least bit interested in getting to know her, though he scored points when he revealed that he volunteered for Doctors Without Borders. By the time the dessert course was served, she'd had enough.

"Are you always this rude?" she asked when they were alone. The others at their table had drifted onto the dance floor when the band had struck up, even her hearing-impaired seatmate, who was dancing with his wife.

"What?" Trevor looked up from his phone, blinking as if to bring her into focus.

"You've barely said a word to me all evening. What's your problem?"

"I wasn't aware there was a problem."

"So this is how you normally behave? Or is it because you're embarrassed?"

"Embarrassed?"

"The last time I saw you, you were trying to cop a feel when you weren't stepping on my toes."

His face reddened. "I don't know what you're talking about."

"Seriously? You don't remember dancing with me?"

"Jesus. We were teenagers, and it was one dance."

"Ha. So you do remember."

His face turned even redder. "Yes. But if I stepped on your toes while we were dancing, it was unintentional, and I assure you I wasn't trying to cop a feel." He lowered his voice. "It was actually my not-so-subtle attempt to wipe the sweat from my palms without you noticing. I suffered from excessive sweating as a teenager."

"That's your excuse?"

"Girls made me nervous. They still do," he admitted, his expression somewhere between a smile and a grimace.

"Women, you mean. Unless you like them young."

He groaned. "Give me a break. I'm trying here, and I'm sorry for any distress I caused you in the past."

"I accept your apology, but it doesn't excuse your being a dick tonight."

"That I own. I was mad at my parents and took it out on you."

"Why were you mad at them?"

"Because I'm fed up with their meddling. Tonight was the last straw."

"Ah. So my parents weren't acting alone."

"In tonight's matchmaking? No. I'd bet a paycheck mine are in on it, too. I suspected they were up to something when we were introduced earlier. When I saw we were seated next to each other, it confirmed my suspicion. This isn't the first time I was roped into going to one of these functions only to find myself seated next to the one other person at the table who was both single and below the age of sixty."

"A female person, presumably."

"Right. My folks won't rest until all their children are married. I'm the last holdout."

She ate the maraschino cherry from her chocolate mousse and spooned some of the whipped-cream topping into her mouth. "Mine had hoped I'd stay here and marry a local boy. Instead I moved to California, where I met my husband. They haven't given up on their dream, though, and now that my husband is gone . . ." She swallowed. "They want to look after me."

"You don't seem like you need looking after."

"I don't, but I suppose to them I'll always be their little girl. They also want to see more of their grandchildren."

"How many children do you have?"

She softened toward him. It was the first sign of interest he'd shown in her all evening. Maybe he wasn't irredeemable. "Two, both girls, ages seven and five." She pulled out her phone. "That's Jess, my big one." She showed him a picture of a gap-toothed Jess that was taken just after she lost her first tooth before scrolling down to a photo of Emma in her ballerina costume. "And this is Emma."

"She looks just like you," he said, studying the photo of Emma.

"I get that a lot. Jess takes after her dad."

"I'd like to meet them sometime."

She raised an eyebrow at him. "Why, Dr. Wheatleigh, are you proposing that we meet again?"

"What I'd like is a do-over. Do you think that's possible?" With his eyes dancing and his mouth curved in a smile, he looked like a different person from his dark-and-brooding persona of earlier.

"I don't know. It may be too late for that."

"Please accept my sincere apology, then. You're right. I behaved abominably tonight, and if you never want to see me again, it'd serve me right. But I'm hoping you'll give me another chance."

"Well . . ."

Before she could answer, Trevor stood and extended his arm toward her as the band, a four-piece pop ensemble aptly named the Silver Tones in keeping with the average age of its members, segued from a lively fox trot to a slow waltz number. "Jo, may I have this dance?"

Trevor's dancing had improved over the years, Jo was relieved to discover. They danced several more dances before she whispered, "We'd better sit the next one out, or they'll get ideas." His and her parents were no doubt congratulating themselves on what they imagined to be a successful match, from the approving looks they were giving her and Trevor. He nodded, and they returned to their seats, where they chatted until the band stopped playing and it was time to go. She didn't expect to see him again and was surprised when he asked if she was free for lunch the next day. She was even more surprised to hear herself say yes.

"But our parents can't know," she cautioned him.

"Roger that," he agreed with a conspiratorial wink.

They met for lunch on Sunday at Gennaro's, a cozy trattoria a block from his medical practice in a mixed residential-commercial section of Houston, where Trevor had made a reservation. "What excuse did you give for leaving the house today?" he asked as they ate their shared appetizer of steamed mussels.

"I said I had to shop for a birthday present for my mom—she has a birthday coming up. So I need to hit the mall after lunch to back up my cover story." She'd noticed an outdoor mall down the street. "I also promised to bring something back for my girls. They weren't happy that I went without them."

"I'll come with." He pried a mussel from its shell with his fork and ate it. Today, wearing jeans and a quarter-zip pullover, loafers without socks, with his body language relaxed and his features animated, he looked like a different person from the coldly distant man she'd encountered last night.

"I don't know if that's such a good idea. Someone might see us."

"In this neighborhood? It's off the beaten track, miles from Fairview. Why do you think I chose this restaurant?"

"Good thinking. It's bad enough my parents saw us dancing last night. If they knew we were having lunch today, they'd have us engaged already."

"Mine would be booking the church."

She paused as she was dipping a piece of garlic toast into the mussel broth, fixing him with a stern look. "Seriously, you can't breathe a word to them. If you do, I might have to kill you."

"Or marry me," he teased.

"Ha."

A memory from her wedding day surfaced, causing her to smile even as it brought a throb of loss. When the minister asked, "Sean Joseph Myers, do you take this woman as your lawful wedded wife?" Sean had answered, in a voice loud enough to carry into the rafters of the old church, "I DO!"

Now that same voice whispered, *He seems nice.*

Now. But what about last night? We didn't get off to a good start.

Neither did we, if you recall.

The difference is, we were meant for each other.

Or maybe you think that because you know how our story ends.

Our story ended with you dying.

Yes, but the story of the rest of your life is just beginning.

Jo couldn't imagine ever falling in love again, much less remarrying. Another man would suffer by comparison. She recalled something Len, the director of her grief group, had said on the subject of dating again after the death of one's spouse: *"If you don't get out of your head, you'll trip over your own feet before you've taken the first step."* She made a conscious effort to be in the moment. To not overthink it.

"My lips are sealed," Trevor vowed. "Although, if we keep on seeing each other, our parents are bound to find out eventually."

Jo didn't know how that would even work with her living in California and him living in Texas. They both had demanding careers, and she was a mom. "We'll cross that bridge when we get to it."

After they finished their appetizer, their server brought their main courses. Trevor had ordered the pasta a la Norma and she the crab ravioli, which was delicious. After they ate and Trevor paid the bill, they headed for the mall down the street, where they strolled its sheltered walkways lined with shops. At a Sunglass Hut, she bought a pair of sunglasses to replace the pair she'd misplaced on this trip, and a souvenir T-shirt for each of the girls. Next stop was a kiosk that sold imported handcrafted jewelry, where she found a pretty amethyst pendant on a silver chain for her mom that was affordable.

"So how do you see this working?" Trevor asked as they were crossing the plaza in the center of the mall. "Us," he clarified when she shot him a quizzical look. "I'd like to see you again, in case I didn't make myself clear."

She didn't know how to respond. She liked Trevor, but would it be fair to lead him on, given her situation and how conflicted she was? "It hasn't been that long since I lost my husband." Or at least that was how it seemed. "Today was . . . lovely, but to be honest, I don't know that I'm ready to date."

He looked disappointed but was cool about it. "I've never been in your shoes, so I can only imagine. And the last thing I want to do is pressure you. If you decide to give it a shot, you have my number."

"Yes, and thank you for understanding."

"Of course." He paused as they were passing an Amorino gelateria. "Fancy a gelato?"

"Sure, but only if you let me pay," she said. "You treated me to lunch."

"Did you know 'Amorino' is the Italian word for Cupid?" he asked when they were seated on a shaded bench in the plaza overlooking its splashing fountain, eating their gelato.

"No. You speak Italian?"

"Just enough to get me in trouble. I was a nerd in high school, in case you haven't already guessed. I took an Italian class because I thought it'd make me seem cool and impress the ladies."

"How'd that work for you?"

"Not good. I accidentally called this girl I was chatting up at a party a *puta*, which means 'whore' in Italian. She was insulted and stormed off. That was the end of my career as a Casanova."

Jo laughed. She noticed he ate his scoop as Sean had been in the habit of doing, licking from side to side while rotating the cone, rather than from bottom to top. She wondered if it was a sign.

"What do you like most about being a photographer?" he asked.

"Capturing images that tell a story. The best ones give you a peek into the lives of their subjects or depict an object or landscape in an unusual way. Like Dorothea Lange's photos of migrant workers and Ansel Adams's landscapes. Not that I'm in the same league as them, but I aspire to be, and sometimes I can make magic." She recalled the thrill of seeing the world through the viewfinder of her camera for the first time when she was thirteen. If only she could recapture that joy, which had eluded her since Sean's death. "Why did you decide to become a doctor?"

He shrugged. "I never wanted to be anything else."

"Same here."

"Another thing we have in common besides our meddling parents. We both knew from a young age what we wanted to be when we grew up."

"Except I bet you were encouraged to pursue your dream, while my parents did everything they could to discourage my photography. Once they realized it wasn't just a hobby, they tried to steer me toward a more 'productive' career path. Dad urged me to get a business degree as a backup plan. Mom believes women should have careers, but only until they marry and become stay-at-home moms."

"I'm glad you didn't listen to them. I took a look at your website. You're a good photographer, Jo. Maybe even a great one. I'm no expert, by any means, but I was impressed by your work."

She warmed at his compliment. "Thank you. That's nice of you to say."

"I'm not saying it to be nice. I mean it—you have a gift. As for my parents, as much as they love boasting about their son the doctor, they'd love it even more if I had a wife and children."

"Is that why you're still single at your advanced age? To spite your parents?" she teased.

He laughed. "Actually, it's not by choice."

"Or from lack of opportunity."

"I don't count my parents' matchmaking attempts. Apart from last night's." He cut her a meaningful glance that caused her to squirm. "The truth is, I'd like to get married and have a family someday."

"Ever been in a serious relationship?"

"One or two, but while I was in med school and during my internship and residency, I was focused on my studies and work. It's only now that I'm in a group practice that I have time for a social life. You caught me on the upswing."

She smiled but didn't comment.

After they finished their gelato, he walked with her to where her car was parked. She was driving her mom's Mercedes today while her mom stayed home with the girls. "When do you go back to California?" he asked.

"Tomorrow."

She saw a flash of disappointment in his eyes, but he hid it well, keeping his tone light as he replied, "I guess our secret is safe, then. For now."

"Thanks for lunch. It's been fun," she told him when she reached her car.

"Hopefully, I'm forgiven for my bad behavior last night."

"You are. I also forgive you your transgressions as a teenager."

"I didn't grope you. I only fantasized about it."

"Oh my God." She stared at him. "Seriously?"

He shrugged. "I was fifteen. Sex is the only thing teenage boys think about. I would've kissed you, but you probably would've slugged me if I had."

"Damn right."

His amused expression gave way to a serious one. "Would it be okay if I kissed you now?"

Jo hesitated, remembering how she'd reacted the last time she'd been kissed. But she'd been caught off guard. And Trevor wasn't Scott. She might not mind. She might even like it. Swallowing her reservations, she nodded, and he moved in. She tensed slightly as his mouth closed over hers, then surrendered to the kiss when she didn't go into automatic freak-out mode. His lips were warm and soft, and thankfully there was no tongue involved. She even felt a tingle . . . of something.

She wondered if there was room for him in her heart, which still belonged to Sean.

18

Jess and Emma were both buzzing from excitement and the pancakes they'd eaten for breakfast, drowned in maple syrup, when Jo's dad dropped Jo and the girls off at the airport the next morning. Jo could hardly contain them as they made their way through the terminal to their gate. When they weren't running ahead of her, they were either peppering her with questions or plying her with requests.

"Mommy, can we go for a ride?" Emma pointed to one of the airport's electric carts as it whizzed past, carrying a pair of elderly passengers.

"No, sweetie," Jo told her. "That's just for people who can't walk very fast and need help getting around."

"I can't walk fast. My legs are short."

"Yes, but you can run."

"Mommy, can I have a hot chocolate?" asked Jess while they stood in line at a Starbucks, where Jo had stopped to get a coffee.

"You've had enough sugar for one day," Jo told her.

"Nuh-uh."

"What about the pancakes you ate for breakfast?"

"But I'm *thirsty*."

"I'll get you a water."

Jo sank into an empty seat with a sigh of relief when they finally reached their gate. Once she'd gotten the girls settled with the coloring books and crayons she'd packed, she was able to drink her coffee in peace. She'd slept fitfully the night before and was tired today. At one point she'd dreamed she was dancing with Trevor, only to discover when the music stopped playing that her dance partner was Sean. She'd woken with a start and had trouble getting back to sleep afterward.

Their flight was delayed, as luck would have it. It was lunchtime by the time they boarded. On the plane, they ate the bagged lunches that Juana had prepared for them. They landed in Sacramento shortly after three, and it was another thirty minutes before they collected their baggage and made their way to her car in the extended parking lot. It was 5:12 when she crossed the town line into Gold Creek ninety minutes later. The day was sunny, with a mild breeze blowing, which carried the faint scent of smoke. It'd been the driest summer in recent memory. Passing the forest ranger's station on 49, she noticed the arrow on the color wheel of the wooden sign posted outside, which indicated the current fire danger was in the red zone, the highest threat level.

Here in Washburn County they were never more than a dry lightning strike, an unattended campfire, or a kid playing with matches from a fire outbreak during the dry season. Several wildfires had broken out in recent weeks. Fortunately, they'd been contained before widespread damage was done, but everyone remained on alert, knowing the next one could spread out of control, like the Caldor fire of five years ago that had consumed over 600,000 acres of timberland and caused the evacuation of more than one community and, most recently, the fires in LA.

Jo was greeted by the sight of Hank mowing the lawn and Snickers lazing in the shade of the porch, her graying muzzle resting on her forepaws, when she pulled into her driveway. It was good to be home. Hank waved to them and cut the engine on the mower before he started toward them. Snickers climbed down from the porch, her tail waving.

"Hank, look what I got!" Jess showed him her new smartwatch, which was just one piece of her loot from the shopping spree her grandfather had taken her and Emma on. He'd bought a bike for Emma, which was being shipped to their address. "It has GPS and everything!"

Jo wished her dad had consulted her before buying the girls expensive gifts, but seeing Jess's beaming face, she couldn't be too annoyed at him for spoiling them.

"Fancy." Hank admired the watch. "Now if you ever get lost, you can always find your way back home."

"I won't get lost," Jess said. "But if I did, I wouldn't be scared."

Jo had never expected to hear those words come out of Jess's mouth. She continued to be amazed by the strides Jess was making in her therapy. And maybe their change of circumstances had something to do with it, too. Jess had adapted to her home, and Hank had become a friend and father figure. She might never be as adventurous as Emma, but she'd become more open to new experiences. She was processing her grief, according to Dr. Shaw.

"Hank, did you remember to feed Homer?" asked Emma. Homer was the pet goldfish Jo had gotten her in lieu of the kitten she'd begged for. After Jo explained that she couldn't afford another pet that would cost money to feed and incur vet bills, or that would shed all over the rugs and furniture, Emma had been okay with it. Hank had been in charge of Homer while they were away.

"I sure did," he said. "And I'm happy to report he's full of beans."

Emma's eyes grew wide. "You fed him *beans*?"

He chuckled and tweaked her nose. "Figure of speech. It's another way of saying he's perky as ever."

"We don't know that it's a 'he.' It could be a girl," said Jess in her know-it-all voice. When Jo had offered to get her a goldfish, too, she'd declined. She was holding out for an aquarium stocked with tropical fish, like the one in Dr. Shaw's office. Jo suspected she was regretting that decision.

"Is not," protested Emma.

Jess turned to Hank. "Hank, how can you tell if a fish is a boy or a girl?"

He scratched his head bemusedly before answering, "Well, I'm no expert, but Homer strikes me as a bit of a show-off, like most boys, so I'm guessing a name change won't be in order."

"Good answer," Jo said after the girls had gone inside carrying their backpacks, which were stuffed with more loot from their trip. Hank was helping her unload the suitcases from the trunk.

"I'll leave the birds-and-the-bees lecture to you," he said as they wheeled the suitcases up the driveway.

"Jess already knows the facts of life. I had to tell her how babies are made after a boy in her class told her babies were 'pooped out' and she asked me if it was true. Minus the details, of course. Please God, may the day I'll need to talk to her about birth control not come anytime soon." It was yet another painful reminder that she was on her own, without Sean to help with the hard conversations.

"They don't stay innocent for long, do they?"

"No." Her children had already learned the hardest fact of life when they'd lost their dad.

They were growing up too fast. Jess would be in third grade and Emma in kindergarten when school started in the fall, a week from today. It seemed like only yesterday they'd been in diapers and onesies, crawling before they learned to walk. One day in the not-too-distant future, they'd both be grown.

Jo pushed aside the gloomy thought. As she entered, dragging her suitcase over the threshold, she was met by delicious cooking smells. "Something sure smells good. What are you making?"

"Shrimp and grits," called a familiar voice.

Frannie emerged from the kitchen, wearing an apron over shorts and a T-shirt. "I figured you'd be too tired to cook after your travels, so I made supper."

Jo grinned at her. "I can't think of anything nicer than coming home to a home-cooked meal, especially your shrimp and grits." Frannie was welcome anytime, not just because she was Hank's guest and a good friend, but because she was a better cook than either of them. She'd learned to cook from her grandmother CeCe, and many of the Creole dishes she was known for had been passed down from one generation to the next in her family. "My mouth is watering already."

"How was your visit with your folks?" asked Hank when the adults were in the kitchen, him peeling the shrimp while Frannie stirred the grits on the stove and Jo made a green salad, and the children in their room. Jo had last seen Emma conducting a one-sided conversation with Homer. Jess was with her new best friend Shoshanna, who'd shown up within minutes of their arrival.

"Not what I expected," Jo said.

"Which part?" asked Frannie.

"Remember the boy I told you about? The one I danced with at the dinner-dance I went to when I was fifteen?"

"The one who stepped on your toes and had more arms than an octopus?"

"The very one. He was my seatmate at last Saturday's dinner-dance. Not by coincidence, either."

"It was a setup?" Hank guessed correctly.

"Yep. We were both blindsided."

Frannie sampled the grits and added a pinch of salt. "Has he improved with age?"

"I didn't think so at first, but he turned out to be a nice guy. He claims he didn't try to grope me when we were teenagers. He allegedly suffered from excessive sweating back then. He was hoping I wouldn't notice his sweaty palms if he didn't keep his hands in any one spot on my body for very long."

"Oh my." Frannie smothered a laugh.

"Nothing more brutal than a boy trying to impress a girl and doing the opposite," said Hank.

"Are you speaking from experience?" Frannie asked him.

"I was hopeless as a teenager," he confirmed.

"You've improved with age, too." Frannie leaned sideways to give Hank a one-armed hug. They exchanged an affectionate look.

"So your evening wasn't a total bust?" Hank asked Jo.

"No. That was the most surprising part." After swearing them to secrecy, Jo told them about her lunch date with Trevor the next day, leaving out only the part about them kissing. "Our parents would be planning a wedding if they knew. I don't want the girls to know, either. Unless there's something to know," she added.

"Do you plan on seeing him again?" Frannie asked.

"I don't know. I haven't decided." Jo felt her stomach flip. Trevor had made his intentions known. Now the ball was in her court. "I like him, but I don't know if I'm ready for anything more than friendship. Besides, everybody knows long-distance relationships don't work."

"Someone should tell that to Marisol," said Frannie dryly. Marisol and her boyfriend, Cal, were still going strong, despite their temporary separation while he was doing his postgrad at NYU.

Jo remembered feeling tingly when Trevor kissed her. But while it was good to know her hibernating libido had emerged from its long winter's sleep, she still couldn't see herself in a relationship.

She changed the subject. "What did you two get up to while I was away?"

"She wants to know if you slept over," Hank said to Frannie, his face creased with amusement.

"I'll have you know we boomers were doing it long before your generation thought they invented it," said Frannie with a toss of her curly silver head. "And that's all I'm saying on the subject."

Jo didn't need to know the details. The glow in her friend's cheeks and sparkle in her eyes said it all. Her vision blurred and she felt something twist in her chest, remembering when she'd been on cloud nine, madly in love with Sean. A love that hadn't always been carefree but had sustained through the years they were together. The last words they'd spoken to one another were "I love you."

"Hello, Emma. My name is Miss Morales, and I'm very glad to meet you."

Somewhere in her mid-twenties, bright-eyed, with brown hair she wore in a ponytail, Emma's teacher didn't look old enough to be a qualified teacher. Jo was seized with anxiety. How could she entrust her baby to someone who was a mere child herself?

Becoming aware that she was holding Emma's hand too tightly, Jo loosened her grip. Emma was excited to start kindergarten. So why was Jo having such a hard time with it?

"I'm five and a half!" Emma announced. She wore one of the outfits her grandma had bought for her during their recent visit, a pink jumper and kelly-green jersey with elephants on it and ruffled sleeves. "I didn't get to go to kindergarten last year, but I'm a big girl now."

Emma had a birthday coming up, so technically she'd been eligible to enroll in kindergarten last year at this time. Jo had decided to hold off for a year, however, because Emma had still been dealing with her dad's death. She seemed to have bounced back since then. She sucked her thumb only occasionally now, and it'd been weeks since she'd last wet the bed or had a bathroom accident.

Now they stood outside the kindergarten classroom where Miss Morales was greeting the arriving students and their parents. The teacher smiled at Emma. "You certainly are, and I'm delighted to have you in my class. I have so many fun things planned for this year. Now, why don't you go inside? Miss Tori will show you where your cubby is and you can meet the other children."

Jo hugged her goodbye, and Emma disappeared into the classroom without a backward glance. Jo felt like crying, watching her go. Shouldn't it be the other way around? Why was she experiencing separation anxiety when Emma clearly had no problem being apart from her? And why now? She hadn't felt this way seeing her youngest off to camp with Jess every day this past summer.

"I'm sorry. I didn't expect to get this emotional," she apologized as she brushed away a tear.

"Believe me, you're not the first parent to get the weepies on their child's first day of kindergarten," said Miss Morales. "Happens all the time. Last year, one of the moms refused to leave. She waited outside the classroom, in case her son needed her."

"Did he?"

"No. He told her it was okay to leave, in fact."

Obviously, this wasn't Miss Morales's first year teaching, despite her youthful appearance. Jo felt a little better, discovering she wasn't a newbie. "I wasn't like this with my older daughter." Maybe because Sean had been there helping to calm Jess when she'd had a meltdown on her first day of kindergarten. Although she'd seemed fine today when Jo had dropped her off at her classroom. The fact that her friend Shoshanna was in her third grade class had something to do with it, she suspected.

"Emma's your youngest?"

"How can you tell?"

"It's harder when it's your baby, from what I've observed."

"I just didn't expect it to be this hard."

"If it's any consolation, Emma should have no problem adjusting. She seems like a great kid."

"She's amazing." Jo handed her the paper sack she carried, with Emma's name written on it in Magic Marker, that contained a change of clothing. "Just in case. She doesn't always make it to the bathroom in time."

The teacher thanked her and said, "I'll put it in her cubby."

Jo thought there was a good chance Emma wouldn't need it. The change of clothing Jo had left for her at Little Explorers had been returned, unworn, on the last day of camp at the end of summer. But you never knew. "It's just . . . I wouldn't want her to be embarrassed."

"We do our best to make sure that doesn't happen. When one of the children has an accident, it's no big deal. We usually have them cleaned up and in dry clothes before anyone even notices."

"Good to know."

Jo fought back tears as she made her way to the exit. She stayed busy after she got home to keep her mommy blues at bay. She did the breakfast dishes, started a load of laundry, and vacuumed. She spent the rest of the morning removing the remaining wallpaper in the dining nook. After lunch she worked in her office until 2:45, then left to go pick the girls up from school. After today, they'd take the school bus, but she wanted to be there to meet them on their first day. She arrived shortly before the last bell rang and children began pouring from the building.

On the drive home, Emma chattered excitedly about all the fun things she'd done in class. Jess was less animated, but at least she wasn't glum. She reported that she liked her teacher but hadn't made any new friends. "It's okay, though," she said. "I played with Shoshanna during recess."

"All you need is one friend," Jo agreed.

Of which she was reminded that night when she gave up on getting any sleep after tossing and turning for hours. She switched on her bedside lamp, eyeing her phone, in its charger on her nightstand. She wished there were someone she could call, but who would be awake at this hour? It was past midnight. Then she remembered something Ian had said. *I'm the friend who's awake when the friends who might be your first call are asleep.* Before she knew it, she was picking up her phone.

He answered on the second ring. "Jo! What a pleasant surprise."

"Is this a bad time?"

"No. I'm on duty, but we're practicing simulated flights right now, so it's safe for me to step away for a minute. No one will die if their plane goes down," he assured her. "What's up? Everything okay?"

"Nothing bad happened. It's just—" She broke off with a choked sound.

"Talk to me." His voice was as comforting as a glass of warm milk. Tears welled in her eyes.

"Today was Emma's first day of kindergarten."

She expected to hear him say what she'd been telling herself. *It's kindergarten, not college. You'll still see her every day when she's not in school.* Instead, he said the exact right thing. "Big day."

"Yeah." She let out a shaky breath. "She loves being in school. It's me who's a hot mess."

"You're a mom," he corrected her. "It's normal to have separation anxiety, I would imagine."

"My case might be more extreme than most."

"Everyone's different. And your situation is . . ."

"An emotional minefield," she filled in. She gazed at the empty side of the bed, her heart aching. "That's part of it."

"You're also sending your child out into the world, entrusting her to be taught by other adults whose opinions you may not share and exposing her to kids who might be mean to her."

"Right." He'd hit the nail on the head. "You sure know a lot for someone who doesn't have kids."

"I learned from my mom. She's an OR nurse. She deals with life-and-death situations every day at work, but she told me being a parent was the hardest job she's ever done. On my first day of kindergarten, she allegedly binge-watched home movies while eating a tub of ice cream."

"Wow. And I thought I had it bad. Although if this is a preview of what's to come when I'm facing an empty nest, I'll need to stock up on ice cream in advance. And tissues," she added, plucking one from the box on her nightstand.

"You have a few years before then."

"When my girls were babies, I thought this day would never come."

"By the time you're an empty nester, you'll be in a different place in your life than you are now."

"I'll always want them near, no matter what." It occurred to her she wasn't so different from her mom in that regard. Growing up, when she'd been pushing her mom away in establishing her independence, she'd been breaking her heart without being aware of it. She felt new sympathy for her.

"Sure, but if you were with someone, maybe your nest wouldn't seem so empty."

She blew her nose into the tissue. "I don't see that happening."

"Why not?"

"I'd feel like I was being disloyal to my husband. I know it makes no sense, but I can't help how I feel."

"My mom said the same thing about my dad, and he's been dead for over thirty years."

"She didn't date after he died?"

"Not that I know of. She may have had the occasional lover, but if she did, she kept it on the DL."

"I haven't ruled out the possibility of . . . companionship."

"Hypothetically, or do you have someone in mind?"

She hesitated before answering, "I met someone."

She heard a low whistle at the other end. "Wow. This is a major development."

"His name's Trevor. His parents and mine are old friends. We met at a dinner-dance at their club when I was visiting over Labor Day weekend. Or rather, we became reacquainted—we'd met once before when we were teenagers. He took me out to lunch the next day."

"How was it left?"

"He wants to see me again."

"How do you feel about it?"

She sighed. "I don't know. It's complicated. I'm not sure if I'm ready to date."

"Maybe it'd be easier if you were in a long-distance relationship than if you were seeing someone on a regular basis. You could take it slow."

"I hadn't considered that aspect."

"Food for thought, anyway."

Jo was feeling better by the time she ended the call. Whatever she decided in regard to Trevor, a friendly voice in the dark was just what she'd needed tonight. She had no trouble getting to sleep after that.

She awakened the next morning with a clear head and renewed vigor. The girls were still asleep and the house quiet, except for the padding of her footsteps and clicking of her dog's toenails against the floor as Snickers followed her down the hall. After letting the dog out to do her business, she started the coffee. While she waited for it to brew, she sent Trevor a text. Thinking of you.

19

Over the next couple of weeks, Jo and Trevor fell into the habit of talking daily, usually at night after she'd put the girls to bed. The more she got to know Trevor, the more she found to like about him. He was intelligent and dedicated to his work, as well as kindhearted. He'd gotten choked up at one point while telling her about a young patient of his, a boy who'd lost an arm in an accident. He also had interests beyond medicine: rock climbing, surfing, and wild-mushroom foraging, to name a few. Another thing Jo was discovering was how liberating a long-distance relationship could be. In the absence of physical intimacy, she didn't have to worry that she was cheating on Sean. Marisol put it best when she'd said, "It's like phone sex without the sex."

So when Trevor asked her to go away with him for a weekend, it threw her into a panic. This was during the third week of September. She was on the phone with him one night chatting via Bluetooth, as she tidied up in the living room, when he said, "Say, Jo, something's come up that I'd like to run by you. I just found out I'll be speaking at a medical conference in New York City the first week in October. It's last minute—I'm replacing another speaker who canceled due to a family emergency—or I would've told you about it sooner. Anyway, I was thinking about staying through the weekend, if you'd care to join me. Any chance of making that happen?" His voice was casual, elaborately so, as if he didn't want to scare her off by coming on too strong.

She should've seen it coming. Of course he'd want to take their relationship to the next level. He was a man with needs, who, unlike her, wasn't content to idle in neutral indefinitely. But still . . . she was unprepared. She rocked back onto her heels as she was fishing a stray Lego piece from under the sofa, overcome by a sense of panic. Her heart pounded. She took a moment, and a deep breath, before answering, "Gee, I don't know. I'll have to check my schedule. How soon do you need to know?"

"As soon as possible, so I can book the flights."

"I'll get back to you tomorrow."

Work was slower this time of year than during the summer months. She'd picked up some work doing family portraits, fall being the time of year when people's minds turned to their Christmas cards, and freelance assignments for the local paper, *The Washburn Bugle*, photographing local events that were held every fall, such as the county fair in Gold Creek, the pumpkin festival in Pinehurst, and the Renaissance Faire in Redwood Falls. But she had nothing booked for the first weekend in October, she saw when she checked her calendar after ending the call.

Leaving the girls was another matter. She did so rarely unless it was a work-related trip. A romantic weekend in New York City seemed frivolous, if not downright irresponsible. It was only when she spoke with Reggie and he offered to come stay with the girls that weekend—he was just back from filming a movie in London and between acting gigs—that she was given the opportunity to get away without feeling guilty. There was just one remaining impediment . . .

"I'm free that weekend, as it turns out," she told Trevor when they spoke the next day. "But I still don't see how we can make it happen."

"Why not?" he asked.

"Because I'm not sleeping with you unless I'm feeling it, and I can't afford to pay for my own hotel room." She'd checked hotel prices online. At some of the nicer hotels in New York City, rooms rented for up to three thousand a night. "I wouldn't feel comfortable having you pay, either."

"I figured you'd say that," he replied. "Which is why I arranged for the conference organizers to cover all your travel expenses, including a separate room at the hotel where I'll be staying."

"How'd you manage that? What are you, the keynote speaker?"

"No, just the guy who's replacing the speaker who canceled at the last minute. They're so grateful, they're going out of their way to accommodate me. Naturally, I'd love nothing more than to share a room with you, but I respect your boundaries. You can set the pace. We'll take it as slow as you like."

She relaxed. He'd satisfied her concerns, and Fate had intervened in the form of Reggie as her babysitter. The girls adored Uncle Reggie. "In that case, how can I refuse? Besides, I've always wanted to see New York City. I've never been. And of course it'll be wonderful to see you again."

The Thursday before she was due to leave on her trip, Reggie arrived with his usual flair for making a dramatic entrance. "Fee-fie-fo-fum, do I smell the blood of a Munchkin?" he called from the entryway.

Jo heard a door slam down the hall and the sound of running feet before the girls burst into the living room, crying in delight, "Uncle Reggie! Uncle Reggie!" as they flung themselves at him.

He dropped his bags in the foyer and scooped them up. "Hello, my pets. Good Lord, what has your mommy been feeding you? You're both HUGE." They giggled as he lowered them onto their feet.

"Did you bring us presents?" Emma wanted to know.

"You think I'd visit without bringing presents? Better yet, I brought them all the way from London."

"Uncle Reggie was filming a movie in London," Jo reminded them.

"When can we watch it?" Jess wanted to know.

"When your mommy decides you're old enough. It's rated PG," he told her.

"What's pee-gee?" asked Emma.

"It means it's not for young children," Jo explained.

"I play an American abroad who discovers he's the bastard son of a British duke. The twist is that neither of them has a nickel to rub between them and they become partners in crime."

"Uncle Reggie said a swear word," said Emma, giggling.

"You'll be hearing a lot more swear words before the weekend is over," he said with a devilish grin.

Jo laughed and punched his arm. "Don't you dare."

"Party pooper," he whispered. "Buckle up, Munchkins, because you're in for a wild ride. And your little dog, too." He bent to give Snickers, who'd come over to greet him, a scratch under her snout. "Mommy might want to cover her ears so she won't hear about any r-u-l-e-s that'll be broken."

"You're incorrigible," said Jo.

She showed Reggie to her room, where he'd be sleeping. She planned to sleep on the sofa tonight and leave first thing in the morning for her early flight. After he unpacked, they went out onto the deck. There was a nip in the air, but the sun was shining, which made it seem warmer than the actual temperature. The forest to the east was brushed here and there with fall colors. Jo served refreshments and the girls opened the presents Reggie had brought them—a doll's tea set for Emma and a painted wooden nutcracker for Jess, both from the gift shop at Buckingham Palace. Reggie had brought Jo a bottle of cherry brandy and a tin of shortbread from the duty-free shop at Heathrow.

"Guess what, Uncle Reggie? I'm in kindergarten!" announced Emma after she'd admired her tea set.

"So I heard," he said. "Your mom tells me you have so many new friends she has to schedule your playdates weeks in advance."

Emma had turned six the week before. They'd celebrated her birthday with a party here at the house to which everyone in her class was invited. The activities, which Hank had helped organize, included a three-legged race, pin the tail on the donkey, and limbo. Jess and her friend Shoshanna had been enlisted to assist Jo and Hank as party hosts. Jo remembered how Jess's face had lit up when Hank had praised her and Shoshanna for doing a good job of making everyone feel included.

"If somebody invited me over and I said no, their feelings might get hurt," Emma explained.

"It's not always easy being popular," Reggie agreed with a sage nod. He turned to Jess. "What about you, Miss Priss? How are you liking your new school?"

"It's okay," she told him. "I like hunting for arrowheads during recess with my friend Shoshanna."

"Find many arrowheads on your school playground, do you?"

"We haven't found any yet, but we will if we keep looking," she replied confidently. "My teacher says it was a hunting ground of the Miwok tribe in the olden days. Did you know the Miwoks are hunter-gatherers? Or at least they were back then."

"I did not know that," said Reggie. "You remind me of your dad. He used to collect facts about all kinds of stuff. He was a walking encyclopedia."

Jo felt a twinge of sadness, wishing Sean were here to see how their daughters were turning out. Jess, who was smart and inquisitive, with a mind like a mousetrap—she never forgot anything. Emma with her sunny nature and big heart, who was nice to everyone so no one would feel left out.

After supper, Jo and Reggie played Chutes and Ladders and Candy Land, two of the board games from the treasure trove of sixties playthings that had come with the house, with the girls until it was their bedtime. Then Reggie read them a chapter from *James and the Giant Peach*, doing the different voices of the characters, which had them captivated. Once they were tucked into their beds, he and Jo retired to the living room, and she poured them each a small glass of the cherry brandy he'd brought her.

"Thanks again for doing this," she said. "I wouldn't be going on this trip if you hadn't made it possible."

"It's my pleasure." He looked like a *Saturday Night Live* comedian spoofing a *Masterpiece Theatre* presenter, wearing the burgundy velvet smoking jacket he'd "borrowed" from the wardrobe department on the set of *The Duke of Dubuque*. "I've missed the Munchkins, and there's nothing I wouldn't do for you, baby girl. Also, it's for a good cause. Speaking of which, please tell me you packed sexy underwear." He cut a glance at her suitcase, parked by the door in readiness for her early departure. "Because, honey, your big-girl panties ain't gonna cut it."

"My big-girl panties have served me well so far."

"Maybe, but one thing they haven't done is get you laid."

"I'm not planning to sleep with Trevor. We're staying in separate rooms."

Reggie raised an eyebrow. "With a connecting door, I take it?"

She shrugged. "I'm playing it by ear."

"And hopefully a few other body parts as well."

Jo wondered again what might be in store for this weekend. She was nervous, but proud of herself for taking a leap of faith. Sean would be proud, too.

"Wow. It's like we're on top of the world!" Jo exclaimed as she took in the views from the glass sky deck of the Edge in Hudson Yard the following Sunday.

"The Western Hemisphere, anyway," said Trevor.

According to the literature they'd picked up at the ticket booth, the Edge was the tallest building in the Western Hemisphere. From where they stood, Jo could see as far as the East and Hudson Rivers to the east and west and Brooklyn and the Bronx to the north and south. Central Park, from this distance, resembled a carpet woven of fall colors.

It was the last day of her trip, which had been a whirlwind of activities from the moment she'd arrived. On Friday night there was dinner at Jean-Georges followed by a Broadway show. On Saturday, they'd explored the city from the Upper West Side to the Lower East Side, where they'd shared a mile-high pastrami sandwich at Katz's Deli. This morning, after a leisurely breakfast at their hotel, they'd strolled Fifth Avenue, taking in an exhibit at the Metropolitan Museum before heading downtown for more sightseeing. The entire weekend, Trevor had refused to let her pay for so much as a subway ride. He'd insisted it was his treat and had pointed out it was also a tax write-off. She wasn't entirely comfortable with the arrangement but had gone along out of necessity. Her budget didn't allow for pricey vacations. She was saving up for a trip to the Grand Canyon with the girls next summer, a long-held dream of Jess's.

"What do you say we head back to the hotel and freshen up before dinner?" suggested Trevor as they took the elevator back down to the street level. He'd managed to score a hard-to-get reservation at Per Se for tonight through a colleague from the medical conference with connections.

"Perfect," she said. "I'm pooped after all the sightseeing we did today."

"I hope you don't mind eating early. Six thirty was the only reservation I could get."

"I prefer it, actually," she said. "You get into the habit of eating early when you have kids. I'm usually in my pj's by the time most people are having dinner."

Put that way, her life sounded boring. Especially after the whirlwind of the past couple of days. She glanced over at Trevor as they exited the building. So far, all they'd done was kiss, once while lying on the bed in his room adjoining hers at their hotel. Each time, she'd stopped herself from going any further, but it was becoming increasingly difficult to come up with reasons why she should. Trevor was the full package: handsome and intelligent, and charming when he wasn't being set up by his parents. More importantly, being with him had reminded her she was a woman with needs.

Dinner that evening was magical. When they arrived at the restaurant on the fourth floor of the Time Warner Center, they were immediately shown to their table, where they enjoyed views of Columbus Circle as darkness fell and the lights came on in the surrounding buildings, while sipping complimentary glasses of the house-brand sparkling wine. They both ordered the nine-course vegetarian menu. Neither was a vegetarian, but they opted for the lighter fare to make up for all the food they'd eaten over the weekend. One spoonful of the borscht with red-beet agnolotti, however, and Jo decided she could easily become a vegetarian if every meatless dish tasted this good. Each successive dish was as delicious as the last. She was stuffed by the time dessert, star fruit sorbet with ginger-beer granite on a bed of mango slices, arrived at the table, but she ate it anyway, as she did the complimentary chocolates that came with the check.

"I don't know about you, but I could do with a walk after all that food we ate," Trevor said as they were leaving after he'd paid the bill. "How about a stroll in Central Park?"

"Is it safe to walk in the park after dark?"

"If we stick to the more populated areas. This time of year, the park is usually as busy at night as it is in the daytime." Trevor had attended Columbia's medical school, so he knew the city like the back of his hand.

"I'm up for it, then." It was a mild evening, and she wasn't ready to call it a night.

They exited the building, passing the statue of Christopher Columbus that dominated Columbus Circle as they crossed the street, heading for the Central Park West entrance to the park. They ambled along one of the paths that crisscrossed the park, which wound through trees and grassy meadows, passing park buildings, statuary, and ball fields. When they grew weary, Trevor hailed one of the horse-drawn carriages that were a fixture of the park, instructing the driver to take them to their hotel. They rattled over roadways closed to motorists, populated with pedestrians, dog walkers, and joggers. New York City was indeed the city that never slept, she'd discovered. She heard a saxophone playing somewhere in the distance, likely that of a street musician.

"It doesn't get better than this," she said as she snuggled with Trevor under the plush blanket spread across their laps. "I get to rest my sore feet and channel my inner Carrie Bradshaw at the same time."

He smiled. “I’m glad you’re enjoying it.”

“This entire trip has been magical. I don’t want it to end.”

“You don’t miss your children?”

“Only a little,” she lied. After the fourth or fifth time she’d phoned to check up on the girls, Reggie had ordered her to go have fun and not call again unless it was an emergency. “But I wouldn’t have wanted to miss this. It’s been a dream weekend.”

He locked gazes with her. “For me, too. And if you get lonely tonight, you know where to find me.”

Jo shivered a little. True to his word, he’d allowed her to set the pace and hadn’t pressured her to have sex with him. Now he was letting her know how he’d prefer to spend their last night together in New York. She glanced down at her wedding ring. Although she wore it on her right hand now, it still reminded her of her commitment to Sean, which hadn’t ended with his death. She felt torn. *This is what he wanted for you. To honor what you and he had without letting it hold you back.*

“Who says I’m going anywhere?” she replied, coming to a decision.

She saw a flash of desire in Trevor’s eyes, and he dipped his head to kiss her. The feel of his mouth against hers ignited a spark in her, which caught and spread, warming even the parts of her body she’d forgotten still functioned. Somewhere in the night, she heard the haunting melody of the street musician’s saxophone playing “Someone to Watch Over Me.” It seemed like a sign.

Back at their hotel, they took the elevator to the fourth floor and walked the corridor to their connecting rooms. This time, though, instead of saying their good nights, she followed him into his room. She was trembling with a combination of nerves and excitement. She’d never been with anyone other than Sean. Would she freak out? Or worse, what if she enjoyed it and felt guilty afterward?

At one point when they were lying in bed together naked, she stiffened as Trevor nuzzled her breast. He lifted his head to give her a questioning look. “We don’t have to do this if you’re not ready.”

"No, it's just . . ." *You're not him.* "Don't stop." If she stopped now, she might never get another opportunity as perfect as this or find the courage to go for it again. Besides, it felt good. Her body, starved for physical closeness, sprang to life at his touch, despite her mental resistance.

Trevor was a gentle and attentive lover. He took it slow and brought her to a satisfying climax. Still, their lovemaking felt . . . flat. Jo chalked it up to it being their first time, but after the second time, she knew. She remembered something Suzy had once said: *It's different with every partner. Sometimes it's fireworks. Sometimes it's a sparkler. Sometimes it's a lit candle on a table for two.* Lying next to Trevor in the dark, Jo realized that, although she might never again experience the heights of passion she had with Sean, she wasn't willing to settle for less. And because she knew Trevor wanted more than she was prepared to give and it'd be unfair to lead him on, she felt obliged to be honest with him the next day when they were saying their goodbyes at the airport.

"Trevor, I had the most amazing time with you this past weekend, and I think you're an amazing guy, but I don't think we should see each other again." She felt like a jerk, watching his face fall.

He looked confused. "Did I do something wrong? Did you feel I was rushing you last night?"

"No. You were great. And the sex was great," she added, remembering another piece of advice from Suzy on dating: *The male ego is fragile. Handle with care.* "It's just that I don't see a future for us. You deserve more than I can give you right now."

"Is it the long-distance thing? Because it doesn't have to be a deal-breaker. I'd be open to relocating if it was to come to that. I don't expect you to uproot your family and your business for me."

"I appreciate that, but distance isn't the only obstacle."

"What else is there?"

"I'm not in love with you."

"I didn't expect you to be. It's too soon for that."

"Yes, and I don't presume you're in love with me, either."

"I could be, in time."

"I'm sure I could grow to love you, too. What's not to love? But it wouldn't be the kind of love that inspires poetry." Or a tattoo like the heart on her left ankle with her and Sean's initials on it.

"How do you know?"

"Because I had it once. I'm sure she's out there somewhere, the woman you're meant to be with . . ." She gestured around her at the passengers streaming past. "And when you find her, you'll know, like I did with my husband."

"It doesn't always happen like in the movies."

"For me it did."

"Not everyone gets that lucky," he replied sourly.

"Look at the bright side," she said in an attempt to lighten the mood. "At least we won't have our parents throwing us a surprise wedding."

"There is that." He chuckled weakly, and she was heartened to see he'd recovered somewhat. "Look, I won't pretend I'm not disappointed. I'd hoped . . . well, it doesn't matter now. But I get it. I didn't know your husband, but from the way you talk about him, I imagine he'd be a tough act to follow."

"He was one of a kind," she agreed.

Babe, if you hold out for your next Mr. Right, you could be in for a long wait.

Maybe, but I'm not settling.

Nor would I expect you to. But in the meantime, leave the door open.

As she continued to her gate, she reflected on recent events, starting with her date with Scott and ending with her romantic weekend with Trevor. Those experiences, both good and bad, had informed the way forward, showing her what she didn't want as well as what was possible. And one positive thing had come out of it all. It made her realize she didn't want to spend the rest of her life alone.

There was nothing like a six-year-old and a seven-year-old greeting you like you were Santa Claus and the Easter Bunny rolled into one as you walked in the door. No sooner had Jo arrived than Jess and Emma were pouncing on her, nearly knocking her off balance in their excitement at seeing her. She bent to gather them into her arms, while Snickers wriggled her way into the scrum. Despite their having been thoroughly spoiled by Uncle Reggie while she was gone, her daughters had obviously missed her.

She felt bad about how she'd ended it with Trevor—although she had no regrets, her timing could've been better—but her mood improved as she hugged her daughters. "Am I glad to see you! I missed you both so much."

"I thought you were never coming back!" said Emma as if she'd been away for weeks instead of days. She wore her pink corduroy overalls and her hair was braided, inexpertly, Jo couldn't help noticing. Reggie had done his best, but there was no substitute for a mother's touch.

"Snickers slept on my bed while you were gone," reported Jess as their dog grinned and wagged her tail, unrepentant. "Uncle Reggie said it was okay."

"Tattletale." Reggie stuck his tongue out at her, and she giggled.

Jo crouched to run her hands over her dog's flanks while Snickers licked her face. "I see. So you weren't the only ones who got away with murder while I was away," she said to the girls. "Don't get any ideas," she told her dog. "You'll be sleeping in your own bed again now that I'm home."

When they were all sitting down in the living room, she showed the girls pictures from her trip and gave them the souvenirs she'd brought back for them, a pair of embroidered Chinese slippers from the Pearl River Market in Chinatown and a Yankees jersey from a gift shop in Times Square for each of them in their sizes. She didn't get a chance to speak with Reggie alone until later, when she was unpacking in her room, while the girls played outside.

"So you had a good trip?" he asked.

Jo removed a dress from her suitcase and hung it in her closet. "It was amazing. So much to see and do. And the food! We ate our way through Manhattan. I even got to see a Broadway show."

"Which one?"

"*The Book of Mormon*. It was wonderful."

"Oh my God." He made like he was swooning. "I've seen it twice, the first time on Broadway with the original cast." He started to hum one of its numbers—show tunes were his love language—and stopped. "What else did you do? And don't give me the G-rated version. I want to know if you slept with Dr. McDreamy. Spill, girlfriend," he demanded when she didn't immediately respond. "After my animated-movie marathon of this past weekend, you owe me."

"Fine. Okay. I slept with him," she admitted. "I was going to tell you. I was just choosing my moment."

"And?"

"It was good."

"'Good' as in good? Or 'good' as in mind-blowing?"

"It wasn't mind-blowing."

Reggie sighed, looking disappointed. "Well, at least it got you over the hump. No pun intended."

"It also made me realize something."

"What?"

"I want more."

"Naturally. Why settle for so-so sex when there are plenty of other fish in the sea?"

"I wasn't talking about sex, though of course that's a big part of it. What I meant was, I want more than to be with someone I like but could never love. The chances of lightning striking twice are slim to none, but if I ever meet someone I could love as much as I loved Sean, I'll know it was worth the wait."

"How was it left with Dr. McDreamy?"

"I broke it off with him."

"Ouch. How'd he take it?"

"He was disappointed, but it's not as if he's in love with me, either." She felt a stab of remorse. She hadn't purposely led Trevor on or planned to break up with him, but the fact was, she'd let him down.

"You shouldn't settle," Reggie agreed when she plopped down next to him on the bed after she'd finished unpacking. "Although my perspective as a gay man might be different from yours. I had sex with multiple partners before I met Marco. The universe saved the best for last," he added with a smile.

"Speaking of the devil, are you two getting along now that the wedding drama is over?"

"I'm happy to report my groomzilla, like the Wolf Man with the waning of the moon, has reverted to his human guise. Praise Jesus, and do I hear an amen?" Reggie raised his eyes and arms heavenward, reminding her that, while he claimed to be a philistine, he was the son of a preacher.

Jo grinned. "I'm glad to hear it."

He laced his fingers through hers. "I hope you find what you're looking for, baby girl."

"I'm not looking, but thank you."

"Neither was I, but love has a way of finding you when you least expect it."

"It'd have to walk in without knocking because I'm done with dating. Anyway, I'm happy." *Or I'm getting there.* "I have my family and friends." She tightened her fingers around Reggie's. "This house, my work." If the pleasure she'd once taken in her photography had proved elusive of late, she hadn't given up hope that it would return eventually. "It's enough." *For now.*

20

As the golden days of second summer stretched into mid-October, life in the house on Mountain Laurel Lane was busy and full. Both Jess and Emma now had after-school activities. Emma was taking a ballet class, which Jo's mom had insisted on paying for because "brains will only get you so far in life," as she'd put it. Jess was taking swimming lessons at their local community center. She'd graduated from the guppies class when she was four but had only recently decided it was safe to venture past the shallow end. She was now in the minnows class. Jo, watching her kick and splash her way across the pool doing an approximation of the crawl or breaststroke, couldn't have been prouder if it were the English Channel she was swimming. It was another indication of the progress Jess had made in her therapy. She was doing so well, in fact, that Dr. Shaw had recommended her sessions be cut back from once a week to every other week.

They were healing as a family. Even at her lowest, Jo took heart in seeing how far they'd come over the past two years. Getting a fresh start in a new place had a lot to do with it, as did Hank, who provided the stability they'd sorely lacked in Sean's absence. But she'd played a part in it as well. She'd steered their ship of state through a rocky passage to safe harbor. She was also achieving what she had once believed impossible: making a life for herself and her children without Sean.

But there was always some new threat. She was reminded of this driving home, one morning in October, when she noticed the current fire danger in their area, as indicated by the sign outside the forest ranger station, was still at its high of the summer, its arrow seemingly stuck in the red zone, despite the fall's cooler temperatures. She shivered a little, worry nibbling at her insides. Their region hadn't seen any rain in months. Its waterways had either slowed to a trickle or dried up altogether in some areas, and its lakes' water levels were at record lows. Indoor fires were now banned by local ordinance along with outdoor fires. It wouldn't take more than a single windblown ember from a chimney or a campfire to start a blaze, with the understories of the forests as dry as tinder.

Please keep us safe.

The next day, she rose at her customary early hour. She was letting Snickers out to do her business when she smelled smoke. She stepped out onto the deck, wearing Sean's old UCD T-shirt, which she'd slept in, and saw smoke rising from somewhere in the forest to the east. A prickle of anxiety ran up the back of her neck and across her scalp as she stared at the dark smudge against the dawn sky. Catching movement out of the corner of her eye, she looked down to see Hank, in his robe and slippers, standing on the patio below gazing at the same view.

"Morning!" she called. "Should we be worried?" She pointed toward the smoke on the horizon.

"Could be a controlled burn," he said.

They both knew that was highly unlikely, but she appreciated he wasn't pressing the panic button before they knew the cause of the fire. "Do you know of any buildings or campgrounds out that way?"

His words confirmed her suspicion. "Can't say that I do."

"If it's a wildfire, how far out do you figure it is?"

"Hard to say from this distance. Let me grab my binoculars."

He disappeared below the deck overhang, then reappeared shortly carrying a pair of field binoculars. He climbed the stairs to the deck and peered through the binoculars. "Looks to be somewhere in the vicinity of Tomahawk Ridge." Tomahawk Ridge, named after its distinctive rock formation in the shape of a tomahawk, was often featured in photos of the region and was a popular destination of hikers and rock climbers. "That'd be forty, fifty miles from here as the crow flies."

Precisely forty-eight miles due east, Jo learned when she did a Google Earth search. "There's an old logging road that runs through there, but it's not used anymore, and who knows if it's even still navigable." She pointed to the gray line snaking across the aerial view of the area on her phone. "If the firefighters can't get access except by air or on foot . . ." She looked up at Hank with worried eyes.

"Fortunately for us, the wind's blowing in a southeasterly direction," he said, looking at the weather app on his phone. Away from them. But the wind could shift at any moment. "I'll check with my friend Monty. He might know something." Howard "Monty" Montgomery was a fellow Graybeard and a ham radio enthusiast. "He must be picking up some chatter on his police-band radio."

"I have to get the girls ready for school," she said when her dog rejoined her on the deck after doing her business. "Let me know if you find anything out."

"Will do. In the meantime, try not to worry. Just remember, for every wildfire that spreads out of control, there's a dozen more that are contained." He gave her shoulder a light squeeze before heading back downstairs. "Chances are this fire will be put out by the time the girls get home from school."

His words were both a comfort and a painful reminder of when Sean had been her rock in emergencies. Like when she'd gone into labor with Emma and her labor had been progressing faster than anticipated. Sean had not only driven her to the hospital through torrential rain, arriving minutes before she gave birth, but had also been the voice of calm throughout.

The girls were still asleep when she poked her head in their room. "Wake up, sleepyheads! Time for school." Jess stirred but kept her eyes squinched shut. Emma sat up in bed, rubbing her eyes. "Hurry, or you'll miss your bus."

Leaving them to get dressed, she went to the kitchen, where she found Snickers parked by her food bowl, staring up at her piteously. "Oh, for heaven's sake," she declared as she bent to pick up the empty bowl. "Anyone would think you hadn't been fed in days, and we both know better." Her Lab disputed this with a woof.

She scooped premium kibble for senior dogs into the bowl, mixed in some warm water and cooked chicken parts, and placed it back on the floor. While her dog wolfed down her food, Jo started breakfast. She was stirring raisins into the cooked oatmeal when the girls appeared wearing the outfits she'd helped them pick out the night before. Fifteen minutes later, they were fed, with their hair combed and their teeth brushed and their lunches packed. Jo was hustling them out the door to take them to their school bus stop, five minutes away at the Little Library on Beech Road, when Jess paused to look up at the smoke rising above the rooftop.

"What's burning?" she asked.

"A wildfire," Jo informed her. Hank's friend Monty had reported that firefighters had been dispatched to put out the fire, according to the chatter on his police-band radio. "But it's nothing to worry about. We're not in any danger. The firefighters are on it." She remained uneasy, nonetheless.

"What about the animals in the forest?" asked Emma worriedly when they were in the car.

"If they're in any danger, they'll go to where it's safe," Jo assured her.

"What if the whole forest burned down?" asked Jess.

"Honey, it's no use worrying about things that haven't happened and probably won't." It was hard not to worry, though, with the recent fires in LA still fresh in her memory. Those fires had burned for days, whipped by the Santa Ana winds, and caused widespread devastation.

Many of the residents of the affected communities had lost their homes and some had lost their lives.

After dropping the girls off at their bus stop, she spent the rest of the morning preparing for an evacuation. Just in case, she told herself. It probably wouldn't come to that, but better to err on the side of caution than to be caught unprepared. She packed clothes and necessities she and the girls would need. She went through her kitchen cupboards and pantry, assembling a supply of nonperishable foods to take with them and making a list of the items to buy. She checked in with her friends, none of whom lived in areas where they were in imminent danger from the fire, fortunately.

Throughout the day, she monitored the rapidly evolving situation via the news feed on her phone. The Gold Creek and Washburn County fire departments had combined forces in battling the wildfire, and they'd called in fire departments in neighboring counties to assist. The state authorities in charge of emergency relief had deployed its planes and helicopters that were equipped for firefighting. Despite the swift and aggressive response on the part of the agencies involved and the firefighters both on the ground and in the air, however, the fire continued to spread.

Jo awakened the next morning to find the view of Tomahawk Ridge obscured by a cloud of thick, dark-gray smoke, at the center of which glowed the hot spot like a live coal in a bed of ash. The visual came as a shock, even though she'd half expected it. It was a stark reminder that there was no safe ground in life. One never knew when or where lightning, in the form of a catastrophe, would strike. Like Sean getting cancer and dying. And now this. Her stomach was a fist shoved up into her rib cage as she drove the girls to their bus stop. Despite her worries, she did her best to reassure her daughters.

"Mommy, why isn't the fire out yet? You said the firefighters would put it out," fretted Jess.

"They're working on it, sweetie, but wildfires are unpredictable. It depends on the conditions, like which way the wind is blowing and how hard, and whether there's deadfall or dry brush feeding the fire." Jess was the kid who, from the time she learned to talk, had wanted to know why the sun shone and why grass was green and how rocks were formed. Jo hoped her quasi-scientific explanation would distract her from catastrophizing. "Luckily, we have the best firefighters in the country."

"That's what you said about Daddy's doctor."

In the rearview mirror Jess's eyes stared at her accusingly. When Sean had been battling cancer, Jo had told the girls how lucky he was to have Dr. Wong as his oncologist. Dr. Wong was Harvard trained and had been chief of the oncology department at MD Anderson in Dallas, Texas, before he'd relocated to their area for family reasons. But even Dr. Wong couldn't save Sean. As a result, her children had learned at a young age that adults didn't always come through, despite their best efforts. She mourned their lost innocence.

On her way home after dropping them off, she stopped at the supermarket to pick up the items on her grocery list. In addition to her normal weekly purchases, she bought a ten-pound bag of kibble, a skid of bottled waters, and flashlight batteries. She arrived home to the buzzing of a chain saw. Hank was up on a ladder removing a dead limb from the oak tree in the front yard.

"Fire prevention," he called, gesturing toward the tree limbs scattered on the ground below.

Jo swallowed against the knot of anxiety in her throat. What good would preventive measures do in the event their neighborhood was engulfed in flames? "What's the latest?" she asked, hoping against hope for a positive development in the thirty minutes since she'd last checked her news feed.

Hank's grim expression squashed that hope. "Wind's picked up."

"So I see." She glanced up at the tree branches swaying in the wind and felt her dread mount.

"Good news is, it's still blowing east. If the direction holds, we might get lucky." Meaning the fire would spread away from them instead of toward them. He began picking up the smaller branches on the ground and stuffing them into a lawn-and-leaf bag. "By the way, I'm headed over to the senior center after I finish up here, if there's anything you need while I'm in town."

"I just got back from the supermarket, but if you're going to the senior center, you can drop off the stuff I got for Frannie." Frannie was the head of a group of local volunteers who supplied food and beverages to firefighters and disaster relief workers during emergencies. Its official title was the Gold Creek Women's Auxiliary, but they called their organization Meals on Heels, although Jo had never seen any of the women in heels; they were more the sneakers and Birkenstocks type. They were currently operating out of the senior center downtown. When Jo had called Frannie earlier to ask what she needed, Frannie had given a list.

"Sure thing," he said.

He helped her carry the groceries inside. She was putting the gallon of milk she'd bought in the fridge when she noticed a large Tupperware container filled with individually wrapped sandwiches on Hank's shelf in the fridge. "I see you were busy while I was out," she remarked. It explained why he was going to the senior center. Jo's contribution to the Meals on Heels ladies' efforts—a can of ground coffee, a jar of powdered creamer, and a pack of protein bars—seemed puny in comparison.

"I like to do what I can," he said with a shrug.

He and Frannie were well matched in terms of their characters as well as their temperaments. Both were community minded and generous to a fault. Either one would give you the shirt off their back. Sean had been like that. Once, when she and Sean had been volunteering for their church's annual coat drive around the holidays, a shabbily dressed man had shown up at the church on the last day, after all the coats had been distributed. Seeing him shivering in his thin jacket, Sean had felt so bad for him, he'd given the man his own jacket. Jo smiled at the memory even as it shattered her.

The wildfire continued to rage throughout the day and into the next. Volunteer firefighters were pouring in from all over the country to assist local firefighters. But neither the boots on the ground nor the aerial drops of fire retardant had stopped the fire's spread. By day three, it had consumed over 10,000 acres of forest. Authorities had ordered the communities situated directly in its path to evacuate. Wildlife habitats had also been affected, as evidenced by the unusual number of reported wildlife sightings over the past couple of days. Yesterday, Suzy had surprised a coyote rooting through her garbage can when she'd gone to take out the trash.

"Shouldn't you be home getting ready to evacuate?" asked Frannie when Jo arrived at the senior center to drop off today's contribution: the two dozen chicken salad sandwiches she and Hank had made together. They were in the center's rec room, which was normally used for club meetings and crafting and the like but today was a beehive of activity with volunteers bustling about, organizing and loading everything into the Meals on Heels van to be delivered to the firefighters' command center, and people dropping off donated food. Tubs of prepared foods, bagged and boxed snacks, paper goods, bottled waters, coffee supplies, and several industrial-size coffee makers covered the long folding tables that stood against the walls and in rows down the middle of the room. Frannie, clipboard in hand, was at the center of it all overseeing operations.

"We're all packed," Jo reported. "Ready to go at a moment's notice. The girls wanted to pack every book and toy they own, but after I explained that it wouldn't all fit in our car, they pared it down to just the stuff they couldn't live without. But I'm praying we won't have to evacuate." If they did, what might they return home to? Smoking ruins where their neighborhood had been? Her stomach clenched.

"Let's hope it doesn't come to that. But if it does, at least you won't have to stay at a motel or one of the emergency shelters." At the baffled look Jo wore, she went on, "You and Hank and the girls will stay with me, of course. Didn't Hank tell you? I told him to, or I thought I did. It's been such a madhouse here . . ." Her gaze took in the swirl of activity around her. "It may have slipped my mind."

"He didn't say anything to me."

"He probably thought I had. Well, anyway, now you know. You're staying with me."

Jo was touched by her friend's generosity, but felt obliged to point out, "That's kind of you, but you don't have room for us all." The one guest room at Frannie's cabin was currently in use by her daughter. "Where would we all sleep?"

"Let me worry about that. Promise you'll drive straight to my place at the first sign of danger."

Jo knew better than to argue once Frannie's mind was made up. Besides, she could think of no better place to shelter than Frannie's cabin. Not only was it ideally situated on a body of water a safe distance from the hot spot, but it was cozy and comfortable. She grinned. "Yes, ma'am."

After leaving, she drove to the girls' school to pick up Jess and Emma. She'd been notified that classes were letting out early today. School had been canceled until further notice to accommodate the teachers and students who lived in areas that were either facing imminent evacuation or had been evacuated already. She waited in the pickup and drop-off lane in front of the school building with the other parents until the bell sounded and kids began flooding from the building. Her heart lifted at the sight of her daughters running toward her.

"It's snowing!" exclaimed Emma, buckled in next to her sister in the back seat, as they drove home. Outside, the air was hazy with smoke. Ashes drifted down. The landscape through which they passed, one of scattered buildings interspersing open fields and wooded areas, was covered in a gray layer of ash.

"It's ashes from the fire," Jess corrected her. "It only snows in the winter."

"I know," huffed Emma. "But I can pretend."

"It does look like snow," Jo said. "Girls, remember that big storm we had last winter? The snow was so deep, we couldn't leave our house until Mr. Peters came and dug us out with his snow mover?"

Her attempt to redirect, to prevent a squabble from breaking out and keep Jess from going into doomsday-crier mode, failed. "Mommy, I'm scared," Jess whimpered.

"I know, sweetie. It's scary," Jo acknowledged. She remembered something Dr. Shaw had said: *Failure to confront one's fears only makes things worse, never better.* When Sean had been ill and they were scared he'd die, she'd told the girls what she thought they needed to hear. But in the end, painting a falsely optimistic picture and making promises she couldn't keep had done more harm than good. It had cost her the trust of her eldest. Now she did her best to assuage Jess's fears without telling a lie. "But when I'm afraid, I look at the facts, which usually aren't as scary as what I imagine."

"The fire is burning. That's a fact," said her seven-year-old, who was sometimes too smart for her own good.

"Yes, but it's nowhere near us and the wind is blowing it in the opposite direction."

"What if it gets to us?"

"There's a good chance it won't, but even if it did, we'd go stay at Frannie's. We'd be safe there."

"What if our house burned down while we were gone?"

Jo didn't know what to say. The threat of losing their home, which had become her sanctuary, was as terrifying for her as it was for Jess. Because she'd lose more than the roof over her head; if the life she'd built were taken away, she'd lose faith that it was possible to have a life without Sean.

"Brittney, this girl in my class? Her house burned down in the last fire. Her and her mom had to go live at her aunt and uncle's for, like, a whole year. Her cousins were horrible to her, and her cat ran away and never came back." Jess's voice quavered. She appeared on the verge of tears.

"Sweetie, I'm sorry about what happened to your friend, but no matter what, we'll be okay because we have each other—you, me, and Emma. That's the most important thing to remember."

Jess lapsed into thoughtful silence before she spoke again. "I'm glad we don't have a cat."

"Why is that?"

"I'd be sad if it ran away."

"That's one less thing to worry about," Jo agreed.

That evening after supper she and the girls piled onto the sofa with a bowl of popcorn to watch *Despicable Me* for the umpteenth time. When Hank came upstairs at one point, she invited him to join them. He did, and for a time, she could make believe the four of them were a family, safe in their fortress.

The next day brought more worrisome news. The wind had shifted overnight, sending the wildfire spreading in their direction. At 1:18 p.m., an evacuation order was issued for their area. Jo's phone rang minutes after it was announced. It was Frannie. "Have you heard the news?" She sounded anxious.

"Yes, and we're getting ready to roll out. We'll leave as soon as we're done loading everything into our vehicles," Jo said as she heaved a suitcase into the trunk of her Toyota, while Hank loaded a box into the bed of his truck.

"Hank has a spare key to my place. No one's home at the moment. I'm at the senior center and Hannah's staying with her boyfriend. But I should be back by five or thereabouts. I'll bring stuff for supper. If you get hungry before then, help yourself to anything you find in the fridge or pantry."

Jo was moved by Frannie's kindness, and it took the edge off her anxiety knowing she and her children wouldn't be sleeping in a motel or on cots in an emergency shelter. "Thanks again for putting us up."

Frannie brushed aside her thanks. "You're family. This is what families do."

"I love you."

"Love you, too. Be safe. And let me know when you get there."

"I'll text you as soon as we arrive."

They were pulling out of the driveway by two, their vehicles loaded. Snickers rode with Hank in his truck. Homer rode with Jo and the girls, in a Ziploc bag filled with water that Emma carried on her lap. In addition to the clothes and necessities they'd packed, and the sleeping bags Hank had obtained from a sporting goods store owned by a buddy of his, they'd brought their valuables, everything that fell under the heading of *Things You Take In a Fire*: Jo's Nikon and camera equipment, Emma's stuffed animals, Hank's sports memorabilia, and Jess's rock and mineral collections.

The roads were a nightmare, with vehicles backed up for miles along the evacuation route, car horns blaring as drivers vented their frustration. After crawling through bumper-to-bumper traffic for over an hour, Jo was discouraged to see that they'd traveled less than a mile. Only another fourteen miles to go. Meanwhile, the smoke outside was growing thicker by the minute. At one point, she could've sworn she saw an ember fly past her windshield. Which, of course, was all in her head. Or was it?

After they'd driven another hour and a half, traffic came to a full stop. The cause became apparent when Jo spied a county unit parked at a roadblock five or six car lengths up ahead, its lights swirling. A male deputy wearing the uniform of the Washburn County Sheriff's Department was redirecting traffic. The driver of the vehicle at the front of the line, a blond woman in a silver CRV, stuck her head out the window to speak with the deputy, gesticulating in an agitated fashion.

Directly ahead of Jo was Hank's truck. When he pulled over onto the shoulder, she followed. She watched as he climbed from the driver's side and jogged toward the deputy manning the roadblock.

"Mommy, what's happening? Why are we stopping?" asked Jess.

"There's a roadblock up ahead. Hank's gone to see what the problem is," Jo told her.

After a brief exchange with the deputy, Hank returned to inform her, "Road's unsafe past this point. They're only letting emergency vehicles through." His voice was hoarse from the smoke in the air.

Dear God. "How did this happen? It was supposed to be safe." When the evacuation order was issued, they'd been advised as to which routes to take.

"Apparently, the fire is spreading faster than the traffic is moving."

His words struck terror in her heart. "Is there a detour we can take?"

"No, and even if we could get through, the freeway ramps are closed. We have to turn back."

"And go where?"

"Home."

"We might not be safe there. Wouldn't it be wiser to keep going until we get where it is safe?" The road to home would take them to town and from there to the highway. If they continued north on the highway, they'd get to Pine City, where they'd find safety and shelter.

He shook his head. "We wouldn't make it to town with all the road closures. They're saying both the northbound and southbound lanes of the highway are closed from the Freemont Avenue to the Burnett Street exits."

Her anxiety ramped up. She spoke in a controlled voice to keep from alarming her children. "What are we supposed to do once we get home?"

"I was advised to stay inside until help arrives."

"When might that be?"

His bleak expression said it all: There was no way of knowing.

"I wanna go to Frannie's!" whined Emma as they headed back the way they'd come.

You and me both. Jo felt sick, knowing she was instead leading them back into danger. They could become trapped. The fire might reach them before the responders did. This was her worst nightmare.

The call came an hour later, when she was halfway home. It was late in the day. The sun shone through the trees lining the road, its glow muted by the thick gray haze. The girls were both asleep in the back seat. Jo answered via her AirPods rather than her car's Bluetooth feature so as not to disturb her children, leaving one ear free to listen for any emergency vehicles. She expected it to be Hank, with whom she'd been in communication throughout the drive, and was surprised to hear Ian's voice.

"Jo, it's me. Ian. I just got off the phone with Pop-Pop. He told me you were evacuating but had to turn back. Are you okay?"

"I'm fine." The tightness in her chest eased. Suddenly, she could breathe again. It felt as though she hadn't drawn a full breath since they'd set out on their journey. "There was a road closure. They were only letting emergency vehicles through." She kept her voice low so as not to wake her children.

"Yeah, I know, but Pop-Pop said it was nothing to worry about. *Should* I be worried?"

"I don't know." She struggled to stay calm. "We were advised to return home and wait for help to arrive, but who knows when that'll be?"

"Damn. I wish there was something I could do." She could hear the frustration in Ian's voice.

"There is. Keep talking." *And keep me from losing it.*

"About what?"

"Anything. Sports. The weather. What you ate for breakfast. Anything."

So he did. He told her about growing up in Seattle and his earliest memory, watching the takeoffs and landings at Sea-Tac Airport with his grandpa when he was four. He talked about life on his military base and his difficulties learning to speak German, which according to him was "like trying to form a sentence while gargling." He told her about going horseback riding once in the Black Forest and skiing in the Austrian Alps. She didn't say much. Mainly, she just listened, his voice guiding her like a lighthouse beacon through the turbulent waters of her worst-case imaginings.

He rode with her the rest of the way home.

21

Arriving home, she took in the view above the rooftop after she climbed from her car. Flames advanced like a marauding army down the hills to the east. Their neighborhood wasn't in immediate danger, but it was only a matter of time. "How much longer do you figure we have?" she asked Hank.

"Twenty-four hours, give or take, if the current conditions hold," he estimated. "Pray for rain." Tomorrow's forecast showed a 50 percent chance of showers.

Desperation clawed at her. They were screwed unless Mother Nature intervened.

The girls climbed from the car, looking out of sorts, despite having napped during most of the ride home. Jess started to cry, which set Emma off. Jo took them by the hand, pulling them along with her as she hurried toward the house, while Hank called to Snickers, who was sniffing at the grass a few feet away. "It's going to be okay," she reassured them. "Help is on the way." Or at least she hoped it was.

"What if it doesn't get here in time? What if we get burned up?" Jess whimpered.

"That won't happen." She prayed Fate wouldn't make a liar of her.

Power outages in their area were frequent, and given the current conditions, it seemed nothing short of miraculous when the lights came on after she flipped the switch inside the door. She didn't expect the power to stay on much longer, but she'd take advantage of it while it lasted. She got Jess and Emma settled on the sofa in front of the TV and returned Homer to his fishbowl after filling it with fresh water. It was suppertime, but the girls had been snacking in the car and both claimed they weren't hungry. She'd fix them something to eat later.

"What can we do?" she asked Hank when they were conferring in the kitchen while the girls watched TV.

"We can hose the roof down," he said.

"Good idea." Her house, like most of the others on their street, was of wood construction. A windblown ember landing on a dry roof could cause it to go up in flames. "I once saw a news photo of a lone house still standing after the rest of the neighborhood had burned down. Probably because the owner had the same idea."

"It's worth a try. I'll get the ladder and meet you outside." He headed back out.

Jo fired off a group text to her friends, responding to the stream of messages she'd received from them while driving, assuring them she was all right. Hank had kept Frannie updated on the situation. Next, she found two dish towels, soaked them in water, and wrung them out. They'd have to do in the absence of N95 face masks to protect against smoke inhalation.

The girls were absorbed in the adventures of Dora the Explorer and her animated friends Boots and Backpack when she passed through the living room on her way out. "Girls, I have to go help Hank with something," she told them. "I'll be outside if you need me." They both nodded distractedly.

Outside, she tied one of the dish towels around her head so it covered her nose and mouth. She gave the other to Hank when she caught up with him, in the narrow side yard that ran along the south side of the house where he'd placed the ladder, next to the water spigot the garden hose was attached to. Above the wooden fence that separated her property from the one next door, the upper-floor windows of the Clemmonses' two-story stared down at her like milky blind eyes through the haze of smoke. There were no signs of activity. She hoped her neighbors, Burt and Janine, had gotten out safely. She thought she heard the crackling of flames in the distance and shivered a little, but it was only the rustle of leaves blowing in the wind.

"Hold the ladder steady and see that the hose doesn't get tangled," Hank instructed as he started up the ladder, pulling the hose with him.

"Wait!" she called when she saw him wobble. She was reminded he was in his seventies, which she tended to forget, he was so energetic. "Why don't I go up while you hold the ladder?"

He stopped and looked down at her, frowning. "If you're thinking I'm too old to be climbing ladders—"

"I wouldn't dream of it. But if anyone falls and breaks a leg, it should be me, since it's my name on the deed."

He eyed her skeptically but didn't argue. They switched places. When she climbed to the top of the ladder and saw the view from the roof, it caused her to gasp in horror. The fire advancing down the hillside seemed closer from this height. She could almost feel the heat of its flames and became momentarily paralyzed before she shook off her panic and got to work.

She thoroughly hosed the roof down as far as she could reach with the spray, and then they moved the ladder and hose to the other side of the house, where there was another spigot. Together, they got the job done in no time. Jo was descending the ladder when she heard a voice call, "Mommy!"

She dashed around to the rear of the house and saw her children standing on the deck, peering over the railing. Jess's face was white. She was pointing in the direction of the house directly behind theirs on Dogwood Court. Dogwood ran parallel to Mountain Laurel Lane, the last street before the state forestlands began, which formed the easternmost border of their neighborhood. Beyond stretched layers of forest and mountains. "Mrs. Beadle's house is on fire!" she cried.

Eleanor Beadle was the only neighbor on Dogwood Court with whom Jo was acquainted. This was due to the fact that she was also the head librarian at their local public library. A middle-aged woman with grown children, she'd worked at the library for decades and always had a book recommendation or two for the girls when they visited. She'd introduced Jess to classics like *Matilda* and the Encyclopedia Brown series, with which Jess had become obsessed.

Now Jo was horrified to see flames dancing on the roof of Mrs. Beadle's Craftsman bungalow, which was visible above the fence separating their properties. Her heart climbed into her throat. Horror morphed into terror when it occurred to her that Eleanor might be trapped inside.

"Christ."

She turned to see Hank standing behind her, staring grim-faced in the same direction. "Do you know if anyone's home?" she asked.

"I don't think so," he said. "I passed Eleanor on the road earlier. Looked like she was going on a trip. She has a son in Auburn. Maybe she's gone to stay with him."

Jo pulled her phone out to call 911 and cursed. No bars. Of course. The nearest cell tower would be toast by now. Her panic mounted. When she looked up from her phone and saw Hank heading toward the front of the house at a fast jog, she called to him, her voice sharp with alarm, "Wait! Where are you going?"

"To put the fire out!" he called back.

By the time she caught up with him, he was on his way to his truck carrying the hose and ladder. "You can't do it alone."

"Maybe not, but I can't sit back and do nothing."

"I'd come with, but—"

"You need to stay with the girls. I'll manage."

Jess was crying and Emma on the verge of tears when she returned to them. She hustled them back inside, where the smoke wasn't as thick, and pulled them into her arms, hugging them.

"Mommy, is Mrs. Beadle's house gonna burn down?" asked Jess.

"Hank went to put the fire out," she stated rather than offer false reassurance.

With any luck, someone would come forward to help him. But what were the chances? Their neighborhood had become a virtual ghost town. Some of the evacuees would have made it to safety, and of those who'd been turned back at the roadblock, some might not have heeded the advice to return home and gone to stay with friends or relatives instead. She hadn't noticed any signs of activity when she'd been driving through the neighborhood earlier. If only she could call for help!

Then she remembered her neighbor across the street had a landline. She'd noticed it the day she'd gone to return the Tupperware after Mrs. Atkins had brought them brownies to welcome them to the neighborhood. Probably no one was home. In any event, what good would it do to call 911 when they were effectively cut off from the outside world? But she had to try. She had to do *something*. If nothing else, she ought to check up on her elderly neighbor, in case she hadn't evacuated.

She clipped on her dog's leash, threw on a jacket and got the girls into theirs, and the four of them set out. It was sundown, the light fading from the sky, and they cast elongated shadows as they crossed the street. No lights shone from any of the houses on either side of the street as far as she could see.

"Mrs. Atkins! You're here!" she cried in surprise when the old lady answered her knock. "I didn't expect anyone to be home."

Mrs. Atkins was in her eighties with a round face crumpled with age, framed by a cap of gray hair. Pale-blue eyes peered from behind corrective lenses. "My granddaughter was on her way to pick me up and got turned back at the roadblock," she explained. "You?"

"Something like that." There was no time to explain. "May I use your phone?"

"Of course." Mrs. Atkins stepped back, holding the door open to let them in. "Though I'm surprised to be asked. Nobody ever uses landlines anymore except us old fogies."

"My phone's not working, and I need to make a call. It's an emergency."

"Oh dear. Is it a medical emergency? Or—" She cast an anxious glance toward the front window as if expecting to see flames dancing in her front yard.

"I'll explain later. Wait here," she told the girls and hurried toward the landline, a sixties-era model in baby blue, sitting on the hall table just past the foyer. When she lifted the receiver to her ear and heard a dial tone, she blessed Mrs. Atkins and the gods of analog.

"Nine-one-one. What's your emergency?" asked the male dispatcher after she placed her call.

"House fire on Dogwood Court." She gave her name and address. She didn't know Mrs. Beadle's address but provided the general location. "How soon can you get a fire crew out here?"

"I can't give you an exact ETA, with all the road closures," she was told, "but we have crews working on it. Roads are expected to be cleared for emergency vehicles sometime within the next hour."

Jo was relieved to hear the roads were being cleared, but she feared help might arrive too late. If the fire at Mrs. Beadle's spread, they'd all be in peril. This entire neighborhood could go up in flames.

"A house fire? Oh my word," exclaimed Mrs. Atkins after Jo ended the call. "And just when I thought it couldn't get any worse."

Jo met her worried gaze. "Hank went to see about putting the fire out, but it's more than one person can handle, and I was told the soonest the firefighters could get here is sometime within the hour."

Mrs. Atkins cut a glance at the girls, who stood stock-still in the entryway, quiet as mice. Even their dog was still, as though she sensed the tension in the air. "Why don't you go? Leave the girls with me."

Jo hesitated, torn between her responsibility to her children and the strong urge to go to Hank's aid. Would the girls be frightened if she left them, even with a trusted neighbor? Given the situation, and with Jess's issues . . .

She was distracted from her thoughts by a small hand slipping into hers. She glanced down to see Jess standing beside her, looking up at her with a brave face. "It's okay, Mommy. We can stay here."

Emma chimed in, taking her cue from her big sister. "We'll be okay, Mommy."

Oh, my darling girls. Her heart full, she bent to hug Jess, whispering in her ear, "I'm proud of you." She straightened, asking her neighbor, "Are you sure it's no trouble?"

"Of course. I'll take good care of them, don't you worry. Your dog, too." Mrs. Atkins bent to give Snickers a scratch behind her ears. "I taught fourth grade for over forty years. I think I can handle your two sweet girls." She cast her smiling gaze on Jess and Emma, who smiled back at her.

"Thank you," Jo said. "Hopefully, I won't be too long."

"Frankly, I'm glad for the company. Beats sitting home alone worrying about . . . well, things you worry about in the dark." That was when Jo noticed there were no lights on. "Power outage," Mrs. Atkins explained after she remarked on it. "But we'll be fine. I have a flashlight and candles."

As Jo hurried off, she heard her neighbor say, "Girls, how about a game of cards? Have you ever played gin rummy? No? I'll teach you. But first let's rustle up some candles and matches . . ."

Back home, Jo dashed inside just long enough to grab her car keys. Two minutes later she was braking in front of Mrs. Beadle's Craftsman bungalow on Dogwood. She'd expected to find it engulfed in flames and was surprised and relieved to see it intact. She saw signs of fire damage—the roof was partially collapsed and the exterior charred in spots—but it appeared the fire had been put out. It seemed nothing short of miraculous. She didn't see Hank but knew he had to be somewhere on the property, because his truck was parked out front. She went in search of him.

She called his name as she headed toward the rear of the house, picking her way around the bits of charred debris that littered the side yard. She grew worried when he didn't respond. As she let herself in through the gate to the backyard, two things caught her eye. The first was the ladder propped against the back porch. The second was the still figure lying on the ground, one hand loosely curled around the nozzle of the hose snaking across the grass. She froze in shock for a second before springing forward with a sharp cry.

"Hank!"

22

She felt for a pulse and gave a cry of relief when she found one. It was weak, but he was alive. His breathing was so shallow as to be nearly undetectable, however, and his face, she saw when she pulled down his towel, was ashen, with a bluish tinge to his lips. He was having a heart attack. She recognized the signs from when her grandpa Bob had had a heart attack when she was fourteen. She'd been alone with him at the time, and she remembered her terror and sense of helplessness like it was yesterday. She hadn't known what to do except call 911. Luckily, her grandfather had survived and made a full recovery, but she'd been deeply shaken by the experience. She'd taken the CPR class offered by their local fire department so she wouldn't be caught unprepared the next time there was an emergency.

Which was how she knew what to do now.

She'd never put her training into practice in a real life-and-death situation, but it came back to her as she tended to Hank, operating on autopilot. She covered him with her jacket to keep him warm. She cleared his airway before administering mouth-to-mouth, alternating with timed chest compressions. When his breathing grew more regular, she stopped giving him mouth-to-mouth but continued with the chest compressions. Talking to him all the while, in the hope he could hear her.

"Stay with me, buddy. I've got you. You're gonna be okay. I won't let you die. But you've got to hang on. You hear me? You've got to hang on until help arrives and they can get you to the hospital."

His eyes fluttered open at one point. "Jo?"

She squeezed his hand, which was ice cold. "Where does it hurt?"

He grimaced as if in pain and tried to raise his right arm before letting it drop back onto the ground as though it weighed a hundred pounds. "Feels . . . like . . . an elephant . . . on my chest."

"You're having a heart attack. But you're gonna be okay. So . . . please. Hang in there. Help is on the way."

"You . . . got . . . through?"

"I used Mrs. Atkins's landline. Who knew that old relic would come in handy? The sixties can keep its shag carpeting, but once this is over, I'm getting a landline of my own."

"Good . . . idea."

"You'll be my first call."

A smile passed over his lips, and then his expression grew troubled. "I'm . . . sorry."

"Sorry for what?"

"I wish . . . I could've done more."

"More than keep this house from burning down and the entire neighborhood along with it? No one could put out a wildfire single-handedly. Hank, you may be a hero, but you're no superhero."

He huffed a laugh. "You . . . haven't seen . . . my cape."

Jo choked back a sob and forced a smile onto her face. Her eyes were watering, and she knew it wasn't just from the smoke in the air. She remembered the day Sean died. They'd talked about ordinary, everyday things—Jess's latest report card, Emma's potty training, the new soup recipe Jo was trying out—and then Sean had looked her in the eye and said, as if he'd known it would be the last time he would say the words, "I love you, babe." She'd told him she loved him back before he lapsed into unconsciousness. He never woke up. The memory gutted her. She couldn't bear the thought of losing Hank, too.

Please, don't let him die.

◆ ◆ ◆

Within thirty minutes of her 911 call, emergency responders were at the scene, blue and red lights strobing in the darkness, the air crackling with two-way radio communications. Along with the fire crew, there was a deputy from the Washburn County Sheriff's Department. Fortunately, the fire department had taken the precaution of sending one of its paramedic units in addition to a fire engine. While members of the crew cleared the building, others tended to Hank, checking his vitals and lifting him onto a wheeled stretcher before placing an oxygen mask over his nose and mouth. Jo didn't let go of his hand until he was loaded into the paramedic unit.

By the time she returned to Mrs. Atkins's after the sheriff's deputy had taken her statement, she was drained. It seemed like an eternity had passed. She found Jess and Emma seated at the kitchen table playing cards. A candle burned on the table alongside a half-eaten plate of gingersnaps. Snickers was curled up at their feet. For a moment she stood in the hallway outside the kitchen with her neighbor drinking in the sweet scene before the girls spotted her and came running.

"Where's Hank? Why isn't he with you?" Jess wanted to know.

"Did Mrs. Beadle's house burn down?" asked Emma.

"No, sweetie, Mrs. Beadle's house didn't burn down. Hank put the fire out before the firefighters got there. But he . . . he wasn't feeling well, so they're taking him to the ER to get checked out."

"But he'll come home when he's feeling better?" Jess eyed her anxiously.

"Yes, but he may have to stay overnight at the hospital."

"Was it his heart?" asked Mrs. Atkins when she and Jo were having a word in private, while the girls finished their game.

"How did you guess?" asked Jo.

"My husband, Charlie, died of a heart attack when he was a few years younger than Hank. I pray to God Hank has a better outcome."

"I did what I could for him." Jo briefly described the actions she'd taken, from when she'd arrived at the scene to find Hank collapsed on the ground to when the emergency responders showed up. "I just hope it was enough."

"Oh my. You must have been so frightened. And Hank! The dear man. To think he risked his life trying to keep our neighborhood safe. I can't say I'm surprised. Did you know he was a war hero? Of course you do. I see you kept the sign honoring his service that Martha put up."

"Yes, and he was a hero today," Jo said in a choked voice.

"So were you, my dear." Mrs. Atkins patted her hand. "Most people panic in an emergency, but you kept a cool head. You did what needed to be done. Thanks to you, Hank has a fighting chance."

Jo prayed he would live to fight another day.

Before leaving, she made two more calls on the landline. First, she phoned Frannie, to tell her the news about Hank. Frannie was someone who could be counted on to keep cool in a crisis. She'd dealt with any number of crises involving Hannah through the years. She remained calm now, too, and asked all the right questions, although Jo could hear the barely suppressed panic in her voice. Then she heard something else—the sound of a car engine firing. Frannie was already in her car, headed for the ER, by the time she ended the call.

Next, she called Kyra and arranged for her and the girls to stay the night at Coop and Kyra's. They'd be safe there, and her friends could watch the girls while Jo visited Hank in the hospital. Kyra said she'd love to have them. "And Lord knows we have the room." Their renovated farmhouse in the countryside had two guest rooms and was dog friendly. "You're welcome to stay as long as you need."

Not wanting to abandon her neighbor, Jo waited until Mrs. Atkins's granddaughter had arrived to pick her up before leaving. She stopped for gas on the way to Coop and Kyra's and saw that she had a signal on her phone. At last! She had one missed call and a voicemail message, from a number with a Seattle area code. She played back the message. It was from Hank's daughter-in-law, Cherise. As his emergency contact, she'd been informed about Hank by someone at the hospital. She'd be there as soon as she could, she said in her message. Jo returned the call and they spoke briefly. Cherise sounded frustrated because the earliest flight she could get wasn't until tomorrow morning.

After she got off the phone with Cherise, Jo tried calling Ian. She assumed he'd gotten the news about Hank by now. Knowing how close he was to his grandpa, she imagined he was sick with worry. She wanted him to know she was there for him. But he didn't pick up.

Jo felt like a refugee disembarking from a ship after a lengthy ocean voyage when she finally stepped into the cozy warmth of Coop and Kyra's house. But her day wasn't over yet. Once the girls were settled and asleep in the guest room they'd been assigned, she headed for the hospital.

It was half past ten by the time she arrived. Entering the terrazzo-tiled lobby of Washburn Medical in Pine City, she remembered when she used to come with Sean when he was a patient here. Their visits had been so frequent—between his doctor appointments, endless rounds of tests, and chemo treatments—Sean had once joked that they'd worn a path from the entrance to the oncology department on the first floor. She felt the same emotions she had then: a mixture of hope, fear, dread.

After checking in at the reception desk, she took the elevator to the third floor and followed the signs to the cardiac care unit. She found Frannie sitting alone in the family visiting room looking at something on her phone. Frannie lifted her gaze as Jo entered. Her eyes were bleak.

Jo sat down next to her, and they hugged. "How's he doing?"

"Hanging in there. I wasn't able to get much out of the cardiologist who's on call tonight, being as I'm not a family member. All I know is that he's in critical condition." Her voice cracked.

"We'll know more once Cherise gets here."

"When will that be?"

"She said the soonest she could get here is tomorrow morning. She was hoping to get an earlier flight, but they were all booked. How are you holding up?"

"About as well as you might expect under the circumstances. I'm glad you came." She squeezed Jo's hand.

"I got here as quick as I could. I had to wait until my neighbor's granddaughter picked her up before I could leave."

"Where are the girls?"

"At Coop and Kyra's. We're staying with them until it's safe to return home."

Frannie gave a weary smile. "So much for making plans. We planned on you sheltering at my place, where I'd envisioned a relaxed evening of supper followed by a movie. Instead, here we are at the hospital, us holding vigil while Hank . . ." She trailed off. "Meanwhile, I've been getting an education." She glanced down at her phone. "Google 'heart attack' and you can scare yourself into having one. Did you know the first symptom of a heart attack in fifty percent of the cases is death?"

Jo shuddered. "No, and that's one statistic I'd have preferred not to know. What I don't understand is why Hank? My dad was overweight and hadn't exercised in years apart from swinging a golf club when he had his heart attack. But Hank's in great shape and stays active."

"Who knows? All I know is, the man I love is fighting for his life."

Jo knew just how she felt. She'd been there. When Sean had been battling cancer, her moods had oscillated daily between high hopes and the depths of despair. "Have you been in to see him yet?"

"Once, and only a few minutes."

"How did he look?"

Frannie just shook her head. "What if he doesn't make it through the night? What if I never get the chance to tell him—" She broke off, bringing a fist to her mouth to stifle a sob.

"Tell him what?"

"That I love him."

"You haven't told him yet?"

"I was waiting for the right time. Like we had all the time in the world. Like either of us is getting any younger. Stupid, huh?"

"Something tells me he already knows." Jo was grateful that nothing had been left unsaid between her and Sean. They'd talked about everything that mattered and shared everything that was in their hearts. Even on her darkest days after he died, she'd had the comfort of knowing she'd been well and truly loved by the man she'd loved.

Frannie's sister and daughter showed up half an hour later. Hannah, a Jennifer Beals look-alike with her big brown eyes and cloud of dark curls, flung herself into Frannie's arms. "Mom! I'm sorry we couldn't get here sooner. Traffic was a nightmare! It was backed up for miles. How's Hank? Is he going to be all right? What did the doctor say? You must be going out of your mind!"

Frannie smiled and gave her a motherly pat on the back. Hannah was a woman in her forties, but in many ways, she was a perpetual child. "He's hanging in there, and so am I."

Vanessa carried a tray of coffees and a large box of pastries from Cowboy Coffee. After Jo and Frannie had each helped themselves to a coffee and a pastry, Vanessa took the rest to the nurses' station. "While I'm sure Hank's getting the best possible care, it doesn't hurt to show the nurses some appreciation," she said. "I'll never forget their kindness when Buck was a patient here." A shadow of some old pain crossed her face as she spoke of her husband, who'd died four years earlier.

"Thanks, sis." Frannie smiled at her. "Trust you to think of everything."

Suzy showed up minutes later, bouncing in like a cheerleader at halftime during a losing game. "I heard something about a party. Oh, honey." She took one look at Frannie's face and abandoned her false cheer. Instead of attempting to lift her spirits, she comforted her oldest friend with a hug.

Marisol came next, carrying a bag with the Buckboard Books logo on it, a line drawing of a cat perched on a stack of books. "I thought you might like something to read while you wait." She pulled a book from the bag. "I think you'll like this one. It's a love story set in World War II Paris. The hero is an American journalist and the heroine is a spy for the French Resistance."

"Does it have a happy ending?" asked Frannie warily.

"Neither of them dies," she assured Frannie.

Kyra was the last to arrive, with Ranger. "The girls were still asleep when I left," she told Jo. "And Coop has strict instructions to call if anything changes." Jo wanted to be there when Jess and Emma woke up.

"How'd you get this guy past the reception desk?" asked Hannah as she crouched to ruffle Ranger's ears while he licked her face. They were old friends. "I didn't know dogs were allowed."

"Ranger's not just any dog. He's a licensed therapy dog." Kyra bent to unclip his leash. The shepherd mix showed why he was her partner in interviewing witnesses and victims of crimes when he went over to Frannie and placed his head on her lap as though sensing her distress.

"How'd you know this was just what I needed?" Frannie stroked the thick fur of his neck.

As the women sat and talked, the conversation turned inevitably to the wildfire. The good news was, the area that had been directly in the path of the wildfire, where Jo lived, had been spared due to a shift in the wind, which had caused the fire to spread to the forested area to the northeast instead. The bad news was, the firefighters' best efforts hadn't slowed the fire's spread. Everyone was praying for rain.

Around midnight, Jo said her goodbyes and headed back to Kyra's. If she didn't get some rest, she'd drop from exhaustion. She also wanted to be there when her children woke up. She was passing through the corridor lined with patient rooms when she spied Hank in one of them. The sight of him lying so still in his hospital bed, hooked up to machines with tubes running out of him, came as a shock even though she'd seen him looking worse tonight. Maybe it was the machines and beeping monitors. They might have been keeping him alive, but they also served to remind her of the fragility of his existence.

She slipped into the room after glancing around to see if anyone was watching. She didn't know what the rules were here in the CCU, but she was pretty sure patient visits were restricted. Hank didn't move or open his eyes when she took his hand in hers.

Her eyes became wet, and she swallowed to get her voice past the lump in her throat. "Hank, it's me, Jo. I don't know if you can hear me. I hope so because there's something you need to know, if you haven't guessed already. Best decision I ever made besides marrying my husband was buying a house with you in it. Some thought it was risky, me included at first, but you taught me that good things can come from taking risks. You've been a friend and a father figure for my children, and I'm pretty sure my dog likes you better than she does me. In fact, I sometimes think Sean sent you, never more than tonight. Next time I hear a bell ring, I'll know it's because you got your wings."

She couldn't have sworn to it, but she thought she saw the ghost of a smile pass over his lips.

She slipped in quietly when she arrived back at Coop and Kyra's, using the spare key she'd been given. She crept up the stairs and down the hall to the guest rooms at the far end. The first one she came to was occupied by her girls and their dog. All three were fast asleep when she peeked in on them. As was she, almost as soon as her head hit the pillow after she got to her room. She slept soundly. The next morning, she was awakened by voices and someone breathing on her.

"Wake up, Mommy!"

Jo cracked one eye open to see Jess and Emma had crawled into bed with her, their faces pressed close to hers. She couldn't help smiling, though she could've done with another hour or two of sleep. "Oh, it's you. I thought I was being eaten alive by a pair of bunny rabbits who mistook me for a carrot."

They both giggled, and it warmed her heart to find them looking none the worse for yesterday's ordeal.

"Why are you wearing your clothes?" asked Emma.

Jo glanced down to see she still wore the shirt she'd had on yesterday, though she'd apparently removed her pants at some point. "I was too tired to change into my pajamas when I got back last night."

"Did you visit Hank at the hospital?"

"I did."

"Is he better?"

"We won't know until we talk to his doctor, but he was resting comfortably when I left him." She felt a lurch in her chest, wondering if that was still true. She needed to check on him. But first she needed to reassure her daughters.

"When's he coming home?" asked Jess.

"I don't know, sweetie, but when I do, you'll be the first to know. What are you two doing up so early?"

"We couldn't sleep anymore," said Emma. Her baby-fine hair was sticking up in some spots, and she wore her Tinker Bell nightgown. Tinker Bell was her second-favorite animated character after Princess Ariel. Jo suspected it had to do with the ballerina costume.

"What time is it, anyway?" The fact that she was seeing daylight told her she'd slept past the hour when she normally got up.

"Time for breakfast," Jess announced. "Uncle Coop is making waffles."

The smell of waffles cooking drifted up the stairs. The girls must've smelled it, too, because they climbed down from the bed, and a moment later, she heard the pounding of their feet on the stairs. It was 7:20, she saw when she picked up her phone. She dialed Frannie's number.

"How's he doing? Any change?"

"No." Frannie sounded exhausted. "But he's still with us."

"Thank God for that. Where are you?"

"At the hospital." Said in a tone that suggested she'd never left. "Where else?"

"Did you get any sleep last night?"

"I closed my eyes for a couple hours after everyone left. I made them leave, by the way. They wanted to stay."

Of course they had. "I'll be there as soon as I've eaten breakfast and gotten the girls sorted out."

After ending the call, Jo took a quick shower and threw on some clean clothes. Downstairs in the big country kitchen, she found Coop standing at the butcher block island prying a waffle from the waffle iron with a fork, while her girls ate the waffles on their plates at the pine trestle table overlooking the "north forty," as he called it. The two dogs sat below licking their chops, in hope of a dropped crumb.

"Morning," he greeted her. "I would've let you sleep in, but the girls had other ideas."

"Thanks anyway. And thanks for feeding us." She yawned. "What time did Kyra get home last night?"

"Sometime around two, I think. She's still asleep. Waffle?"

"Yes, please." She suddenly realized she was starving. She hadn't eaten a proper meal since lunch yesterday.

Coop placed the waffle on a plate. As he passed it to her, his gaze held hers. She shook her head in answer to his unspoken question, letting him know there was no update on Hank's condition. "If you're planning to head back over to the hospital after you eat, I could watch the girls," he offered.

"Are you sure? I can make other arrangements if you're busy."

"I've already rescheduled my morning appointments. Girls!" he called in his booming voice. "What do you say we head down to the creek after breakfast? We have some tadpoles to catch."

"Yay!" The girls seemed excited, so Jo didn't feel as guilty about leaving them.

"Anyone ever tell you you're a keeper?" she said to Coop as she headed out after eating.

"Yeah, me. I tell Kyra all the time. One of these days I'll persuade her to marry me," he added with a confident grin.

It was 9:42 when Jo pulled into the hospital parking lot. It was chilly. The haze of smoke that had covered the sky for the past few days was mixed now with clouds. It seemed their prayers had been answered. But it would take a soaking rain to put the fire out. She couldn't determine whether the clouds overhead were storm clouds or boded scattered showers. She found an empty space and parked. As she climbed from her car, she spied a man walking in her direction from the other end of the parking lot. Tall and lean with short dark hair and a loose-limbed stride. He looked familiar. She couldn't make out his features from that distance, but something about him caused her pulse to quicken.

"Ian? Is that you?" she called as he approached.

He stopped and stared. "Jo? Oh my God. I don't believe it."

"Your mom didn't tell me you were coming."

"She didn't know until I called her from the airport a couple of hours ago. I've been in transit since I got the news about Pop-Pop. I hopped on the first cargo plane out of Ramstein bound for the US. It got me as far as Boston, and from there I caught the red-eye to Sacramento."

Jo couldn't get over the reality of him in the flesh. The man standing before her was even better-looking than his virtual self, his eyes bluer than any pixels could capture—the blue of a mountain lake in summer. They stood out in contrast to his brown skin. The one thing about him that was the same in person as over the phone was his voice. The voice that had instantly put her at ease when they'd first met, comforted her on more than one occasion, and calmed her when she'd been so scared driving home the other night. The voice that sent a thrill coursing through her hearing it now. He wore khakis and a button-down underneath a navy windbreaker, both rumpled as though he'd slept in them. His jaw was shadowed with beard stubble. "Please tell me you're not AWOL."

"No, although I might've been if things had worked out differently. As it so happened, my CO, Captain Kellogg, not only granted my request for compassionate leave, but he also personally arranged for my transport out of Ramstein. Turns out the 'old bastard' has a heart after all. Who knew?"

"I tried to call you."

"You did? Why didn't you leave a message?"

"I didn't know if you'd heard the news about your grandpa. I didn't want to be the one to break it to you, at least not in a voicemail."

His expression clouded over at the reminder of why they were both here. "Mom's with him now."

"What did she find out from his doctor?"

"He suffered a major coronary, but you already know that. Mom tells me you saved his life. He might've died if you hadn't gotten there when you did and given him CPR." His eyes were soft with gratitude.

"I did what I could." *I just hope it was enough.* "What's his prognosis?"

"My mom can tell you more than I can, being a nurse. She's also been consulting with his doctor. All I know is, he needs surgery to replace a damaged valve among other repairs, and they can't operate until his vitals stabilize. The next twenty-four hours are critical."

Jo shivered, and was once again in the doctor's office with Sean on the day she'd heard the words "inoperable brain cancer" for the first time outside *Grey's Anatomy* and *Scrubs.* Words that hadn't registered until she'd seen the shadowy mass on the MRI. "How did this happen? Was it sudden, or were there symptoms he ignored?"

"I never heard him complain about chest pains. And he got a clean bill of health after his last physical. But that was a while ago. He doesn't go for his annual physical as often as he should. Mom's been bugging him about it. I guess she should've leaned on him harder. Hey, are you okay? You look a little shaky." He took her by the shoulders, steadying her as she swayed on her feet.

It was catching up with her all at once—the aftereffect of yesterday's adrenaline rush coupled with the anxiety gnawing at her. She suddenly felt drained and lightheaded. Ian's strong hands gripping her shoulders acted on her like a jumper cable on a dead car battery, jolting her back to life. She felt suddenly energized, her body tingling. "I'm fine. Just tired. I didn't get much sleep last night."

Ian's eyes locked with hers and she noticed he hadn't let go of her, even though she'd regained her balance. "Would it be okay if I hugged you? It might seem weird if I shook your hand. Even though this is the first time we've met in person, I think we're beyond the formalities, don't you?"

She nodded and leaned into him as he drew her close. There was none of the usual awkwardness of strangers embracing. They fit. *Like peas and carrots.* Ian held her gaze after they drew apart, and she fell into the clear, depthless blue of his eyes. The tingling awareness he'd sparked in her had intensified, zinging through her body like electrical pulses. "Shall we?" he said, tipping his head the direction of the hospital building where Hank was fighting for his life. "Mom's eager to meet you. Although I should warn you. She doesn't do handshakes, either. She's a hugger."

"I think we could all use a hug right now."

They were nearing the building when Jo felt something cold and wet splash against the top of her head. She glanced up to see the sky had darkened. Seconds later, the heavens opened up and rain poured down. She grabbed Ian's hand and together they dashed for cover.

23

The call came the next day, while she was mopping the kitchen floor. She'd been on edge waiting for news since Hank had gone into surgery several hours earlier. Keeping busy to keep from picturing him on the operating table with his chest cut open—or worse—and becoming consumed by her fears. Yet it startled her when her phone rang, and when she lunged forward to grab it from the kitchen counter, she slipped on the wet floor and nearly fell before she snatched it up. The call was from Ian.

"Is he out of surgery?" she asked in a breathless voice.

"That's why I'm calling," he said.

As she listened to what he had to say, she leaned against the mop handle, using it as a crutch to support herself as her knees buckled. When she ended the call a minute later, it became a firehouse pole down which she slid. She landed on her butt on the wet floor and burst into tears.

The sound of her weeping brought the girls running, followed by Snickers. They'd been playing out on the deck, and there were strands of Silly String caught in their hair and in their dog's fur. The danger from the wildfire had passed, due to the four inches of rainfall that had soaked the region yesterday and doused the fire, so it was safe for them to be outdoors again.

"Mommy, what's wrong?" asked Emma as the girls approached.

Jo held out a hand, traffic cop–style. "D-don't come any c-closer. You might s-slip and f-fall." They both froze like baby deer in headlights. Not because they were following orders or because the floor was wet, she suspected, but because they were shocked by the sight of their mother weeping. Any weeping she'd done after Sean died had been in private.

"Why are you crying?" asked Jess, her eyes dropping to the phone Jo clutched. She sounded anxious. They were all worried about Hank.

Jo drew in a shuddery breath and knee-walked across the wet floor to where her daughters stood. She pulled them into her arms, holding them close while Snickers tried to squeeze in between them. "These are happy tears. Hank's grandson just called to say he's going to be all right."

The operation had been a success, and Hank was expected to make a full recovery.

Hank remained hospitalized for a full week after his surgery, during which time Ian and Cherise stayed in his quarters downstairs at the house on Mountain Laurel Lane. Jo enjoyed getting to know them both and hanging out with them at home when they weren't visiting Hank at the hospital. Cherise was a formidable-looking woman, with broad cheekbones and salt-and-pepper hair she wore braided in an elaborate weave, piled on top of her head. She had a ready smile and an infectious laugh, but woe unto any hospital staffer who crossed her—she was as fierce an advocate as she was devoted to Hank. Jo imagined few in her workplace, including doctors, could stand up to her when she was in badass-nurse mode. Jo was sorry to see her go at the end of the week, but she and the girls had a standing invitation to visit Cherise in Seattle anytime.

She was even sorrier to see Ian go when the time came. They hadn't known each other for long, but it felt as though she were saying goodbye to an old friend, one she might not see again for some time. "Thanks for your hospitality," he said. "And thanks for talking me off the ledge." On the day of Hank's surgery, after he was wheeled into the OR, Ian had called her and they'd talked for over an hour.

"We talked each other off the ledge," she corrected him. "So I still owe you."

They stood on the front porch, Ian with his duffel bag parked at his feet. It was midmorning, and the girls were in school. They'd said their goodbyes to Ian earlier. He'd thoroughly charmed them both during his visit, and Jo suspected Jess had a crush on him. She didn't blame her.

Ian tipped her a salute. "Until next time."

Jo felt bereft as she watched him walk away, his duffel slung over one broad shoulder, headed for his rental car in the driveway. Would there be a next time? She hoped so. She missed him already.

Hank didn't come home. Instead, after he was discharged from the hospital, Frannie took him back to her place, where he wouldn't have stairs to climb while he recuperated. Before that, she'd been a constant presence at his bedside during visiting hours. When she announced that she and Hank were engaged to be married and planning a December wedding, no one was surprised.

"Nothing like a health scare to take the chill off cold feet," joked Suzy after Frannie made the announcement.

Jo was reminded of Aesop's fable about the North Wind and the Sun quarreling over which was more powerful. Just as the Sun succeeds in getting a passing traveler to remove his cloak where the North Wind failed, Hank's devotion had opened Frannie's eyes and heart to a future she couldn't envision before.

Love is the sun.

There was, of course, the matter of the vacancy created by Hank's departure. He felt bad about it and offered to make it up to her by paying for the months he still had left on his lease. Jo wouldn't hear of it, and as it turned out, she didn't need the money in the end. Thanks to an article in the November issue of *Bride* magazine, in which she was named as one of the up-and-coming wedding photographers in the

West, she was seeing a dramatic increase in bookings. She might decide to rent out the downstairs again someday. Or not.

You never know what life will throw at you. The trick was to be prepared for anything and everything.

◆ ◆ ◆

As her gaze swept the packed church on the day of the wedding, Jo marveled at how everything had come together in just two and a half months. This was mainly due to Frannie's efforts combined with her ties to the community. She had the church booked, the officiant lined up, and the flowers ordered with a few phone calls. Everyone who knew and loved her was happy to lend a hand. Hank, in compliance with his doctor's orders, was assigned the easiest task, addressing the wedding invitations, which he could do sitting down. Frannie had done the rest, with the help of her daughter, sister, and friends. Vanessa was hosting the reception at Cowboy Coffee, which Suzy, Marisol, and Kyra had helped organize. Jo had volunteered her professional services for the wedding, although she would be attending the reception strictly as a guest, at Hank's and Frannie's insistence. Presently, she was positioned to the right of the altar, camera at the ready, with the procession due to commence shortly.

It was the day before Christmas Eve. Outside, the temperature was below freezing and patches of snow covered the ground. Inside, the sun streaming through the stained glass windows of the sanctuary cast a jewel-toned glow. The historic church, constructed of stone with a vaulted roof and bell tower, was drafty, as old buildings tended to be, but today no one seemed to mind. The mood was joyful and the decor festive. Seasonal flowers in baskets spray-painted gold and tied with white ribbons—a mix of red and white poinsettias, amaryllis, and pink-frost hellebores—were interspersed along the altar and middle aisle. Garlands made of pine boughs were twined around doorframes and railings. The air was fragrant with the mingled scents of incense, flowers, and evergreen.

Jo was remembering the spring day, just over twelve and a half years earlier, when she'd stood in this church as a bride. She saw her and Sean's younger selves, she in her satin-and-lace wedding dress, which had been her mother's, altered to fit her, he in his one good suit, facing each other at the altar. She'd been trembling, but her certainty that Sean was the One had never wavered. As they'd exchanged vows, she'd pictured them celebrating other occasions in the years to come—birthdays, anniversaries, christenings, graduations. She'd seen babies and grandbabies, and imagined them, someday in the distant future, as one of those cute older couples who still held hands after decades of marriage.

Except Sean hadn't lived long enough for them to grow old together.

Emotions swirled in her like the cool draft swirling around her ankles, but for the first time, it didn't hurt to remember. Her life was not as she'd once envisioned, no, but she'd discovered you could be happy with what you were given in the absence of your heart's desire. She might never find love again, but she had her memories of Sean and their two beautiful children, who were presently behind the scenes preparing to make their entrances as flower girls.

For now, it was enough.

She idly rubbed her finger, from which she'd removed her ring to squeeze her hand through the narrow opening of a vase she'd been washing at the time. When she'd gone to slip it back on, something had stopped her. Or rather, someone. Sean's voice, saying, *You don't need to wear it anymore.*

Just then, the groom emerged from the vestry, followed by his best man, and they took up their positions at the altar. Hank looked handsome in his navy suit, a sprig of stephanotis tucked into one lapel, thinner than before his heart attack but no less dapper—Clint Eastwood minus his Dirty Harry squint. But it was the best man on whom Jo's gaze lingered. Ian was the picture of an officer and a gentleman in his dress uniform, its brass buttons gleaming and his shoes shined. They'd stayed in touch since his visit in October, and she'd come to look forward to their regular phone and FaceTime chats. If she'd developed feelings for him, she'd been in denial about it. Until he'd shown up again. Today, and at last night's rehearsal dinner, she'd found herself tracking him with her gaze and noticing details about him she hadn't noticed before, like how one side of his mouth tipped up slightly higher than the other when he smiled, and his nervous habit of sawing at his thumb with his index finger. It was unsettling, to say the least. Now when their eyes met, it jolted her like the electrical charge that had coursed through her body when they'd hugged for the first time. Her cheeks flushed.

She got busy snapping photos, hoping no one would notice, with her face hidden behind her camera, that it was the color of the red poinsettia at her feet.

She was distracted from her thoughts when the organ in the choir loft began to play. The familiar melody of "Ave Maria," accompanied by a soprano voice singing the vocals, resonated throughout the church, so beautiful it made the tiny hairs on the back of her neck stand up. The members of the wedding party began to file in through the double door. Vanessa came first, as the matron of honor, followed by Hannah and the three other bridesmaids: Suzy, Kyra, and Marisol. In a break from tradition, due to time constraints, each wore an outfit of her choosing, as opposed to them wearing matching dresses. Vanessa appeared regal in a lavender silk wrap dress with sprigs of baby's breath tucked into her braided coronet. Hannah wore a lacy white top and long purple taffeta skirt. Marisol looked like a younger, more stylish version of Mrs. Claus in a wine-colored velvet dress trimmed with faux white fur at the neckline, one of her vintage finds. Kyra wore a calf-length dress in a silky pale-blue fabric sewn with metallic threads that glittered with her movements. But it was Suzy who stole the show in her fitted emerald-green shantung-silk suit, four-inch black patent-leather heels, and cute little hat with a veil that dipped down over one eye, which made her look like a forties film star.

Next came the ring bearer and flower girls. Jo couldn't decide who looked more adorable, her daughters in their matching tartan dresses scattering rose petals, or her dog sporting a ribbon around her neck, from which hung a small heart-shaped pillow with the rings pinned to it. Jess and Emma performed their roles as they'd rehearsed, without a hitch until they got to the end of the aisle, when they broke rank and scampered over to Jo. Snickers looked like she was about to follow but was brought to a standstill by a low whistle from Hank. He'd worked with her on her obedience training when he'd lived with them, disproving the old adage "you can't teach an old dog new tricks."

Jo bent to hug her children, whispering, "You did good."

Last but not least came the bride. She walked unescorted—because, as Frannie had put it, "I'm past the age of being given away, and anyone who might've done the honors is long gone"—a vision in her ankle-length dress, made from ivory silk that fell in graceful lines over her slender body, with long sleeves and a cowl neck. She carried a bouquet, a mix of anemones and narcissus and pink peonies, and wore a garland of rosebuds in lieu of a veil. No makeup except for a touch of tinted lip gloss. The blush on her cheeks was natural. She looked beautiful and, most of all, like herself. When she joined Hank at the altar, they were both glowing. Jo grew misty-eyed as she snapped photos of them.

Lydia Fowler, an old friend of Frannie's and an ordained minister, officiated. She told guests about how Hank and Frannie had met and why they were perfect for each other. She followed with a Bible reading from Proverbs. Then it was time for the bride and groom to say a few words, starting with Hank. "First time I met you, at Jo's house-painting party, I thought you were the most beautiful woman I'd ever laid eyes on. When I asked you to join me in the bedroom and you said yes, I felt like the luckiest son of a gun on the planet. Didn't matter that we were doing nothing more than painting walls, I knew you were the one for me. And as I stand before you today—damned grateful to still be standing, I might add—I promise to spend every day of the rest of my life proving myself worthy of your love."

"You, Hank Goodwin, were just what I needed when I didn't know I needed it," Frannie said when it was her turn. "Before I met you, I'd have told any man who asked me to marry him he was barking up the wrong tree. Yet as I stand before you today, I've never been so sure of anything in my life as I am about marrying you. Because, you see, you're not just any man—you're *the* man. The one I was meant to be with. It only took us a few decades to find each other. And after I almost lost you, I decided I wasn't going to waste another minute of however much time we have together."

Jo, feeling a mix of joy and nostalgia, paused to brush away a tear as she snapped a photo of them kissing after they were pronounced husband and wife. When she caught Ian's eye again as she lowered the camera, the look he gave her was . . . intense. Suddenly, the drafty old building felt too warm.

She took more pictures of the bride and groom making their way down the aisle and exiting the church amid an eco-friendly shower of birdseed tossed by the guests, Hank with his arm firmly around Frannie's waist so she wouldn't slip and fall on the icy steps. Jo knew without looking at the photos she'd taken today that they'd be among her best. Because she'd *felt* it. She had her mojo back.

Afterward, she drove home with the girls to drop off her camera and equipment, and her dog, before heading to the reception. She arrived at Cowboy Coffee to find a sign on the door that read CLOSED FOR A SPECIAL EVENT. Inside the place was transformed. The dining area in back was festooned with crepe-paper streamers and heart-shaped Mylar balloons. A Christmas tree stood in one corner, its lights twinkling. The tables were covered in white linen cloths, each with a potted Christmas cactus at its center, and rearranged to create space for a dance floor.

Food and beverages were being served at two long tables placed side by side. One held platters of antipasti, salads, and hot foods in chafing dishes, the other wine and champagne and nonalcoholic fruit punch. The wedding cake, a glorious multilayered confection piped with swirls of frosting in pastel shades and topped with miniature bride and groom figurines, occupied its own spotlit table. The DJ who'd been hired for the occasion was playing "My Girl" from his playlist of hit tunes from the sixties and seventies.

The place was crowded and the mood merry. Jo spotted her neighbors Mrs. Atkins and Mrs. Beadle standing over by the beverage table holding drinks, their gray heads bent together in conversation. Hank's brother, Paul, from Ohio was chatting with one of Hank's biker buddies, "Monty," the ham radio hobbyist. She recognized several staff members and residents from the Morningside Veterans' Care Home from when she and the girls had attended the talent show Hank had put on there. People were gathered around the newlyweds, congratulating them, including Frannie's old friends Kurt McNally, whom she'd babysat when she was a high schooler and whom she still bossed around even though he was now the sheriff of Washburn County, and Gertie Naylor, who'd worked at the sheriff's office before she retired.

Jo greeted people she knew as she made her way to the buffet table with the girls in tow. Her mouth watered seeing the spread, which included Creole dishes representative of Vanessa and Frannie's heritage: jambalaya and dirty rice, étouffée, shrimp and grits, and orzo with sausage. The girls, however, were homing in on the sloppy joe sliders from the Cowboy Coffee menu.

"Smart choice," said Marisol, coming up alongside them, holding a plate of food. "I can't resist their sloppy joes, either."

She was with her boyfriend, who was visiting for the holidays. Cal resembled an adorable cartoon character with his wide mouth and sandy hair that stuck straight up like broom straw on top, and he and Marisol made the perfect couple, despite and maybe because of their twenty-year age gap. Jo wondered if Marisol might be the next Tattooed Lady to get engaged, though Kyra was the more likely prospect, given that she lived with her boyfriend. Out of the corner of her eye, Jo caught sight of Coop and Kyra sitting at one of the tables with Suzy and her current Mr. Right For Now, Cliff the pharmacist, the four of them chatting over their plates of food. Jo couldn't help noticing that Suzy seemed a bit distracted, possibly because of her family drama involving her dad.

After the food and toasts, there was dancing. Hank and Frannie were the first to take to the dance floor. They slow danced to the tune of "At Last," and then others began drifting over to join them. Marisol and Cal. Suzy and Cliff. Coop and Kyra. Coop's parents, Shirley and Ed. At one point, Jo saw her neighbor Mrs. Atkins dancing a lively foxtrot with one of the spryer residents of the old soldiers' home, a Korean War vet named Calvin. It seemed everywhere Jo looked, she saw couples. It was a bittersweet reminder of when she'd been part of a couple. Which was why she'd avoided Ian today, ducking him whenever it seemed their paths might cross and finding other people to chat with when it appeared he was headed her way. In her current emotional state, while she was missing Sean, being around a man to whom she was strongly attracted might prove combustible.

The dancing was interrupted at one point by the cutting of the cake, of which Jo snapped photos with her phone—even without her Nikon, she could still make magic—and more speeches. By the time they'd eaten their cake, it was past the girls' bedtime. Jo said her goodbyes and was donning her coat after helping Jess and Emma with theirs when she heard a voice say, "Leaving so soon?"

She looked up to see Ian. For a moment, she could only stare at him. He was a one-man force field, immobilizing her and rendering her speechless. "It's past the girls' bedtime," she finally managed.

"Shoot. And I was hoping one of you lovely ladies would do me the honor of dancing with me again," he said to the girls, flashing his slightly crooked smile, which caused Jo's pulse to quicken. He'd danced with them earlier, to their delight, and they now gazed up at him adoringly.

"We really should get home," Jo said before either of them could answer.

"Can we talk later?" he said to Jo. "Tomorrow maybe?"

Before she could respond, Mrs. Atkins appeared from behind the coatrack, wearing her coat. It became apparent she'd overheard them talking when she said, "It's past my bedtime, too. Jo, dear, why don't I take the girls home with me, and then you could stay and dance with your young man? My granddaughter's waiting outside." She gestured in the direction of the front entrance.

"He's not my—" Jo started to say before Jess interrupted.

"Can we, Mommy?" she pleaded.

"Pretty please," Emma chimed in. "Then I can play with Black Bart."

Black Bart was the cat that Mrs. Atkins had recently adopted from the feline rescue shelter that Buckboard Books partnered with. He was a sweetheart, despite being named after the notorious Wild West outlaw. The girls adored him, especially Emma, who was obsessed with cats. They also adored Mrs. Atkins, who'd become their new best friend since the night of their ordeal by fire.

Jo ignored them, saying to her neighbor, "It's kind of you to offer, but I wasn't planning on staying."

"I could keep them overnight." Either Mrs. Atkins was pretending not to have heard, or she'd suddenly become hard of hearing. Jo guessed it was the former from the sly glint in her eye behind her glasses. "Emily's staying in the guest room, but I could make up the sofa bed in the living room for the girls. If you trust me with your house key, I could collect their things and leave it under the mat for you."

"Great idea," Ian jumped in.

Jo shot him a narrow glance, but she relented, seeing as how she was outvoted. "All right, if you're sure it's no trouble. But if you girls change your mind, call me and I'll come get you," she said to Jess and Emma.

"We won't," Jess said firmly.

Ian put his coat on and escorted them out. "I'll see you both in the morning," Jo told the girls as she kissed them goodbye at the curb, where Mrs. Atkins's granddaughter's red Toyota idled. "Be good, and mind Mrs. Atkins." She watched them climb into the back seat before the car drove off.

"Walk with me?" asked Ian.

Jo nodded, the pull of temptation proving stronger than her fears about where it might lead.

They strolled the main drag, their breaths forming frosty plumes in the chill air. The downtown was a storybook village decked in its holiday finery. Rooflines and doorways and window frames were outlined in fairy lights. Every door boasted a wreath. The lampposts resembled peppermint sticks, twined in red ribbons. They passed holiday-themed window displays, each more creative than the last. The Christmas tree fashioned from books in the window at Buckboard Books was Jo's favorite, although the life-size cowboy-hatted Santa riding a bucking bronco at Boots and Saddle was a close second. In the distance the LED star atop the iron bell tower on Signal Hill glowed bright against the night sky.

The sidewalks, as usual after dark, were deserted except for the people coming and going at popular watering holes like the Whiskey Barrel. A stagecoach strung with blinking lights and tinsel garlands rattled past on the street. Tourists and day-trippers flocked to Gold Creek at Christmastime, which meant tourist attractions like stagecoach rides enjoyed a seasonal boost in ticket sales.

When they reached Sutter Park, Jo and Ian headed down one of its winding paths, stopping to admire the fourteen-foot Christmas tree presiding over its central plaza. At the other end of the plaza stood a sculpture of Santa and his reindeer made of woven willow branches and threaded with fairy lights. Both were seasonal features of the park this time of year.

"Is it my imagination, or have you been avoiding me today?" asked Ian. "Are you upset with me for some reason?"

They'd been chatting about the wedding and their holiday plans a moment ago, so his question came out of the blue. A guilty flush crawled across her face. "What gave you that idea?"

"It seemed like every time I got anywhere near you, you pulled a disappearing act."

"And yet here I am."

"Only because I roped you into going for a walk with me."

"Ha. I came of my own free will."

"After your neighbor and I ganged up on you."

She laughed, and then said, becoming serious, "It's me, not you. The reason I seemed distant earlier. You didn't do anything wrong. I'm sorry if I gave you that impression. It's just . . ." She was about to explain that the wedding had brought up a lot of feelings that she needed to process, but instead heard herself say, "I was married in that church." Didn't that say it all?

"Ah." He nodded in understanding, his forehead creased in sympathy. "I can imagine how that would be hard, and I'm sorry if it caused you any pain. But it doesn't explain why you were avoiding me. Could it be . . ." His eyes searched her face. "Because you also have feelings for me?"

She winced. He'd cut right to the heart of it. "Am I that transparent?"

"No. I guessed, or maybe I just hoped."

Was he saying he had feelings for her, too? Suddenly, her heart was beating too fast.

Ian's gaze dropped to her hand. "I noticed you're not wearing your ring." She had her gloves on, so he must've observed it earlier. What else had he noticed?

She nodded. "It . . . it was time."

"Time to put the past behind you?"

"No. Sean will always be a part of my life, but the ring had become my Do Not Disturb sign. So I took it off and unlocked the door." She drew a breath and looked him in the eye. "And you walked in."

His face lit up. "And that scares you?"

She nodded again, her heart in her throat. "I'm having feelings I never expected to have again. And yeah, that scares me because I hate being out of control, and part of me still feels like I'm betraying my husband. I also don't think it'd be fair to lead you on when I don't know where this is going."

"How about you let me worry about that? I'm a big boy."

She didn't point out that they'd also be separated by an ocean and two continents once he returned to Germany. The obstacle didn't seem as insurmountable as her fears about entering into a relationship.

From somewhere in the distance, she heard Christmas carolers chorusing, "Silent night, holy night, all is calm, all is bright . . ." The sweet sounds resonated in the quiet of the night. Suddenly, it seemed like they were the only two people in the world. "So what happens next? Where do we go from here?"

"I have an idea about that, if you'll allow me." She nodded and he took a step toward her, cupping her chin in one hand as he bent to kiss her. At the press of his mouth against hers, she melted into him. She parted her lips and felt the tip of his tongue play over hers. Every nerve in her body sprang to life. She felt like a shaken snow globe with all the sensations swirling inside her.

"That wasn't so difficult, was it?" he asked when they drew apart, his voice husky with emotion.

"Um." In her shell-shocked state, she couldn't come up with an intelligible response.

"We'll figure out the rest as we go along. One step at a time. Starting with dinner tomorrow night, if you're free."

"When do you have to go back to Germany?"

"Day after tomorrow, but I should be back soon."

"What, the air force is suddenly handing out free hall passes? That's twice in a row you were granted leave. A third time might be pressing your luck." She didn't know if compassionate leave counted, but even so.

"Next time I come, I won't be on leave."

She eyed him in confusion. "Why is that?"

"My tour of duty is up at the end of this month, and I decided not to reenlist. So you won't see me again in uniform after today. Next time we meet, I'll be a civilian."

"Wow. That's huge. Why did you decide not to reenlist?"

"I'd like to get married and have kids someday, and life in the military can be hard on families. I don't want to be the kind of husband and father who only sees his family between deployments."

"What will you do? Where will you go?"

"I'm interviewing for a job as manager of the airport in Pine City." Rodgers Air Field in Pine City, named after a local war hero who'd been a bomber pilot during World War II, consisted of a single landing strip, half a dozen hangars, an air traffic control tower, and a small terminal. It was the closest airport to Gold Creek and could accommodate lightplanes, private jets, and smaller commercial aircraft. "I have the qualifications. I'm trained both as a pilot and a flight instructor. I also have experience in air traffic control and a degree in aeronautic engineering."

"Sounds like you may be overqualified," she said as she struggled to absorb the mind-boggling news that Ian was both retiring from the military and looking to relocate to their area.

"I'd make more money working at one of the larger airports or flying for a commercial airline, sure, but then I wouldn't get to live in one of the most beautiful spots on God's green earth, where I'd also get to visit Pop-Pop more than once or twice a year. Plus, there's the winter sports."

She lifted a brow. "The winter sports?"

"Among other attractions." His blue eyes sparkled with the reflected glow of the Christmas tree lights as they exchanged a meaningful look that sent her heart into overdrive. "I aced my Zoom interview and they seemed impressed by my résumé. Tomorrow I go for my in-person interview."

"So you'll take the job if it's offered?"

"If we can come to terms. Just think, this time next month, we could both be living in the same time zone."

"It has definite possibilities," she agreed.

"If you'll have dinner with me tomorrow night, hopefully we'll have something to celebrate."

She was reminded that she had yet to give him an answer. "I'd love to, but would you mind if we ate in?" She didn't like leaving the girls with a babysitter if she could avoid it. "I'll cook."

He grinned. "How can I refuse a home-cooked meal? And this way I get to spend more time with your daughters. What can I bring?"

"Just yourself." He was more than enough. "And Ian? I'm . . . I'm really happy about your news."

"Are you? Because I don't want you to feel pressured. We could take it slow. We wouldn't even have to date. We could just, you know, hang out. Whatever you're comfortable with."

She rose on tiptoe and kissed him, and as he drew her close and their kiss deepened, she was once more caught up in the swirl of sensations that swept through her. "Does that answer your question?"

"Oh yeah." They stood entwined for another minute or so, her face tucked against his chest and his chin resting on the top of her head. He smelled of winter and damp wool and vanilla frosting. She felt the steady thumping of his heart underneath the layers of fabric separating them.

Jo didn't know where the road she was on would take her but looked forward to discovering what lay around the next bend.

ACKNOWLEDGMENTS

If you're under the illusion, as I was before I became a published author, that writing a novel is a solo undertaking, you couldn't be more wrong. To write one that anyone other than your spouse or your mother might want to read takes a village. That's because most novels, leaving aside the rare masterpiece that springs fully formed from the mind of its author like Athena from Zeus's brow, require editing and oftentimes research. I had plenty of help in both departments in writing this book.

First, a shout-out to my team at Lake Union: editors Melissa Valentine, Chantelle Osman, Carmen Johnson, and Tiffany Yates Martin; copyeditor Tara Whitaker, proofreader Kellie Osborne, and cold reader Jessica Poore; and production manager Karah Nichols, marketing manager Rachael Clark, art director Mandy Kain, and cover designer Eileen Carey. They helped me realize my vision for this book and make it the best it could possibly be. Thank you, ladies. I couldn't have done it without you.

Thanks, too, to the following "villagers": My agent, Paula Munier, who believed in me when no one else did, and who's also a talented author in her own right. My critique partner, Donna Ball, who not only gives me useful feedback on my manuscripts but keeps me humble by managing to write three novels for every one of mine. She's also my go-to expert in all things canine, as a dog owner and former trainer who writes dog mysteries (seriously, I want to be one of Donna's dogs in my next life).

Because this book is about a widow, I relied on stories told to me by those who've walked that difficult path in depicting my heroine's grieving process. The women from the Widows' Journey of Dallas, Texas—Kay Murcer, Babs McMahan, Beth Pribulsky, and Claudia Knake Spears—who were kind enough to share their experiences with me provided valuable insights, and I was inspired by their strength and courage. Each found a way forward after the death of her husband and created her own "epic encore." As did my friend and loyal reader Bunny Soloman, who worked as a grief counselor after the loss of her husband. I was fortunate to have Bunny share her professional expertise as well as personal experiences with me.

Since my heroine works as a photographer, I needed help researching that subject as well. I was lucky enough to meet the incredibly talented, award-winning photographer Olga Ginsburg through my husband, Sandy, who covered entertainment and the arts as a former reporter for WABC-TV in New York City. Olga was kind enough to answer all my questions. Although she doesn't normally do weddings, I learned a lot from her about the life of a professional photographer. Thanks to her, I was able to recreate a day in the life of a wedding photographer, as I imagined it.

Since no "village" is without family and friends, I must pay tribute to mine. My dear friends and writing pals, the Beach Babes—Jen Tucker, Julie Valerie, Meredith Schorr, Samantha Bailey, Francine LaSala, and Josie Brown—regularly remind me, with their love and support, that although the life of a writer is often a solitary one, I'm not alone in it. I miss our annual writers' retreat at the beach, but they are always in my heart when we're not texting or emailing one another or visiting in person. My sister Karen, in addition to being a marvelous painter and poet, is also an avid reader with a critical eye, so when she says she liked a book I wrote, it's high praise indeed—thanks, Lil Sis. Last but not least, a big kiss to my husband, Sandy Kenyon, who reads every draft I write, points me in the right direction when I'm lost in the weeds, reminds me of why I write when I lose faith, and also gives awesome foot rubs. I love you, babe.

Finally, thank you to everyone who has read, borrowed, or spread the word about my books. You are the reason I write. Your love of books and the many ways in which you support us are the bedrock of every author's career. I literally couldn't keep doing this without you. Visit me on social media or my website at www.eileengoudge.com. I always welcome a virtual cup of tea and a chat with my readers and fellow book lovers.

ABOUT THE AUTHOR

Photo © Sandy Kenyon

Eileen Goudge is the *New York Times* bestselling author of more than twenty novels, including *Garden of Lies*, *One Last Dance*, and *All They Need to Know*. Together, they have sold over six million copies worldwide. Eileen draws from her own experiences in writing women's fiction, exploring recurring themes of sisterhood/friendship bonds, the joys and heartaches of romance, and reversals of fortune. Eileen got her start as a ghostwriter for the popular teen series Sweet Valley High, which spawned multiple spin-offs and a TV show. Between cooking up plots for her novels, Eileen can often be found in her kitchen kneading bread or rolling out pie dough. In 2005 she published a cookbook, *Something Warm from the Oven*, filled with family recipes and recipes contributed by readers. She lives with her husband, Sandy Kenyon, the former entertainment reporter and film critic for New York City's WABC-TV, in the 1940s home they remodeled in Sacramento, California. For more information, visit www.eileengoudge.com.